Ben Counter

BATTLE FOR THE ABYSS

My brother, my enemy

With special thanks to Nick Kyme.

A BLACK LIBRARY PUBLICATION

First published in Great Britain in 2008 by
BL Publishing,
Games Workshop Ltd.,
Willow Road, Nottingham,
NG7 2WS, UK.

10 9 8 7 6 5 4 3 2 1

Cover and page 1 illustration by Neil Roberts.

A CIP record for this book is available from the British Library.

ISBN 13: 978 1 84416 549 0
ISBN 10: 1 84416 549 3

Distributed in the US by Simon & Schuster
1230 Avenue of the Americas, New York, NY 10020, US.

See the Black Library on the Internet at
www.blacklibrary.com

Find out more about Games Workshop
and the world of Warhammer 40,000 at
www.games-workshop.com

Printed and bound in the US.

THE HORUS HERESY

It is a time of legend.

Mighty heroes battle for the right to rule the galaxy. The vast armies of the Emperor of Earth have conquered the galaxy in a Great Crusade – the myriad alien races have been smashed by the Emperor's elite warriors and wiped from the face of history.

The dawn of a new age of supremacy for humanity beckons.

Gleaming citadels of marble and gold celebrate the many victories of the Emperor. Triumphs are raised on a million worlds to record the epic deeds of his most powerful and deadly warriors.

First and foremost amongst these are the primarchs, superheroic beings who have led the Emperor's armies of Space Marines in victory after victory. They are unstoppable and magnificent, the pinnacle of the Emperor's genetic experimentation. The Space Marines are the mightiest human warriors the galaxy has ever known, each capable of besting a hundred normal men or more in combat.

Organised into vast armies of tens of thousands called Legions, the Space Marines and their primarch leaders conquer the galaxy in the name of the Emperor.

Chief amongst the primarchs is Horus, called the Glorious, the Brightest Star, favourite of the Emperor, and like a son unto him. He is the Warmaster, the commander-in-chief of the Emperor's military might, subjugator of a thousand thousand worlds and conqueror of the galaxy. He is a warrior without peer, a diplomat supreme.

As the flames of war spread through the Imperium, mankind's champions will all be put to the ultimate test.

~ DRAMATIS PERSONAE ~

The Ultramarines Legion

CESTUS
: Brother-captain and fleet commander, 7th Company

ANTIGES
: Honour Guard, Battle-brother

SAPHRAX
: Honour Guard, Standard Bearer

LAERADIS
: Honour Guard, Apothecary

The Word Bearers Legion

ZADKIEL
: Fleet Captain, *Furious Abyss*

BAELANOS
: Assault-captain, *Furious Abyss*

IKTHALON
: Brother-Chaplain, *Furious Abyss*

RESKIEL
: Sergeant-commander, *Furious Abyss*

MALFORIAN
: Weapon Master, *Furious Abyss*

ULTIS
: Battle-brother

The Mechanicum of Mars

KELBOR-HAL
: Fabricator General

GUREOD
: Magos, *Furious Abyss*

The Space Wolves Legion

BRYNNGAR
: Captain

RUJVELD
: Battle-brother

The Thousand Sons Legion

MHOTEP   Brother-sergeant and fleet
                       captain, *Waning Moon*

The World Eaters Legion

SKRAAL   Brother-captain

The Saturnine Fleet

KAMINSKA   Rear Admiral, *Wrathful*
VENKMYER   Helmsmistress, *Wrathful*
ORCADUS   Principal Navigator, *Wrathful*

ONE

**Bearers of the Word/Let slip our cloaks
The death of Cruithne**

OLYMPUS MONS BURNED bright and spat a plume of fire into the sky. Below the immense edifice of rock lay the primary sprawling metropolis of Mars. Track-ways and factorums bustled with red-robed acolytes, pursued dutifully by lobotomised servitors, bipedal machine-constructs, thronging menials and imperious skitarii. Domed hab-blisters, stark cooling towers and mono-lithic forge temples vied for position amidst the red dust. Soaring chimneys, pockmarked by millennia of endeavour, belched thick, acrid smoke into a burning sky.

Hulking compressor houses vented steam high over the industrious swell like the breath of gods from arcane blasting kilns carved into the heart of the world; so vast, so fathomless, a labyrinthine conurbation as intricate and self-involved as its fervent populous.

Such innumerate, petty meanderings were as inconse-quential as a fragment of coal in the blast furnaces of the mountain forges, so great was the undertaking of that day. Few knew of its significance and fewer still witnessed the anonymous shuttle drone launch from the hidden caldera in the Valles Marineris. The drone surged into the stratosphere, piercing cloud-like crimson smog. Through writhing storms of purple-black pollution and wells of geothermal heat that hammered deep bruises into the sky, it breached the freezing mesosphere, the drone's outer shell burning white with effort. Plasma engines screaming, it drove on further into the thermosphere, the rays of the sun turning the layer into a blazing veil of relentless heat. Breaking the exosphere at last, the shuttle's engines eased. This was to be a one-way trip. Preset tracking beacons found their destination quickly. It was far beyond the red dust of Martian skies, far beyond prying eyes and questions. The shuttle was headed for Jupiter.

THULE HAD ORBITED the shipyards of Jupiter for six millennia. Suspended high above the gaseous surface of its patron planet, it dwelled innocuously beyond the greater Galilean moons: Callisto, Ganymede, Europa and Io. It was an ugly chunk of rock, its gravity so weak that its form was misshapen and mutated.

Such considerations were of little concern to the Mechanicum. What place did appearance and the aesthetic have in the heart of the machine? Precision, exactness, function, they were all that mattered.

Though of little consequence, Thule was to become something more than just a barren hunk of rock. It had been hollowed out by massive boring machines and filled with conduits, vast tunnels and chambers. Millions of menials, drones and acolytes toiled in the subterranean labyrinth, so great was the deed that they

were charged to perform. In effect, the dead core of
Thule had become a giant factorum of forge temples
and compressors, a massive gravity engine its beating
heart. This construction extended from the surface via
metal tendrils that supported blister domes, clinging
like limpets to the rock, and pneumatic lifter arrays.
Thule was no mere misshapen asteroid. It was an orbital
shipyard of Jupiter, and one that had guests.

'WE STAND UPON the brink of a new era.' Through the
vox-amplifier built into his gorget, Zadkiel's voice resonated powerfully in the gargantuan chamber. Behind
him, the exo-skeletal structure of Thule shipyard
loomed large and forbidding against the cold reaches of
space. Here, within one of the station's blister domes,
he and his charges were protected from the ravages of
the asteroid's surface. Solar winds scoured the rock,
bleaching it white, the inexorable erosion creating a
miasma of nitrogen-thick rolling dust.

'A red dawn is rising and it will drown our enemies in
blood. Heed the power of the Word and know it is our
destiny,' Zadkiel bellowed as he delivered the sermon,
animated and fervent upon a dais of obsidian. Scripture
carved into his patrician features and bald skull added
unneeded gravitas to Zadkiel's oratory. His grey, turbu-
lent eyes conveyed vehemence and surety.

His fists encased in baroque gauntlets, Zadkiel
gripped the edge of the lectern and assumed an insistent
posture. He wore his full battle armour, a fledging suit
of crimson ceramite yet to bear the scars of conflict.
Replete with the horns of Colchis, in honour of the primarch's home world and the symbol of a proud and
distinguished heritage, it represented the new era of
which Zadkiel spoke.

The Word Bearers Legion had been denied their true nature for too long. Now, they had shed the simulacra of obedience and capitulation, the trappings of compromise and denial. Their new power armour, fresh from the forges of Mars and etched with the epistles of Lorgar, was a testament to that treaty. The grey-granite suits of feigned ignorance were destroyed in the heart of Olympus Mons. Clad in the vestments of enlightenment, they would be reborn.

A vast ocean of crimson stretched before Zadkiel, as he stood erect behind his pulpit of stone. A thousand Astartes watched him dutifully, a full Chapter split into ten companies, each a hundred strong, their captains to the fore. All heeded the Word.

The Legionaries were resplendent in their power armour, bolters held at salute in their armoured fists, clutched like holy idols. Zadkiel's suit was the mirror-image of those of his warriors, although sheaves of prayer parchment, scorched trails of vellum writ over with litanies of battle, and the bloodied pages ripped from sermons of retribution were affixed to it. When he spoke, it was with the zealous conviction of the rhetoric he wore.

'Heed the power of the Word and know this is our destiny.'

The congregation roared in affirmation, their voices as one.

'We have our lance of vengeance. Let it strike out the heart of Guilliman and his weakling Legion,' Zadkiel bellowed, swept up by his own vitriolic proclamations. 'Long have we waited for retribution. Long have we dwelt in shadow.'

Zadkiel stepped forward, his iron-hard gaze urging his warriors to greater fervour. 'Now is the time,' he said, smashing his clenched fist down upon the lectern to punctuate the remark. 'We shall cast off falsehoods and the shackles of our feigned obeisance,' he snarled as if the words left a bitter taste in his mouth, 'let slip our cloaks and reveal our true glory!

'Brothers, we are Bearers of the Word, the sons of Lorgar. Let the impassioned words of our dark apostles be as poison blades in the hearts of the False Emperor's lapdogs. Witness our ascension,' he said, turning to face the great arch behind him.

A vast ship dominated the view through the hardened plexi-glass of the blister dome. It was surrounded by massively over-engineered machinery, as if the scaffold supporting the hordes of menials and enginseers had been built around it, and thick trails of reinforced hosing bled away the pneumatic pressure required to keep the gargantuan vessel elevated.

Cathedra soared from the ship's ornate hull, their spires groping for the stars like crooked fingers. So armoured, it could withstand even a concerted assault from a defence laser battery. In fact, it had been forged with that very purpose in mind.

Its blunt bullet prow, and the way its flanks splayed out to encompass the enormous midsection, spoke of strength and precision. Three massive crenellated decks extended from it like the sharpened prongs of a stygian trident. Twin banks of laser batteries gleamed in dull gunmetal down its broadsides. A single volley would have annihilated the loading bay and everyone in it. Cannon mounts sat idle on angular blocks of metal filled with viewpoints that hinted at the myriad chambers within. The rapacious bristle of the defensive turrets along the dorsal and ventral spines, and the dark indentations of the torpedo tubes, shimmered with violent intent.

Spiked antenna towers punched outward from multitudinous sub-decks, interspersed with further weapon arrays and torpedo bays. The ship's ribbed belly shimmered like oil and was replete with dozens of fighter hangars.

At the stern, the huge cowlings of the exhausts flared over the deep glow of the warming engines, primed to unleash enough thrust to force the warship away from Thule. Like chrome hexagons, the engine vents were so vast and terrible that to stare into their dormant hearts was to engulf all sense and reason in a fathomless darkened void.

Finally, sheets of shielding peeled off the prow, revealing a massive figurehead: a book, wreathed in flame, wrought from gold and silver. Words of Lorgar's choosing were engraved on the pages in letters many metres high. It was the greatest and largest vessel ever forged, unique in every way and powerful beyond reckoning.

Such was the sight of it, like some creature born from the depths of an infinite and ancient ocean, that even Zadkiel fell silent.

'Our spear is made ready,' Zadkiel said at last, his voice choked with awe. 'The *Furious Abyss.*'

This ship, this mighty ship, had been made for them, and here in the Jovian shipyards its long-awaited construction had finally reached an end. This was to be a blow against the Emperor, a blow for Horus. None could know of the vessel's existence until it was too late. Steps had been taken to ensure that remained the case. The launch from little known, and even less regarded, Thule was part of that deceit, but only part.

Zadkiel turned on his heel to face his warriors.

'Let us wield it!' he extolled with vociferous intensity. 'Death to the False Emperor!'

'Death to the False Emperor,' his congregation replied like a violent blast wave.

'Horus exultant!'

Discipline broke down. The assembled throng bellowed and roared as if possessed, smashing their fists against their armour. Oaths of hatred and of devout loyalty were shouted fervently and the building sound rose to an unearthly clamour.

Zadkiel closed his eyes amidst the maelstrom of devotion and savoured, drank deep of the zealotry. When he opened his eyes again, he faced the archway and the landscape of the *Furious Abyss*. Smiling grimly, he thought of what the vessel represented, and he imagined its awesome destructive potential. There was none other like it in all of the Imperium: none with the same firepower; none with the same resilience. It had been forged with one deliberate mission in mind and it would need all of its strength and endurance to achieve it: the annihilation of a Legion.

IN THE DARKER recesses of the massive loading bay, now an impromptu cathedra, others watched and listened. Unfeeling eyes regarded the magnificent array of soldiery from the shadows: the product of the Emperor's ingenuity, even perhaps his hubris, and felt nothing.

'Curious, my master, that this Astartes should exhibit such an emotional response to our labours.'

'They are flesh, Magos Epsolon, and as such are governed by petty concerns,' remarked Kelbor-Hal to the bent-backed acolyte stooped alongside him.

The fabricator general had purposely taken the long journey from Mars to Thule aboard his personal barge. He had done so under the pretence of a tour of the Jovian shipyards, overseeing atmospheric mining on the surface of Jupiter, reviewing the operations on Io, and observing vehicle and armour production within the hive cities of Europa. All of which would explain his presence on Thule. The truth was that the fabricator general wanted to witness this momentous event. It was not pride that drove him to do it, for such a thing was beyond one so close to absolute communion with the Omnissiah, rather it was out of the compulsion to mark it.

One endeavour was much like any other to the fabricator general, the requirements of form and function outweighing the need for ceremony and majesty. Yet, here he stood swathed in black robes, a symbol of his allegiance to the Warmaster and his commitment to his cause. Had he not sanctioned Master Adept Urtzi Malevolus to forge Horus's armour? Had he not also allowed the commissioning of vast quantities of materiel, munitions and the machines of war? Yes, he had done all of this. He had done it because it suited his purposes, the burgeoning desire, or rather intrinsic programming, within the servants of the great machine-god to gradually become one with their slumbering deity. Horus had unfettered Mars in its pursuit of the divine machine, countermanding the Emperor's chastening. For Kelbor-Hal the question of his allegiance and that of the Mechanicum was one of logic, and had required mere nanoseconds of computation.

'He sees beauty where we see function and form,' the fabricator general continued. 'Strength, Magos Epsolon, strength made through fire and steel, that is what we have wrought.'

Magos Epsolon, also robed in black, nodded in agreement, grateful for his overlord's enlightenment.

'They are human, after a fashion,' the fabricator general explained, 'and we are as far removed from that weakness as the cogitators aboard that ship.'

Immensely tall, his ribcage exposed through the ragged edge of his robes with ribbed pipes and tendril-like servos replacing organs, veins and flesh, Kelbor-Hal was anything but human. He no longer wore a face, preferring a cold steel void implanted with a curious array of sunken green orb-like diodes in place of eyes. A set of mechadendrite claws and arms stretched from his back, like those of an arachnid, replete with blades, saws and other arcane machinery. His voice was devoid of all emotion, synthesised through a vox-implant that droned with artificial coldness and indifference.

As Kelbor-Hal watched the phalanx of Astartes boarding the ship through the tube-like umbilical cords that snaked from the vessel's loading ramps to the blister dome, their bombastic leader swelling with phlegmatic pride, the internal chron within his memory engrams alerted him that time was short.

Dully, the *Furious Abyss*'s thrusters growled to life and the great vessel strained vertically against the lifter clamps. A low, yet insistent hum of building power from the awakening plasma engines followed, discernible even through the plexi-glass of the blister dome. With the Astartes and their crew aboard, the *Furious Abyss* was preparing to launch.

A data-probe snicked from the end of one of the fabricator general's twitching mechadendrites and fed into a cylindrical console that had emerged from the hangar floor. Interfacing with the device, Kelbor-Hal inputted the code sequence required to launch the ship. A series of icons upon the face of the console lit up and a slowly building hum of power resonated throughout the launch chamber.

Lead Magi Lorvax Attemann, part of the coterie of acolytes and attendant menials who had gathered to observe the launch, was permitted to activate the first sequence of explosions that would release the *Furious Abyss*. He did so without ceremony.

Lines of explosions, like stitches of fire, rippled along the side of the dock. Lifters, assembly arrays and webs of scaffolding fell away into the darkness, where magnetic tugs waited to gather the wreckage. Slabs of radiation shielding lifted from the ship's hull. The last dregs in the refuelling barges ignited in bright ribbons of fire.

The plasma engines roared, loud and throaty, scorching a blue swathe of fire and heat across the surface of Thule. A new star was rising in the darkling sky, so terrible and wonderful that it defied expression. It was a thunderous metal god given form, and it would light the galaxy aflame with its wrath.

At last the *Furious Abyss* was underway. As Kelbor-Hal watched it lift majestically into the firmament and registered the heavy thrum of its engines, a single tiny vestige of emotion blinked into existence within him. It was an ephemeral thing, barely quantifiable. Accessing internal cogitators, interfacing with his personal memory engrams, the fabricator general found its expression.

It was awe.

THE DRONE SHIP waited deep within the heart of Thule, accessed through a series of clandestine tunnels and lesser-known chambers. As it made its approach, the still toiling menials and servitors paid it no notice, programme wafers ensuring that they remained intent on their work. So, the shuttle passed them by slowly, unchallenged, unseen. Once through the myriad tunnels, the drone waited for several hours docked in a small antechamber that fed off the vast gravity engine at the asteroid's core.

An hour earlier, Fabricator General Kelbor-Hal's personal barge had departed the station, the head of the Mechanicum leaving his subordinate, Magos Epsolon, to organise the clean up after the launch of the *Furious Abyss*. It was to be the last vessel that left Thule.

Pre-programmed activation protocols abruptly came on line in the servitor pilot slaved to the drone shuttle. A mix of chemicals, separated within the body of the servitor pilot became merged as they were fed into a shared chamber. Once combined, the harmless chemicals became a volatile solution capable of incredible destructive force. A second after the solution became fully merged a small incendiary charge ignited their fury. The immediate firestorm engulfed the ship and spread out, the growing conflagration billowing down tunnels and through access pipes, incinerating labouring menials. When it struck the gravity engine the resultant explosions began a cataclysmic chain reaction. It took only minutes for the asteroid to break into flame-wreathed fragments. There was no time to flee to safety and no survivors. Every adept, servitor and menial was burned to ash.

The debris field would spread far and wide, but the asteroid was far enough away, locked at the farthest point of its horseshoe orbit, not to trouble Jupiter. It would not escape notice, but it was also of such little consequence that any investigation would take months to effect and ratify. None would discover the thing that had been wrought upon the asteroid's surface until it was much, much too late.

Much technology was lost in Thule's destruction. It was a steep price to pay for absolute and certain secrecy. In the end, the fabricator general's will had been done. He had willed the death of Thule.

TWO

Hektor's fate/Brothers of Ultramar/In the lair of the wolf

IT WAS DARK in the reclusium. Brother-Captain Hektor kept his breathing measured as he prosecuted another thrust with his short-blade. He followed with a smash from his combat shield and then twisted his body out of the committed attack to make a feint. Crouching low, blackness surrounding him in the chapel-like antechamber, he spun on his heel and repeated the manoeuvre in the opposite direction: swipe, thrust, block, thrust; smash, feint, turn and repeat, over and over like a physical mantra. With each successive pass he added a flourish: a riposte here, a leaping thrust there. The cycles increased in pace and intensity, the darkness enveloping him, honing his focus, building to an apex of speed and complexity, at which point Hektor would gradually slow until at peace once more.

Standing stock-still, maintaining control of his breathing, Hektor came to the end of the training regimen.

'Light,' he commanded, and a pair of ornate lamps flared into life on either wall, illuminating a spartan chamber.

Dressed in only sandals and a loincloth, Hektor's body was cast in a sheen of sweat that glistened in the artificial lamplight. The curves of his enhanced musculature were accentuated within its glow. Indulging in a moment of introspection, Hektor regarded the span of his hands. They were large and strong, and bereft of any scars. He made a fist with the right.

'I am the Emperor's sword,' he whispered and then clenched his left. 'Through me is his will enacted.'

Two robed acolytes waited patiently in the shadows, cowls concealing their augmetics and other obvious deformities. Even without being compared to the tall slab of muscle that was an Astartes, they were bent-backed and diminutive.

Hektor ignored their obsequiousness as he released the straps affixing the combat shield to his arm and handed it over along with his short-blade to the acolytes. He looked at the ground as his attendants retreated silently into the shadow's penumbra at the edge of the room. An engraved 'U' was carved into the centre of the chamber, chased in silver on a circular field of blue. Hektor stood in the middle of it, in exactly the position that he had started.

He allowed himself a smile as he beckoned his attendants to bring forth his armour.

A great day was fast approaching.

It had been a long time since he had seen his fellow Ultramarines. He and five hundred of his battle-brothers had been far from their native Ultramar for three years, as they helped prosecute the Emperor's Great Crusade to bring enlightenment to the galaxy and repatriate the lost colonies of man by fighting the

Vektates of Arkenath. The Vektate were a deviant culture, an alien overmind that had enslaved the human populous of Arkenath. Hektor and his warrior brothers had shattered the yoke that bound their unfortunate human kin and in so doing had destroyed the Vektates. The human populace owed fealty to the Imperium, and demonstrated it gladly when they were free of tyranny. It had been a grim war. The *Fist* had been involved in a brutal ship-to-ship action against the enemy, but had prevailed. Repairs had been conducted on Arkenath, as well as the requisitioning of a small tithe of men, eager to venture beyond the stars, to help replenish elements of the ship's crew. Once the war was over, Hektor and his battle-brothers had been summoned to the Calth system and the region of space known as Ultramar. At long last, they would be reunited with their brothers and their primarch.

Hektor was full of pride at the thought of seeing Roboute Guilliman again, his gene-father and noble leader of the Ultramarines Legion. The deciphered messages from the *Fist of Macragge's* astropaths had been clear. The Warmaster himself, mighty Horus, had ordered the Legion to the Veridan system. Guilliman had ratified the Warmaster's edict and instructed all disparate Ultramarine forces to muster at Calth. There they would take on supplies and rendezvous with their brothers in preparation to launch a strike on an ork invasion force besieging the worlds of neighbouring Veridan. A short detour to the Vangelis space port to take on some more battle-brothers stationed there and the campaign to liberate Veridan would be underway.

FULLY ARMOURED, HEKTOR strode down an access tunnel and headed towards the bridge. His ship, the *Fist of*

Macragge, was a Lunar-class battleship, named in honour of the Ultramarines' home world. Deck hands, comms-officers and other Legion serfs bustled past the Astartes down the cramped confines of one of the vessel's main thoroughfares.

The faint hiss of escaping pressure greeted Hektor's arrival on the bridge as the automated portal allowed him entry, before sliding shut in his wake.

'Captain on the bridge,' bellowed Ivan Cervantes, the ship's helmsmaster. Cervantes was a human, and despite being dwarfed by the mighty Astartes, he remained straight-backed and proud before the glorious countenance of his captain. Cervantes snapped a sharp salute with an augmetic hand; his original body part had been lost on Arkenath, together with his left eye, during the boarding action against the Vektates. The bionic replacement glowed dull red in the half-light of the bridge.

Screen illumination from various consoles threw stark slashes into the gloom, the activation icons upon them grainy and emerald. Crewmen, hard-wired directly into the vessel's controls from access ports bolted into their shaved scalps worked with silent diligence. Others stood, consulting data-slates, observing sensor readings and otherwise maintaining the *Fist of Macragge*'s smooth and uninterrupted passage through real space. Lobotomised servitors performed and monitored the ship's mundane functions with precise, circadian rhythm.

'As you were, helmsmaster,' Hektor replied, climbing a short flight of steps that led to a raised dais at the forefront of the bridge, and sitting down at a large command throne at its centre.

'How far are we from Vangelis space port?' Hektor asked.

'We expect to arrive in approximately–'

Warning icons flashed large and insistent on the forward viewport in front of the command throne, interrupting the helmsmaster in mid-flow.

'What is it?' Hektor demanded, his tone calm and level.

Cervantes hastily consulted a console beside him. 'Proximity warning,' he explained quickly, still poring over the data that had started churning from the console.

Hektor leaned forward in his command throne, his tone urgent.

'Proximity warning? From what? We are alone in real space.'

'I know, sire. It just… appeared.' Cervantes was frantically consulting more data as the organised routine of the bridge was thrust into immediate and urgent action.

'It's another ship,' said the helmsmaster. 'It's huge. I've never seen such a vessel!'

'Impossible,' barked Hektor. 'What of the sensorium, and the astropaths? How could it have got so close to us, so quickly?' he demanded.

'I don't know, sire. There was no warning,' said Cervantes.

'Bring it up on the viewscreen,' Hektor ordered.

Blast shields retracted smoothly from the front viewscreen, revealing a swathe of real space beyond. There, like black on night, was the largest ship Hektor had ever seen. It was shaped like a long blade with three massive decks that speared out from the hull like prongs on a trident.

Points of intense red light flared in unison down the vessel's port side as it turned to show the *Fist of Macragge* its broadside. The light illuminated more of the ship, so that it stretched the entire length of the viewscreen. It was even larger than Hektor had first assumed. Even several kilometres from the *Fist of Macragge*, it was rendered massive in the glow of its laser batteries

'Name of Terra,' Hektor gasped when he realised what was happening.

The terrible vessel that had somehow foiled all of their sensors, even their astropathic warning systems, was firing.

'Raise forward arc shields!' Hektor cried, as the first impact wave struck the bridge. A bank of consoles on the left suddenly exploded outward, shredding a servitor with shrapnel and all but immolating one of the deck crew. The bridge shuddered violently. Crewmen clutched their consoles to stay upright. Servitor drones went immediately into action dousing sporadic fires with foam. Hektor gripped the arms of his command throne as critical warning klaxons howled in the tight space, and crimson lightning shone like blood as emergency power immediately kicked in.

'Forward shields,' Hektor cried again as a secondary impact wave threw the Astartes from his command throne.

'Helmsmaster Cervantes, at once!' Hektor urged, getting to his feet.

No answer came. Ivan Cervantes was dead, the left side of his body horribly burned by one of the many fires erupting all across the bridge.

What was left of the crew worked frantically to reroute power, close off compromised sections and find firing solutions so that they might at least retaliate.

'Somebody get me power, lances, anything!' Hektor roared.

It was utter chaos as the carefully drilled battle routines were made a mockery of by the sudden and unexpected attack.

'We have sustained critical damage, sire,' explained one of Cervantes's subordinates, blood running freely down the side of his face. Behind him, Hektor saw other crewmen writhing in agony. Some were prone on the bridge floor and not moving at all. 'We're dead in the void.'

Hektor's face was grim in the gory glow of the bridge, a burst of sparks from a shorting console casting his features in stark relief.

'Get me an astropath.'

'A distress call, sire?' asked the crewman, fighting to be heard above the chaotic din. The silhouettes of his colleagues rushed back and forth to stem the damage, desperately trying to restore order in spite of the fact that it was hopeless.

'We are beyond help,' Hektor uttered with finality as the *Fist of Macragge*'s systems started failing. 'Send a warning.'

CESTUS KNELT IN silent reflection within one of the sanctums in the Omega quarter of Vangelis space port. The vast orbital station was built into a large moon and based around several hexagonal blisters into which docks, communion temples and muster halls were housed. A labyrinthine tramway connected each and every location of Vangelis, which was organised into a series of courtyards or quarters to make navigation rudimentary.

The bustling space port was crammed with traders, naval crewmen and mechwrights. A large proportion of its area had been given over to the Astartes. Vangelis was a galactic waymarker and small numbers of Astartes involved in more discreet missions used it as a gathering point.

Once their objective was completed, they would congregate at one of the many muster halls designated for their Legion and await pick-up by their battleships. Though little more than a company from any given Legion would be expecting transit at any one time, sectors Kappa through Theta were at the complete disposal of the Legions. Few non-Astartes were ever seen there, barring ubiquitous Legion serfs and attendants, though occasionally remembrancers would be granted brief access in concordance with maintaining good relations with the human populous.

Cestus drank in the darkness of the sanctum and used it to clear his thoughts. He was fully armoured, and pressed his left gauntlet against the sweeping, silver 'U' emblazoned on the cuirass of his power armour, symbol of the great Ultramarines Legion, whilst keeping his head bowed.

Soon, he thought.

He and nine of his battle-brothers had been on Vangelis for over a month. They had been acting as honour guard for an Imperial dignitary at nearby Ithilrium and were consequently separated from the rest of their Legion. Their sabbatical had passed slowly for Cestus. At first, he had thought it curious and enlightening to mix with the human population of the space port, but even bereft of his power armour and swathed in Legionary robes he was greeted with awe and fear. Unlike some of his brothers, it wasn't a reaction that he relished. Cestus had kept to Astartes quarters after that.

The fact that transit was inbound to extract them from Vangelis and ferry him and his brothers to Ultramar and their primarch and Legion filled Cestus with relief. He longed to embark on the Great Crusade again, to be out on the battlefields of a heathen galaxy, bringing order and solidity.

Word had reached them that the Warmaster Horus had already departed for the planet of Isstvan III to quell a rebellion against the Imperium. Cestus was envious of his Legion brothers, the World Eaters, Death Guard and Emperor's Children who were en route with the Warmaster.

Though Cestus craved the esoteric and was fascinated by culture and erudite learning, he was a warrior. It had been bred into him. To deny it was to deny the very genetic construct of his being. He could no more do that than he could go against the will and patriarchal wisdom of the Emperor. Such a thing could not be countenanced. So, Cestus sought the seclusion of the meditative sanctum.

'You have no need to genuflect on my account, brother.' A deep voice came from behind Cestus, who was on his feet and facing the intruder in one swift motion.

'Antiges,' said Cestus, sheathing his short-blade at his hip. Normally, Cestus would have rebuked his battle-brother for such a disrespectful remark, but he had formed an especially strong bond with Antiges, one that transcended rank, even of the Ultramarines.

It was a bond that had served the battle-brothers well, their whole much more than the sum of their parts as it was for the Legion in its entirety. Where Cestus was governed by emotion but prone to caution, Antiges was at times choleric and insistent, and less intense than his brother-captain. Together, they provided one another with balance.

Battle-Brother Antiges was similarly attired to his fellow Astartes. The sweeping bulk and curve of his blue power armour reflected that of Cestus, together with the statutory icons of the Ultramarines. Pauldrons, vambrace and gorget were all trimmed with gold, and a gilt brocade hung from Antiges's left shoulder pad to the right breast of his armour's corselet. Neither Astartes wore a helmet; Antiges's fastened to a clasp at his belt, whilst Cestus's head was framed by a silver laurel over his blond hair, his battle helm cradled beneath his arm.

'A little on edge, brother-captain?' Antiges's slate-grey eyes, the mirror of his closely cropped skull, flashed. 'Do you desire to be out amongst the stars, commanding part of the fleet again?'

As well as a company captain, Cestus also bore the rank of fleet commander. During his sojourn on Ithilrium that aspect of his duty had been briefly suspended. Antiges was right, he did desire to be back with the fleet, fighting the enemies of the Emperor.

'At the prospect of you lurking in the shadows, waiting to reveal yourself,' Cestus returned sternly and stepped forward.

He managed to maintain the chastening expression for only a moment before he smiled broadly and clapped Antiges on the shoulder.

'Well met, brother,' Cestus said, clasping Antiges's forearm firmly.

'Well met,' Antiges replied, returning the greeting. 'I have come to take you away from here, brother-captain,' he added. 'We are mustering for the arrival of the *Fist of Macragge*.'

IT WAS A short journey from the sanctum of Communion Temple Omega to the dock where the rest of

Cestus's and Antiges's battle-brothers awaited them. A narrow promenade, lined with ferns and intricate statuettes, quickly gave way to a wide plaza with multiple exits. The Ultramarines, who spoke with warm camaraderie, took the western fork that would eventually lead them to the dock.

Turning a corner, at the lead of the two Astartes, Cestus was hit square in the chest. The impact, though surprising, moved the Astartes not at all. He stared down at what had struck him.

Quivering amidst a bundle of tangled robes, a lithoslate clasped reassuringly in his hands, was a scholarly-looking human.

'What is the meaning of this?' Antiges demanded at once.

The pale scholar cowered beneath the towering Astartes, shrinking before his obvious power. He was sweating profusely, and used the sleeve of his robe to wipe his head before casting a glance back in the direction he had come from in spite of the monolithic warriors in front of him.

'Speak!' Antiges pressed.

'Be temperate, my brother,' Cestus counselled calmly, resting his hand lightly on Antiges's shoulder pad. The gesture appeased the Ultramarine, who backed down a little.

'Tell us,' Cestus urged the scholar gently, 'who are you and what has put you in this distemper?'

'Tannhaut,' the scholar said through ragged breaths, 'Remembrancer Tannhaut. I only wanted to compose a saga of his deeds, when a madness took him,' he blathered. 'He is a savage, a savage I tell you!'

Cestus exchanged an incredulous look with Antiges, who turned back to fix the remembrancer with his imperious gaze once more.

'What are you talking about?'

Tannhaut pointed a quivering finger towards the arched entrance of a muster hall.

A stylised rendering of a lupine head was etched into a stone panel beside it.

Cestus frowned when he saw it, knowing full well who else was on the space port with them at that time.

'The sons of Russ.'

Antiges groaned inwardly.

'Guilliman give us strength,' he said, and the two Ultramarines strode off in the direction of the muster hall, leaving Remembrancer Tannhaut quailing behind them.

BRYNNGAR STURMDRENG'S BOOMING laughter echoed loudly around the muster hall as he felled another Blood Claw.

'Come, whelplings!' he bellowed, taking a long pull from the tankard in his hand. Most of the frothing, brown liquid within spilled down his immense beard, which was bound in a series of intricate knots, and swept over the grey power armour of his Legion. 'I've yet to sharpen my fangs.'

In recognition of the fact, Brynngar displayed a pair of long incisors in a feral grin.

The Blood Claw Brynngar had just knocked prone and half-conscious crawled groggily on his belly in a vain attempt to get clear of the ebullient Wolf Guard.

'We're not done yet, pups,' Brynngar said, clamping a massive armoured fist around the Blood Claw's ankle and swinging him across the room one-handed to smash into what was left of the furnishings.

The three Blood Claws left standing amongst the carnage of broken chairs and tables, and spilled drink and victuals, eyed the Wolf Guard warily as they began to surround him.

The two facing Brynngar leapt in to attack, their shorter fangs bared.

The Wolf Guard drunkenly dodged the swipe of the first and hammered a brutal elbow into the Blood Claw's gut. He took the punch of the second on his rock-hard chin before smashing him to the floor with his considerable bulk.

A third Blood Claw came from behind, but Brynngar was ready and merely sidestepped, allowing the young warrior to overshoot, before delivering a punishing uppercut into his cheek.

'Never attack downwind,' the bawdy Wolf Guard told the Blood Claw rolling around on the floor. 'I'll always smell you coming,' he added, tapping his flaring nostrils for emphasis.

'As for you,' Brynngar said, turning on the one who had struck him, 'you hit like you're from Macragge!'

The Wolf Guard laughed out loud, before stomping a ceramite boot in mock salute of his triumph on top of the last Blood Claw, who had yet to stir from unconsciousness.

'Is that so?' a stern voice from the entrance way asked.

Brynngar swung his gaze in the direction of the speaker, and his one good eye brightened at once.

'A fresh challenge,' he cried, swigging from his tankard and delivering a raucous belch. 'Come forth,' Brynngar said, beckoning.

'I think you've had enough.'

'Then let us see.' The Wolf Guard gave a feral grin and stepped off the inert Blood Claw. 'Tell me this,' he added, stalking forward, 'can you catch?'

* * *

CESTUS HURLED HIMSELF aside at the last moment as the broad-backed chair flew at him, smashing into splinters against the wall of the muster hall. When he looked up again, he saw a broad and burly Wolf Guard coming towards him. The Astartes was an absolute brute, his grey power armour wreathed in pelts and furs, numerous fangs and other feral fetishes hanging from silver chains. He wore no helmet, his long and ragged hair swathed in sweat together with a beard drenched in Wulfsmeade, swaying freely about his thick shoulders.

'Stay back,' Cestus advised Antiges as he hauled himself to his feet.

'Be my guest,' the other Ultramarine replied from his prone position.

Adopting a crouching stance as dictated by the fighting regimen of Roboute Guilliman, Cestus rushed towards the Space Wolf.

Brynngar lunged at the Ultramarine, who barely dodged the sudden attack. Using his low posture to sweep under and around the blow, Cestus rammed a quick forearm smash into the Space Wolf's elbow, tipping the rest of what was in the tankard over his face.

Brynngar roared and came at the Ultramarine with renewed vigour.

Cestus ducked the clumsy two-armed bear hug aimed at him and used Brynngar's momentum to trip the Space Wolf hard onto his rump.

The manoeuvre almost worked, but Brynngar turned out of his trip, casting aside the empty tankard and using his free hand to support his body. He twisted, using the momentum to carry him, and landed a fierce punch to Cestus's midriff when he came back too swiftly for the Ultramarine to block. An overhand blow followed as Brynngar sought to chain his attacks, but

Cestus moved out of the striking arc and unleashed a fearsome uppercut that sent Brynngar hurtling backwards.

With the sound of more crushed furniture, the Space Wolf got to his feet, but Cestus was already on him, pressing his advantage. He rained three quick, flathanded strikes against Brynngar's nose, ear and solar plexus. Staggered after the barrage, the Wolf Guard was unable to respond as Cestus drove forward and hooked both arms around his torso. Using the weight of the attack to propel him, Cestus roared and flung Brynngar bodily across the muster hall into a tall stack of barrels. As he moved backwards, Cestus watched as the rack holding the barrels came loose and they crashed down on top of Brynngar.

'Had enough?' Cestus asked through heaving breaths.

Dazed and defeated, and covered in foaming Wulfsmeade, a brew native to Fenris and so potent that it could render an Astartes insensible should he drink enough, Brynngar looked up at the victorious Ultramarine and smiled, showing his fangs.

'There are worse ways to lose a fight,' he said, wringing out his beard and supping the Wulfsmeade squeezed from it.

Antiges, standing alongside his fellow battle-brother, made a face.

'Up you get,' said Cestus, hauling Brynngar to his feet.

'Fair greetings, Cestus,' said the Wolf Guard, when he was up, crushing Cestus in a mighty bear hug. 'And to you, Antiges,' he added.

The other Ultramarine backed away a step and nodded.

Brynngar put his arms down and nodded back with a broad smile.

'It has been a while, lads.'

It was on Carthis during the uprising of the Kolobite Empire in the early years of the crusade that the three Astartes had first fought together. Brynngar had saved Cestus's life that day and had been blinded in one eye for his trouble. The venerable wolf had fought the Kolobite drone-king single-handed. The mighty rune axe, Felltooth, which Brynngar wielded to this day, had part of its blade forged from the creature's mandible claw by the rune-priests and artificers of Fenris in recognition of the deed.

'Indeed it has, my noble friend,' said Cestus.

'Drunk and brawling? Are the drinking holes of this space port insufficient sport, Brynngar? Did you build this muster hall for just such a purpose, I wonder?' said Antiges with a hint of reproach.

Lacquered wood panelled the walls, and a plentiful cache of barrels, filled with Wulfsmeade, were stationed at intervals throughout the hall. Huge, long tables and stout wooden benches filled the place, which was empty except for Brynngar and the groaning Blood Claws. Tapestries of the deeds of Fenris swathed the walls. The muster halls of the Ultramarines were austere and regimented; this one, fashioned by the artisans of Leman Russ's Legion, looked more like a rustic long-house from the inside.

'A pity you could not have joined in sooner,' Brynngar remarked. 'Perhaps tomorrow?'

'With regret, we must decline,' Cestus replied, secretly relieved; he had no desire to go a second round with the burly Space Wolf. 'We leave today for Ultramar. War is brewing in the Veridan system and we are to be reunited with our brothers in order to prosecute it. We are heading to the space dock now.'

Brynngar smiled broadly, clapping both Astartes on the shoulder, who both felt the impact through their armour.

'Then there is only one thing for it.'

Antiges's expression was suspicious.

'What is that?'

'I shall come to see you off.'

With that, the Wolf Guard turned the two Ultramarines and, putting his massive arms around their shoulders, proceeded to walk them out of the muster hall.

'What about them?' Cestus asked as they were leaving, indicating the battered Blood Claws.

Brynngar cast a quick look over his shoulder and made a dismissive gesture.

'Ah, they've had enough excitement.'

THREE

God of the *Furious Abyss*/Psychic scream/Visions of home

CORALIS DOCK WAS one of many on Vangelis. A wide, flat plain of plate metal stretched out from its many station houses and listening spires, ending in a trio of fanged docking clamps where the various visiting craft could make harbour and take on or drop off cargo.

Arriving at the main control hub of Coralis, the three Astartes found themselves in a tight chamber that overlooked the dock. Thick, interwoven cables looped from the ceiling and dim, flickering halogen globes illuminated the bent-backed menials and cogitator servitors working the hub. A backwash of sickly yellow light thrown from numerous pict screens and data-displays fought weakly against the gloom.

An azure holosphere was located in the centre of the chamber, rotating above a gunmetal dais. It depicted Vangelis space port in grainy, intermittent resolution and a wide arc surveyor net that projected several thousand metres from the surface.

A large, convex viewport confronted the Astartes at the far wall through which they could see the magnificent vista of real space. Distantly, writhing nebulae patterned the infinite blackness with their iridescent glory and fading suns. Starfields and other galactic phenomena were arrayed like the flora and fauna of some endless obsidian ocean. It was a breathtaking view and stole away the fact that the recycled air within the control hub was sickly and stifling. A machine drone accompanied it from the space port's primary reactor located in the subterranean catacombs of Vangelis. The insistent hum of latent power could be felt through the reinforced plasteel floor. It was hot, too, the stark industrial interior barely shielded against the dock's generatorium.

Saphrax was already on the command deck of the control hub, consulting with the hub's stationmaster, when the other Astartes arrived. Saphrax was the honour guard squad's standard bearer, and the Ultramarines honour banner was rolled up in its case slung over his back. The rest of Saphrax's battle-brothers were below at the hub's gate, preparing for their imminent departure.

'Greetings, Saphrax. You know Brynngar of the Space Wolves,' said Cestus, indicating the brutish Wolf Guard who gave a feral snarl.

'What news?' the brother-sergeant asked his banner bearer.

'Captain, Antiges,' said the Ultramarine to his battle-brothers. 'Son of Russ,' he added for Brynngar's benefit. Saphrax was a bald-headed warrior with a long scar that ran from his left temple to the base of his chin: another souvenir from the Kolobite. Cestus often mused that none in the Legion were as straight-backed as Saphrax, so much so that he seemed permanently at attention. Dependable and solid, he was seldom given to great emotion and wore a stern expression like a mask over chiselled stone features. Pragmatic, even melancholic, he was the third element to the balance that existed between Cestus and Antiges. Even so, the banner bearer's mood was particularly dour.

'We have received an astropathic message,' Saphrax informed them.

There were three astropaths in residence at the hub, and more in the space port at large. They were sunk into a deep, circular vestibule, just below floor level, and swathed in shadow. Dim lights set into the edge of the vestibule cast weak illumination onto their faintly writhing forms. A skin of translucent, psychically conditioned material was draped over the trio of astropaths like a clinging veil. Beneath it, they looked like they were somehow conjoined, as if feeling each other's emotions as one being. Other, less obvious, wards were also in place. All were designed to safeguard against the dangerous mental energies that could be unleashed during the course of their duties.

Withered and blinded, the wretched creatures – two males and a female – like all of their calling had undergone the soul-binding ritual; the means by which the Emperor moulded and steeled their minds, so that they might be able to look into the warp and not be driven insane. Astropaths were vital to the function of the Imperium; without them, messages could not be communicated over vast distances, and forces could not be readied and co-ordinated. Even so, it was an inexact science. Messages both sent and received by the Astra Telepathica were often nought but a string of images and vague sense-impressions. Wires and thick cables snaked from the vestibule, slaving the astropaths to the control hub, where their 'messages' could be logged and interpreted.

'It started fifteen minutes ago,' said the stationmaster, an elderly veteran of the Imperial Army with cables running from under his shaved scalp, plugged into the command ports of the consoles set above the astropathic chamber. 'We've only received fragments of meaning, so far. All we know for certain is that they come from a distant source. Thus far, only part of the message has reached us. Our astropaths are endeavouring to extract the rest as I speak to you.'

Cestus turned to regard the stationmaster and in turn the gibbering astropaths. Beneath the protective psyskin, he could see their wasted bodies, swaddled in ragged robes. He heard the hissing of sibilant non sequiturs. The astropaths drooled spittle as they spoke, their sputum collecting against the inner material of the skin enveloping them. Their bone-like fingers were twitching as their minds attempted to infiltrate the empyrean.

'Falkman, sire,' said the stationmaster by way of introduction with a shallow bow. His right leg was augmetic and, judging by his awkward movements, most of his right side, which was probably why he had been sidelined to age and atrophy at Vangelis, no longer fit to taste of the Imperium's glory on the battlefield. Cestus pitied his fragility and that of all non-Astartes.

'Could it be a distress beacon sent from a ship?' Antiges broke through Cestus's thoughts with his assertive questioning.

'We have been unable to discern that yet, sire, but it is unlikely,' said Falkman, his face darkening as he turned to Saphrax.

'The nature of the message was… broken, more like a psychic cry delivered with extreme force. With the warp in tumult the energy used to send it was unpredictable,' said Saphrax, 'and it was no beacon. There was a single message; the pattern does not repeat. We think perhaps it was an astropathic death scream. 'And that is not all.'

Cestus's gaze was questioning.

Saphrax's face was grim.

'We have yet to receive word from the *Fist of Macragge*.' The banner bearer of the honour guard let the words hang there, unwilling to voice what was implied.

'I will not make any negative conclusions,' Cestus replied quietly, unwilling to give in to what he feared. 'We must believe that–'

The three astropaths slaved to the control hub began convulsing as the full force of the psychic scream made its presence felt. Blood spurted inside the psy-skin covering them and looked hazy and bright viewed from outside it. The wasted limbs of the astropaths pressed against the material, forcing it tight, their muscles held in spasm as they writhed in agony. Cogitators set around the hub above them were spewing reams of data as the astropaths fought to control the visions rushing into their minds.

Smoke clouded the already hazy interior of the psy-skin as it rose from their decrepit bodies. Consoles sparked and exploded as wrathful electricity arced and spat. It earthed into the wizened frames of the astropaths, carried by the wires and cables, now little more than human conductors for its power. As one, they threw their heads back and a backwash of pure psychic force was unleashed in a terrible death scream that resonated throughout the room. The astropaths became a conduit for it, the strength of the

psychic emission made many times more powerful by
the volatile state of the warp.

Walls shuddering against the onslaught, the lights of
Vangelis space port went out.

THE BRIDGE OF the *Furious Abyss* was like a sprawling city in
miniature. The banks of cogitators were like hive-stacks rising above the streets formed by the exposed industrial
ironwork of the deck. The various bridge crews sat in
sunken command posts like arenas or deep harbours.
Three viewscreens dominated one end of the bridge, while
a raised acropolis at its heart was formed by the captain's
post. A strategium table stretched out before it from which
he could raise an orrery display, showing the ship and its
foes wrought in rotating brass rings.

High above the sprawling bridge was a decked
clerestory where the astropathic choir of the mighty
warship were slaved. The vaulted space was shared by
the Navigator's sanctum, concealed in an antechamber
so as to be secluded whilst traversing the perils of the
warp.

The command throne, raised upon a hard-edged pen-
tagonal dais, was the seat of a god.

Zadkiel was that god, looking down upon a city
devoted to him.

'Listen,' Zadkiel bade those kneeling before him in
supplication. The dulcet roar of the *Furious Abyss*'s
plasma engines, even dulled by the thick adamantium
plating surrounding the ship's hull and interior, was
like a war cry.

'Listen and hear the sound of the future...' Zadkiel was
on his feet, sermonising, '...the sound of fate!'

Three warriors, true devotees of the Word, heeded
Zadkiel's rhetoric and stood.

'We pledge our service to you, Lord Zadkiel,' said the tallest of the three. He had a voice like crushed gravel and one of his eyes was blood-red, surrounded by a snarl of scar tissue. Even without the injury, his granite slab of a face would have made him a figure of fear even among his fellow Word Bearers. This was Baelanos, assault-captain and Zadkiel's private terror weapon. A potent warrior, Baelanos lacked imagination, which made him the perfect follower in Zadkiel's eyes. He was obedient, deadly and fiercely loyal, all fine qualities in an underling.

'As do we all,' Ikthalon interjected blithely. Another Astartes, Ikthalon was a company chaplain, demagogue and expert torturer. Unlike Baelanos, he wore his helmet in the presence of his commander, a skull-faced piece of armour with a pair of discreet horns on either side of the temple. Even through it, Ikthalon's thinly veiled contempt was obvious. 'Perhaps we should address the matters at hand, brother,' he counselled, lingering sarcastically on the last word.

Zadkiel sat back down in the command throne. It was sculpted to accept his armoured frame, as if he had been born to take command of this bridge, to be the god of this warship.

'Then let us tarry no further,' he said, his viperous gaze lingering on Ikthalon.

'Sensorium reports that the *Fist of Macragge* was destroyed and all weapon's systems tested successfully, sire.' It was Reskiel who spoke. He was a youth compared to the other Astartes on the command dais, gaunt of face with a keening hunger in his black eyes, a strange quirk of his birth. Reskiel was a veteran of many battles, despite his age, and he wore the newly fashioned studded armour of his Legion proudly, keen to baptise it with the scars of war. He was widely regarded as Zadkiel's second, if not in an official capacity – that honour fell to Baelanos – and made it his business to know all the happenings aboard the *Furious Abyss* and report them to his master. Where Baelanos was the dutiful lapdog, Reskiel was the eager sycophant.

'It was as expected.' Zadkiel's response was terse.

'Indeed,' said Ikthalon, 'but our astropaths also suggest that the stricken ship, though smitten by our righteous fury, managed to send out a distress call. I would not like to think that all our caution at commissioning the vessel's construction in the Jovian shipyards has been undone so swiftly and needlessly.'

Zadkiel allowed a flutter of emotion to cross his features for a moment at the news. He considered drawing his power mace and staving in Ikthalon's skull for his persistent insubordination, but in truth, he valued the chaplain's council and his Word. Though he was a barb in Zadkiel's side, even since the Great Crusade had been in its infancy, he did not couch expressions with sycophantic frippery as Reskiel was prone too, nor was he so singled-minded that he was unable to convey subtlety and the need for delicacy when required like Baelanos. Zadkiel did not trust him, but he trusted his Word and so he was tolerated.

'It is possible that a message reached a way station, or some isolated listening spire at the edge of the segmentum, but we are well underway and there is little that any vessel can do to prevent our destiny. So it is written,' Zadkiel said at last.

'So it is written,' the assembled commanders intoned.

'Reskiel, you will maintain a close watch on the sensorium. If anything should stray into surveyor range, I want to know immediately,' Zadkiel ordered.

'It will be done, my lord.' Reskiel bowed obsequiously and retreated from the dais.

'Baelanos, Ikthalon, you have your own duties to attend to,' Zadkiel added, dismissively, not waiting to watch them depart as he turned to regard the viewscreens before him.

'Engines,' said Zadkiel, and at once the central viewscreen blinked into life, the bridge lights dimmed and the image on the screen lit the miniature city in hard moonlight. It showed the *Furious Abyss*'s cavernous engine room, the prostrate cylinders of the plasma reactors dwarfing the crewmen who scrabbled around them in their routine duties. The crew wore the deep crimson of the Word Bearers; they were servants of Lorgar just as the Word Bearers were, devoted to the primarch's Word and grateful for such a certain place in the universe.

They did not know the details of the Word, of course. They were ignorant of the web of allegiances and oaths that Lorgar had created among his brother primarchs, or of the mission that would seal the inevitability of the Word Bearers' victory. They did not need to know. It was enough for them that they laboured under the wishes of their primarch.

Amongst the piteous menials, a tall figure stood out. Looming from the darkness, he was swathed in black robes and bore the cog symbol of the Mechanicum around his neck on a chain of bolts.

'Magos Gureod, you are to keep us at a steady speed, but be ready to increase our plasma engines to maximum capacity.'

'It will be done,' the magos replied, his artificial voice relayed through a series of synthesisers. Gureod's face was hidden by the massive cowl over his head, but a pair of blinking red diodes was vaguely discernible in the void where his eyes should have been. Odd protrusions in the sweep of his long robes suggested further augmetics, and his withered hands, crossed over his abdomen, offered the only clue that Magos Gureod was indeed human. At the order, he withdrew into the shadows again, doubtless heading for the sanctum and deep communion with the machine spirit.

Turning to another screen, Zadkiel uttered, 'Ordnance.'

The crowded munitions deck was displayed there. Weapon Master Malforian was in residence, barking harsh commands to crews of sweating orderlies and gang ratings, toiling in the steam-filled half dark of the cluttered deck. Full racks of torpedoes stood gleaming, fresh from the Martian forges. The ordnance deck stretched across the breadth of the *Furious Abyss* beneath the prow, and like the rest of the ship it was wrought in a bare industrial style that had an elegance of its own.

Realising he was being summoned, Malforian attended to his captain at once.

'Keep broadsides primed and at ready status, Master Malforian,' Zadkiel instructed him. 'The test against the *Fist of Macragge* was to your satisfaction, yes?'

'Yes, my lord. Your will shall be done.' The lower portion of the weapon master's face was supplanted by a metal grille and he spoke in a tinny monotone as a result; most of his jaw and chin had been destroyed during the early years of the Great Crusade while he was aboard the *Galthalamor*, fighting the ork hordes of the Eastern Fringe. The vessel, an ancient Retribution-class battle cruiser, was all but annihilated in the conflict.

Zadkiel dismissed the weapons master and blanked the pict screens. Coding a sequence into his command throne, Zadkiel felt the hydraulic pistons at work in the dais as he was slowly, majestically, raised above the bridge and brought level with the massive viewport overlooking the vessel's prow. The endless expanse of real space stretched beyond it. Somewhere within that curtain of stars was Macragge, home world of Guilliman's Legion. It was the stage of his destiny.

'Navigator Esthemya,' said Zadkiel, staring into the infinite.

'My lord,' a female voice chimed through the vox set into the command throne.

'Take us to Macragge.'

'Vectors are locked, captain,' Esthemya informed him from the secluded cocoon in the clerestory, a hard-edged blister that was surrounded by spines of data medium like the spires of a cathedral.

Zadkiel nodded, turning to face the viewscreen in front of him as the Navigator went to her duties.

The infinite gaped before him, and Zadkiel was acutely aware of the power that lay beyond the veil of real space and the pacts he had made to harness its limitless strength. Before the countenance of his enemies, aboard this mighty vessel, he would be god-like. There was no other ship in existence that could do what the *Furious Abyss* was destined to do. It alone had the power to achieve the mission that Kor Phaeron had charged them with. Only the *Furious Abyss* could get close enough, could endure the awesome defences of Macragge to unleash its deadly payload.

Icons in his command throne lit up with the acquisition of their new heading, bathing Zadkiel in an aura of his own personal heaven.

'Like a god,' he whispered.

* * *

EVERY EMERGENCY KLAXON had gone off at once in the control hub of Coralis Dock at Vangelis space port. Cestus could barely hear the thoughts in his head. Light flickered sporadically from the warning readouts on every command surface, casting the darkened control hub like some monochromatic animation. The astropathic choir bucked and kicked, and spat blood beneath the psy-skin in a collective seizure.

'Station captain, report,' bellowed Cestus.

Falkman was reeling, trying to tear the cables from his skull as they pumped a screaming torrent of information into his mind.

Brynngar went to the side of the human at once, preventing Falkman from ripping out more cables, determined that the station master would do his duty.

'The hub reactor is overloading,' the station captain snarled through gritted teeth, trying desperately to hold on. 'The psychic jolt must have started a chain reaction in our electrical systems. The reactor must be shut down or it will destabilise.'

Cestus's face, lit up intermittently in readout flares and the bursts of warning strobes, held a question.

'The resulting explosion will vapourise the station, this dock and all of us.'

The Ultramarine captain turned to the assembled Astartes in the control hub.

'Saphrax, stay here and maintain control over the situation,' he ordered with a meaningful glance at Falkman. 'Try to salvage whatever you're able to from the astropathic choir.'

'But my captain–'

'Do it!' Cestus would not be argued with, even with a battle-brother so seldom disposed to querying orders as

Saphrax. 'Whatever was in that message was important; I can feel it in my very marrow. It must be recovered.'

'What of the rest of us?' asked Antiges, barley registering the flying embers of sparks spitting across the chamber.

'We're going to save the dock.'

'YOU ARE NO Techmarine. How do you plan on shutting down the reactor?' Brynngar shouted against the din, sparks showering him from cogitator cables above.

Although the Space Wolf's face was almost next to Cestus's ear, the Ultramarine could only just hear him. The droning reactor was a thunderous pulse in the subterranean access tunnels. After verbally guiding the Astartes to an antechamber below the control hub and a reinforced access portal that would lead them to the reactor, Falkman had neglected to provide them with the necessary instruction to shut the device down, the fact of his passing out from shock a major contributing factor to the oversight.

Usually, this area of the dock would be thronging with menials and engineers, but the rapid outflow of escape reactor radiation had prompted an evacuation alert. The Astartes had passed a number of fleeing tech adepts as they'd made their way down to the reactor. Those that were left were either dead or critically injured. The Astartes ignored them all, immune to their pleas for help with the safety of the entire dock at stake.

'I am hoping a solution will present itself,' Cestus replied as they made their way through the cramped tunnel. The corridor the Astartes were in spiralled around the main reactor shell down to the power source at the base of the station.

'To think the Legion of Guilliman are regarded as master strategists,' said Brynngar with bellowing laughter.

'Directness is a valid strategy, Space Wolf,' Antiges reminded him, shouting to be heard above the horrendous noise of lurching metal, as if an inner storm was at play within the conduit. 'I would have thought one of the Sons of Russ would find it familiar.'

Brynngar's amused response was raucous and deafening.

Shouldering past the last of the surviving crewmen and panicked tech adepts as they fled, Cestus led the Astartes to the reactor chamber. Only one of the Emperor's Angels, replete in his power armour, could hope to survive the reactor's intense radiation at such close range. Like his battle-brothers, Cestus had donned his helmet before entering the tunnel. Extreme radiation warning icons flashed insistently in the lens display. Time was running out.

Atmospheric pipes fractured and sprayed freezing gas across a pair of gargantuan blast doors closing off the interior of the reactor shell from the rest of the station. Doubtless, they'd been activated as soon as the psychic power surge from the astropaths had hit. The servos on the massive door had shorted and were a tangled mass of wires and machinery.

'Prepare yourselves,' cried Cestus, ignoring the sub-zero gas. He seized the edge of the blast door in an effort to prise it open.

'Stand back,' snarled Brynngar, using his bulk to muscle the Ultramarine aside. He hefted Felltooth with practiced ease, sweeping the rune axe around in a lazy arc.

'No sport when the enemy stays still,' he growled and split the blast door in two with one mighty swing, sparks cascading from the blade.

Stowing the weapon, Brynngar peeled back the rent metal with both hands, making a space wide enough for the Astartes to enter.

The reactor was a swirling mass of glowing blue-green energy, rippling in on itself as it drew in power from the plasma conduits looping around it like eccentric orbits around a star. It pulsed, streaked with black and purple, and chunks of scorched machinery tumbled into it. A hot blast of air, tingling with radiation, washed over them in a back-draught. More warning runes flickered against Cestus's helmet lens, transmitted through onto the display from the acute sensor readouts on his armour.

'Now what?' shouted Antiges above the howl of the reactor.

Cestus watched the writhing mass of energy, taking in the confines of the small chamber that housed it and the control console, all but destroyed by its wrath.

'How many charges do you have?'

'A cluster of fragmentation and three krak grenades, but I don't understand, captain,' Antiges replied, his perplexity concealed by his helmet.

'A full belt of krak,' Brynngar growled. 'Whatever you are planning, lad, we'd best be about it,' he added. Being blown to smithereens by a malfunctioning reactor was not the death saga he wanted for his epitaph.

'We prime the chamber with set charges, everything we've got,' said Cestus with growing conviction, 'and bury it.'

'That would cause catastrophic damage to the station,' Antiges countered, turning to regard his captain.

'Yes, but it would not destroy it,' said Cestus. 'There is no other choice.'

Cestus was about to detach the grenades from his clip harness when the reactor abruptly collapsed like a dying star imploding into a black hole. In its place a glowing sphere of deep purple blossomed, flickering like an image on a faulty pict screen. Purple lightning licked from the surface, playing over Cestus's armour. He took a step back.

Yowling static flared suddenly into life and the Astartes were floored by the wave of noise. A bright flash lit the entire chamber, overloading their helmet arrays in an instant. There, amidst the intense flare of light, Cestus saw an image, so fleeting and indistinct that it could have been an illusion from the overwhelmed optics in his helmet. He blinked once, seeing only white haze, and shook his head, trying to recapture it. The flare died down and when Cestus's vision returned the afterglow haunted the edge of his retinas, but the image was gone and the reactor was dead. The core had turned dark. Cracks of static electricity glowed over its surface. It shrank and became abruptly inert. The warning lights inside the reactor shell dimmed and went out.

Elsewhere on the station, secondary and tertiary reactors, registering the loss of the primary reactor, diverted power to the dock, allowing the tech-seers time to make the necessary repairs. The storm had howled itself out.

'What in the name of Terra just happened?' asked Antiges, a cluster of frag grenades still in his hand.

'Mother Fenris,' Brynngar breathed at what he had just witnessed.

'Did you see that?' asked Cestus. 'Did you see it in the blast flare?'

'See what?' Antiges replied, relieved that they didn't have to collapse the reactor chamber after all.

Cestus's posture displayed his shock and disbelief as sure as any facial expression disguised by his armour.

'Macragge.'

SHARDS OF BROKEN images flashed on the psy-receiver, what was left of the astropathic transference from the psychic scream.

Falkman, looking gaunt and haggard from his earlier experience, but otherwise intact, pored over them, running analysis protocols and clarity procedures with what little machinery still worked in the hub. Saphrax stood pensively beside him, awaiting the return of his captain.

'Brother-captain!' he said with no small amount of relief as Cestus and the others emerged from the tunnel, their armour scorched black in several places.

When Cestus removed his helmet, his face was ashen and a cold sweat dappled his brow.

Saphrax was taken aback; he had never seen a fellow Astartes, certainly not his captain, look so afflicted.

'The astropathic message,' Cestus stated coldly, going to the psy-receiver before Saphrax could verbalise his concern. 'What's left of it?'

'All is well, brother,' said Antiges, following in his captain's wake and placing his hand on the banner bearer's shoulder, though his tone was anything but reassuring.

Brynngar waited further back, deliberately distancing himself, and stony silent as if processing what had happened in the reactor. He touched a fang totem attached to his cuirass with an inward expression.

'There is little left,' confessed Falkman, who, though he had managed to restore lighting and some of the basic functions of the hub, had failed to recover the entire astropathic message. 'I need to get one of the logic engines functioning if I'm to decipher it with any degree of certitude, but this is what we have.'

Cestus glared at the pict-slate of the psy-receiver as the broken images cycled slowly: a gauntleted fist wreathed in a laurel of steel, a golden book, what appeared to be the hull of a ship and a cluster of indistinct stars. Cestus knew of a fifth image. Though his rational mind told him otherwise, in his heart, the Ultramarine knew what he had seen – the range of mountains, the lustrous green and blue – it was unmistakable. He also knew what he had felt: a sense of belonging, like coming home.

'Macragge,' he whispered, and felt suddenly cold.

FOUR

Divine inspiration/A gathering/Contact

Mhotep stared into the water, so still and clear its surface was like silver. The face that stared back at him had hard and chiselled features with a handsome bone structure, despite the velvet cowl that partly concealed it. Hooded eyes spoke of intelligence, and skin, so tan and smooth that it was utterly without imperfection, suggested the nature of his Legion: the Thousand Sons.

Mhotep was dressed in iridescent robes that pooled like deep red liquid around him as he knelt with head bowed. Stitched in runes, his attire suggested the arcane. He was at the heart of his private sanctum.

The ellipse-shaped chamber had a low ceiling that enhanced the sense of claustrophobia created by the sheer volume of esoteric paraphernalia within. Stacks of scroll cases and numerous shelves, replete with well-thumbed archaic tomes, warred for space with crys-glass cabinets filled with bizarre arcana: an oculum of many hued lenses, a bejewelled gauntlet, a plain silver mask fashioned into an ersatz skull. Upon a raised dais, there was a planetarium in miniature, rendered from gold, the stellar bodies represented by gemstones. Gilt-panelled walls were swathed in ancient charts in burnished metal frames, cast in the azure glow of eldritch lamps.

A red marble floor stretched across the entire room, engraved with myriad paths of interlocking and concentric circles. Runes of onyx and jet, etched into the stone, punctuated the sweeping arcs without regularity. Mhotep was at the nexus of the design, at the point where all of the interweaving circles converged.

A chime registered in a vox-emitter built into the sanctum's entry system, indicating a guest.

'Enter, Kalamar,' said Mhotep.

A hiss of escaping pressure accompanied the aide as the door to the sanctum opened and he shuffled into the room.

'How did you know it was I, Lord Mhotep?' asked Kalamar, his speech fraught with age and decrepitude.

'Who else would it be, old friend? I do not need the prescience of Magnus to predict your presence in my sanctum.'

Mhotep bent towards the bowl, plunging both hands into the water to lightly splash his face. As he came back up, he withdrew his cowl and the lamp light reflected from his bald scalp.

'And I need no sophisticated augury to divine that you bring important news, either,' Mhotep added, dabbing his face with his sleeve.

'Of course, sire. I meant no offence,' said Kalamar, bowing acutely. The serf was blind, and wore ocular implants; the augmetic bio-sensors built into his eye cavities could not 'see' as such, but detected heat and provided limited spatial awareness. Kalamar supplemented his somewhat unorthodox visual affliction with a silvered cane.

'My lord, we have docked at Vangelis,' he added finally, confirming what his captain already knew.

Mhotep nodded, as if possessed of sudden understanding.

'Have the Legion serfs prepare my armour, we are leaving the ship at once.'

'As you wish,' Kalamar said, bowing again, but as he was retreating from the sanctum he paused. 'My lord, please do not think me impertinent, but why have we docked here at Vangelis when our journey's end lies at Prospero?'

'The paths of destiny are curious, Kalamar,' Mhotep replied, looking back down at the bowl.

'Yes, my lord.' Even after over fifty years in his service, Kalamar did not fully understand his master's cryptic words.

When the Legion serf had gone, Mhotep rose to his feet, his voluminous robes gathering up around him. From within the folds of his sleeves, he produced a stave-like object, no longer than his forearm and covered in arcane sigils.

Stepping away from the circle, a single eye was revealed at its centre as he took a bizarre course through the labyrinthine design of the room. It represented the wisdom of Magnus, Primarch of the Thousand Sons Legion and gene-father to Mhotep. Locked in his cabalistic route, Mhotep arrived at an ornate, lozenge-shaped vessel and reverently placed the stave within it. The vessel was much like a gilded sarcophagus, similar to that in which the rulers of ancient Prospero had once been entombed. The item secured, Mhotep sealed the vessel shut, a vacuum hiss of escaping pressure emitting from its confines, and inputted a rune sequence disguised within the sarcophagus's outer decoration.

'Yes,' uttered Mhotep, the task done, absently caressing a scarab-shaped earring, 'very curious.'

'IT IS A low turn out,' muttered Antiges beneath his breath.

Within the stark, grey ferrocrete austerity of the Ultramarines muster hall three Astartes awaited Cestus and his battle-brothers. The three were seated around a conference table inset with a single arcing 'U'. A huge tapestry, depicting the auspicious day when the Emperor came to Macragge in search of one of his sons, framed the scene. Clad in glorious armour of gold, a shining halo about his patrician features, the Emperor stretched out his hand to a kneeling Roboute Guilliman, who reached out to claim it. That day, their primarch had been truly born and their Legion's inception cemented.

Even now, and rendered as mere artistry, Cestus could not help but feel his heart lift.

'With such short notice, I had expected less,' the Ultramarine confessed, approaching the gathering with Antiges. Cestus's battle-brother had briefed his captain on the attendees. Brynngar he knew, of course, but the two others, a Thousand Son and a World Eater, he did not.

Cestus and Antiges were joined by four more of their brothers – Lexinal, Pytaron, Excelinor and Morar, for the sake of appearances. The rest, Amyrx, Laeradis and Thestor, were with Saphrax on a separate duty. The Ultramarines had called the gathering, so it was only proper that they arrived at it in force to show their commitment.

'Greetings brothers,' Cestus began, taking his seat alongside his fellow Ultramarines. 'You have the gratitude of Guilliman and the eighth Legion for your attendance here this day.'

'As is well,' said a bald-headed Astartes with richly tanned skin, 'but we beseech you to illuminate us as to your plight.' His voice was deep and powerful. Clad in the panoply of the Thousand Sons Legion, a suit of lacquered dark red and gold power armour, as angular and proud as the monuments of Prospero, he cut an intimidating figure. Antiges had already informed Cestus that the Thousand Son was Fleet Captain Mhotep.

Darkly handsome, bereft of the usual battle scars and functional facial bionics wrought by years of unremitting warfare, this Mhotep had a curious, aloof air. His shining eyes seemed to bore into Cestus's very soul.

Not all of the assembly were so respectful of his obvious power.

'The Great Wolf values silence over idle chatter, so that he might heed wise words otherwise lost in needless interrogation,' snarled Brynngar, the animosity he felt towards the son of Magnus obvious.

It was the Wolf Guard, already pledged to Cestus's cause, together with Antiges, that had summoned the Legions on Vangelis to this meeting. They had done so with passion and curt request, divulging little of what Cestus needed of them. The Space Wolf had at first railed against the inclusion of the Thousand Sons to be their potential sword-brothers in this deed. The conflicting character of the two Legions did not lend itself to a ready accord, but Cestus had reasoned that they needed every soul, and Mhotep had answered the call. What was more, he also had his own ship, a fact that only served to bolster the small fleet he was trying to assemble.

The captain of the Thousand Sons ignored the Space Wolf's thinly veiled insult and leant back in his seat with a gesture for Cestus to proceed.

The Ultramarines captain told the assembly of his squad's scheduled extraction from Vangelis by the *Fist of Macragge*, and of the astropathic message that had very nearly wrecked the control hub of Coralis dock. He even confided in them his fears that some unknown enemy had destroyed the ship, but he did not mention his experience in the reactor core. Cestus was still processing what he had seen. Visions were the province of sorcery and to divulge that he, an Ultramarine, had witnessed one would undermine his credibility and arouse suspicion as to his motives.

'Perhaps this deed was committed by an alien ship. Ork hulks have been fought and crushed by my Legion as far as the Segmentum Solar,' said a voice like iron. Skraal was a World Eater, an Astartes of the XII Legion, and the third of the invited warriors, including Brynngar.

He wore battered Mark V power armour, rendered in chipped blue and white, the colours of his Legion, clearly eschewing the Corvus pattern suits worn by his battle-brothers. The armour was heavily dented in several places, sporting numerous replacement parts, and the battlefield repair work was obvious. Formed of basic materials, the plates were held together by spikes, the manifest studs clearly visible on the left pauldron, greaves and gorget. The helmet rested on the table next to the warrior. It was similarly adorned and bore a fearsome aspect of blade and ballistic damage that revealed bare, grey metal beneath.

Skraal's face was the mirror of his armour, cross-hatching scar tissue a map-work of pain and suffering. A thick vein across his forehead throbbed as he spoke. His bellicose demeanour, coupled with a nervous tic beneath his right eye, gave him the outward appearance of being unhinged.

The World Eaters were a fearsome Legion. Much like their primarch, Angron, they were a primal force that fought with fury and wrath as their weapons. Each and every warrior was a font of rage and barely checked choler, bloody echoes of the battle-lust of their primarch.

'That is possible,' said Cestus, deliberately holding the gruesome warrior's gaze, despite Skraal's obvious belligerence. 'What is certain is that a ship of the Emperor's Astartes has been attacked by enemies unknown and for some nefarious purpose,' he continued with building anger and got to his feet. 'This act cannot go unreckoned!'

'Then what would you have us do, noble son of Guilliman?' asked Mhotep, ever the epitome of calm.

Cestus spread his hands across the table, laying his palms flat as he regained his composure. 'Astropathic decryption revealed a region of space that has been identified by the station's astrocartographer. I believe this is where the *Fist of Macragge* met its end. I also believe that since the ship was headed for the Calth system and a rendezvous with my lord Guilliman, it is possible that their attacker was heading in the same direction.'

'A substantial leap of logic, Ultramarine,' Mhotep countered, unconvinced by Cestus's impassioned arguments.

'It cannot believe that the very ship carrying five companies of my battle-brothers and en route to Calth was destroyed before reaching Vangelis in a random act of xenos contrition,' Cestus reasoned, his need for urgency fuelling his frustration.

'How are we to find this slayer vessel, then?' asked Skraal, thumbing the hilt of his chainaxe, the urge for carnage obvious. 'If what you say is true, and the distress call you received from the vessel is old, the prey will be far from that location.'

Cestus sighed in agitation. He wished dearly that he could make his brothers see what was in his heart, what he knew in his gut. For now, though, he dared not, at least, not until he could make some sense of what he had seen. There was no time for delay.

'Our position on Vangelis bisects the route of the *Fist of Macragge*; the route it would have taken to Calth. In short, it is ahead of the site of its demise. If we make ready at once, it is possible we may be able to catch the enemy's trail.'

Silent faces regarded him. Even Brynngar did not look certain of the Ultramarine's reasoning. Cestus realised that it was not logic that guided him on this course, but instinct and inner belief. The image of Macragge seen for an instant in the flash of the reactor burned fresh in his mind, and he spoke.

'I do not need your aid in this venture. I have already sent one of my battle-brothers to commandeer a vessel from this very station and I will take it to the site of the *Fist of Macragge*'s last transmission. With luck we can pick up a trail to follow and find whoever is responsible for what happened to it. No, I do not *need* your aid, but I *ask* for it, humbly,' he added, pushing the seat back and kneeling reverently before his fellow Astartes with head bowed.

Antiges was aghast at first, but then he too left the table and kneeled. The other Ultramarines followed his

lead, and soon all six of Guilliman's sons were genu-
flecting before the rest of the council.

'The sons of Russ do not refuse an honour debt,' said
Brynngar, getting to his feet and laying Felltooth upon
the table. 'I will join you in this endeavour.'

Skraal stood next and set his chainaxe with the Space
Wolf's rune blade.

'The fury of the World Eaters is at your side.'

'What say you, son of Magnus?' Brynngar growled, his
savage gaze falling upon Mhotep.

For a moment, the Thousand Son sat in calm reflection, considering his answer. He laid his ornate scimitar
with the other weapons, its gilded blade humming with
power as he unsheathed it.

'My ship and I are at your disposal, Ultramarine.'

'Bah! This council's greatest opponent; I should like
to know why,' said Brynngar.

Mhotep smirked with amusement at the Space Wolf's
rancour, but refused to be baited.

'You all know of the events at Nikea concerning my
primarch and Legion, and the sanctions placed upon us
that day,' the Thousand Son said plainly. 'I am keen to
foster improved relations with my fellow Legions and
where better to start than the vaunted sons of Roboute
Guilliman.' Mhotep nodded respectfully at the final
remark, a deliberately weak attempt to cover the slight.

Cestus cared little for the discord between the two
Astartes and arose, Antiges following his example.

'You do me great service this day,' Cestus said with
genuine humility. 'We meet at Coralis dock in one
hour.'

THE SATURNINE FLEET had existed before the Great Crusade, carving out a miniature empire among the rings of

Saturn. Its strength and longevity had been based on a tradition of navigational skill, essential to negotiate the infinitely complex puzzle of the rings. Its rolls of honour noted the first time it had encountered the warships of the fledgling Imperium. Its admirals saw a brother empire, based on the demonstration of power and not just empty words or fanaticism, and signed a treaty with the Emperor that still held pride of place in the Admiralty Spire on Enceladus. Its ships had accompanied the Great Crusade to all corners of the galaxy, but their spiritual home had always been in the rings, the endless circle of Saturn boiling above them.

The *Wrathful* was a fine ship, Cestus admitted to himself as he stood upon the bridge alongside Antiges. It was old and lavish, panelled and decorated with the heritage of a naval aristocracy that pre-dated the Imperial Army and its fleets. Its bridge looked like it had been lifted from a naval academy on Enceladus, all dark wood map tables and glass-fronted bookcases, with only the occasional pict screen or command console to break the illusion. A ring of nine viewscreens was mounted on the ceiling, where they could be lowered to provide an all-angles view of what was happening outside the ship. The command crew were in the dark blue brocaded uniforms of the Saturnine Fleet, all starch and good breeding.

In commandeering this vessel, Saphrax and his battle-brothers had performed their task well.

'Rear admiral,' said Cestus as he approached the captain's post, a grand throne surrounded by racks of charts.

The throne rotated to reveal Rear Admiral Kaminska. Cestus could almost see the proud heritage etched upon her face: strong jaw, fine neck, high cheekbones, with a slight curl to the lip that suggested acute arrogance.

'Captain Cestus, it is an honour to serve the Emperor's Astartes,' she responded coolly. Saphrax had described the admiral's reaction to the acquisition of her ship to Cestus as he and the rest of the Ultramarine honour guard had boarded. It was prickly and vociferous.

She gave a near imperceptible nod by way of acknowledgement. The gesture was all but lost in the high collar of her uniform and the thick, furred mantle that hung around her shoulders. Admiral Kaminska was a stern-faced matriarch. A monocle over her left eye partly obscured a savage scar that cracked that side of her face. The monocle's sweeping chain was set with tiny skulls and pinned to the right breast of her jacket. She carried a control wand at her waist, secured by a loop of leather, and a naval pistol sat snugly in a holster at her hip. Gloved hands bore a lightning flash emblem made from metal; they were tense and gripped the supports of her command throne tightly.

'The *Wrathful* is an impressive ship,' said Cestus, attempting to dispel the fraught atmosphere. 'I am glad you could respond to our summons.'

'Indeed it is, Lord Astartes,' Kaminska said in clipped tones. 'It would be a great pity to sacrifice it upon the altar of futile vengeance. As for your summons,' she added, face pinching tight with anger, 'it was hardly that.'

Cestus held his tongue. As an Astartes fleet commander, it was within the remit of his authority to take command of the ship. For now, he decided he would allow the admiral some leeway. He was sketching a suitable reproach in his mind, when Kaminska continued.

'Captain Vorlov of the *Boundless* has also requested to accompany us, although you'll find he is of a more placid demeanour.'

Cestus had heard of the vessel, and of Captain Vorlov. It was a warhorse ship of the fleet, its combat scars too numerous to count. Its star was in decline, as better, more powerful ships made their presence felt in the greater galaxy. Cestus suspected that the *Boundless* had been docked at Vangelis for some time, its role in the Great Crusade somewhat diminished, and that Captain Vorlov did not wish to submit to atrophy just yet.

'Very well,' said Cestus, deciding against rebuking the admiral. He had, after all, taken her ship for a mission of dubious reasoning. Her attitude, he told himself, was to be expected.

'You have your heading, admiral. There is little time to lose.'

'The *Wrathful* is the fastest vessel in the Segmentum Solar. If your enemy is out there in the void then we will catch him,' Kaminska assured him, and whirled her command throne back around to her instrument panels.

ADMIRAL KAMINSKA BRISTLED furiously as the Astartes departed the bridge. She had come to Vangelis to effect repairs and take on supplies and replacement crew. She had been looking forward to a week or so of recuperation. Yet, at the word of the Emperor's Angels, lord regents of the galaxy it seemed, she and her ship were pressed back into service with barely a moment's notice. 'By the authority of the Emperor of Mankind', those words were an unbendable edict that Kaminska could not refuse. It was not that she resented serving – she was a dutiful soldier of the Imperium who had distinguished herself on numerous occasions for its greater glory – no, she took umbrage at the fact that this particular mission was fostered on hunches and, as far as she could tell, whimsy. It did not sit well with Kaminska, not at all.

'Lord admiral, the escort squadron is in position,' said Helmsmistress Athena Venkmyer. Her long hair was tied up severely, and her shoulders were forced to attention by the brocade of her uniform.

'Good,' Kaminska replied. 'Screens down!'

The ring of viewscreens descended and glowed to life. The bright, hard gleam of Vangelis was visible from the assembly point, surrounded by a fuzzy shoal of lesser lights: satellite listening spires, fleets at anchor and orbital debris. A distant sun was a brighter point, automatically dimmed by the viewscreens' limiters.

Icons blinked onto the screens, showing the positions of the other ships in the makeshift fleet. The four escorts – *Fearless*, *Ferox*, *Ferocious* and *Fireblade* – were flying in a slanted diamond around the *Wrathful*. The vessel of the Thousand Sons and Captain Mhotep, the *Waning Moon*, was a short distance away. Even at this distance, the Astartes craft was impressive, a sleek dart of red and gold. The *Boundless*, a cruiser like the *Wrathful*, but fitted out with decks for attack craft, was further out, still making its approach.

Satisfied that they were about ready to disembark, Admiral Kaminska flicked a control stud on the arm of her throne and the bridge vox-caster opened up. 'Loose escort pattern, keep the *Waning Moon* in our lee. Advance to primary way point, plasma engines three-quarters.'

'Three-quarters!' came the yell from Helms-mate Lodan Kant at the engine helm.

'Mister Orcadus, the Terraward end of the Tertiary Core Transit if you please,' said Kaminska, having opened up a line to her principal Navigator.

'At your word, lord admiral,' was the dour response from the Navigator's sanctum.

The Tertiary Core Transit was the most stable warp route from Segmentum Solar to the galactic south-east. It would take them to their destination expediently, and hopefully allow the *Wrathful* to gain some ground on whatever foes, real or imagined, awaited them in the void. It was also the route that any void-farer, if he or she did not want to take a four to five year detour, would take to arrive at the Calth system. The Astartes had been very specific about that. Admiral Kaminska would have liked to question it, but there was no bringing the Emperor's Angels to account on such a triviality. She would defer to the Astartes's order, since he was in charge. It would have been unseemly to do otherwise. Kaminska resolved to discover the truth later.

The *Wrathful*'s engines kicked in, banishing the admiral's thoughts to the back of her mind. She could feel the vibration through the panelled floor of the bridge. The escort squadron moved into formation on the viewscreens, followed by the *Waning Moon* and the *Boundless*.

Whatever was out there, they would find out soon enough.

'THERE IS AN energy trail here. It's degraded but discernible,' said Principal Navigator Orcadus's voice from his inner sanctum on the *Wrathful*.

The Imperial ship and her fleet had reached the region of real space as indicated by the co-ordinates provided by Captain Cestus, the supposed site of the destruction of the *Fist of Macragge*, in short order. They found no sign of the Ultramarine vessel. There was merely a faint energy trace that matched the *Fist of Macragge*'s signature. Unlike battles on land, where evidence of a fight could be seen clearly and obviously, conflicts in space were not so easily identifiable. Wrecks drifted, ships could be caught and destroyed in black holes, space debris drawn into the gravity well of a passing moon or small planet, even solar wind could scatter the final proof of a battle ever having taken place. So it was that Kaminska had instructed her Navigator to search for whatever energy traces remained behind, those last vestiges of plasma engine discharge that lingered in spite of all other evidence dissipating due to the ravages of space.

'By Saturn, the output must have been massive,' Orcadus continued with rare emotion. 'Whatever ship left this wake is gargantuan, admiral.'

'It is possible to follow it then?' Kaminska asked, swivelling in her command throne to regard Captain Cestus standing silently alongside her.

Orcadus's reply was succinct.

'Yes, admiral.'

'Do it,' Cestus told Kaminska grimly, his expression far away.

Kaminska scowled at what she perceived as arrogance, and returned to her original position.

'Then do so. Set radar array to full power, Mister Orcadus. Take us onward.'

'BROTHERHOOD,' SAID ZADKIEL, 'is power.'

Surrounded by novices in the sepulchral gloom of the cathedra, he loomed high above the assembly within a raised pulpit of black steel.

'It is at the core of all authority in the known galaxy, and the source of humanity's dominion. This is the Word of Lorgar, as it is written.'

'As it is written,' echoed the novices.

Over fifty Word Bearers had gathered for the seminary and knelt in supplication before their lord, wearing grey initiate robes over their crimson armour. The cathedral's ceiling soared on stone-clad struts overhead, adding acoustic power to Zadkiel's oratory, and the air was as still and cold as a vault. The floor, tiled with stone pages cut with passages from the Word, emphasised that this was a place of worship. It was the very thing that the Emperor had forbidden in his Legions. Idolatry and zealous faith had no place in the Master of Mankind's new age of enlightenment, but here, in this place, and in the hearts of all Lorgar's children, faith would be honed into a weapon.

One of the initiates stood among the congregation, indicating his desire to respond.

'Speak,' said Zadkiel, quelling his annoyance at the impromptu interruption.

'Brother can turn on brother,' said the novice, 'and thus become weakened. Where, then, is such power?'

In the half-light, Zadkiel recognised Brother Ultis, a zealous youth with ambitious temperament.

'That is the source of its true power, novice, for there is no greater rivalry than that which exists between siblings. Only then will one seek to undo the works of the other with such vehemence, giving every ounce of his being to claim victory,' Zadkiel said, arrogantly, enjoying the feeling of superiority.

'Upon gaining mastery over his kin, that brother will have forged a mighty army so as to overthrow him. He will have plumbed deep of his core and unleashed his hate, for in no other way can such a victory be achieved.'

'So you speak of hate,' said Ultis, 'and not brotherhood at all.'

Zadkiel smiled thinly to conceal his impatience.

'They are two wings on the same eagle, equal elements of an identical source,' Zadkiel explained. 'We are at war with our brothers, make no mistake of that. In his short-sightedness, the Emperor has brought us to this inexorable fate.

'With our hate, our devotion to the credos of our primarch, the all-powerful Lorgar, we will achieve our victory.'

'But the Emperor holds Terra, and in that surely there is strength,' Ultis countered, forgetting himself.

'The Emperor is brother to no one!' cried Zadkiel, stepping forward as his words crushed Ultis's challenge easily.

Silence persisted for a moment, Ultis shrinking back before his master as he was being chastened. None in the cathedral dared speak. All were cowed by Zadkiel's obvious power.

'He lurks in his dungeons on Terra,' Zadkiel continued with greater zeal, but now addressing the entire congregation. 'The eaxectors and bureaucrats, the flock of Malcador, who run Terra's regency, they shy away from all ties of brotherhood. They sit on a pedestal, above reproach, above their brothers, above even our noble Warmaster!'

The crowd roared in ascent, Ultis among them, kneeling once more.

'Is that brotherhood?'

The novices roared again, gauntleted fists pounding the breast plates of their armour to emphasise their fervour.

'These regents create a stale, meaningless world where all passion is dead and devotion is regarded as heresy!' Zadkiel spat the words, and was suddenly aware of a presence in the shadows behind him.

One of the *Furious Abyss*'s crew, Helms-mate Sarkorov, a man with delicate data-probes instead of fingers, was patiently awaiting Zadkiel's notice.

'My apologies, lord,' he said, once he had crossed the few metres between them, 'but Navigator Esthemya has discovered a fleet of pursuing vectors in our wake.'

'What fleet?'

'Two cruisers, an escort squadron and an Astartes strike vessel.'

'I see.' Zadkiel turned back to the congregation. 'Novices, you are dismissed,' he said without ceremony.

The assembled Word Bearers departed in silence into the shadows around the edge of the cathedral, heading back to their cells to ruminate on the Word.

'They are gaining ground, my lord,' said Sarkorov once they were alone. 'We are powerful, but these ships are smaller and outmatch us for speed.'

'Then they will reach us before we arrive at the Tertiary Core Transit.' It was a statement, not a question.

'They will, my lord. Should I instruct the magos to force the engines to maximum power? It is possible we could make warp before we are intercepted.'

'No,' said Zadkiel, after some thought. 'Maintain course and keep me updated as to the fleet's progress.'

'Yes, sire,' replied Sarkorov, saluting and then turning sharply to return to the bridge.

'My Lord Zadkiel,' said a voice from the gloom. It was Ultis, concealed by the shadows, but now stepping into the light at the centre of the cathedra.

'Novice,' said Zadkiel, 'why have you not returned to your cell?'

'I would speak with you, master, of the lessons imparted.'

'Then illuminate me, novice.' There was the slightest trace of amusement in Zadkiel's tone.

'The brothers of whom you spoke, you were referring to the primarchs,' Ultis ventured.

'Go on.'

'Our current course will bring us into conflict with the Emperor. To the unenlightened observer, it would appear that the Emperor rules the galaxy and the throne of Terra cannot be usurped.'

'What of the enlightened, novice, what do they see?'

'That the Emperor's power is wielded through his primarchs,' Ultis said with growing conviction, 'and by dividing them, the power of which you spoke is realised.'

Zadkiel's silence bade Ultis to continue.

'It is how Terra can be defeated, when Lorgar's brothers join with him, when we bring war to those who will inevitably side with the Emperor. We will yoke our hatred and use it as a weapon, one that will not be denied!'

Zadkiel nodded sagely, suppressing a prickle of annoyance at this precocious, yet insightful, youth. Ultis, however, had overreached himself. Zadkiel saw the naked ambition in his eyes, the flame within that threatened to devour Zadkiel's own.

'I merely seek to understand the Word,' Ultis added, exhaling his fervour.

'And you shall, Ultis,' Zadkiel replied, a plan forming in his mind. 'You will be an important instrument in the breaking of Guilliman.'

'I would be honoured, lord,' said Ultis, bowing his head.

'Truly blind men like Guilliman are few,' Zadkiel counselled. 'He believes religion and devotion to be a corrupting force, something to be abhorred and not embraced as we followers of the Word do. His pragmatic retardation is his greatest weakness and in his dogmatic ignorance we shall strike at the heart of his favoured Legion.'

Zadkiel spread his arms wide to encompass the cathedral, its high vaults and fluted columns, its pages of the Word, its altar and pulpit. 'One day, Ultis, the whole galaxy will look like this.'

Ultis bowed once more.

'Now, return to your cell and think on these lessons further.'

'Yes, my lord.'

Zadkiel watched the novice go. A great passage in the sermon of the Word was unfolding and Ultis would play his part. Zadkiel turned back to the pulpit, behind which was a simple altar. Zadkiel lit a candle there for the soul of Roboute Guilliman. Blind he might be, but he was a brother of sorts, and it was only right that his future death be commemorated.

ABOARD THE WRATHFUL, on one of the ship's training decks, two World Eaters clashed furiously in a duelling pit. It was one of several arenas in a much wider gymnasium that was replete with dummies, weights and training mats. Weapon ranks lined the walls. The Astartes had brought their own stocks of training weapons with them, and sword-breakers, short-blades, bludgeons and spears were all in evidence. It appeared that the concept of simple training was anathema to the duelling sons of Angron. Amidst the storm of blades and unbridled blood-lust the World Eaters fought as if to the death.

Armed with unfettered chainaxes and stripped to the waist, wearing crimson training breeches and black boots, their muscled bodies revealed gruesome welts and long, jagged scars.

With a roar, they broke off for a moment, and began circling each other in the sunken chamber of the pit. White marble showed up dark splashes from where the gladiators had wounded each other early on in the contest. A narrow drain at the centre of the pit was already clogging with blood.

'Such anger,' Antiges commented, overlooking the contest from a seated position at the back of the auditorium before which it was staged.

'They are Angron's progeny,' said Cestus, alongside him, 'it is their way to be wrathful. Properly employed, their wrath is a useful tool.'

'Yes, but their reputation is a dire one, as is their lord's,' replied Antiges, his expression stern. 'I for one do not feel at ease with their presence on this ship.'

'I have to concur with my brother, Captain Cestus,' added Thestor, who was watching the show alongside Antiges. The burly Astartes was the biggest of the honour guard. Unsurprisingly, his bulk went well with his role of heavy weapons specialist. The rest of the honour guard were nearby, except for Saphrax, watching the ferocious display with mixed interest and disdain. Thestor echoed the thoughts of all his brothers when he next spoke.

'Was it necessary to bring them with us at all?' he asked, his gaze shifting back from his captain to watch the fight. 'This is the business of the Ultramarines. What has it got to do with our Legion brothers?'

'Thestor, do not be so narrow-minded as to think we do not need their aid,' Cestus chastened the heavy-set Astartes, who glanced over at his captain. 'We are a brotherhood: all of us. Though we each have our differences, the Emperor has seen fit for us to conquer the galaxy in his name together. The moment we seek our own personal glories, when we abandon solidarity for pride, is the moment when brotherhood will be shattered.'

Thestor regarded the floor when his captain had finished, shamed by his selfish remarks.

'You may take your leave, Thestor,' said Cestus. It wasn't a request.

The big Astartes got to his feet and left the training arena.

'I agree with you, Cestus, of course I do,' said Antiges, once Thestor had gone, 'but they are like savages.'

'Are they, Antiges?' Cestus challenged. 'Are Brynngar and the wolves of Russ not savages, too? Do you hold them in such disregard also?'

'Of course not,' Antiges replied. 'I have fought with the Space Wolves and know of their courage and honour. They are savages in their own way, yes, but the difference is that they are possessed of a noble spirit. These sons of Angron are blood-letters, pure and simple. They kill for the simple joy of it.'

'We are all warriors,' Cestus told him. 'Each of us kills in the Emperor's name.'

'Not like them we don't.'

'They are Astartes,' Cestus said, biting out his words, and turning on his battle-brother. 'I will hear no more of this. You forget your place, Antiges.'

'I apologise, captain. I spoke out of turn,' Antiges replied after a moment of stunned silence. 'I only meant to say that I do not approve of their methods or their deeds.' At that, the Ultramarine turned back to watch the battle.

Cestus followed his battle-brother's gaze. The Ultramarine captain did not know either of the World Eaters in the duelling pit. He knew precious little of their leader, Skraal. This was ritual combat. No slight, no besmirching of honour had occurred to bring it about. Yet it was bladed and deadly.

'I do not, either,' Cestus admitted, watching as one of the combatants nearly lost his arm to a wild swing of his opponent's chainaxe.

The Ultramarine had heard stories from his fellow Legionnaires about the so called 'cleansing' of Ariggata, one of the World Eaters' more infamous battle actions. The Legion's assault on the citadel there had reputably left a charnel house in its wake. Cestus knew full well that Guilliman still sought a reckoning with his brother primarch, Angron, concerning the dire events of that mission, but this was no time for recrimination. Necessity had forced Cestus's hand, and whether he liked it or not, this is what he had been dealt.

Skraal led twenty World Eaters on the *Wrathful* and Cestus was determined to make the best use of them. Brynngar had brought the same number of Blood Claws, and while they were raucous and pugnacious, especially when forced into idleness in the confines of the ship, they did not harbour the same homicidal bent as the bloody sons of Angron. Mhotep was the only Astartes not aboard the *Wrathful*. He had his own ship, the *Waning Moon*, but no squads of Thousand Sons, just cohorts of naval arms-men at his command.

Barely fifty Astartes and the vessels of their makeshift fleet, Cestus hoped it would be enough for whatever was in store.

'What troubles you, brother?' asked Antiges, their brief altercation swiftly forgotten. The Ultramarine finally turned his back on the battling World Eaters, deciding he had seen enough.

'The message at Coralis dock sits heavily on me,' Cestus confessed. 'The clenched fist, crested by a laurel crown represents Legion... our Legion. The golden book – I don't know what that means, but I saw something else.'

'In the reactor flare,' Antiges realised. 'I had thought I was hearing things when you asked us if we'd seen anything.'

'You were not, and yes, I saw it in the reactor flare, so fleeting and indistinct that at first I believed it was my imagination, that my mind was articulating what my heart longed for.'

'What did you see?'

Cestus looked Antiges directly in the eyes.

'I saw Macragge.'

Antiges was nonplussed. 'I don't–'

'I saw Macragge and I felt despair, Antiges, as if it presaged something terrible.'

'Signs and visions are the province of witchery, brother-captain,' Antiges counselled warily. 'We both know the edicts of Nikea.'

'Brothers,' a voice broke in before Cestus could respond. It was Saphrax, come from the bridge where Cestus had instructed he maintain a watch on proceedings.

Both Saphrax's fellow Ultramarines turned to him expectantly.

'We have made visual contact with the ship from the site of the *Fist*'s destruction.'

* * *

'THAT IS A Legion ship, captain. You are not suggesting that a vessel of the Imperium fired upon one of its own?' Admiral Kaminska warned the Astartes.

Following Saphrax's report, Cestus and Antiges had made for the bridge at once. What they saw in the viewscreen when they got there had stunned them both.

The vessel they tracked in the void was of Mechanicum design and clearly made for the Legion. It was bedecked in the iconography of the Word Bearers.

It was the largest ship that Cestus had ever seen. Even at a considerable distance it was massive, easily three times the size of the *Wrathful*, and would have dwarfed an Emperor-class battleship. It bore an impressive array of weapons; tech-adepts aboard the *Wrathful* had suggested port and starboard broadside laser batteries and multiple torpedo tubes to the prow and stern. It was the monolithic statue towering at the vessel's prow, however, that gave Cestus the most concern: a gigantic golden book, the echo of the fragmented image in the astropathic message on Vangelis.

'We're at extreme strike range,' said Captain Commander Vorlov. 'What are your orders, admiral?'

'Hold them back,' said Cestus, deliberately interrupting Kaminska. 'They are our Legion brothers. I am certain they will be able to account for themselves. They may have information regarding the *Fist of Macragge*.'

Vorlov was a paunchy man with jowls that wobbled independently of the rest of his body. He had a gnarled red nose that spoke of long nights drinking to keep away the cold of space, and dressed in the heavy furs typical of his Saturnine heritage. His presence filled the viewscreen through which he was communicating with the bridge of the *Wrathful*. 'Yes, my lord,' he said.

'No point rattling the sword without reason,' Cestus muttered to Antiges, who nodded his assent. 'Hang back and keep them within range, but do not approach. Admiral Kaminska, bring the *Wrathful* in at the lead. Keep the *Waning Moon* and the escort fleet in our wake.'

'As you wish, my lord,' she said, swallowing her annoyance and her pride. 'Relaying orders now.'

The tension around the bridge was palpable. Brynngar, having joined them a moment before, growled beneath his breath.

'What is your plan, Cestus?' he asked, eyes locked on the viewscreen and the mighty vessel visible beyond it.

'We draw in close enough to hail them and demand to know their business.'

'On Fenris, when stalking the horned orca, I would swim the icy depths of the ocean taking care to stay in the beast's wake,' Brynngar said with intensity. 'Once I drew close enough I would slip my baleen spear from my leg and launch it into the orca's unprotected flank. Then I would swim, long and hard, to reach the beast before it could turn and impale me on its horn. Within its thrashing swell I would seize upon it and with my blade pare its flesh and gut its innards. For the orca is a mighty beast, and this was the only way to be sure of its demise.'

'We will hail them,' Cestus affirmed, noting the savagery that played across Brynngar's features with unease. 'I won't commit us to a fight over nothing.'

'Admiral,' the Ultramarine added, turning to Kaminska.

'Helms-mate Kant, open up a channel to the vessel at once,' she said.

Kant did as ordered and indicated his readiness to his commander.

Kaminska nodded to Cestus.

'This is Captain Cestus of the Ultramarines Seventh Chapter. In the name of the Emperor of Mankind, I am ordering you to state your designation and business in this subsector.'

Static-fringed silence was the only reply.

'I repeat: this is Captain Cestus of the Ultramarines Seventh Chapter. Respond,' he barked into the bridge vox.

More silence.

'Why do they not answer?' asked Antiges, his fists tightly clenched. 'They are Legionaries, like us. Since when did the sons of Lorgar fail to acknowledge the Ultramarines?'

'I don't know. Perhaps their long-range vox is out.' Cestus was reaching for answers, trying to deny what he had known in his heart ever since Vangelis, that something was wrong, terribly, terribly wrong.

'Signal one of the frigates to make approach,' Cestus ordered after a brief silence, eyes fixed on the viewscreen like every other soul on the bridge. 'I don't want to come in with our cruisers,' he reasoned. 'It might be perceived as a threat.'

Kaminska relayed the order in curt fashion and the *Fearless* closed on the unknown vessel.

'I shall follow them in,' said Mhotep from a second viewscreen on the bridge. 'I have half a regiment of Prospero Spireguard standing by to board.'

'Very well, captain, but keep your distance,' Cestus warned.

'As you wish.' The viewscreen went blank as Mhotep took active command of the *Waning Moon*.

A tactical array abruptly activated, depicting the closing vessels that were virtually lost from sight in the viewport. The Word Bearers ship was a red icon on the display surrounded by sensor readings of the approaching frigates, little more than green blips in its presence.

'This reeks,' snarled Brynngar, who had begun prowling the bridge with impatience, 'and my nose never lies.'

Cestus kept his eyes on the tactical array.

Macragge. The image of his Macragge, seen as part of the astropathic warning in the reactor core, came to mind once more. How were the fates of this vessel and his home world entwined?

The Word Bearers were his brothers; surely they had nothing to do with the destruction of the *Fist of Macragge*? Such a thing was unconscionable.

Cestus would have his answers soon enough.

The *Fearless* had reached its destination.

FIVE

A line is drawn/Silver Three down/Open book

'YOUR ORDERS, CAPTAIN?' came the vox from the ordnance deck.

Zadkiel sat back on his throne. The feeling of power was intoxicating. The battleship was his to command, like an extension of his body, as if the torpedo tubes and gun turrets were his hands. He could simply spread his fingers and will destruction on the enemy.

'Hold,' said Zadkiel.

The central viewscreen showed the closing vessels: a frigate with a strike cruiser in its wake. The frigate did not interest the Word Bearer captain, but the cruiser was an entirely different prospect: fast, well-armed and designed for precision attacks and boarding actions. It was painted in the livery of the Thousand Sons.

'Magnus's brood,' said Zadkiel, idly. Astride his command throne, he glanced at a supplementary screen that depicted a tactical readout of the ship. The *Furious Abyss*'s archive had identified it as the *Waning Moon*. It had many battle honours, and had followed the Thousand Sons Legion across half the galaxy prosecuting the Great Crusade. 'I have always admired their imagination.'

Assault-Captain Baelanos was standing behind the command throne.

'They're within range, sire.'

'There is no hurry, captain,' said Zadkiel. 'We should savour this moment.' Additional readings flicked up on the viewscreen. The *Waning Moon* was showing life-signs equivalent to a full regiment of troops gathering at the boarding muster points.

'Helms-mate Sarkorov, open up a clandestine channel to the *Waning Moon*,' Zadkiel ordered.

'At once, my lord,' came the reply from deep inside the dark city of the bridge.

After a moment, Sarkorov added.

'Channel is secure.'

'On screen.'

The central image was replaced with a view of the *Waning Moon*'s gilded bridge. The Astartes in the command throne, which was massively ornate and inset with numerous jewels and engraved runes, looked up in mild surprise. He had light brown skin and hooded eyes, with a face that spoke of discipline and resolve.

'This is Captain Zadkiel, addressing you from the *Furious Abyss*. Am I speaking to the captain of the *Waning Moon*?' asked Zadkiel.

'You are. I am Captain Mhotep of the Thousand Sons. Why have you not responded to our hails?'

'No, captain, I demand to know what this display of force means,' Zadkiel said, unwilling to be interrogated by his brother Astartes. 'You have no authority here. Disengage at once.'

'I repeat, why have you not responded to our hails and what do you know of the *Fist of Macragge* and its fate?' Mhotep was relentless and would not be cowed.

'I do not appreciate your tone, brother. I know nothing of the vessel you speak of,' Zadkiel replied. 'Now, disengage.'

'I do not believe you, brother,' said the Thousand Son with certainty.

Zadkiel smiled mirthlessly.

'Then I shall give you the truth. Great deeds are unfolding, Captain Mhotep. Lines will be drawn. Flame and retribution is coming, and those who are on the wrong side of that line will be burned to ash.' Zadkiel paused for a moment, allowing his words to sink in.

Mhotep remained impassive. The Thousand Sons were quite the experts at concealing their true emotions.

'We are on a secure channel, Captain Mhotep, and the Legion of the Word have ever been supporters of your lord Magnus. The events of Nikea must rankle.' That got a reaction, near imperceptible, but it was there.

'What are you suggesting, Word Bearer?'

Hostility now, the icy reserve was thawing at the mention of what many in the Legion regarded as Magnus's trial and that what happened at Nikea was performed by a council in name only.

'Lorgar and Magnus are brothers. So are we. What side of the line will you stand on, Mhotep?'

The retort was curt. The Thousand Son's face was set like stone.

'Prepare to be boarded,' he said.

'As you wish,' replied the Word Bearer.

The vox link to the *Waning Moon* was cut.

'Master Malforian,' said Zadkiel, levelly.

The ordnance deck flashed up on the viewscreen, a deep metal canyon beneath the prow crowded with sweating ratings hauling massive torpedoes.

'My lord.'

'Fire.'

A spread of torpedoes flew from the *Furious Abyss* towards the *Waning Moon*, which had positioned itself before the massive ship's prow. Starboard, a bank of laser batteries lit up at once, and beams of crimson light stabbed into the void. They struck the *Fearless* and the frigate was broken apart in a bright and silent flurry of blossoming explosions.

'THRONE OF TERRA!' Cestus could not believe what he was seeing through the *Wrathful*'s viewscreen. Powerless, and benumbed, he watched the *Fearless* fragment like scrap as a firestorm ravaged it, hungrily devouring the oxygen on board and turning it into a raging furnace. It was over in seconds, and after the conflagration had died all that remained was a blackened ruin. Then the torpedoes hit the *Waning Moon*.

'SHARKS IN THE void!' cried Helms-mate Ramket from the sensorium on the bridge of the *Waning Moon*. The crew were all at battle stations, carefully monitoring the actions of the Word Bearer ship. The lights in the elliptical chamber were dimmed as was protocol for combat situation, and the tiny blips that represented the ordnance launched by the *Furious Abyss* glowed malevolently on one of the bridge's tactical display slates.

'Evasive manoeuvres. Turrets to full! Withdraw boarding parties to damage control stations!' Mhotep scowled and gripped the lip of the command console in front of him. Shields were useless against torpedoes; he had to hope their hull armour could bear the brunt of the *Furious Abyss*'s opening salvo.

'At your command, my lord,' came Ramket's reply.

Warning runes flashed on multiple screens at once, presaging the missile impacts. Mhotep turned again to his helms-mate.

'Open a channel to the *Wrathful*,' he ordered as the first of the torpedoes hit, sending damage klaxons screaming as a massive shudder ran through the bridge.

'Mhotep, what's happening out there?' asked Cestus over the ship-to-ship vox array.

'The *Fearless* is gone. We are taking fire and attempting to evade. The Word Bearers have turned on their own, Cestus.'

A burst of crackling static held in the air for the moment combining with the din of relayed orders and cogitator warnings.

When he finally spoke, the Ultramarine's voice was grim.

'Engage and destroy.'

'Understood.'

THE BRIDGE OF the *Wrathful* moved to battle stations, Kaminska barking rapid orders to her subordinates with well-drilled precision and calm. The professionalism of the Saturnine Fleet's officer class was evident as the weapons were brought to bear and shields focused prow-ward.

'How shall we respond, lord Astartes?' she asked, once they were at a state of readiness.

Cestus fought a cold knot of disbelief building in the pit of his stomach as he watched the spread of blips on the tactical display move into attack positions.

The Word Bearers have turned on their own.

Mhotep's words were like a hammer blow.

His words, the words that Cestus had spoken earlier on the training deck to Thestor and Antiges, of brotherhood and the solidarity of the Legions, suddenly turned to ash in his mouth. He had admonished his brothers for even voicing mild dissent against a fellow Legionnaire, and now, here they were embattled against them. No, they were not World Eaters. They were not the murderous, blood-letters that Antiges had described. They were the devout servants of the Emperor. Ostensibly they were his most vehement and staunchest supporters.

How far did this treachery go? Was it confined merely to this ship, or did it permeate the entire Legion? Surely, with the vessel crafted by the Mechanicum it had the sanction of Mars. Could they be aware of the Word Bearers' defection? Such a thing could not be countenanced. With these questions running through his mind like a fever, Cestus could not believe what was happening. It did not feel real. From disbelief, anger and a desire for retribution was born.

'Break that ship in two,' Cestus said, full of righteous conviction. He could feel the ripples of shock and disbelief passing through the non-Astartes as the full horror of what they had witnessed sank in. He would show them that the true servants of the Emperor did not tolerate traitors and any act of heresy would be summarily dealt with. Cestus's feelings and the ramifications of what had transpired would have to wait and be rationalised later. 'Relay astropathic messages to Macragge and Terra at once,' the Ultramarine added. 'The sons of Lorgar will be held to account for this. Admiral Kaminska, you have the helm.'

'As you wish, my lord.' Kaminska said. Trying her best to maintain her cold composure in the face of such developments, she swivelled the command throne as the screens around her shifted to show every angle around the ship. 'Captain Vorlov, are you with me?'

'Say the word, admiral.' Vorlov's enthusiasm was obvious, despite the static flickering through the fleet's vox array.

'Take the lead behind the *Waning Moon*. If they stay on the Astartes ship, swing up in front of them. Give them a bloody good broadside up the nose, and scramble attack craft. Keep their gunners busy. I'll send what's left of our escorts with you. In the name of Emperor.'

'At your command, admiral,' replied Vorlov with relish. 'Main engines to full, all crew to battle stations. Watch my stern, admiral, and the *Boundless* will pick this swine apart! In the name of Emperor.'

'Mister Castellan,' Kaminska barked, terminating the vox link with the *Boundless*. The *Wrathful*'s Master of Ordnance appeared on screen, toiling ratings just visible behind him on the gun decks.

'A lance salvo to their dorsal turret arrays and engines, if you please,' said Kaminska. 'Load prow plasma torpedoes, but hold in reserve, I want something up our sleeve.'

'At your command, admiral,' came the clipped response from Master of Ordnance Castellan, who snapped a curt salute before the screen blanked.

CESTUS WATCHED AS the organised chaos of battle stations unfolded. Every crewman on the bridge had his own role to play, relaying orders, monitoring sensorium and viewscreens, or making minute adjustments to the ship's course. One of the tables on the bridge unfolded into a stellar map where holographic simulacra were moved around to represent the relative positions of the ships in the fleet.

'Traitorous whoresons,' snarled Brynngar, 'it'll be Lorgar's head for this.'

Cestus could see the hairs on the back of the Space Wolf's neck rise. In this fell mood and with the dimmed battle stations gloom, he took on a feral aspect.

'Scuttle her and I'll lead the sons of Russ aboard,' he growled darkly. 'Let the wolves of Fenris gut her and I'll tear out the beating heart myself.'

Brynngar hawked and spat a gobbet of phlegm onto the deck as if what was transpiring in the void had left a bitter taste. There were a few raised eyebrows, but the Wolf Guard paid them no heed.

Cestus's reply was terse. 'You'll get your chance.'

Brynngar roared, baring his fangs.

'I can no longer sit idle,' he snapped savagely, turning on his heel. 'The warriors of Russ will make ready at the boarding torpedoes. Do not make us wait long.'

Cestus couldn't be certain if the last part was a request or a threat, but he was, for once, glad of the Wolf Guard's departure. His mood, since they'd hit the void and encountered the Word Bearers had grown increasingly erratic and belligerent. The Ultramarine sensed that the wolves of Russ did not relish such encounters. The fact that Brynngar was so eager to spill the blood of fellow Astartes only caused Cestus greater discomfort.

At war with our Legion brothers, the very idea scarcely seemed possible, yet it was happening.

Cestus watched the space battle unfold with curious detachment and felt his sense of foreboding grow.

* * *

THE WANING MOON had burned its retro engines to kill its speed, and fired all thrusters on its underside to twist upwards and present its armoured flank to a second torpedo volley shimmering towards it.

The first torpedoes missed high, spiralling past the ship to be lost in the void.

A handful detonated early, riddled with massive-calibre fragmentation shells from the defence turrets mounted along the flank of the *Waning Moon*.

Several found their mark just below the stern. Another streaked in with violent force, and then two more amidships. Useless energy shields flared black over the impact points as hull segments spun away from the ship, the torpedoes gouging their way through the outer armour.

'Damage report!' shouted Mhotep above the din of the bridge.

'Negligible, sire,' Officer Ammon answered from the engineering helm.

'What?'

'Minimal hull fractures, my Lord Mhotep.'

'Sensorium definitely read four impacts,' confirmed Helms-mate Ramket watching over the readouts.

Embedded deep in the hull of the *Waning Moon*, the outer casing of each torpedo split with a super-heated incendiary and six smaller missiles drilled out from their parent casing. They were ringed with metallic teeth and bored through the superstructure of the strike cruiser as they spun. Drilling through the last vestiges of hull armour, the missiles emerged into the belly of the vessel and detonated with a powerful explosive charge. With a deafening *thoom-woosh* of concussive heat pressure, the gun decks were ruined. Ratings and indentured workers died in droves, burned by the intense conflagration. Heaps of shells exploded in the firestorm, throwing lashes of flame and chunks of spiralling shrapnel through the decks. Master Gunner Kytan was decapitated in the initial barrage, and dozens of gunnery crew met a similar fate as they scrambled for cover as the gun-decks became little more than an abattoir of charred corpses and hellish screaming.

THE WANING MOON shuddered as explosions tore through its insides. A destructive chain reaction boiled through the upper decks and into crew quarters. Stern-wards, detonations ripped into engineering sections, normally well shielded from direct hits, and ripped plasma conduits free to spew superheated fluid through access tunnels and coolant ducts.

Damage control crews, waiting at their muster points to douse fires and seal breaches, were torn asunder by the resultant carnage from amidships. Orderlies at triage posts barely had time to register the pandemonium on the gun decks before the blunt bullet of a warhead thundered through into the medicae deck and annihilated them in a flash of light and terror.

Chains of explosions ripped huge chunks out of the *Waning Moon's* insides. Like massive charred bite marks, whole sections were reduced to smouldering metal and hundreds of crewmen were lost to the cold of the void as the vessel's structural integrity broke down.

'REPORT THAT!' ORDERED Mhotep, clinging to his command throne on the bridge as sections of the ship collapsed around him, revealing bare metal and sparking circuitry. The lights around the bridge were stuttered intermittently as the *Waning* registered power loss and damage across all decks. Mhotep's crew were doing their best to marshal some semblance of order, but the attack had been swift and far-reaching.

'Massive internal and secondary explosions,' replied Officer Ammon, struggling to keep pace with the warning runes dancing madly over the engineering helm, and snapping off further reports. 'Plasma venting from reactor seven, gun crews non-responsive and medicae has taken severe damage.'

'Tertiary shielding is breached,' said Mhotep as the ship-to-ship vox crackled into life.

'Mhotep, report your status at once! This is Captain Cestus.' The impacts had shaken the vox array and the Ultramarine's voice was distorted with static.

'We are wounded, captain,' said Mhotep grimly. 'Some kind of Mechanicum tech that I have never seen before burned our insides.'

'Our lances are firing,' Cestus informed him. 'Can you stay engaged?'

'Aye, son of Macragge, we're not done yet.'

A further crackle of static and the vox went dead.

The bridge of the *Waning Moon* was alive with transmissions from the rest of the ship: some calm, reporting peripheral damage to minor systems; others frantic, from plasma reactor seven and the gun decks, and there were those that were unintelligible through raging fire and screaming: the last words of men and women dying agonising deaths.

'Be advised, captain, they are coming about.' Principal Navigator Cronos was eerily calm as his voice came through the internal vox array. Mhotep scrutinised the tactical holo-display above the command console. The *Furious Abyss* was changing course. It was suffering lance impacts from the *Wrathful* and was turning to present its heavily armoured prow to the aggressors.

'What folly from this Bearer of his Word,' Mhotep intoned. 'He thinks we will flee like the jackal, but his only victory is in raising the ire of Prospero! Mister Cronos, bring us across his bow. Gun decks port and starboard, prepare for a rolling broadside!'

THE WANING MOON rotated grandly, as if standing on end in front of the *Furious Abyss*. The Word Bearer vessel had not reacted, and its blunt prow faced the damaged strike cruiser.

Deep scores, like illegible signatures, were seared into the prow armour of the traitors' ship by the *Wrathful's* laser batteries. An insane crosshatch of crimson lance beams erupted between the two vessels with pyrotechnic intensity as they traded blows, silent shield flares indicating absorbed impacts.

Errant bursts glittered past the *Waning Moon* as it opened up its gun ports and the snouts of massive ship-to-ship cannon emerged. Behind them, sweat-drenched ratings toiled to load the enormous guns and avenge their dead. They chanted in gun-cant to keep their rhythm strong, one refrain for hauling shells out of the hoppers behind them, another for ramming it home, and yet another for hauling the breech closed.

The signal to fire reached them from the bridge. The rating gang leaders brought hammers down on firing pins and inside the ship, thunder screamed through the decks.

Outside, jets of propellant and debris leapt the gap between the two ships. A split second later the shells impacted, explosive charges blasting deep craters into the enemy vessel.

* * *

THE BRIDGE OF the *Furious Abyss* stayed calm.

Zadkiel was pleased. His ship, the city over which he ruled, was not governed by panic.

'My lord, should we retaliate?' asked Helms-mate Sarkorov.

'For now, we wait,' said Zadkiel, content to absorb the punishment as he sat back on the command throne watching images of the *Waning Moon*'s assault on the viewscreens above him. 'There is nothing they can do to us.'

'You would have us sit here and take this?' snarled Reskiel at his master's side.

'We will prevail,' said Zadkiel, unperturbed.

Dozens of new contacts flared on the viewscreens, streaking from the launch bays of a ship identified as the *Boundless*.

'Assault boats, sire,' Sarkorov informed him, monitoring the same feed. 'Escorts are closing.'

Zadkiel pored over the hololithic display.

'They intend to attack from all angles and confuse us, and while we weather this storm, their assault boats and escorts will pick us apart.' Zadkiel provided the curt tactical analysis coldly, his face aglow in the display.

'What is our response?' asked Reskiel.

'We wait.'

'That's it?'

'We wait,' repeated Zadkiel, his voice like iron. 'Trust in the Word.'

Reskiel stood back, watching the fire hammering in from the *Waning Moon*, and listening to the dull thuds of explosions from within the *Furious*'s prow.

THE ATTACK CRAFT wing of the *Boundless* swept in tight formation through the veil of debris building up from the damage to the two ships ahead of them. The *Waning Moon* and the *Furious Abyss* were locked in the Spiral Dance: the long, painful embrace that saw one ship circle another pumping broadsides into the enemy as it spun. Like everything else in space the Spiral Dance had its own mythology, and to a lifelong pilot of the Saturnine Fleet it meant inevitable doom and the spite of one ship lashing out at the enemy in its death throes. It was desperation and tragedy, like a dying romance or a last stand against vast odds.

The fighters, ten-man craft loaded with short-range rockets and cannon, streaked past the *Waning Moon*, the pilots saluting their fellow ship as custom dictated. They locked on to the *Furious Abyss*, the squadron leaders marking out targets on the immense dark red hull already pocked with lance scars and broadside craters from the battering the *Wrathful* had given it. Shield housings, sensor clusters and exhaust vents all lit up on the tactical display in a backwash of emerald light. Targeting cogitators locked on and burned red.

Silver Three, flown by Pilot Second-Class Carnagan Thaal, matched assigned approach vectors and built to full attack run speed. Through the shallow forward viewscreen, Thaal could see the *Furious Abyss* crisscrossed by laser battery barrage, its prow a flickering mass of smouldering metal.

He ordered his weapons officers to lock on to their target, a stretch of gun turrets along the *Furious's* dorsal spine. The port guns obeyed, the lascannon mounts swivelling into position.

The starboard guns did not move.

Pilot Thaal repeated his order through the ship's vox. His co-pilot, Rugel, checked the array, but found nothing amiss.

'Rugel, go down to the armaments deck and align those guns,' Thaal ordered, deciding there was enough time before they hit their final approach vector.

The co-pilot nodded and tore out the wires attaching him to his seat and the console in front of him, and swung around in his chair.

'Scell, what are you doing?' Thaal heard his co-pilot ask and turned to get a good look at what was going on.

He started when he saw Weapons Officer Carina Scell standing there with her autopistol in her hand. Thaal was about to tell her to get back to her post and get the damn cannons locked on when Scell shot him in the face.

She took Rugel in the chest, stepping forward to deliver the shot point-blank. Bleeding badly, the co-pilot scrabbled to get his sidearm out of its holster.

'It is written,' Scell said, and shot him twice more in the head.

Silver Three continued on its attack vector. Scell headed below decks to finish her work.

'SILVER THREE'S DOWN,' said Officer Artemis on the fighter control deck of the *Boundless*. The deck ran almost a third of the length of the *Boundless* to accommodate the numerous tactical consoles.

Captain Vorlov, his face awash in the reflected ochre glow of datascreens, paid it little heed as he prowled the ranks of fighter controllers. Attack craft were always lost. It was the way of the void.

Vorlov continued his tour, preferring to witness first-hand the actions of his fighters rather than make do with the fragmented reports filtering through to the bridge. The *Boundless* was a dedicated carrier for attack craft and his duties were here, listening to the fates of his fighter wings. His helms-mate was perfectly capable of keeping the ship running in his absence.

'Any defensive fire?' asked Vorlov of the nearest control overseer.

'None yet,' said the overseer, whose shaved scalp was festooned with wires feeding information from each controller into her brain.

'But we're in range of their countermeasures,' said Vorlov, a thought occurring to him. 'You! What took down Silver Three?'

The controller looked up from his screen. 'Unknown. The pilot went off my screen. Possible crew casualties.'

'Non-standard transmissions from Gold Nine,' said another controller hunched over his screen. He held one of his earphones tight against his head and winced as he tried to hear more clearly. 'Some kind of commotion aboard ship, sire. They're not responding to protocols.'

'Bring them in. The rest of you, report any further anomalies!' Vorlov harrumphed in annoyance and leaned forward on his cane. The Saturnine Fleet had the best small craft pilots this side of the galactic centre. They didn't just flake out during a firefight.

'Gold Nine is lost, captain,' reported the controller. 'I detected small-arms fire in the cockpit.'

'Get me word on what the hell's going on or I'll have your commission,' barked Vorlov at the overseer.

'Yes, captain.'

'Fragmented reports are coming in from Silver Prime,' interrupted yet another controller. 'They say they've lost control of the engine crew.'

'Get all this on air!' shouted Vorlov. The overseer fiddled with a couple of settings and cockpit transmissions crackled through the deck's vox-caster.

'…gone insane! He's barricaded himself in the aft quarters. Esau's dead and he's venting the bloody air. I'm pulling out from attack vectors and going down there to shoot him.'

'I am the light that shines always. I am the lord of the dawn. I am the beginning and the end. I am the Word.'

'Agh, I'm… I'm bleeding out… Heral's dead, but I'm not going to make it.'

'Gold Twelve just opened fire on us! We're hit aftwards, pulling back and venting engine three.'

Vorlov was assailed by the desperate voices and distorted screams, dozens of them, all from experienced assault pilots, all tinged with fear or disbelief, or pain. Reports of colleagues sabotaging engines or murdering crew, ranting paranoia and delusion spewed forth from the vox. Vorlov couldn't believe what he was hearing. His wings were in total disarray and the glorious attack run he had envisaged had failed utterly without the enemy firing off a shot. He had never even read about such a thing in the histories of the Saturnine Fleet.

'It's as if they're going mad, captain,' said the overseer, struggling to keep her voice level, 'every one of them.'

'Abort!' shouted Vorlov. 'All wings! Abort attack run and return to the *Boundless*!'

'WE ARE SUCCESSFUL, lord,' the sibilant voice of Chaplain Ikthalon said through the vox array. 'The supplicants have effectively neutralised their fighter assault.'

'You are to be commended, chaplain. Ours is a divine purpose and you have ensured your name will be remembered in the scriptures of Lorgar,' Zadkiel replied coldly from the command throne, before turning to address Helms-mate Sarkorov.

'Let the escort craft close and then open the book.'

'Yes, my lord.' Sarkorov relayed the order at once.

Zadkiel watched a close-up of the sector of space through which the *Boundless*'s attack wings were flying. Fighters were already tumbling, glittering short-lived explosions as their colleagues shot them down. Others were spiralling off-course. The pathetic assault was in ruins.

'Behold,' Zadkiel said to his second standing alongside him, 'the power of the Word, Reskiel.'

'It is indeed humbling,' Reskiel replied, bowing deeply to his lord.

Zadkiel found the obvious toadying distasteful. Even so, this was a great moment, and he allowed himself to bask in it before returning to the vox.

'Ikthalon, how many supplicants did we lose?'

'Three, Lord Zadkiel,' the chaplain replied. 'The weakest.'

'Keep me appraised.'

'As you wish.' Ikthalon said, and terminated the link.

Zadkiel ignored the impudence and sat back in his command throne to watch the damage control reports flicker by. The prow was mangled, chewed up by the *Waning Moon*'s broadsides and torn by the lances of the *Wrathful*, but the prow was merely armour plating and empty space. It didn't matter. It could soak up everything they could throw at it for hours before the shells penetrated live decks. Even then, only Legion menials would perish, the unaugmented humans pledged to die for Lorgar.

'This is the *Fireblade*,' came the transmission intercepted by the *Furious Abyss*'s advanced sensorium from one of the approaching escort ships. 'We've got a clear run. Lances to full.'

'On your tail, *Fireblade*,' came the reply from a second frigate.

'Master Malforian, bring turrets to bear and reload ordnance,' said Zadkiel. He followed the blips of the escorts as they negotiated the graveyard of fighter craft, intent on helping the *Waning Moon* finish off the *Furious*.

Zadkiel allowed himself a thin smile.

'THE FIGHTERS ARE lost,' said Vorlov. His face was ruddy with frustration as it glowered out of the viewscreen on the bridge of the *Wrathful*.

Almost to a man, the crewmen of the ship were watching Captain Vorlov's report of the total failure of the attack run.

'What, all of them?' asked Admiral Kaminska.

'Twenty per cent are en route back to the *Boundless*,' said Vorlov. 'The rest are gone. Our crews turned on each other.'

'You think this was a psychic attack, captain?' asked Cestus, suddenly glad that Brynngar was off the bridge.

'Yes, lord, I do,' Vorlov breathed, fear edging his voice.

This was a worrying development. All the Legions knew full well what had been decided on Nikea, and the censure imposed by the Emperor on dabbling in the infernal powers of the warp and the use of sorcery. The Ultramarine turned to Admiral Kaminska.

'What of our remaining escorts?'

'Captain Ulargo on the *Fireblade* is leading them in,' she replied. 'No problems so far.'

Cestus nodded, processing everything unfolding on the bridge.

'Maintain lance barrage from the *Wrathful* and the *Waning Moon*. Captain Vorlov, add the *Boundless*'s from distance and let the escorts engage. No ship, however massive, can withstand such a concentrated assault.'

'At your command, my lord,' Vorlov returned.

Cestus turned to regard Kaminska, seething at her command throne.

'As you wish, captain,' she responded coolly.

THE FIREBLADE STITCHED the first volleys of lance fire down against the upper hull of the *Furious Abyss*. It had nothing like the firepower of the fleet's cruisers, but up close it could pick its targets, and each lance fired independently to blast off hull plates and shear turrets from their emplacements with fat bursts. Defensive guns retaliated in kind and shots blistered against the *Fireblade*'s shields, some making it through to the escort's dark green hull. The *Fireblade* twisted out of arcs of fire and sent a chain of incendiaries hammering down into the dorsal turret arrays. Silent explosions blossomed and were swallowed by the void, leaving glittering sprays of wreckage like silver fountains.

The *Fireblade*'s hull was resplendent with kill markings and battle honours. It had done this many times before. It was small, but it was agile and packed a harder punch than its size suggested. Behind it was the *Ferox*, its younger sister ship, using the heat signatures of the *Fireblade*'s strikes to throw bombs and las-blasts through the tears opened up in the upper hull.

The *Fireblade* finished its first run and corkscrewed up over the *Furious*'s engine housings, letting the heat wash of the battleship's engines lend a hand in catapulting it void-wards before it lined up for another pass.

Below the two escorts, the last of the squadron, now just the *Ferocious* with the dramatic and sudden demise of the *Fearless*, was making its run along the underside of the massive vessel, pouring destruction into the ventral turrets. All three remaining escorts came under fierce fire, but their shields and hull armour held, their speed too great to allow a significant number of defensive turrets to bear at once and combine their efforts.

Captain Ulargo, at the helm of the *Fireblade*, commented to his fellow escort captains that the Word Bearers appeared to want to die.

ANOTHER BROADSIDE THUNDERED from the *Waning Moon* as the strike cruiser turned elegantly, keeping level with the *Furious Abyss*'s prow. The void was sucking fire out of the prow, so it looked like the head of a fire-breathing monster made of smouldering metal.

The enormous book that served as the ship's figurehead was intact. Slowly, silently, the metal book cracked open and folded outwards.

The massive bore of a gun emerged from behind it.

The end of the barrel glowed red as reactors towards the rear of the ship opened up plasma conduits to the prow and the weapon's capacitors filled. Licks of blue flame ran over the ruined prow, ignited by the sheer force of the building energy.

The prow cannon fired. A white beam leapt from the *Furious Abyss*. At the same time thrusters kicked in, rotating the *Furious* a couple of degrees so that the short-lived beam played across the void in front of it.

It struck the *Waning Moon* just fore of the engines. Vaporised metal formed a billowing white cloud, like steam, condensing into a silver shower of re-solidified matter. Secondary explosions led the beam as it scored across the strike cruiser's hull, until finally it was lost in the shower of debris and vapour as its energy expended and the glowing barrel began to cool down in the vacuum.

Further explosions rippled across the *Waning Moon* in the wake of the crippling barrage, and the rear third of the strike cruiser was sheared clean off.

SIX

The void/Squadron disengage/A way with words

THE PACE OF space battles was glacially slow. Even when
seen through viewscreens it was carried out at extreme
ranges, with laser battery salvoes taking seconds to
crawl across the blackness.

The battle had been raging for over an hour when the
cannon on the prow of the *Furious Abyss* fired its maiden
shot. The broadside from the *Waning Moon* had crossed
a gulf of several hundred kilometres before impacting
on the enemy ship's prow and that had been point-
blank by the standards of ship-to-ship warfare. The
Boundless's fighter wings had flown distances that would
have taken them across continents on a planet's surface.

When something happened quickly, it was a sudden,
jarring occurrence that threw everything else out of kil-
ter. The slow ballet of a ship battle was broken by the
discordant note of a rapid development, and all plans
had to be re-founded in its wake. An event that could
not be reacted to, that was over too quickly to change

course or target, was a nightmare that many ship captains struggled to cope with.

It was unfortunate for the captains of the Imperial fleet, then, that the death of the *Waning Moon* happened very quickly indeed.

'BY TITAN'S VALLEYS,' gasped Admiral Kaminska on the bridge of the *Wrathful*. 'What was that?'

The instruments on the bridge suddenly lit up as one as an intense flare of light filled the forward viewscreen.

'Massive energy reading,' came the confused reply from Helmsmistress Venkmyer. 'Energy sensorium's blind.'

'Did the *Waning Moon* just go plasma-critical?'

'There were no damage control signs that suggested major engine damage. They'd got the reactor-seven leak locked down. Maybe a weapons discharge?'

'What weapon could do that?'

'A plasma lance,' replied Cestus.

Kaminska turned to face the Ultramarine, whose grim expression betrayed his emotions.

'I did not know such a device had been wrought and fitted,' he added.

The admiral's initial shock turned to stern pragmatism.

'My lord, if I am to risk my ship and the souls onboard, I would have you tell me what we are up against,' she said, with no little consternation.

'I have little idea,' Cestus confessed, staring into the viewscreen, analysing and appraising tactical protocols in nanoseconds as he considered Kaminska's question. 'The Astartes are not privy to the secret works of the Mechanicum, admiral.' The Ultramarine sensed the challenge from Kaminska, her growing discontent, and was determined to crush it. 'Suffice to say that the plasma lance was developed as a direct fire close-range weapon for ship-to-ship combat. In any event, it matters not. Your orders are simple,' said Cestus, turning his steely gaze upon Admiral Kaminska in an attempt to cow her veiled truculence. 'We are to destroy that ship.'

'They are Astartes aboard that ship, Cestus, our battle-brothers,' Antiges said quietly. Until now, the fellow Ultramarine had been content to maintain his silence and keep his own council, but events were unfolding upon the bridge of the *Wrathful* and out in the wide, cold reaches of real space that he could not ignore.

'I am aware of that, Antiges.'

'But captain, to condemn them to–'

'My hand is forced,' Cestus snarled, suddenly turning on Antiges. 'Know your place, battle-brother! I am still your commanding officer.'

'Of course, my captain.' Antiges bowed slightly and averted his gaze from his fellow Ultramarine. 'I would request to leave the bridge to inform Saphrax and the rest of the squad to prepare for a potential boarding action.'

Cestus's face was set like stone.

Antiges met it with a steely gaze of his own.

'Granted.' His captain's curt response was icy.

Antiges saluted, turned on his heel and left the bridge.

Kaminska said nothing, only listened to what Cestus ordered next.

'Raise Mhotep at once.'

The admiral turned to regard her helms-mate monitoring communications with the *Waning Moon*.

'We cannot, sire,' Kant replied. 'The *Waning Moon*'s vox array is not operational.'

Kaminska swore beneath her breath, turning to the tactical display in the hope that a solution would present itself. All she saw was the massive enemy ship manoeuvring for a fresh assault against the *Boundless*.

'Captain Vorlov,' she barked into the vox, 'this is the *Wrathful*. She's heading for you next. Get out of there.'

There was a crackle of static and Vorlov's voice replied, 'What is this monster you have us hunting, Kaminska?'

There was a slight pause, and suddenly Kaminska looked very old as if the many juvenat treatments she'd undertaken to grant her such longevity had been stripped away.

'I don't know.'

'I never thought I'd hear you at a loss for words,' said Vorlov. 'I'm breaking off and hitting warp distance. I suggest you do the same.'

Kaminska looked at Cestus. 'Do we run?'

'No,' said Cestus. His jaw was set as he watched the debris from the *Waning Moon* rain in all directions as the ship's hull split in two.

'That's what I thought. Helmsmistress Venkmyer, relay orders to engineering to make ready for full evasive.'

THE BRIDGE OF the *Waning Moon* was in ruins. Massive feedback had ripped through every helm. Crewmen had died as torrents of energy had hammered through their scalp sockets and into their brains. Others were burning in the wreckage of exploded cogitators. Some of them had got out, but there was little indication that anywhere on the ship was better off. There was smoke everywhere, and all sound was swamped by the agonising din of screaming metal from the rear of the ship. The ship's spine was broken and it could no longer support its own structure. The *Waning Moon's* movement was enough to force it apart with inertia.

The blast doors had buckled under the extreme damage inflicted upon the stricken vessel and would not open. Mhotep had drawn his scimitar and cut through them with ease, forcing his way out of the bridge.

Engineering was gone, simply gone. The last surviving readouts on the bridge had been tracking the engines as they spun away below the ship, ribbons of burning plasma and charred bodies spilling from the ship's wounds like intestines.

No order had been given to abandon ship. Mhotep hadn't needed to give it.

'Captain, power is falling all across the ship,' shouted Helms-mate Ramket, his voice warring against the din of internal explosions somewhere below decks.

'We are beyond saving, helms-mate. Head for the starboard saviour pods immediately,' Mhotep replied, noting the savage gash across Ramket's forehead where he'd been struck by falling ship debris.

Ramket saluted and was about to turn and do as ordered when a sheet of fire rippled down the corridor, channelled through the *Waning Moon's* remaining oxygen. It flowed over Mhotep in a coruscating wave, spilling against his armour as it was repelled. Warning runes within his helmet lens display flashed intense heat readings. Ramket had no such protection, and his scream died in his burning mouth as the skin was seared from his body. Smothered by fire, as if drowning, Ramket thundered against the deck in a heap of charred bone and flaming meat.

Mhotep forced his way through the closest access portal and hauled it shut against the blaze. The fire had caught on the seals of his armour and he patted them out with his gauntleted palm. He had emerged from the conflagration into one of the ship's triage stations, where the wounded had been brought from the torpedo strikes on the gun decks. The injured were still lying in beds hooked up to respirators and life support cogitators. The orderlies were gone; ship regulations made no provision for bringing invalids along when abandoning ship.

They had given their lives to the Thousand Sons. They had known that they would die in service, one way or another. Mhotep ignored the dead and pressed on.

Beyond the triage station were crew quarters. Men and women were running everywhere. Normally, they would know exactly where to head in the event of an abandon ship, but the *Waning Moon*'s structure was coming apart and the closest saviour pods were wrecked. Some were already dead, crushed by chunks of torn metal crashing through the ceiling or thrown into fiery rents in the deck plates. In spite of the confusion, they stood aside instinctively to allow Mhotep clear passage. As an Astartes and their lord, his life was worth more than any of theirs.

'Starboard saviour pods are still operational, captain,' said one petty officer. Mhotep remembered his name as Lothek. He was just one of the many thousands of souls about to burn in the void.

Mhotep nodded an acknowledgement to the man. The Thousand Son's own armour was still smouldering and he could feel points of hot pain at the elbow and knee joints, but he ignored them.

Abruptly, the crew quarters split in two, one side hauled sharply upwards in a scream of twisting metal. Lothek went with it, smashed up into the ceiling and turned to a grisly red paste before his mouth had even formed a terrified scream.

A huge section of the *Waning Moon*'s structure had collapsed and given way. Its inertia ripped it out of the ship's belly and air shrieked from the widening gaps. Mhotep was staggered by the unexpected rupture and grabbed the frame of a door as air howled past him. He saw crewmen wrenched off their feet and dashed against torn deck plating that bent outwards like jagged, broken teeth. The tangled mass before him gave way and tumbled off into the void, over a dozen souls screaming silently as they went with it. Their eyes widened in panic even as they iced over. They gasped out breaths, or held them too long, and ruptured their lungs, spewing out ragged plumes of blood. Hitting space, their bodies froze in spasm, limbs held at awkward angles as they drifted away into the star-pocked darkness. The scene was bizarrely tranquil as Mhotep regarded it, the swathe of black-clad nothing silent and endless where distant constellations glittered dully and the faded luminescence of far off suns left a lambent glow in the false night.

Gravity gave way as the structure was violated.

Mhotep held on, armoured fingers making indentations in the metal, as the last gales of atmosphere hammered past. A corpse rolled and bumped against his armour, on its way to the void. It was Officer Ammon, his eyes red with burst veins.

They were dead: thousands all dead.

Mhotep felt some grim pride, knowing that, had they seen it would end this way, the crew would all still have given their lives to Magnus and the Thousand Sons. With no time for reverie, the Astartes pulled himself along the wall, finding handholds among shattered mosaics. With the air gone, the only sound was the groaning of the ship as it came apart, rumbling through its structure and up through the gauntlets of Mhotep's armour. His armour was proof against the vacuum, but he could only survive for a limited time.

The same was not true of anyone else aboard ship.

Mhotep passed through the crew quarters. In the wake of its demise, the *Waning Moon* had become an eerily silent tomb of metal. As power relays failed, lights flashed intermittently, the illumination on some decks made only by crackling sparks. Gobbets of blood broke against Mhotep's armour as he moved, and icy corpses bobbed with the dead gravity as if carried by an invisible ocean. The Astartes shoved tangled bodies aside, faces locked in frozen grimaces, as he fought his way to a pair of blast doors and opened them. The air was gone beyond them, too, and more crewmen floated in the corridor leading down to the saviour pod deck. One of them grasped at Mhotep's arm as the Astartes went past him. It was a crewman who had emptied his lungs as the air boomed out and had, thus, managed to stay conscious. His eyes goggled madly. Mhotep swept him aside and carried on.

The starboard saviour pods were not far away, but the Thousand Son had to take a short detour first. Passing through a final corridor, he reached the reinforced blast door of his sanctum. Incredibly, the chamber still retained power, operating on a heavily protected, separate system from the rest of the ship. Mhotep inputted the runic access protocol and the door slid open. The oxygen that remained in the airtight sanctum started to pour out. Mhotep stepped over the threshold quickly and the door sealed shut behind him with a hiss of escaping pressure.

Ignoring the damage done to the precious artefacts within the room, Mhotep went straight to the extant

sarcophagus at the back of the sanctum. Opening it
with controlled urgency, he retrieved the short wand-
stave from inside it and secured the item in a
compartment in his armour. When Mhotep turned,
about to head for the saviour pods, he saw a figure
crushed beneath a fallen cry-glass cabinet. Shards of
glass speared the figure's robed body, and vital fluids
trickled from its bloodless lips.

'Sire?' gasped Kalamar, using what little oxygen
remained in the chamber.

Mhotep went to the ageing serf and knelt beside him.

'For the glory of Magnus,' Kalamar breathed when his
lord was close.

Mhotep nodded.

'You have served your master and this vessel well, old
friend,' the Astartes intoned and stood up again, 'but
your tenure is at an end.'

'Spare my suffering, lord.'

'I will,' Mhotep replied, mustering what little compas-
sion existed in his cold methodical nature and, drawing
his bolt pistol, he shot Kalamar through the head.

THE SAVIOUR POD deck was situated next to the hull, a
hemispherical chamber with six pods half-sunk into the
floor. Two had been launched and another was damaged beyond repair, speared through by a shaft of steel
fallen from the ceiling.

Mhotep pulled himself down into one of the remaining pods. Contrary to naval tradition, he would not be
going down with his ship. In his chambers, just prior to
docking at Vangelis, he had seen a vision of himself
standing upon the deck of the *Wrathful*. This was his
destiny. The hand of fate would draw him here for
some, as of yet, unknown purpose.

Mhotep engaged the icon that would seal the saviour pod. It closed around him. There was room for three more crew, but no one was alive to fill it. He hit the launch panel and explosive bolts threw the pod clear of the ship.

He watched the *Waning Moon* turning above him as the pod spiralled away. The aft section had burned out and was just a black flaking husk, disappearing against the void. The main section of the ship was tearing itself apart. The fires were mostly out, starved of fuel and oxygen, and the *Waning Moon* was a skeleton collapsing into its component bones.

In the distance, thousands of sparks burst around the *Furious Abyss,* as if it were at the heart of a vast pyrotechnic display.

Mhotep was as disciplined as any Thousand Son, and Magnus made the conditioning of his Legion's minds the most important part of their training. He could subsume himself into the collective mindset of his battle-brothers, and as such was rarely troubled by emotions that did not serve any immediate purpose.

He was disturbed. He very much wanted to exact the hatred he felt on the *Furious Abyss*. He wanted to tear it apart with his bare hands.

Perhaps, Mhotep told himself, if he was patient, he would find a way to do that.

THE FIGHTERS HAD come from nowhere.

With the violent death of the *Waning Moon*, the remaining escort ships, the *Ferox* and the *Fireblade*, were locked in a deadly duel with the massive enemy vessel. Even with the *Boundless* in support and the *Wrathful* inbound they would not last long against the Word Bearer battleship. The frigates would have to use their superior speed to endure while aid arrived. That advantage was summarily robbed with the appearance of crimson-winged fighter squadrons issuing from the belly of the *Furious Abyss* in an angry swarm.

It was impossible for such a ship, even one of its impressive size, to harbour fighter decks and the weapons system that had destroyed the *Waning Moon*. This fact had informed every scenario the escort squadron's captains had developed for any reaction to their attack runs. The *Furious Abyss*, however, was no ordinary ship.

The destruction of the *Waning Moon*, appalling as it was, had at least given the escort ships the certainty that the Word Bearers would not have the resources for attack craft. That was before the launch bays had opened like steel gills down the flanks of the battleship, and twinkling blood-slick darts had shot out on columns of exhaust.

Captain Ulargo stood in a corona of light on the bridge of the *Fireblade*. The rest of the bridge was drenched in darkness with only the grainy diodes of control consoles punctuating the gloom. Arms behind him, surrounded by the hololithic tactical display and with vox crackling, the terrible choreography of war played out with sickening inevitability.

'*Ferox* engaged!' came the alert from Captain Lo Thulaga. 'Multiple hostiles! Fast attack craft, registering impacts. Shutting down reactor two.'

'Shield your engines, for Terra's sake!' snapped Captain Ulargo, watching the grim display from the viewport.

'What do you think I'm doing?' retorted Lo Thulaga. 'I have fighters port, aft and abeam. They're bloody everywhere.'

The *Ferox* spiralled away from its attack run on the underside, pursued by a cloud of vindictive fighters. Tiny explosions stitched over the hindquarters of the escort ship, ripping sprays of black debris from the engine housings. Turrets stammered back fire from the belly and sides of the *Ferox*, but for every fighter reduced to a bloom of plasma residue there were two more pouring fire into it.

It was like a predator under attack from a swarm of stinging insects. The *Ferox* was far larger than any of the fighters, which were shaped like inverted Vs with their stabiliser wings swept forwards. Individually its turrets could have tracked and vaporised any of the enemy before they got in range, but there were over fifty of them.

'I cannot shake them,' snarled Captain Vorgas on the *Ferocious*, his voice ragged through the vox.

'They're bloody killing us!' yelled Lo Thulaga, whose voice was distorted by the secondary explosions coming from the escort's engines.

Ulargo wore a disgusted expression. In his entire career, he had never backed down from a fight. He hailed from the militaristic world of Argonan in Segmentum Tempestus, and it was not in his nature to capitulate. Clenching his fists, he bawled the order.

'Squadron disengage!'

Fireblade pulled away from the *Furious Abyss*, followed by the *Ferocious*. The *Ferox* tried to pull clear, but the enemy fighters hounded it, darting into the wake of the escort's engines, risking destruction to fly in blind and hammer laser fire into its engineering decks.

One of the reactors on the embattled frigate melted down, its whole rear half flooding with plasma. The forward compartments were sealed off quickly enough to save the crew, but the ship was dead in the void, only its momentum keeping it falling ponderously away from the upper hull of the *Furious Abyss*. The fighters circled it, flying in wide arcs around the dead ship and punishing it with incessant fire. Crew decks were breached and vented. Saviour pods began to launch as Lo Thulaga gave the order to abandon ship.

The *Furious Abyss* wasted no time sending fighters to assassinate the saviour pods as they fled the stricken *Ferox*.

The *Ferocious* pulled a dramatic hard turn, ducking back towards the enemy battleship to fox the fighters lining up for their attack runs. It strayed into the arcs of the *Furious Abyss*'s ventral turrets, and a couple of lucky shots blew plumes of vented atmosphere out of its upper hull. The fighters closed and targeted the breach, volleys of las-fire boring molten fingers into the frigate. Somewhere amidst the bedlam the bridge was breached and the command crew died, incinerated by sprays of molten metal or frozen and suffocated as the void forced its way in.

The remaining turrets on the *Furious Abyss* targeted the fleeing *Fireblade*, the last vessel of the escort. Most of the battleship's attention was away from the frigate, representing as it did a mere annoyance. Its vengeful ire was focused squarely on the *Boundless*.

'THE FEROX AND the *Ferocious* are gone,' Kaminska stated flatly, watching the blips on the tactical display blink out. 'How on Titan can that thing support those fighter wings?'

'The same way it has a functioning plasma lance,' said Cestus, grimly. 'The Mechanicum know more about what they're doing than they are letting on, and are ignoring Imperial sanctions.'

'In the name of Terra, what is happening?' Kaminska asked, seeing the enemy battleship turn its cross hairs on the *Boundless*.

For the first time, the Ultramarine thought he could detect a hint of fear in the admiral's voice.

'We cannot win this fight, not like this,' he said. 'Bring the *Boundless* in, we need to regroup.'

Kaminska cast her eye over the tactical display. Her voice was choked. 'It's too late for that.'

'Damnation!' Cestus smashed his fist hard against a rail on the bridge and it buckled. After a moment, he said, 'Contact your astropath, and find out what is keeping that message. I must warn my lord Guilliman at once.'

Kaminska raised the astropathic sanctum on the ship-to-ship vox, even as Helmsmistress Venkmyer relayed disengagement protocols to engineering.

Chief Astropath Korbad Heth's deep voice was heard on the bridge.

'All our efforts to contact Terra or the Ultramarines have failed,' he revealed matter-of-factly.

'By order of the Emperor's Astartes, keep trying and you will prevail,' said Cestus.

'My lord,' Heth began, unmoved by the Ultramarine's threatening tone. 'The matter is more fundamental than you appreciate. When I say our efforts have failed, I mean utterly. The Astronomican is gone.'

'Gone? That's impossible. How can it be gone?'

'I know not, my lord. We are detecting warp storms that could be interfering. I will redouble our endeavours, but I fear they will be in vain.' The vox went dead and Heth was gone again.

Antiges's return to the bridge broke the silence.

'We must return to Terra, Cestus. The Emperor must be warned.'

'What of Calth and Macragge? Our Legion is there, and our primarch; they are in imminent danger and the ones who must be warned. I do not doubt the strength of our battle-brothers and the fleet above Macragge is formidable, as are its ground defences, but there is something about this ship… What if it is merely the harbinger of something much worse, something that can be a very real threat to Guilliman?'

'Our primarch has ever taught us to exercise pragmatism in the face of adversity,' Antiges reasoned, stepping forward. 'Upon our return, we could send a message to the Legion.'

'A message that would never reach them, Antiges,' Cestus replied with anger. 'No, we are the Legion's last hope.'

'You are letting your emotion and your arrogance cloud your judgement, brother-captain,' said Antiges, drawing in close.

'Your loyalty deserts you, brother.'

Antiges bristled at the slight, but kept his composure.

'What good is it if we sacrifice ourselves on the altar of loyalty?' he urged. 'This way, we at least stand a chance of saving our brothers.'

'No,' said Cestus with finality. 'We would only condemn them to death. Courage and honour, Antiges.'

Cestus's fellow Ultramarine saw the vehemence in his eyes, remembering his conviction that he knew some terrible peril was creeping towards Macragge and the Legion. His brother-captain had been right thus far, and suddenly Antiges felt shamed that his dogged pragmatism had so blinded him to that truth.

'Courage and honour,' he replied and clapped his hand upon Cestus's shoulder in an apologetic gesture.

'So, we follow them into the warp,' Kaminska interrupted, assuming that the matter was settled. 'We feign flight and get on the ship's tail as soon as it readies to go into the Tertiary Core Transit,' she added.

Cestus was about to give his assent when Helms-mate Kant delivered a report from the sensorium.

'Impacts on the *Boundless*.'

THE BOUNDLESS TOOK longer to die than the *Waning Moon*.

Another volley of torpedoes sailed out from the *Furious Abyss*, this time in a tight corkscrew like a pack of predators arrowing in on the prey instead of spread out in a fan.

High explosives tipped the torpedo formation. They penetrated shields and used up the first volleys of turret fire from the *Boundless*.

The main body of the torpedoes were the same kind of bore-header cluster munitions that had ripped into the *Waning Moon*. A few magnetic pulse torpedoes were part of the volley, too. They ripped through the sensors of the *Boundless* and blinded it. There was no longer any need to conceal the full arsenal of the *Furious Abyss*.

Cluster explosions, like flowers of fire, blossomed down one flank of the *Boundless*. Shock waves rippled through the fighter bays, throwing attack craft aside like boats on a wave. Refuelling tanks exploded, their blooms lost in the torrents of flame that followed the first impacts. Fighter crews that had survived the madness of the attack runs were rewarded by being shredded by shrapnel or drowned in fire. The flank of the *Boundless* was chewed away as if it were ageing and decaying at an impossible rate, holes opening up and metal blackening and twisting to finally flake away like desiccated flesh.

The final torpedo wave had single warheads that forced enormous bullets of exotic metals at impossible speeds. They shot like lances from their housings, shrieking right through the *Boundless* and emerging from the other side, sowing secondary explosions of ignited fuel and vented oxygen, transfixing the carrier like spears of light.

Finally, the *Furious Abyss* took up position at medium range from the Imperial ship. It paused, as if observing the wracked vessel, sizing up the quarry one last time before the kill.

The plasma lance emerged, the energy building up and the barrel glowing. The surviving crew of the *Boundless* knew what was coming, but all their control systems were shot through. A few thrusters sputtered into life as the *Boundless* tried desperately to limp away from its would-be executioner, but the carrier was too big and badly wounded.

The plasma lance fired. It hit the *Boundless* amidships, at enough of an angle to rip through to the plasma reactors. The entire vessel glowed, the heat of the fusing plasma conducted through its structure and hull.

Then the plasma overspilled and, spitted like prey on the solid beam of the plasma lance's light, the *Boundless* exploded.

FROM HIS IMPERIOUS position on the bridge of the *Furious Abyss*, Zadkiel watched the burning wreck of the enemy cruiser flicker into lifeless darkness.

'Glory to Lorgar,' said Reskiel, who was standing behind him.

'So it is written,' Zadkiel replied.

'Two vessels remain, my lord,' added his second, obse-quiously.

Zadkiel observed the tactical display. The remaining cruiser was intact, and the final escort being pursued by the *Furious Abyss*'s fighter wings would probably also escape.

'By the time they get to Terra, it will be too late for any warning,' Zadkiel said confidently. 'The warp is with us. We risk far more tarrying here to hunt them down.'

'I will instruct Navigator Esthemya that we are to enter the warp.'

'Do so immediately,' confirmed Zadkiel, his mind on the transpiring events and their impending foray into the empyrean.

Reskiel nodded and activated the ship's vox-casters, transmitting Zadkiel's relayed orders into the engine rooms and ordnance decks. 'All crew, make ready for warp entry.'

'Reskiel, have Master Malforian load the psionic charges,' Zadkiel said as an afterthought. 'Once we are in the warp, you will have the bridge. I will be inspecting the supplicants in the lower decks. Ensure Novice Ultis attends.'

'As you wish, my lord,' said Reskiel, bowing deeply. 'And if the Ultramarines try to follow?'

'Commend their souls to the warp,' Zadkiel replied coldly.

THE WRATHFUL WENT dark, to simulate the diversion of its power to the engines for escape. The entire bridge was drenched in shadow. The crew was stunned into sudden silence and, for a fraction of a second, stillness, as they struggled to comprehend what they had wit-nessed.

Kaminska was as quiet as the ship. She gripped the arms of her command throne tightly. Vorlov had been her friend.

'A saviour pod jettisoned from the *Waning Moon* before its destruction, admiral,' announced Helms-mate Venkmyer at the sensorium helm, breaking the silence.

'Can you tell who is on board?' asked Cestus, alongside the admiral, watching impotently as the Word Bearer vessel grew farther and farther away as the *Wrathful* made its mock retreat.

'Lord Mhotep, sire,' Venkmyer replied. 'He's on his way to us. I've instructed crews to be ready to retrieve him when he docks.'

'Antiges, have Laeradis join the dock crews. Mhotep might be injured and in need of an apothecary.'

'At once, brother-captain.'

Antiges turned and was about to head off again when Cestus added, 'Disband the boarding parties and return to the bridge. Instruct Brynngar to do the same on my authority. Bring Saphrax and the Legion captains with you.'

The other Ultramarine nodded and went to his duties.

SAPHRAX ARRIVED ON the bridge with Antiges as ordered. Brynngar and Skraal joined them, feral belligerence and unfettered wrath increasing the already knife-edge tension.

With this many Astartes present, the bridge of the *Wrathful* felt very small. Saphrax wore his ceremonial honour guard armour, the gold of his armour plates glinting dully. Skraal, on the other hand, made do with little in the way of decoration. Cestus could not help noticing the kill-tallies on his chainaxe, bolt pistol and armour plates: a testament to violence. Killing was a matter of pride for the World Eaters and Skraal had several names etched on his shoulder pad, around the stylised devoured planet symbol of his Legion.

'Battle-brothers, fellow captains,' Cestus began as the Astartes present took position around the dead tactical display table. 'We are to enter the empyrean and give chase to the Word Bearers. Our Navigators have discerned that they are on course for a stable warp route. Following them won't be a problem.'

'Though, facing them will,' said Saphrax, ever the voice of reason. 'That ship destroyed two cruisers and the same in frigates. What is your plan for overcoming such odds?' It wasn't an objection. Saphrax was not given to questioning the decisions of his superiors. In his mind, the hierarchy of command was absolute, and much like the Ultramarine's posture, it would brook no bending.

'If we go back to Terra,' said Cestus, 'we could try to raise the alarm. If the warp quietened then we could get a message to Macragge and forewarn the Legion.' Cestus knew there was no conviction in his words as he spoke them.

'You have already decided against that course, haven't you, lad,' said venerable Brynngar.

'I have.'

The old wolf smiled, revealing his razor-sharp incisors. There was something stoic and powerful in the steel grey of his mane-like hair and beard, implacability in the creamy orb of his ruined eye and the ragged scars of previous battles. But for all the war-like trappings, the obvious martial prowess and savagery, there was wisdom, too.

'When the sons of Russ march to war, they do not cease until battle is done,' he said with the utmost conviction. 'We will chase those curs into the eye of the warp if necessary and feast upon their traitorous hearts.'

'The World Eaters do not flee when an enemy turns on them,' offered Skraal with blood lust in his eyes. 'We hunt them down and kill them. It's the way of the Legion.'

Cestus nodded, appraising the brave warriors before him with great respect.

'Make no mistake about this: we are at war,' the Ultramarine warned them, finally. 'We are at war with our brothers, and we must prosecute this fight with all the strength and conviction that we would bring against any foe of mankind. We do this in the name of the Emperor.'

'In the name of the Emperor,' growled Skraal.

'Aye, for the Throne,' Brynngar agreed.

Cestus bowed deeply.

'Your fealty does me great honour. Prepare your battle-brothers for what is ahead. I will convene a council of war upon Captain Mhotep's return to the *Wrathful*.'

Cestus noticed the snarl upon Brynngar's face at the last remark, but it faded quickly as the Astartes took their leave and returned to their warriors.

'Admiral Kaminska,' said the Ultramarine, once the other Legionaries were gone.

Kaminska looked up at him. Dark rings had sunk around her eyes. 'I shall have to prepare Navigator Orcadus. We can follow once the enemy is clear.' She thumbed a vox-stud on the arm of her command throne. 'Captain Ulargo, report.'

'We've got mostly superficial damage; one serious deck leak,' replied Ulargo on the *Fireblade*.

'Make your ship ready. We're following them,' Kaminska told him.

'Into the Abyss?'

'Yes. Do you have any objections?'

'Is this Captain Cestus's order?'

'It is,' she said.

'Then we'll be in your wake,' said Ulargo. 'For the record, I do not believe a warp pursuit is the most suitable course of action in our current situation.'

'Noted,' said Kaminska. 'Form up to follow us in.'

'Yes, admiral,' Ulargo replied.

As the vox went dead, Kaminska sagged in her command throne as if the battle and the comrades she had lost were weighing down on her.

'Admiral,' said Cestus, noting her discomfort, 'are you still able to prosecute this mission?'

Kaminska whirled on the Ultramarine, her expression fierce and the rod at her back once more.

'I may not have the legendary endurance of the Astartes, but I will see this through to the end, captain, for good or ill.'

'You have my utmost faith, then,' Cestus replied.

The voice of Helms-mate Venkmyer at the sensorium helm helped to ease the tension.

'Captain Mhotep's saviour pod is locked on,' she said, 'and the *Fireblade* has picked up additional survivors from the *Waning Moon*.'

'What of the *Boundless*?' asked Kaminska.

'I'm sorry, admiral. There were none.'

Kaminska watched the tactical display on the screen above her as the *Furious Abyss*'s blip shivered and disappeared, leaving behind a trace of exotic particles.

'Take us into that jump point and engage the warp engines,' she ordered wearily, Venkmyer relaying them to the relevant parties aboard ship.

'Captain Mhotep is secured, admiral,' Venkmyer said afterwards.

'Take us in.'

ABOARD THE FURIOUS *Abyss*, the supplicants' quarters were dark and infernally hot. The air was so heavy with chemicals that anyone other than an Astartes would have needed a respirator to survive.

The supplicants, sixteen of them in all, knelt by the walls of the darkened rooms. Their heads were bowed over their chests, but the shadows and darkness could not hide their swollen craniums and the way their features had atrophied as their skulls deformed to contain their grotesque brains. Thick tubes snaked down their noses and throats, hooking them to life support units mounted on the walls above. Wires ran from probes in their skulls. They were dressed neatly in the livery of the Word Bearers, for even in their comatose states they were servants of the Word just like the rest of the crew.

Three of the supplicants were dead. Their efforts in psychically assaulting the Imperial fighter squadrons had taxed them to destruction. The skull of one had ruptured, spilling rust-grey cortex over his chest and stomach. Another had apparently caught fire, and his blackened flesh still smouldered. The last was slumped at the back of the quarters, lolling over to one side.

Zadkiel entered the chamber. The sound of his footsteps and those of one other broke the hum of the life support systems.

'This is the first time you have seen the supplicants, isn't it?' said Zadkiel.

'Yes, my lord,' said Ultis, though his answer was not necessary.

Zadkiel turned to the novice. 'Tell me, Ultis, what is your impression of them?'

'I have none,' the novice answered coldly. 'They are loyal servants of Lorgar, as are we all. They sacrifice themselves in a holy cause to further his glory and the glory of the Word.'

Zadkiel smiled at the phlegmatic response. Such zeal, such unremitting fervour; this Ultis wore ambition like a medal of honour emblazoned upon his chest. It meant he was dangerous.

'Justly spoken,' offered Zadkiel. 'Was it a worthy sacrifice?' he added, probing the depths of the novice's desire for advancement without him even knowing.

'No one ever served the Word without understanding that they would eventually give the Word their life,' Ultis responded carefully.

He is aware that I am testing him. He is more dangerous than I thought.

'Very true,' Zadkiel said out loud. 'Still, some would think this sight distasteful.'

'Then some do not deserve to serve.'

'You always answer with such conviction, Ultis,' said Zadkiel. 'Are you so sure in your beliefs?'

Ultis turned to regard his lord directly. Neither of the Astartes wore a helmet, and their gazes locked in unspoken challenge.

'I have faith in the Word. It is such that I need not hesitate; I need only speak and act.'

Zadkiel held the novice's vehement gaze for a moment longer before he broke away willingly and knelt down by the third dead supplicant. The Word Bearer tipped its head upwards to reveal burned out eyes.

'This is conviction, Ultis. This is adherence to the creed of Lorgar,' Zadkiel told him.

'Lorgar's Word is powerful,' Ultis affirmed. 'None of his servants would ever forsake it.'

'Perhaps, but think upon it. Many of our Legion have a seductive way with words. We are passionate about our lord primarch and his teachings. We are most talented in spreading that to others. Could it not be said that this blinds lesser men? That to blind them with such passion, and have them do our bidding, is no different to slavery?'

'Even if it could be said,' replied Ultis carefully, 'it does not follow that we would be in the wrong. Perhaps some are more use to the galaxy as slaves than as free men, doing as their base instincts tell them.'

'Were these men suited to being slaves?' asked Zadkiel, indicating the supplicants.

'Yes,' said Ultis. 'Psykers are dangerous when left to their own devices. The Word gave them another purpose.'

'Then you would enslave others to do Lorgar's will?'

Ultis thought about this. The novice was no fool, and would be well aware that Zadkiel was evaluating his every word, but failing to answer at all would be by far the most damning result.

'It is better,' said Ultis, 'that lesser men like this lose their freedom than that the Word remains unspoken. Even if what we do is slavery, even if our passion is like a chain that holds them down, these are small prices to pay to see Lorgar's Word enacted.'

Zadkiel stood up. 'These supplicants will require some time to recover. Their psychic exertions have drained them. It is good that the weaker were winnowed out, at least. The warp will not be kind to them.

You show remarkable tolerance, Novice Ultis. Many Astartes, even those of our Legion, would balk at the use of these supplicants.'

'Those are the lengths to which we must go,' said Ultis, 'to fulfil the Word.'

Yes, very ambitious, Zadkiel decided.

'How far would you go, Brother Ultis?'

'To the very end.'

Driven, too.

Zadkiel smiled thinly.

Dangerous.

'Then, there is little left to teach you,' said the Word Bearer captain.

The vox-emitter in Zadkiel's gorget chirped. 'Master Malforian has indicated that he is ready,' said Helmsmate Sarkorov.

Delegating already, are we Reskiel? thought Zadkiel, seeing rivals and potential usurpers in every exchange, every obsequious nod.

'Deploy at once,' said Zadkiel.

'Yes, sire.'

'They pursue us still?' asked Ultis.

'It was to be expected,' Zadkiel replied. 'Doubtless, some sense of duty compels them. They will soon learn the folly of that emotion.'

'Pray enlighten me, my lord.'

Zadkiel considered the novice as he bowed before him.

'Join me on the bridge, Brother Ultis,' he said, 'and merely watch.'

THE WARP WAS madness made real. It was another dimension where the rules of reality did not apply. The human mind was not evolved to comprehend it, for it had no rules or boundaries to define it. It was infinite, and infinitely varied. Only a Navigator, a highly specialised form of stable mutant, could look upon it and not go insane. Only he could allow a ship to travel the stable channels of the warp, fleeting as they were, and emerge through the other side. To traverse an unstable warp route, even with a Navigator's guidance, would put a vessel at the capricious mercy of the empyrean tides.

The *Furious Abyss* had plunged into this sea. It was kept intact by a sheath of overlapping Geller fields, without which it would disintegrate as its component atoms ran out of reasons to stay neatly arranged in its metals.

From the ordnance bay, wrapped in its own complement of fields, emerged a large psionic mine, spinning rapidly as it tumbled away from the Word Bearers' ship. Though not visible on the outside, within the mine's inner core was a coterie of screaming psykers, insane with a poisonous vapour that had been pumped into the chamber and then hermetically sealed. Their combined death cry would send psionic ripples through the empyrean. With a flash of light, which bled away into emotion as it was absorbed into the warp, the mine and all its raving cargo detonated.

The warp quaked. Love and hate boiled and ran together like paint, the agony of billions of years breaking and shifting like spring ice. Mountains of hope crumbled, and oceans of lust drained into the nothingness of misery.

With a sound like every scream ever uttered, the Tertiary Core Transit collapsed.

SEVEN

Ghosts in the warp/Hellbound/Legacy of Magnus

'ULARGO!' SHOUTED KAMINSKA. 'You're breaking up. I can barely hear you. Keep the fields up and get into our wake!'

The *Wrathful*, with the *Fireblade* in tow, had entered the infinite that was the warp. Interference from the rolling shadow sea had rendered vox traffic all but dead as the last vestiges of realspace fell away. The final transmissions from the escort ship were fraught with panic and desperation as the *Fireblade* encountered unknown difficulties during transit.

Ulargo's voice was heavily distorted as he relayed a fragmentary message, the words dissolving into crackling non sequiturs. Strange waves of static flowed through the *Wrathful's* bridge speakers, the short distance between it and the *Fireblade* filling up with the impossible geometries of the warp.

Entering the warp through a stable route, even guided by a Navigator, was dangerous. To do so once that route had collapsed and without the beacon of the Astronomican was nigh-on suicidal.

Admiral Kaminska swore beneath her breath, smashing her fist against the arm of her command throne in frustration.

'The link is severed,' she muttered darkly.

'We'll get no further contact with the *Fireblade* until we leave warpspace, admiral,' said Venkmyer.

Kaminska and her crew were alone on the bridge. Captain Cestus and the other Astartes had convened in one of the vessel's many conference rooms to receive Captain Mhotep, find out what he knew and formulate some kind of plan.

The mood was subdued because of the warp transit, and the unknown fate of the *Fireblade* had not alleviated the grim demeanour that pervaded on the bridge.

'I know, helmsmistress,' Kaminska answered with resignation.

The *Wrathful* shuddered. Warning lights flickered up and down the bridge, and in the decks beyond klaxons sounded.

'We're on full collision drill,' Helms-mate Kant informed them.

'Good,' said the admiral. 'Keep us there.'

The whole bridge heaved sideways, scattering navigational instruments and tactical manuals. Kant grabbed the edge of a map table to keep his footing with the sudden warp turbulence.

'At your command,' he replied.

Kaminska sat back in her command throne, exhausted. She had finally come up against a problem she couldn't solve with tactical acumen and audacity. The Astartes captain of the Ultramarines had put her in this situation, and for all her loyalty to the Imperium and the greater glory of mankind, she resented him for it. Lo Thulaga, Vargas, Abrax Vann of the *Fearless* and now Ulargo, all gone. Vorlov, of the *Boundless*, had been her friend and he too had fallen ignominiously in pursuit of an unbeatable foe at the behest of a reckless angel of the Emperor.

Now, in the thrall of the warp and impotent as she was, trusting to her Navigator to guide them out safely, Kaminska's anger was only magnified.

'Helms-mate, get me Officer Huntsman of the Watch,' she ordered with forced resolve.

'Admiral,' said Huntsman's voice over the vox array after a few moments.

'Assemble your best men and have them patrol decks. I don't want any surprises or unforeseen accidents during transit,' she replied. 'Any signs, any at all, and you know what to do.'

'I shall prosecute my duty with due and lethal diligence, admiral,' Huntsman responded.

HUNTSMAN KILLED THE vox link and turned to the three armsmen waiting patiently for him in the upper deck barracks. They were equipped with pistols and shock mauls and light flak jackets. The four men stood in a small group, their features cast with deep shadows from the low-level lighting that persisted whilst the *Wrathful* was in warp transit. The rest of the barrack room, all gunmetal with stark walls and bunks, was empty.

'Four teams, decks three through eighteen,' said Huntsman with curt and level-headed precision. 'I want regular reports from the below decks overseers, every half hour.'

The three armsmen nodded and left to gather the enforcers.

As Officer of the Watch, it was Huntsman's job to ensure that order and discipline were maintained aboard ship. He was brutal in that duty, an unshakeable enforcer who suffered no insubordination. He had killed many men in pursuit of his duty and felt no remorse for it.

Warp psychosis could affect any man, and even Huntsman, though possessed of a stronger will than most, felt its presence, even through the shielding of the Geller fields surrounding the ship that acted as a barrier against the empyrean. He had seen many suffering from the malady, and it took many forms. Both physical and mental abnormalities could present themselves: hair loss, babbling, catatonia, even homicidal dementia, were common. Huntsman had the cure for each and every one of them sitting snugly in his hip holster.

Wiping a hand across his closely-cropped hair, Huntsman checked the load in his sidearm and patiently awaited the return of his men.

CESTUS, ANTIGES AND the other Astartes captains sat around a lacquered hexagonal table in one of the *Wrathful's* conference rooms. Wood panelling decorated the room and gave it false warmth, despite its obvious militaristic austerity. Plaques hung on the walls describing the deeds of the many great commanders, captains and admirals that had served in the Saturnine fleet. Kaminska's was amongst them. Her roll of honour was long and distinguished.

There were several artefacts too: crossed cutlasses, an antique pistol and other traditional oceanic trappings. Presiding over all was an icon that spoke of the new age. The Imperial eagle was the symbol of the Emperor's War of Unification and a symbol of the union between Mars and Terra. It was a stark reminder of all they were fighting for and the fragility inherent within it.

'As soon as we leave warp we get into their wake and launch boarding torpedoes at their blind side. Let the fury of the wolf gut this prey from within!' snarled Brynngar. The Wolf Guard, unlike the rest of them, was on his feet and had taken to pacing the room.

'They would shoot our torpedoes down before they even breached their shields,' countered Mhotep. The Thousand Son had been given the all-clear by Apothecary Laeradis after his ship had been destroyed and was keen to attend the council. 'And should they not,' he added, before the Wolf Guard could protest, 'we do not know what kind of armour they have or what forces are onboard. No, we must be patient and wait until the *Furious Abyss* is vulnerable.'

The debate as to how to stop the Word Bearers had been raging for over an hour. In that time, Mhotep had revealed what little he knew: the name of the vessel and its admiral, the weapon systems that had crippled his vessel and the heresy embraced by the Word Bearers. He neglected to speak of Zadkiel's offer of alliance, leaving that to his own counsel. Despite the heated arguments, little had been agreed upon, other than that they were committed to their current course of action and that an all-out assault upon the *Furious Abyss* was tantamount to suicide.

'Bah! Typical of the sons of Magnus to advise caution in the face of action,' bellowed the Space Wolf, his feelings for the Thousand Son as direct and pointed as his demeanour.

'I agree with the wolf,' said Skraal. 'I cannot abide waiting in the dark. If we are to sacrifice our lives to ensure the destruction of our enemies then so be it.'

'Aye!' Brynngar agreed, making the most of the support. 'Any other course smacks of cowardice.'

Mhotep bristled at the slight and looked unshakeably into the feral grin that had crept across the Space Wolf's savage features, but he would not be goaded.

'This gets us nowhere,' Cestus broke in. 'We know for certain that the Astartes aboard that ship have turned traitor. What that means for the rest of the seventeenth Legion, I do not know. Certainly, the Mechanicum built the vessel and that raises further questions about the nature of its construction. The fact it was kept secret suggests complicity on their part, at least to some degree.'

Cestus allowed a moment's pause before he spoke.

'Something is deeply wrong. It is my belief that the Word Bearers are allied against my Legion, and, in so doing, against the Emperor too. They have supporters in the Mechanicum. How else could such a vessel have been made yet none of us have known of it?'

At that remark the Astartes were united in a common purpose. What the Word Bearers had committed was an outright act of war, but it smacked of something more. Though they had their differences, the sons of the Emperor were all siblings after a fashion. They would fight and die together against a common enemy. The Word Bearers were now just such a foe.

'What then are we to do?' Brynngar asked at last, his choleric mood abating, even though he cast a baleful glance at the Thousand Son sitting opposite.

Cestus caught the path of the Space Wolf's gaze, but ignored it for the moment.

'We must find a way to disable the ship. Attack it when it is vulnerable,' the Ultramarines captain told them. 'For we are at least agreed that our enemy is our brother no longer. They shall be destroyed for this treachery, but not before I find out how deep it goes. The Warmaster must know of the enemies arrayed against him. So, for now, we follow the ship and await our opening.'

'Still sounds like cowardice to me,' grumbled Brynngar, taking his seat at last and slouching back in it.

Cestus got to his feet quickly, fixing the Space Wolf with a steely gaze.

'Do not dishonour me or your Legion further,' he warned.

The Wolf Guard matched the Ultramarine's hard stare, but nodded, grumbling his assent beneath his breath.

Mhotep remained silent throughout the exchange, as ever careful to mask his thoughts.

Cestus sat back down, regarding the animosity of his brother Astartes sternly. The Great Crusade had united the Legions in common purpose. Many were the times that he had fought alongside both the sons of Russ and Magnus. Yes, the primarchs each had their differences, and this was passed down to their Legions, and though they bickered like brothers, they were as one. He could not believe that the foundation of their bonds, and the bonds between all of the Legions, were so fragile that by merely putting them in a room together outright war would be declared. What the Word Bearers had done was an aberration. It was the exception, not the rule.

The walls of the conference chamber shook violently, interrupting Cestus's thoughts.

Brynngar sniffed at the air.

'The stink of the warp is thick,' he snarled, with a glance at Mhotep despite himself.

Another tremor struck the room, threatening to tip the Astartes off their feet. Warning klaxons howled in the corridors beyond and the decks below.

Mhotep gazed into the reflective sheen of the conference table, before looking up at Cestus. 'Our passage through the empyrean has been compromised,' he told him.

The Ultramarine returned the Thousand Son's gaze.

'Antiges,' he said, his eyes still upon Mhotep, 'accompany me to the bridge.'

Cestus turned to address the gathering.

'This isn't over. We reconvene once we have left warp-space.'

Muttered agreement answered him, and Cestus and Antiges left for the bridge.

'I TAKE IT you have come to find out why our transit isn't exactly smooth, my lord,' said Admiral Kaminska, who was standing next to her command throne. She had been appraising tactical data garnered from the disastrous battle against the enemy ship and was in close conversation with Venkmyer, her helmsmistress, when Cestus arrived on the bridge. Alongside the strategic display was the sudden fluctuation in the external warp readings.

'Your instincts are correct, admiral,' Cestus replied. Despite their shared experience fighting the *Furious Abyss* and the obvious validation of his mission, Kaminska's demeanour towards the Ultramarine was still icy. Cestus had hoped it would have thawed slightly in the cauldron of battle, but he had effectively taken her ship, despite her experience and her knowledge. Though Cestus was a fleet commander and his naval tactical acumen was superior to Kaminska's, given that he was an Astartes, he had trampled on her command as if it was nothing. It did not sit well with him, but needs must in the situation they were in. Macragge, maybe more besides, was at stake. Cestus could feel it, and that burden must rest squarely on his shoulders. That meant taking command of the mission. If it also meant that he had to put a vaunted Imperial admiral's nose out of joint then so be it.

'I am about to visit my chief Navigator for an explanation, if you would like to accompany me.' Kaminska's attempt at being cordial was forced as she left the command dais.

Both Cestus and Antiges were about to follow when she added.

'The Navigator sanctum is small, captain. There will only be room for one of you.'

Cestus turned to Antiges, who nodded his understanding and took up a ready position at the bridge.

IN THE CLOSE confines of the Navigator sanctum, Cestus felt the bulk of his power armour as never before. The tiny isolation chamber above the bridge, where Orcadus and his lesser cohorts dwelt whilst in warp transit, was bereft of the ornamentation ubiquitous in the rest of the ship. Bare walls and grey gunmetal austerity housed a trio of translucent blister-like pods in which the Navigators achieved communion with the Astronomican and traversed the capricious ebbs and flows of warpspace.

Kaminska who was looking less dignified than usual in the cramped space next to the Astartes, addressed her chief Navigator.

'Orcadus.'

There was a moment's pause and then a hooded and wizened face appeared in the central blister, blurred

through the translucent surface. There was the suggestion of wires and circuitry hanging down from some
unseen cogitator in the domed ceiling of the pod.

'What has happened?' asked Kaminska.

With a hiss of hydraulics, the central blister broke
apart like petals on a rose and Orcadus emerged
through a gaseous cloud of vapour, rising as if from a
pit.

'Greetings, admiral,' said Orcadus, his voice low and
rasping outside of the blister, as if he were struggling to
speak. The Navigator's skin was a sweaty grey and he
wheezed as he breathed. 'When I was preparing to enter
the warp and traverse the Tertiary Coreward Transit as
instructed, the empyrean ocean swirled and split.'

'Make your explanations brief please, Navigator, I am
needed at the bridge,' Kaminska prompted.

Cestus was gladdened to see that her ire was not
reserved for Astartes hijacking her ship.

Though much of Orcadus's face was concealed by his
hood, Cestus could see a tic of consternation on his lip.
All Navigators possessed a third eye, and it was this tolerated mutation that allowed them to plot a course
through the warp. To look into that eye would drive a
normal man insane.

'The Tertiary Coreward Transit is down,' he explained
simply. 'I had detected a worsening of the abyssal
integrity, prior to the collapse, but we were already too
far engaged in the warp to turn back,' he said.

'How is this possible?' Cestus asked. 'How did the
enemy collapse the route?'

Orcadus's attention fell on the Astartes for the first
time during the exchange. If he thought anything of the
Ultramarine's presence in his sanctum, he did not show
it.

'They deployed some kind of psionic mine,' Orcadus replied. 'The effect would have been felt by our astropaths. As of now, we are sailing the naked abyss,' he stated, switching his attention back to Kaminska. 'What are your orders, admiral?'

Kaminska could not keep the shock from her face. To be effectively cut adrift in the warp was a death sentence, one that she was powerless to do anything about.

'We follow the enemy vessel and stay in its wake as best we can,' said Cestus, cutting in. 'They are bound for Macragge.'

'From Segmentum Solar to Ultramar, outside stable routes?'

'Yes.'

'The chances of success would be minimal, my lord,' Orcadus warned without emotion.

'Even so, that is our course,' Cestus told him.

Orcadus considered for a moment before replying.

'I can use their vessel as a point of reference, like a beacon, and follow it, but I cannot speak for the warp. If the abyss sees fit to devour us or make us its prey then the matter is out of my hands.'

'Very well, chief Navigator, you may return to your duties,' Cestus told him.

Orcadus bowed almost imperceptibly and, just before retreating back to his station, said, 'There are things abroad in the empyrean, the native creatures of the abyss. A shoal of them follows the enemy ship. The warp around it is in tumult, as it has been in the abyss these last several months. It does not bode well.'

At that Orcadus took his leave, swallowed up into the blister once more.

Cestus made no remark. In his experiences as a fleet commander, he was all too aware of the creatures that lurked in the warp. He did not know their nature, but he had seen their forms before and knew they were dangerous. He did not doubt that Kaminska knew of them, too.

With a shared looked of understanding, Cestus and Kaminska left the sanctum and headed back down through a sub-deck tunnel that led to the bridge. They had been walking for several minutes before the Ultramarine broke the charged silence.

'Your attitude towards me and this mission has been noted, admiral.'

Kaminska breathed deep as if trying to master her emotions and then turned.

'You took my ship and usurped my command, how would you feel?' she snapped.

'You serve the Emperor, admiral,' Cestus told her in a warning tone. 'You'd do well to remember that.'

'I am no traitor, Captain Cestus,' she replied angrily, standing her ground against the massive Astartes despite his obvious bulk and superior height. 'I am a loyal servant of the Imperium, but you have ridden roughshod over my authority and my ship for a chase into shadows and probable death. I will lay my life on the altar of victory if I must, but I will not do so meaninglessly and without consideration.'

Cestus's face was an unreadable mask as he considered the admiral's words.

'You are right, admiral. You have shown nothing but courage and honour throughout this endeavour and I have repaid it with ignorance and scorn. This is not fitting behaviour for a member of the Legion and I offer my humble apology.'

Kaminska was taken aback, her expression sketched into a defiant response. At last, her face softened and she exhaled her anger instead.

'Thank you, my lord,' she said quietly.

Cestus bowed slowly to acknowledge the admiral's gratitude.

'I shall meet you on the bridge,' said the Astartes and departed.

When Cestus was gone, Kaminska realised that she was shaking. The vox array crackling into life got her attention.

'Admiral?' said Helmsmistress Venkmyer's voice through the conduit wall unit.

'Speak,' Kaminska answered after a moment as she mustered her composure.

'We've made contact with the *Fireblade*.'

AFT DECKS THREE through six of the *Wrathful* were clear. Most of the non-essential crew were locked down in isolation cells for their own protection. For Huntsman and his small band of three armsmen, it was like patrolling the halls of a ghost ship.

'Squad Barbarus, report.' Huntsman's voice broke the grave-like silence as he strafed a handheld lume-lamp back and forth across the corridor. Shadows recoiled from the grainy blade of light, throwing archways and alcoves into sharp relief.

Huntsman could feel the tension of his men, drawn up in 'V' formation behind him as the radio-silence from the vox-bead in the officer's ear persisted.

'Squad Barbarus,' he repeated, adjusting his grip on the service pistol outstretched in his hand next to the lume-lamp by way of nervous reflex.

Huntsman was about to send two of his armsmen in search of the errant squad when the vox crackled.

'Squad Barb... report... experiencing interfer... all clear.' The clipped reply was fraught with static, but Huntsman was satisfied.

The Officer of the Watch was breathing a sigh of relief when a figure darted across a T-junction ahead, picked out briefly in the light beam.

'Who goes there?' he asked sternly. 'Identify yourself at once!'

Huntsman moved to the T-junction quickly, but with measured caution, using battle-sign to order his arms-men to fan out behind him and cover his flanks.

Reaching the end of the corridor, Huntsman looked left, strafing the light beam quickly.

'Sir, I've got him. This way,' said one of the armsmen, checking down the opposite channel.

Huntsman turned, in time to see the same figure disappearing down another corridor. He could swear he was wearing deck crew fatigues, but they weren't the colours for the *Wrathful*.

'This area is locked down,' barked Huntsman, heart racing. 'This is your final warning. Make yourself known at once.'

Silence mocked him.

'Weapons ready,' Huntsman hissed and stalked off down the corridor, armsmen in tow.

AFTER THE DISASTROUS war council in the conference room, Mhotep had taken his leave of the other Astartes and retired to one of the *Wrathful*'s isolation cells, intending to meditate for the remainder of their transit through the warp. In truth, the confrontation with the Space Wolf had vexed him, more-so his loss of control in the face of Brynngar's berating, and he sought the solitude of his own company to gather his resolve.

Mhotep reached down to the compartment in his armour that contained the wand-stave rescued from the *Waning Moon*. Seeing that the item was intact, he muttered an oath to his primarch. Sitting upon a bench in the cell, the only furnishing in an otherwise Spartan room, Mhotep regarded the wand-stave. In particular, he scrutinised a silvered speculum at the item's tip and stared into its depths.

Focusing his thoughts, Mhotep slipped into a meditative trance as he considered the events unfolding, drawing on the mental acumen for which his Legion was famed.

An anomalous flicker, something inconsistent and intangible, flashed into existence abruptly and was gone.

The Geller field, Mhotep realised. It was the soft caress of the unfettered warp that he had felt, so brief, so infinitesimal that only one of Magnus's progeny, one with their honed psychic awareness, could have detected it.

And something else… Though this, for now at least, slipped beyond Mhotep's mental grasp like tendrils of smoke through his fingers.

The Thousand Son broke off the trance at once and returned the wand-stave to its compartment in his armour. Donning his helmet, he headed for the *Wrathful*'s primary dock.

CAPTAIN ULARGO SAT strapped into his command throne as the warp breached the blast doors at the back of the *Fireblade*'s bridge. All around him was chaos as the hapless crew screamed and thrashed in terror as their minds were unravelled by the warp. Some were already dead, killed by flying debris or simply torn apart as the warp vented its wrath upon them. Ulargo's calm in the face of certain disaster, with chunks of metal hull tearing away into nothing as his bridge was disassembled, was unnerving. The entire chamber was cast in an eldritch light and strange riotous winds buffeted crew and captain alike.

'It goes on… it goes on forever,' he said, his voice caught halfway between wonderment and fear. 'I can see my father, and my brothers. I can hear them… calling me.'

They had entered the empyrean in the *Wrathful*'s wake in accordance with Admiral Kaminska's orders, but upon the collapse of the Tertiary Coreward Transit, their Gellar fields had suffered catastrophic failure, leaving them undefended against the raw emotions of warp space.

It had already changed the place. The bridge shimmered with the skies of Io and the canyons of Mimas, the places where Ulargo had grown up and trained as a pilot in the Saturnine Fleet. The corpses of the navigation crew, slumped over the sextant array, had sprouted into Ganymedian mangrove trees, twisted roots looping through the steel floor of the bridge that in turn was seething with river grass. Waterfalls ghosted over reality, shoals of fish leaping through the shattered viewport. Ulargo wanted very much to be there, back in the places that lived on only in his memory, back when he had been a boy and the universe had felt so infinite and full of wonders.

He held out his hands and felt them brush against the reeds that grew by the River Scamandros on Io. Reptilian birds wheeled in a sky that he could somehow see beyond the torn ceiling of the bridge, as if the torn metal and loops of severed cabling were in another dimension and the reality in his head was bleeding through.

He stepped forwards. The rest of the crew were dead, but that did not mean anything any more. They were ghosts, too.

The stuff of the warp seethed through the blast doors and caught Ulargo up in a swirl of raw emotions. He filled up with regret, then fear, then love, each feeling so powerful that he was just a conduit for them, a hollow man to be buffeted by the warp: the way his father's eyes lit up with pride when he received his first commission. The grief in his mother's eyes, for she knew so many who had lost sons to the void. The fury of space, the ravenous vacuum, the thirsting void, that he always knew one day would devour him. In the warp they were ideas made as real as the mountains of Enceladus.

The side of the bridge gave away. The air boomed out and flung the corpses of the bridge crew out with it. One of the bodies was not yet dead, and in the back of his mind, Ulargo recognised that another human being was dying.

Then he saw the warp beyond the *Fireblade*.

Titanic masses of emotion went on forever, seen not with his eyes, but with his mind: rolling incandescent mountains of Passion, an ocean of grief, leading down to infinity through caves of misery, dripping with the poison of anger.

Hatred was a distant sky, heaving down onto the warp, smothering. Love was a sun. The winds that stripped away the hull of the *Fireblade* were fingers of malice.

It was wondrous. Ulargo was filled with the sight of it; no, not the sight, but the sheer experience, for the warp was not composed of light, but of emotion, and to experience it was to let it speak to the most fundamental parts of his soul.

The sky of hatred split apart and a yawning mouth opened up above Ulargo's soul. Teeth of wrath framed the maw. Beyond it was a black mass, seething like a pit of vermin. It was terror.

Mouths were opening up everywhere. Mindless things, like sharks made of malicious glee, slid between the thunderheads of passion. They snatched at the soul-specks of the *Fireblade*'s crew, teeth like knives through what remained of their minds.

Even love was turning on them, filling them in their last moments of existence with a horrendous longing for all the things they would never have, and appalling, consuming grief for everything they once had, but would never see again.

The maw bore down on Ulargo. Teeth closed in on him, an appalling coldness sheared through him and he knew that it was the purity of death.

The boiling mass seethed. The last vestiges of his physical self recoiled as worms forced themselves into a nose and mouth that no longer existed.

The warp turned dark, and Ulargo drowned in fear.

ADMIRAL KAMINSKA REACHED the bridge to find an ashen-faced crew before her. Cestus had just arrived, his countenance stern and pensive as the distress signal emanating from the *Fireblade* repeated on the ship-to-ship vox.

'This… Ulargo… Fireblade… damaged in transit… request dock… repairs…'

'Impossible,' said Kaminska, feeling all colour drain from her face as she heard the voice of a man she thought was dead. 'Vox traffic is rendered null whilst in warp transit.'

'Admiral, the *Fireblade* claims to be abeam to our port side,' offered Helms-mate Kant as he monitored further communications.

Kaminska looked instinctively over to the viewport and, despite the shimmering interference caused by the

Geller field, she could see Ulargo's ship, a little battered by the initial sortie against the *Furious Abyss*, but otherwise fine.

Common sense warred with the emotions of her heart. Ulargo was a comrade in arms. Kaminska had thought him lost and now she had an opportunity to save him.

'Guide them in to make dock at once.'

HUNTSMAN HAD CHASED the elusive figure to a dead end in the complex of corridors aboard Aft Deck Three of the *Wrathful*. Doors punctuated the apparently endless passageways that led into more barrack rooms and occasionally isolation cells.

As he approached slowly, drawing the lume-lamp across the figure's body, he noticed that his quarry faced the wall. He also saw the fatigues it was wearing more clearly. It was the deck uniform of the *Fireblade*.

'Halt,' he ordered the figure sternly, with a quick glance behind to ensure that his armsmen were still in support.

From the back, he judged the figure to be male, but a scraggly wretch to be sure with unkempt hair like wire and a stench that suggested he hadn't washed in many days.

Huntsman activated the vox-bead.

'Bridge, this is Officer Huntsman. I have detained a male deck crew in Aft-Three,' he said. 'He appears to be wearing a *Fireblade* uniform.'

Helms-mate Kant's response came through crackling static.

'Repeat. Did you say the *Fireblade*?'

'Affirmative – a deck hand from the *Fireblade*,' Huntsman replied, edging closer.

'That's impossible. The *Fireblade* has only just docked with us.'

Huntsman felt a cold chill run down his marrow as the figure turned.

Somehow, the light from the lume-lamp wasn't able to illuminate a belt of shadow across the top of the figure's head and eyes, but Huntsman saw its mouth well enough. The deck hand made a wide, gash-like smile with rotten lips caked in dry blood.

'In the name of Terra,' Huntsman breathed as the figure's jaw distended impossibly wide and revealed dozens of needle-like teeth. Fingers lengthened into talons, nails drenched in blood and razor-sharp. Eyes flashed red in the darkness, like orbs of hate. Huntsman fired.

ON THE BRIDGE, rending screams and scattered gunfire emitted from the vox followed by an almighty static discharge that ended in total silence.

'Raise the Officer of the Watch at once!' Kaminska ordered.

Kant worked at the array, but looked up after a few minutes.

'There is no response, admiral.'

Kaminska snarled, hammered an icon on her command throne and opened another channel.

'Primary dock, respond. This is Admiral Kaminska. Disengage from the *Fireblade* at once,' she said, shouting the orders.

Nothing. Communications were dead.

A warning klaxon sounded on the bridge. Seconds later, the *Wrathful* shook with external hull detonations.

'Admiral,' cried Helmsmistress Venkmyer, 'I'm reading armour damage to the port side, upper decks. How is that even possible?'

'The *Fireblade* is firing its dorsal turrets,' she answered grimly.

'It seems Ulargo's ship survived after all,' said Cestus, donning his battle helm, Antiges following his lead, 'only not in the way we had hoped.'

'All Astartes,' he barked into his helmet vox, mercifully unaffected by the radio blackout, 'convene on Aft-Three, Primary Dock, immediately.'

A LONG, LOW scream keened through the *Wrathful*, vibrating through the hull, then another and another until a chorus of them was shrieking through the ship. It sounded like the death screams of hundreds of terrified men.

Mhotep lowered his smoking boltgun once he had dispatched the creature back to the ether. He had arrived too late to save the Officer of the Watch and his arms-men who lay eviscerated on the floor and part way up the blood-slicked walls.

The thing had been warp spawn, that much was apparent, wearing a shadow form of one of the *Fireblade*'s crew rather than inhabiting a body directly. The momentary breach in the *Wrathful*'s Geller field had allowed it aboard ship. Mhotep's instincts told him that it was just a harbinger, and he headed off quickly to the Primary Dock.

Crewmen were hurrying down the *Wrathful*'s corridors, and they struggled to get past the bulky armoured Astartes as he fought to gain the Primary Dock. The engine sections started just stern-wards of the shuttle decks and the ship was getting up to full evasion power.

Shouldering past the frantic crew, Mhotep saw another figure impeding his progress, but one of flesh and blood, standing rock-like in grey power armour.

'Brynngar,' said the Thousand Son levelly at the Space Wolf who had just emerged from an adjacent corridor.

The World Eater, Skraal, with two of his Legion brothers appeared suddenly alongside him from the opposite corridor. Standing at the intersection of the crossroads, a strange sense of impasse existed for a moment before the Wolf Guard snarled and turned away, heading for the Primary Dock.

THE FIVE ASTARTES emerged into chaos.

Men and women of the *Wrathful* fled in all directions, screaming and shouting. Some brandished weapons, others sought higher ground only to be torn down and butchered. Blood swilled like a slick on the dock as the attendant deck crews of the *Wrathful* were torn apart by fell apparitions dressed in the garb of the *Fireblade*. The crew of the lost escort ship had changed. Their mouths were long and wide as if fixed in a perpetual sadistic grin. Needle-like fangs filled their distended maws like those of the long-extinct Terran shark, while long, barbed fingers curled like claws tearing at skin, flesh and bone.

They fell upon the human deck crews with reckless abandon and were devouring them, the bloodied rotten faces of the gruesome predators alive with glee.

'In the name of Russ,' Brynngar breathed as he saw the docking ports that joined the two ships disgorge numberless hordes of twisted *Fireblade* crew.

'They are warp spawn!' Mhotep told them, drawing his scimitar, 'wearing the bodies of our allies, whose souls are now hell-bound, lost to the empyrean. Destroy them.'

Brynngar threw his head back and roared, the sound eerie and resonant from within the confines of his battle helm. With Felltooth in one hand and bolt pistol in the other, he charged into the fray.

Skraal and the World Eaters followed, brandishing chainaxes and bellowing the name of Angron.

A TRIO OF vampire-like warp spawn fell under the withering report of Mhotep's bolter as he trudged across the Primary Dock and through the visceral mire sloshing at his feet. The copper stink assailing his nostrils would have overpowered a normal man, but the Thousand Son crushed the sensation and closed with the enemy.

Barks of bolter fire were tinny and echoing through his helmet as he cut down an advancing warp spawn, parting its sternum and decapitating it with the return swing. The hordes were everywhere and soon surrounded him. The muzzle-flare from his weapon illuminated the grim destruction he wrought with flashing intermittence, the keening wail of his scimitar a high-pitched chorus to the din of explosive fire.

He felt something trying to push at the edges of his mind, testing his psychic defences with tentative mental probing. Slogging through the despicable horde, he was drawn closer to the source of it, even as it was drawn to him, and he felt the pressure on his sanity increase.

BRYNNGAR SHRUGGED OFF a creature clinging to his arm and smashed it with Felltooth, the rune axe cutting through wasted bone like air. He thrust his bolt pistol into another and used the warp spawn's momentum to lift it from the ground. Triggering the weapon, he blasted the creature apart in a shower of bone and viscera. Then the Space Wolf lunged and butted a third, almost dissolving its rotted cranium against his battle helm. Gore and brain matter spoiled his vision, and

Brynngar wiped his helmet visor clean with the back of his gauntleted hand.

With the destruction of the physical body, the warp spawn appeared to lose their hold on the material plane and dissipated. They were easy meat. Brynngar had fought far hardier foes, but in such swarms they were starting to tax him. Even his gene-enhanced musculature burned after the solid fighting. For every three the Wolf Guard slew, another six took their place, pouring like rancid ants from the docking portals.

Brynngar realised to his dismay, hacking down another spawn, that gradually he was being pushed back.

He caught sight of Skraal through the melee. The World Eater was similarly pressed, though a bloody mist surrounded him from the churning punishment wreaked by his chainaxe. He could not see Skraal's fellow Legionaries; Brynngar assumed they had been swallowed by the horde.

A sudden tearing of metal, mangled with the sound of tortured souls, rent the air, and Brynngar felt the deck lurch from under him as it seemed to twist in on itself.

The integrity fields, which kept the dock pressurised when the dock ports were open, flickered once, but held. The physical structure did not. A huge chunk ripped out of the deck as if bitten by unseen jaws, three decks high. Debris was tumbling out into the ether. Brynngar looked away, for to do otherwise would be to comprehend the naked warp and embrace madness.

Something stirred beyond the breach, out in the infinite. Brynngar felt it as the hackles rose on the back of his neck and the feral nature of his Legion became suddenly emboldened. For a brief moment, the Space Wolf wanted to tear off his helmet and gauntlets and gorge himself on flesh like a beast of the wild. He backed away of his own volition, realising that something primal and terrible was with them on the dock.

MHOTEP HAD FORCED his way to the docking portals, through a swathe of warp spawn. His armour was dented and scratched from their ether claws and his body heaved with exhaustion. It was not physical prowess that would save them here, but the discipline of the mind that needed to hold fast.

Mhotep had felt the presence, too, and standing before the docking portal he beheld it in his mind's eye. It was dark and seething: a pure predator.

'It has seen me,' he said calmly into his helmet vox, the warp spawn hordes recoiling suddenly from the Thousand Son, regarding him in the same way a Prosperine spirehawk regards its prey. 'I cannot hide from it now.'

BRYNNGAR WAS ALMOST back to back with Skraal, the two Astartes having been fought back to the blast doors, when he heard Mhotep through his vox.

'Seen what?' snarled the Space Wolf, gutting another warp spawn as Skraal cleaved the arm from another.

'You cannot prevail here,' the voice of Mhotep came again. 'Get out and seal the doors. I will remain and activate the dock's auto-destruct sequence.'

Many vessels of the Imperial Fleet came with such precautionary measures built in to their design by the Mechanicum. They were meant as weapons of last resort, should a ship be overrun and in danger of capture. If a ship could not be defended or retaken from an enemy then it would be denied to them utterly, although in this case, Mhotep's sacrifice would not destroy the ship, only vanquish the foes that were besieging it.

'Do so now!' urged the Thousand Son.

Brynngar had lost sight of him, though his view was curtailed as he forced himself to look away from the tear into the naked warp beyond. Although it rankled, the Space Wolf knew when he was chasing a lost cause.

'Come on,' he snarled to Skraal who hacked and hewed with berserk fury, 'we are leaving.'

'The sons of Angron do not flee the enemy,' he raged in response.

'Even so,' Brynngar said, smashing a warp spawn aside. Ducking a blood-maddened sweep of Skraal's chainaxe, he punched the World Eater hard in the chest with the flat of his hand. The stunned Astartes was lifted off his feet and sent sprawling through the open blast doors. Brynngar trudged after Skraal's prone form, carving a path through the horde with Felltooth.

A few of the warp spawn had found their way through to the other side of the blast doors that led from the Primary Dock. Brynngar was about to hunt them down when a barrage of bolter fire scythed through them like wheat.

Inside his battle helm, the Space Wolf grinned as he saw the battered forms of the Ultramarines.

'Down!' cried Cestus who was leading the group, and Brynngar hit the deck as a fusillade of fire erupted overhead.

Arching his neck, the Space Wolf saw the smoking bodies of more warp spawn fall into a heap at the dock threshold. Swinging out a hand, he thumped the portal icon and the blast doors slid shut with a hydraulic pressure-hiss.

'We must seal the doors,' he snarled, rolling on his back as Antiges, Morar and Lexinal charged past him to guard the portal.

STRIPPING AWAY THE verisimilitude of the warp spawn crew, Mhotep saw that they were not separate entities at all. They were the extension of a single conjoined conscious, raw emotion given form. Tentacles snaked from three gaping maws lined with cruel teeth that had once been the docking portals, and flesh sacks like finger puppets danced along them.

As he stepped forward, he brandished his scimitar, a power sword engraved with hieroglyphics: the old tongue of Prospero. Mhotep was acutely aware of the blast doors shutting behind him, though the sound was far off, as if listened to in a separate dimension from the one he currently inhabited. Realising he was alone, the Thousand Son tapped into the innate power of his Legion, the psychic mutation common to all sons and daughters of Prospero that had earned Magnus the condemnation of Nikea. Mhotep's power, like that of all the Astartes of his Legion, was honed to a rapier-like point and when properly channelled could be deadly. The nay-sayers of Nikea had been right to fear it.

Mhotep stowed his bolter, for it would not avail him here, and drew forth the wand-stave. Inputting a rune sequence, played out in the jewels along its short haft, the item extended into the length of a staff. Holding the weapon up to his helmet lens, Mhotep peered through the speculum at the tip. The tiny, silvered mirror became transparent and, through it, the Thousand Son saw the entity for what it was.

The warp had been cruel. It had taken the ship and its crew and transfigured it into something wretched and debased. Tiny black eyes rolled in the armoured carapace and the bodies of its crew writhed all over the surface of the ship, trapped within a translucent membrane that sheathed it like living tissue. They were deformed, fused together with their tortured expressions stretched out as if melted. These were the souls of the *Fireblade*'s crew and they were lost to the warp forever.

The portion of the escort ship that had penetrated the cargo hold eked from the belly of the ship like an umbilical cord, the tentacle strings spilling from the maws at the end of them revealed to be tongues. The sound that emanated from them was appalling. The warp screamed from the *Fireblade*'s throat, a screeching gale that threatened to knock Mhotep off his feet. He stayed upright, however, and found what he was looking for in the partly insubstantial hull of the former Imperial ship.

The Thousand Son intoned words of power and an ellipsis of light burned into the deck plate. The Prosperine hieroglyphics on his staff flared bright vermillion. Spinning the staff around, Mhotep drove the scimitar into it pommel first and it became a spear.

'Back to the deeps!' bellowed the son of Magnus, his aim fixed upon the warp-entity's tainted core. 'There will be no feasting here for you, dead thing! By the Silver Towers and the Ever-Burning Eye, begone!'

Mhotep flung the spear just as the tentacles closed on him, a burning trail of crimson light following its psychic trajectory. It struck the *Fireblade* in the heart of its central maw and a great explosion of light detonated within. Spectral blood fountained and the reaching tentacles withered and burned.

The illumination built, blazing out of the maw and Mhotep was forced to look away from its brilliance. The scent of acrid smoke filled his nostrils, penetrating his helmet filters, and raging flames engulfed his senses together with the primordial scream of something dying in the fathomless ether.

IN THE CORRIDOR beyond the Primary Dock, ceiling plates fell like rain as the walls of the *Wrathful* shuddered with fury. Cestus and Antiges fought to get to the doors as the tremors hit. The rippling shock waves were coming from the Primary Dock.

Staying on his feet, Cestus drew his power sword and was about to beckon forward a group of engineers, who were lingering behind them, to fuse the blast doors when the horrific din emanating from within stopped. Smoke and faint, white light issued through the cracks.

All was quiet and still for a moment.

'Where is Mhotep?' the Ultramarine asked, sheathing the blade. He'd been monitoring the helmet vox transmissions and knew that the Thousand Son had been at the Primary Dock. During the warp phenomenon, battles had erupted all across the *Wrathful*, and the secondary and tertiary docks had also come under attack. Reports were flickering past on Cestus's helmet vox that the warp spawn had abated abruptly for reasons unknown, dissolving back into the ether.

Skraal was still out of it on the deck, babbling in enraged delirium, so Cestus turned to Brynngar for his answer.

'He made a noble sacrifice,' intoned the Space Wolf, as he got to his feet.

'That almost sounds like respect,' Cestus said, his voice tinged with bitterness.

'It is,' growled Brynngar. 'He gave his life for this ship and in so doing saved us all. For that he will have the eternal gratitude of Russ. I am not so proud to admit that I misjudged him.'

Whining servos and the hiss of released pressure made the Space Wolf turn with bolt pistol raised as the blast doors ground open. Cestus and the other Astartes joined him with weapons levelled at the flickering dark beyond.

Mhotep emerged from the scorched ruin of the Primary Dock, staggering, but very much alive. Tendrils of smoke rose from his pitted armour and he was drenched in viscous, translucent gore. In spite of his appearance and obvious injuries, he still retained his bearing, that nobility and arrogance so typical of Prospero's sons.

'It is not possible,' Brynngar breathed, taking a step back as if Mhotep were some apparition from the fireside sages of Fenris. 'None could have survived in such a conflagration.'

Cestus lowered his bolter cautiously and then his hand in a gesture for the other Ultramarines to do the same.

'We thought you were dead.'

Mhotep unclasped and removed his helmet, breathing deep of the recycled air. His eyes were black orbs and a riot of purple veins wreathed his face, but was slowly disappearing beneath his skin.

'As… did… I,' gasped the Thousand Son, helmet clattering to the deck as it fell from nerveless fingers.

Cestus caught his fellow Astartes as he lurched forward and bore him down to the floor, half-cradled in his arms.

'Summon Laeradis at once,' he told Antiges, who was stunned for a moment before he came to his senses and went off to find the Ultramarine apothecary.

'He lives, yet,' Cestus added, noting Mhotep's fevered breathing.

'Aye,' Brynngar muttered darkly, having overcome his superstition, 'and there is but one way that could be so…' The Space Wolf's lip curled up in profound distaste. '…Sorcery.'

EIGHT

Nikea/Advantage/Bakka Triumveron

IN HIS PRIVATE quarters, Zadkiel regarded the pict screen on the console before him with interest. The room was drenched in sepulchral light, the suggestion of idols and craven icons visible at the edge of the shadows. Zadkiel's face was bathed in cold, stark light from the pict screen, making him appear gaunt and almost lifeless.

Battle scenarios were displayed on the surface of the screen. An astral body, the size of a moon, exploded moments after being struck by a missile payload. Debris spread outward in a wide field, showering a nearby planet with burning meteors. An icon in the scenario represented a ship, the *Furious Abyss*, as it moved through the debris field. Trajectory markers with distances indicated alongside were displayed, originating at the ship icon and terminating at the planet's surface. The image paused momentarily and then cycled back to the beginning again.

Zadkiel switched his attention to a vertical row of three supplementary screens attached to the main pict screen. The uppermost one was full of streaming data that bore the Mechanicum seal. Calculations concerning armour tolerances, projected orbital weapon strengths and extrapolated endurance times based upon the first statistic versus the other scrolled by. Angles, probable firepower intensities and shield indexes were all considered in exacting detail. The middle screen contained four stage-by-stage picts showing the effects of a particular viral strain upon human beings. A time code at the bottom right corner of the final pict displayed 00:01:30.

The final screen displayed projected casualty rates: Macragge orbital defences – 49%; Macragge orbital fleet – 75%; Macragge population – 93%. Kor Phaeron and the rest of the Word Bearers' fleet would account for the rest. Zadkiel smiled; with a single blow they would all but wipe out the Ultramarines' home world and the Legion with it.

'I SAW IT myself, with this very eye,' snarled Brynngar, pointing to the non-cloudy orb. 'The Kolobite drone king did not blind me so much that I cannot see what is before my face.'

Brynngar had joined Cestus, Skraal and Antiges in a waiting room outside of the medi-bay where Laeradis ministered to Mhotep after his collapse. The Wolf Guard stalked back and forth across the small, sanitised chamber, which was all white tile and stark lighting, impatiently awaiting the Thousand Son's return.

'No man, not even an Astartes, could have faced those hordes and lived,' offered Skraal, 'although I would have gladly laid down my life to dispatch them to the hell of the warp.' The World Eater was raging as he spoke, blood fever clouding his vision as the endless need for violence and slaughter nagged at him. He had confessed earlier that he remembered little of the fight, engaged as he was in a haze of fury, only waking in the access corridor to the primary dock. Brynngar had deliberately chosen not to enlighten him, deciding that he didn't want to risk the World Eater's wrath.

'Aye, and I can think of no other way that such a deed could have been done,' said Brynngar, coming to rest at last.

'You speak of witchcraft, Space Wolf,' said Antiges with a dark glance at Cestus.

The Ultramarines captain had remained silent throughout. If what Brynngar said was true then it had dire ramifications. What was beyond doubt was that Mhotep's actions had saved the *Wrathful* from certain doom, but the edicts of the Emperor, laid down at Nikea, were strict and without flexibility. Such things could not be ignored, to do so would damn them as surely as the Word Bearers. Cestus would not embrace that fate, however rational it might seem.

'We do not know for certain that Mhotep employed such methods and devices, only that he lived where perhaps he should not have,' he said.

'Is that not proof enough?' Brynngar cried. 'The acts of Zadkiel, of this treacherous vermin is one thing, but to have a heretic aboard ship is quite another. Let me wring the truth out of him, I'll–'

'You will do what, brother?' asked Mhotep, standing in the open archway of the waiting room. Like the other Astartes, he wasn't wearing his helmet, but he was also stripped out of his power amour and clad in robes.

Apothecary Laeradis, together with another of the honour guard, Amryx, there by way of additional security, was visible behind him. The Apothecary was collecting his various apparatus as stooped Legion serfs scurried around him gathering up Mhotep's discarded armour.

Brynngar stared at the Thousand Son, fists clenched, his face reddening as he bared his fangs.

'Laeradis?' asked Cestus, stepping in front of the Space Wolf in order to diffuse the tension.

The Apothecary had just emerged into the room. Amyrx was standing silently next to him.

'No lasting injuries that his metabolism cannot cure,' Laeradis reported.

'Good,' Cestus replied. 'Rejoin your battle-brothers in the barracks.'

'My captain,' said the Apothecary, and gratefully left the charged atmosphere of the waiting room with Amryx, obsequious Legion serfs in tow.

'What happened at the dock?' asked Skraal, weighing in on Brynngar's behalf. 'I lost two Legion brothers to that fight, how were you able to survive?'

The two World Eaters had been discovered later, recovered by blind servitors before the dock was locked down permanently and bulk heads put in place. The unfortunate Astartes had been transfixed by the blade claws of the warp spawn and died gurgling blood. Their scorched remains rested in one of the *Wrathful*'s mausoleums, awaiting proper ceremony.

'When I reached the auto-destruct console I found that the protocols were off-line,' Mhotep explained, his face unreadable. 'Favour smiled on me though as during the battle, a fuel line linked to one of the docking ports had come loose from its housing and I was able to ignite it. I fought my way to a place where I was shielded from the blast and the resultant conflagration destroyed the entities with purging fire.'

'Your silver tongue is fat with lies,' Brynngar accused him, stepping forward. 'The air is thick with the stink of them.'

Mhotep turned his stony gaze on the Space Wolf.

'I can assure you, Son of Russ, whatever odour you are detecting is not emanating from me. Perhaps you should seek your answer nearer to your own bedraggled self.'

Brynngar roared and launched himself at the Thousand Son, bearing him to the ground with his massive bulk.

'Drink it in, witch,' snarled the Wolf Guard, intent on forcing Mhotep's head into the tiled floor. A splash of spittle landed on the Thousand Son's grimacing face as he thrashed against the Space Wolf's superior strength.

Cestus, using all of his weight, smashed into Brynngar's side to dislodge him. The Wolf roared again as he was toppled from the Thousand Son.

Skraal was about to wade in, but Antiges blocked his path, the Ultramarine's hand resting meaningfully on the pommel of his short-blade.

'Stand fast, brother,' he warned.

Skraal's hand wavered near his chainaxe, but he snorted in mild contempt, and in the end relented. This was not the fight he wanted.

Brynngar rolled from Cestus's body charge and swung to his feet. The Ultramarines captain was quick to interpose himself between Space Wolf and Thousand Son, his posture low in a readied battle stance.

'Stand aside, Cestus,' Brynngar growled.

Cestus did not move, but instead kept his gaze locked with the Space Wolf.

'Do so, now,' Brynngar warned him again, his tone low and dangerous.

'This is not the way of the Astartes,' Cestus said, his voice calm and level in response.

Behind the Ultramarine, Mhotep got to his feet, a little shaken, but otherwise defiant in the face of his aggressor.

'No: it is not the way of Guilliman's Legion, you mean,' answered Brynngar.

'Even so, I am in charge of this ship and this mission,' Cestus asserted, 'and if you have issue with my commands, then you will take them up with me.'

'He defies the Emperor's decree and yet you defend him!' Brynngar raged and took a step forward. He stopped when he realised that the Ultramarine's short-blade was at his throat.

'If Mhotep is to answer charges then he will do so at my behest and in a proper trial,' Cestus told him, the blade in his hand steady. 'The feral laws of Fenris are not recognised on this ship, battle-brother.'

Brynngar growled again as if weighing up his options. In the end, he backed down.

'You are no brother of mine,' he snarled, and stalked from the chamber.

Skraal followed him, a thin smile on his lips.

'That went well,' said Antiges, sighing with relief. He had not been relishing the idea of facing one of Angron's Legion, nor had he a desire to see Brynngar go toe-to-toe with his brother-captain.

'Sarcasm does not become you, Antiges,' said Cestus darkly. Brynngar was his friend. They had fought together in countless campaigns. He owed the old wolf his life, and more than once, Antiges too had a similar debt to the Wolf Guard. Cestus had defied him, however, and in so doing had besmirched his honour. Yet, how could he not give Mhotep the benefit of the doubt, without proof of his supposed actions? Cestus admitted to himself that his experience in the reactor chamber at Vangelis, the vision of Macragge he had witnessed, might be affecting his decisions.

'I am grateful to you, Cestus,' said Mhotep, smoothing out his robes after the Space Wolf's rough treatment.

'Don't be,' the Ultramarine snapped, in part angry at himself for his self doubt. His gaze was cold and unforgiving as it turned on the Thousand Son. 'This is not over, nor am I satisfied with your explanation for what happened at the dock. You will be remanded to your quarters until we leave the warp and I have time to decide what is to be done.

'Antiges,' Cestus added, 'have Admiral Kaminska send the new Officer of the Watch and a squad of armsmen to escort Captain Mhotep to his cell.'

Antiges nodded briskly and went off towards the bridge.

'I could overwhelm a mere band of armsmen and defy this order,' Mhotep said, matching the Ultramarine's steely gaze.

'Yes, you could,' said Cestus, 'but you will not.'

'LET IT NOT be said,' uttered Zadkiel, 'that the warp is without imagination.'

Before Admiral Zadkiel, who, having left his private quarters, was in the *Furious Abyss*'s cathedra, stood rank upon rank of Word Bearers. Their presence in the vaulted chamber was an echo of what had faced him at the vessel's inaugural launch at Thule. It was a sight that filled Zadkiel with a sense of power.

The warriors represented the Seventh Company of the Quillborn Chapter, one of those that made up the greater Word Bearers Legion. Every Chapter had its own traditions and its own role within Lorgar's Word. The Quillborn were so named because their traditions emphasised their birth, created in the laboratories and apothecarions of Colchis. They were written into existence, born as syllables of the Word. A dedicated naval formation, the Quillborn were true marines, fighting ship-to-ship, completely at home battling through the cramped structure of a starship. At their head was Assault-Captain Baelanos, the acting captain of the company, although Zadkiel was their overlord.

'The ghost of one of their vessels has waylaid them,' continued Zadkiel with rising oratory. 'It was promised that in the warp we would find our allies. The fate of our pursuers aboard the *Wrathful* has shown that promise to have been kept.'

Baelanos stepped forwards. 'Who will hear the Word?' he bellowed.

As one, a hundred Word Bearers raised their guns and chanted in salute.

'They will be harrying us from here to Macragge,' said the assault-captain, his belligerence a contrast to Zadkiel's authoritative confidence, 'and they will die for it! Perhaps the warp will send them to us in the end, so we can show them how we deal with the blind in real space!'

The Word Bearers cheered. Zadkiel saw Ultis among them, and felt a pang of agitation at his presence in the throng.

His fate is written, Zadkiel thought.

'The warp is yet a strange place to us,' said Zadkiel. 'Though it holds nothing for us to fear, for Lorgar knows it better than any mind ever has, you will be assailed by mysteries. You might dream that which your mind has hidden from you. Perhaps you will even see them, as clear as day. These are the ways of the warp. Remember in all things the Word of Lorgar, and it will lead you back to sanity. Lose sight of the Word, and your mind will be carried away on currents from which it might never return. Make no mistake, the warp is dangerous. It is the Word, and the Word alone, that lets us navigate its waters.

'Soon we must make dock. The earlier battle took more of a toll than we thought. The way-station at Bakka Triumveron is our next destination.'

Zadkiel did not tell them that his over-confidence had resulted in the damage to the ship that meant they were forced into a detour. A lucky hit from the *Waning Moon*'s lances had cut off the engineering teams from the *Furious Abyss*'s stores of fuel oil as well as rupturing the primary coolant line. Without regular supply, they could not function, and so it was imperative that the damage be cleared in order to allow the crews access. That could only be done whilst at dock.

'Shortly after that, we shall be at Macragge,' Zadkiel continued. 'Then our chapter of the Word will be completed. To your duties, Word Bearers. You are dismissed.'

The Word Bearers filed out of the cathedra, many of them heading to reclusium cells.

Baelanos approached the pulpit where Zadkiel was standing. 'We won't have long at Bakka,' he said. 'What are your orders to the astropathic choir?'

'I need to make contact with my lord Kor Phaeron,' said Zadkiel, 'and apprise him of our progress.'

'What of Wsoric?' asked Baelanos, a momentary tremor evident in his outward resolve at mention of the name.

'He stirs,' replied Zadkiel. 'We have only to cement our pact with the empyrean with blood, and then he will act.'

'The lap dogs of the Emperor are ever tenacious, my lord.'

'Then we shall cast them off,' Zadkiel told him, 'but for now, we wait. Asking too many favours of the empyrean may not behove us well.'

'As you wish, my lord,' said Baelanos, bowing slightly, but his reluctance was obvious.

'Trust me to fulfil my duties to the Word, Baelanos, as I trust you,' said Zadkiel.

'Yes, admiral,' replied the assault-captain. Baelanos saluted and headed for the engine decks.

Zadkiel remained in the cathedra, for a moment, deep in thought. It was so easy to lose sight of the Word, to become wrapped up in power. It would have been simple for him to forget what he was and where his place was in the galaxy.

That was why Lorgar had chosen him for this mission. There was no more dedicated servant of the Word, save for Lorgar.

Zadkiel knelt before the altar, murmured a few words of prayer, and headed back up towards the bridge.

'Captain Cestus?' said Kaminska's voice over the Ultramarine's helmet vox. The engine servitors of the *Wrathful* had managed to bring on-ship communications back on line.

'Speaking,' he replied, more irritably than he'd intended. The confrontation with Brynngar in the medi-bay waiting room was weighing on his mind, that and whatever Mhotep was hiding from them behind that veneer of indifference.

'Meet me on the bridge at once.'

Cestus sighed deeply at the admiral's curt response. He had intended to patrol the lower aft decks with Antiges. In the wake of the officer of the watch's death, together with all of his most experienced armsmen, the ship was short-handed. The Astartes captain had taken it upon himself to make up the shortfall and ensure that no other unforeseen difficulties arose for whatever time remained of their warp passage.

Given Admiral Kaminska's tone, the patrol would have to wait, so Cestus and Antiges headed for the bridge.

KAMINSKA KEPT A lean bridge when not in combat. Crewmen at the sensorium, navigation and engineering helms were all that were present. The admiral was standing at a table illuminated by a hololithic star map. She looked ragged as he approached her, with dark rings around her eyes and a greyish pallor to her complexion.

Cestus couldn't help think how long it had been since she had slept. An Astartes could go for several days without, but Kaminska was merely human. He wondered how long she could keep going.

'My lord,' she said, acknowledging the giant Astartes.

'Admiral. What is it you wish to bring to my attention?'

Kaminska indicated the star map in front of her. It showed the sector of the galaxy around the dense galactic core. The core was impassable, and so much of the map was taken up with a blank void. Notations and calculations were scrawled in the margins. Beside the map was a printout from one of the sensorium pict screens. It was a close-up of the *Furious Abyss*'s hull.

'See this?' said Kaminska, indicating a white plume issuing from the side of the Word Bearers ship. The grainy resolution made it look like gas was being vented.

'They have an air leak?'

'Better than that,' said Kaminska. 'It's damage to the coolant lines. If they push the engines, the plasma reactors will burn up, and, pursued by *this* ship, if they want to stay ahead of us, they'll have to push the engines.'

Cestus smiled grimly at the sudden turn in fortune. It was small recompense for all they'd lost.

'So the *Furious Abyss* will have to make dock to effect repairs,' the Ultramarine guessed.

'Yes. They'll also be reloading ordnance and using the time to service their fighters after the battle outside the Tertiary Coreward Transit.'

'Show me the location, admiral,' said Cestus, assuming that Kaminska had already planned their strategy in part.

Kaminska laid her finger on the hololithic display in triumph. 'Outside the Solar System there aren't many orbital docks that can support a ship that size.'

The Bakka system was already circled on the map.

'Bakka,' said Cestus. 'My Legion mustered there for the Karanthas Crusade. It's the Imperial Army's staging post for half the galactic south.'

'It has the only docks between the galactic core and Macragge that could handle the *Furious Abyss*,' Kaminska told him. 'I'd bet my commission that this is where they'll head.'

Cestus thought for a moment. A plan was forming.

'How long before we break warp?'

'Several hours yet, but delay or not, we can't beat the *Furious Abyss* in a straight fight.'

'Tell me this, admiral,' Cestus said, looking into Kaminska's eyes. 'When is a ship most vulnerable?'

Kaminska smiled despite her weariness.

'When she's at anchor.'

Cestus nodded. Turning away from the admiral, he raised the other Astartes captains on the vox array and told them to meet him in the conference room immediately.

'WHAT NEWS HAVE you, Brother Zadkiel?' mouthed the supplicant.

Somehow, the creature's lolling mouth formed the words in such a way that Kor Phaeron's short temper and self-confidence were perfectly enunciated.

'We are on our way, my lord,' said Zadkiel, bowing.

Kor Phaeron was one of the arch commanders of the Legion, foremost in Lorgar's reckoning. He was the primarch's greatest champion and it was he, this ancient warrior of countless battles, that would command the forces to attack Calth where Guilliman mustered and destroy the Ultramarines utterly. It was a singular honour to be in Kor Phaeron's presence, albeit across the infinity of warp space, and Zadkiel was at once humbled by the experience. It was not an emotion he had great affinity with.

The supplicant chamber of the *Furious Abyss* was bathed in darkness, but the presence of the astropathic choir behind the supplicant was powerful enough to remove the need for light. The choir consisted of eight astropaths, but the *Furious*'s astral cohort differed from those on any Imperial ship. The fact that there were eight of them suggested their instability. The *Furious Abyss's* route through the warp, and the forces brought to bear on it, eroded the mind of an astropath with dismaying speed, and while such creatures were all blind, they did not have the heavy ribbed cables running from each eye socket attaching them to the macabre contraption clamped around the supplicant's swollen cranium.

'How goes your progress?' asked the mighty champion of the Word Bearers.

'Half a day longer in the warp, until we reach the fringes of the galactic core. We must make vital repairs at Bakka, before heading onwards to Macragge.'

'I recall no such deviation in the mission plan, Zadkiel.' Despite the fact that Kor Phaeron was doubtless aboard the Word Bearers battle-barge the *Infidus Imperator*, in deep communion with its own astropathic choir and speaking through a flesh puppet, his tone and manner were still dangerous.

'During a brief sortie with a fleet of Imperial ships we sustained minor damage that could not be ignored, my lord,' Zadkiel explained more hurriedly than he liked.

'A military action?' Kor Phaeron's disdain was clear. 'Did any survive?'

'A single cruiser pursues us yet through the warp, liege.'

'So they do not seek to raise a warning back on Terra,' mused the arch champion, his considered tone at odds with the slack-jawed, drooling visage of the supplicant. 'A pity. I suspect Sor Talgron is itching in his traitor's shackles.'

'I trust that Brother Talgron would have acquitted himself with distinction, Kor Phaeron.'

In the eyes of Zadkiel, Sor Talgron's mission was not a desirable one. The lord commander was to remain in the Solar System, his four companies ostensibly guarding Terra, in order to maintain the pretence that Lorgar still sided with the Emperor when in fact, he had been instrumental in the Warmaster's defection.

'It matters not, my lord. The prospect of word reaching Terra should not concern us. The warp's disquiet would prevent any warning getting to Macragge.'

'I disagree.' The supplicant sneered in an echo of Kor Phaeron's idiosyncratic expression. 'Any deviation from the plan as written holds the potential for disaster. The entire Word could go disobeyed!'

'We will be a few hours at Bakka at the most, exalted lord,' said Zadkiel plaintively, wary of his master's wrath. 'Then we will be on our way. If our pursuer catches up with us, she will be destroyed as her sister ships were. In any case we will not be late; our passage through the warp was swift. But what of you, my lord?'

'We've joined up with the other elements of the Legion and all is proceeding as written.'

'Calth has no hope.'

'None, my brother.'

The supplicant lolled back, drooling blood as the connection was broken. The astropathic choir sank into silence, only their ragged breathing suggesting the great effort required to maintain the link across the immaterium.

Zadkiel regarded the dead supplicant with detached interest. It was interesting to him to see how easily their physical forms could be destroyed when their minds were so strong. He considered that he would like to test that theory.

'All is well, my lord?' asked Ultis. The novice was standing behind Zadkiel.

'All is well, novice,' said Zadkiel. 'You will join Bae-lanos at Bakka, Ultis. Take the Scholar Coven. They will know to obey you.'

Ultis saluted. 'It will be an honour, admiral.'

'One you have earned, novice. Now, be about your duties.'

'Yes, my lord.'

Ultis turned smartly and headed for the cell deck where the Scholar Coven would be undergoing their scheduled meditation-doctrine training.

Zadkiel watched him go and smiled darkly. Such potential, such relentless ambition; the upstart would soon learn the folly of overreaching.

Soon, Zadkiel told himself, forcing down a thrill of excitement. *Soon, Guilliman will burn and Lorgar will rule the stars*.

Zadkiel could feel that time approaching. That age was in its infancy, but it only needed time to come about. Zadkiel knew this as surely as he had ever known anything, because it was written.

THE WRATHFUL BROKE out of the warp, almost gasping in relief as it slid back into real space.

The vessel's hull was torn and scorched, and chunks of its engine cowlings were ripped out. The winds of the warp had carved strange patterns into its armour plate around the prow and all over the underside. Claws had raked deep gouges all over the upper hull and torn turrets from their mountings.

Sitting in her command throne, Admiral Kaminska looked out of the viewport and saw that the *Wrathful* had not emerged alone.

Leprous and wretched with its pitted, rusting hull and disease-ridden ports, the *Fireblade* limped into existence alongside them.

It was a ship of the damned, the thousands of souls aboard condemned to endless, torturous oblivion.

Such a thing could not be allowed to endure.

Kaminska gave the order to train laser batteries on the decrepit vessel. There was a few seconds' pause when the *Wrathful* unleashed a blistering salvo of fire. Without operational shields, the *Fireblade* crumpled under the onslaught. A few seconds more and all that remained of the blighted escort ship was a scorched wreck and space debris.

It was a duty that gave Kaminska no pleasure, but necessary all the same, much like the expulsion of their own dead. It was bad luck to keep the deceased on board, not to mention unhygienic. Bodies were never returned to their home port in the Saturnine Fleet. What the void killed, it kept.

The tiny gleaming sparks that fell away from the *Wrathful* were corpses enclosed in body bags, reflecting the light of the star Bakka that burned in a magnesium spark a few light hours away. Much closer was Bakka Triumveron, a titanic gas cloud far bigger than the Solar System's Jupiter, bright yellow streaked with violet and ringed with scores of shimmering bands of ice and rock. Bakka was a mystery, its gaseous form far too stormy and strange to admit any craft, while its rings were death-traps many times more lethal than the rings of Saturn. Bakka's outlying moons, however, were habitable, each one almost the size of Terra and all of them heavily populated. Rogelin, Sanctuary, Half Hope, Grey Harbour: these hive cities were just fledglings compared to the teeming pinnacles of the Solar System, but they were still home to billions of Imperial citizens. The Bakka system was one of the most populated in the segmentum, certainly the largest concentration of human life this close to the galactic core.

Bakka Triumveron's fourteenth moon had no cities, but instead was enclosed within a thin black spider web that looked like some planetary disease. It was, in fact, the underlying structure of its orbital docks, held over the moon so that they could benefit from its enormous stores of geothermal energy. The moon was uninhabited, thanks to its relentlessly shifting tectonic plates and accompanying cataclysms, but the dockyards above Triumveron 14 were some of the main reasons why Bakka was populated at all.

THREE ASSAULT-BOATS HEADED out from the launch bays of the *Wrathful*. They approached the farthest docking spike of Bakka Triumveron 14 and did so with stealth and subterfuge. It was imperative that they not be discovered by the enemy. It also meant that the troops on board would have a long trek to the *Furious Abyss*.

Three assault-boats; three discreet combat formations. Skraal joined his Legion warriors in one. Their mode of approach was a central avenue between overlooking docking towers, decks sprawling out from jutting bartizans, and the World Eaters and their captain were to take the lead. Two flanks branched out from the central avenue and these channels would be taken by the Blood Claws, led by Brynngar in spite of the Space Wolf's earlier altercation with Cestus, and a second group of World Eaters led by the only Ultramarine in the raiding party.

Antiges sat bolt upright in the flight couch of the gloom-drenched troop hold of an assault-boat as they made their way closer to the gaseous expanse that was Bakka Triumveron and the moon that would support their embarkation. He was the only Ultramarine aboard the assault-boat, accompanied, as he was, by two combat-squads of Skraal's remaining World Eaters. To Antiges's mind they were brutal warriors, festooned with the trophies of war, crude kill-markings like badges of honour carved into their armour. Each and every one was possessed of a murderous mien, a faint echo of their primarch's battle rage.

Dimly, as if the infinite expanse of black space that existed between them had smothered it, Antiges recalled his last conversation with his captain.

'STAND ASIDE, ANTIGES,' Cestus barked, bedecked in a stripped down version of his honour guard regalia and battle-ready with short-blade, power sword and bolter.

Adjusting to the half-light of the assembly deck, Cestus saw that his battle-brother was similarly attired.

'I have told you before, Antiges. The sons of Guilliman will remain aboard ship in case anything goes wrong. I shall accompany the mission as its leader to ensure that it goes to plan.'

Cestus had gone over the plan several times since it was first broached in the conference room to the rest of the Astartes captains. If they were to make the most of the *Furious Abyss*'s current disposition, they would need to act in subterfuge and in secret. Even with that caveat in mind, the strike would need to be brutal and at close-quarters. The World Eaters and the Space Wolves had no equals in that regard, save for the sons of Sanguinius, but the Angels were far off in another part of the galaxy. These were the tools at their disposal; they had but to unleash them.

The assault force was to infiltrate Bakka Triumveron 14, where the Word Bearers had made dock, in three teams in a classic feint and strike manoeuvre in order that they get close enough to scupper the ship at close-range. Incendiary charges: krak and melta bombs, were to be carried as standard. It was a faint hope, but it was hope none the less and all had embraced it. Even Brynngar, his demeanour sullen and belligerent, had acceded to the plan, doubtless eager to vent his wrath much like his brother captain, Skraal.

'With respect, brother-captain,' said Antiges levelly, purposefully standing his ground. 'You shall not.'

Cestus's face creased in consternation.

'I did not expect disobedience from you, Antiges.'

'It is not disobedience, sire. Rather, it is sense.' Antiges still did not move. His expression brooked no argument.

'Very well,' said Cestus, letting his battle-brother have this indulgence before he rebuked him for his insolence. 'Explain yourself.'

Antiges's face softened, a trace of pleading behind his eyes.

'Allow me to lead the strike,' he said. 'This mission is too dangerous and our plight too great to risk your life, my captain. Without you, there is no mission. Even now, we hold to our cause by a mere thread. Were you to be lost, then so too would be Macragge. You know this to be true.'

Antiges stepped forward, allowing the light to fall on his face and armour. The effect was not unlike a bodily halo. 'I entreat you, liege, let me do this service. I shall not fail you.'

At first, Cestus had thought to deny him, but he knew his brother Ultramarine was right. Cestus was acutely aware of the other combat squads mustering on the deck behind him, readying to take to the assault-boats.

'It would do me great honour to have you, Brother Antiges, as my representative,' he said and clapped Antiges on the shoulder.

'My lord,' the fellow Ultramarine intoned and bowed to his knee.

'No, Antiges,' said Cestus, grasping his battle-brother's shoulder to stop him mid-genuflect. 'We are equals and such deference is not necessary.'

Antiges rose and nodded instead.

'Courage and honour, my brother,' said Cestus.

'Courage and honour,' Antiges replied and turned to walk away towards the assault-boats.

THE WORDS WERE distant now, and Antiges crushed whatever sentiment they held as he intoned the oaths of battle.

The World Eaters were similarly engaged, their lips moving in entreaty to their weapons and armaments that they should not fail them, and rather that they be covered in glory and speak with righteous anger.

The warriors of the XII Legion were well-armed with chainaxes and storm shields. They bore side arms too, but Antiges suspected that they were rarely drawn. World Eaters fought up close, in face-to-face melee, where the force of a charge and the shock of their ferocity counted the most.

Antiges steeled himself and mouthed the name of Roboute Guilliman as the assault-boat screamed towards its destination.

THE DOCK-MASTER HAD demanded to know why prior notification had not been given for the arrival of such an enormous ship. His obstinate and imperious attitude had faltered and withered upon the arrival of the Astartes on his deck.

Once Ultis had gained entry to the observation balcony, he had had the dock master put his deck crews to work to receive the *Furious Abyss*. Violence, at this point, was unnecessary. To the menials and underlings of Bakka Triumveron 14, they were still Astartes and as such their word carried the authority of the Emperor. No man of the Imperium would dare brook that.

From the observation balcony overlooking the battleship dock, Ultis could see the automated coolant tanks picking their way through the docking clamps and other dockside detritus towards the towering shape of the *Furious Abyss*. The dock was a hive of activity, tracked-servitors and human indentured workers bustling back and forth on loaders, carrying massive fuel drums and swathes of heavy piping. The frenetic scene, fraught with activity, was as a mustering of ants before the towering hive that was the Word Bearers ship.

It was the first time Ultis had been able to truly appreciate the vessel's gigantic size. Like a city of crenellated towers, arching spires and fanged fortress-like decks, it dwarfed the puny dock, easily clearing the highest antennae and cranes. The book, resplendent upon the *Furious*'s prow easily eclipsed the observation building in which Ultis was standing.

'We are in control,' Ultis voxed privately through his helmet array, the dock master busied at his consoles with the massive ship's sudden arrival.

'Good,' said Zadkiel, back on the ship. 'Did you encounter any resistance?'

'They accept the authority of the Astartes like the dutiful and deluded lapdogs they are, my lord,' Ultis replied, looking around at the Scholar Coven.

These warriors had been assembled from the Word Bearers under Zadkiel's command who showed the greatest adherence to Lorgar's Word. They were all more recent recruits to the Legion, all from Colchis and all dedicated scholars of Lorgar's writings. They were motivated not by the glory of the Great Crusade, but by the ideology of the Word Bearers. Zadkiel greatly valued such followers since they could be counted on to support the Legion's latest endeavours, which would be sure to bring the Word Bearers into conflict with elements of the Imperium before long. Ultis looked over at the man he would soon kill, once preparations were fully underway, and reasoned that the conflicts were already beginning to come about.

The fact meant absolutely nothing to him. Ultis had no loyalty save to the Word. There was nothing in the galaxy in that moment, other than that which was written.

The novice smiled.

This day, his destiny would be etched in the Word for all time.

NINE

Infiltration/Ambush/Sons of Angron

THE ASSAULT-BOATS DOCKED quickly and without incident, the pilot having avoided radar and long-range scans to insert the Astartes squads outside the main thoroughfares of Bakka Triumveron 14.

Antiges, clad in the blue and gold of his Legion's honour guard, was first out of the assault-boat, speeding from the embarkation ramp. Chainsword held low at his hip and adopting a crouching stance, he moved stealthily across an open plaza of steel plates, flanked by towering cranes and disused craft in for non-urgent repairs. The few servitors meandering back and forth on tracks and slaved to an aerial rail system ignored the Astartes. Working through pre-assigned protocols as dictated by their command wafers, they were not even aware of their presence.

Close behind the Ultramarine, one of the World Eaters, Hargrath, gave the servitors a wary glance as he piled through the open channel with his battle-brothers.

'Pay them no heed,' Antiges hissed, looking back to check on his charges.

Hargrath nodded and continued on his way towards the massive crimson horizon ahead, visible across the entire length of the shipyard: the *Furious Abyss*, the largest vessel any of them had ever seen.

'Keep in cover,' said Antiges as the plaza gave way to a maze-like refuelling and maintenance bay full of passing loaders and stacks of drums. The Ultramarine was careful to keep his squad out of the view of the labouring indentured workers and other menials busying themselves at the dock. They clung to the shadows, using them like a second skin.

Once they had reached their destination, their targets would be the engines and ordnance ports. The Ultramarine checked a bandoleer of krak grenades at his hip. There was a cluster of melta bombs flanking it on the opposite side and as the *Furious Abyss* drew closer, he hoped it would be enough.

BRYNNGAR WAS FESTOONED with trophies and fetishes: wolf's teeth and claws, and a necklace of uncut gemstones, polished pebbles carved with runes. If he were to go to war at last against his brother Astartes then he would do so in his full regalia. Let them witness the majesty and savage power of the Sons of Russ in their most feral aspect before they were torn asunder for their treachery.

The Wolf Guard was focused on the battle ahead, crushing all thoughts of his altercation with Cestus to the back of his mind for now. There would be time for a reckoning later. It was only a pity that the Ultramarine had eschewed the mission in favour of overall command aboard the *Wrathful*. Brynngar wanted to think him cowardly, but he had fought alongside the son of Guilliman many times and knew this not to be the case. It was probably a display of the XIII Legion's much vaunted tactical acumen.

The Space Wolves' aspect of attack was a narrow cordon riddled with junked carriers used for spare parts. It was more like an open warehouse with machine carcasses piled high and banded tightly together to prevent them toppling when stacked. Servitors slaved to loaders hummed back and forth amongst the towers of rusted metal like bees harvesting a nest. If they cared about the Space Wolf captain and his Blood Claws, tooled up with broad-bladed axes and bolt pistols, and weaving crisscross fashion through their domain, they did not show it.

Brynngar knew that he would spill blood this day, and it would be the blood of his erstwhile brothers. This was no fight against mere heathen men, misguided in their beliefs, nor was it foul xenos breeds ever intent on corralling the human galaxy to their yoke. No, this was Astartes against Astartes. It was unprecedented. Thinking of the devastation the Word Bearers had already wrought, the Space Wolf took a better grip of Felltooth and vowed to make the traitors pay for their transgressions.

'THEY ARE MAKING their final approach towards the dock,' said Kaminska poring over the hololithic tactical display in front of her command throne. Having been preparing the other Ultramarines for potential combat and distributing them around the ship accordingly, Cestus had returned to the bridge and joined the admiral at the tactical display table.

Hazy runes moved over a top-down green-rimmed blueprint of Bakka Triumveron 14, indicating the progress of the three attack waves heading for the immense swathe of bulky red that represented the *Furious Abyss*. The ship's magos, Agantese, had tapped into one of the satellite feeds of the orbital moon and was using it to re-route images to the *Wrathful's* tactical network. It had a short delay, but was an otherwise excellent way to keep track of their forces on the ground. Even so, Cestus felt impotent, directing the action from the relative safety of real space where the cruiser lingered to stay out of radar and sensorium range.

'Antiges, report,' he barked into the ship's vox, synced with his fellow Ultramarine's boosted helmet array.

'Assault protocol alpha proceeding as planned, captain,' Antiges's voice said after a few seconds delay. The reply was fraught with static. Even with the boosted array rigged by the *Wrathful's* engineers, the gulf of real space between them impinged greatly.

'We will be making our initial insertion onto the dock in T-minus three minutes.'

'Well enough, Brother Antiges. Keep me appraised. If you meet any resistance, you have your orders,' said Cestus.

'I shall prosecute my duties with all the fury of the Legion, my lord.'

The vox cut out.

Cestus sighed deeply. To think it had come to this. This was no foray into the jaws of alien overlords or the misguided worshippers of the arcane, not this time. It was brother versus brother. Cestus could barely bring himself to think on it. Fighting across the gulf of real space was one thing, but to be face-to-face with those who had betrayed the Emperor, those who had killed

warriors they once called friend and comrade in cold
blood, was indeed harrowing. It felt like an end of
things, and the sense of it caught in the Ultramarine's
throat.

'Admiral Kaminska,' said Cestus after the momentary
silence, 'you have risked much in the pursuit of this mission. You have done, and continue to do, me great
honour with your sterling service to our cause.'

Kaminska was clearly taken aback and failed to hide
her shock from the Ultramarine completely.

'I thank you, lord Astartes,' she said, bowing slightly,
'but if I am honest, I would have chosen to undertake
this duty, although perhaps of my own volition,' she
added candidly.

Cestus's gaze was mildly questioning.

'I am the last of a dying breed,' she confessed, her
shoulders sagging and not from physical fatigue. 'The
Saturnine Fleet is to be decommissioned.'

'Is that so?'

'Yes, captain. It doesn't do to have such an anachro-
nism on the rostrum of the new Imperium. All those
gentlemen in their powdered wigs talking about good
breeding, it hardly speaks of efficiency and impartiality.
Our ships are to be refitted for a new Imperial Navy. I'm
a part of the last generation. I suppose I should be glad
that at least Vorlov didn't see it.

'You see, captain, this is really my last hurrah, the last
great journey of the *Wrathful* as I know it.'

Cestus smiled mirthlessly. His eyes were cold orbs,
tinged with a deep sense of burden and regret.

'It might be for us all, admiral.'

SKRAAL'S ASSAULT FORCE sped down the central channel
of the dock, a loading bay for fuel and munitions

tankers, with reckless abandon. The berserker fury was
building within the World Eater captain and he knew
his battle-brothers were experiencing the same rush.
They were the sons of Angron and like their lord they
were implanted with an echo of the neural technology
that had unlocked the primarch's violent potential. At
the cusp of battle, the Astartes warriors could tap into
that font of boiling range and use it like an edged blade
to cut their enemies down. After several bloody inci-
dents, the Emperor had censured the further use of
implants in the false belief that they made the World
Eaters unstable killing machines.

Angron, in his wisdom, had eschewed the edict of the
Emperor of Mankind and had continued in spite of it.
They were killing machines, Skraal felt it in his burning
blood and in the core of his marrow, but then what
greater accolade was there for the eternal warriors of the
Astartes?

Though the orders of the Ultramarine, Antiges, had
forbidden it, Skraal encouraged his warriors to kill as
they converged on the *Furious Abyss*. A spate of blood-
letting would sharpen the senses for the battle to come.
The only directive: leave none alive to tell or warn others of their approach. The World Eaters pursued this
duty with brutal efficiency and a trail of menial corpses
littered the ground between the assault-boat insertion
point and their current position.

Such reckless slaying had not, however, gone unnoticed.

'MY LORD,' HISSED Ultis into the vox array of the observation platform.

Zadkiel's voice responded from the *Furious*.

'It seems we are not alone,' Ultis concluded.

The novice in command of the Scholar Coven consulted a holo-map of the entire dockyard. His gauntleted finger was pressed against a flashing diode near one of the many refuelling conduits.

'Where is that?' he demanded of the dock-master, still engrossed in the refit and refuel of the vast starship.

'Tanker Yard Epsilon IV, my lord,' said the dock-master, who looked closer when he saw the flashing red diode. 'An emergency alarm.' The dock-master moved to another part of the console and brought up a viewscreen. Warriors in blue and white power armour were visible in the grainy resolution surging through the tanker yard. Prone forms, dressed in worker fatigues, slumped in their wake surrounded by dark pools.

'By Terra,' said the dock-master, turning to face Ultis, 'they are Astartes.'

The novice faced the dock-master and shot the man through the face point-blank with his bolt pistol. After his head exploded in a shower of viscera and bone-riddled gore, his streaming carcass slid to the deck.

The rest of the dock crew on the observation platform had failed to react before the rest of the Scholar Coven had taken Ultis's lead and shot them, too.

'The Astartes have tracked us here and move in on the *Furious Abyss* as we speak,' said Ultis down the vox. 'I have eliminated all platform personnel to prevent any interference.'

'Very well, Brother Ultis. You have your orders,' said Zadkiel's voice through the array.

Ultis looked down through the building's windows to the expanse of the docking stage. Baelanos's assault squad was standing guard there.

'I shall show them what fates are written for them,' said Ultis, drawing his sword.

'Educate them,' replied Zadkiel.

THE BATTLESHIP DOCK looked like a tangled web of metal as Skraal and his warriors forged onward. Beyond that the massive *Furious Abyss* loomed like a slumbering predator in repose.

The stink of blood from the previous slaughter was heady through the World Eater captain's nose grille as he raced towards the end of the channel and the open dock beyond. The cordon tightened ahead and the Legionaries were forced together as they rifled through it. Just as Skraal was feeling confident that they had not been discovered, a group of Word Bearers in crimson ceramite emerged before them to block their path.

Bolter fire wreathed the opening, lighting up the half-dark of the channel with four-pronged muzzle flares. Kellock, the warrior next to Skraal, took a full burst in the chest that tore open his armour and left him oozing blood. Kellock crumpled and fell, both his primary and secondary hearts punctured.

The combat squads were pinned on either side by fuel drums, stacked against bulky warehouse structures. Fleeing menials and mindless servitors, alerted by the commotion, wandered into their path and were cut down with chainblades or battered by shields as the World Eaters sought to close with the foe and wrest the advantage back. One of the drums was struck by an errant bolter round and exploded in a bright bloom of yellow-white fury. A fiery plume spilled into the air, like ink in water, and a wrecked servitor was cast like a broken doll at the edge of its blossoming blast wave. Three World Eaters were shredded by the concussive force of the explosion and smashed aside into the metallic siding of a warehouse unit. The siding didn't yield to the sudden impact of massed flesh and ceramite, and the two warriors were crushed.

Skraal felt the heat of the explosion against his face even through his helmet as the warning sensors went crazy. He staggered, but kept his footing and yelled the order to charge.

ANTIGES WAS STALKING through the refuelling bay when he heard the explosion from across the dock and saw fire and smoke billowing into the air. They were close. The *Furious Abyss*, a dense dark wall, filled the Ultramarine's sights.

'Antiges, report,' Cestus's voice said through the helmet vox, the tactical display obviously registering the sudden influx of heat.

'An explosion in the central channel. I fear we are discovered, brother-captain.'

'Get over there, unite your forces and push on through to the *Furious*.'

'As you command, captain,' he replied and ordered his combat squads through a maze of piping that connected to the central channel where he knew Skraal and his insertion team were placed. As they moved, Antiges at the lead, a shadow fell across the Ultramarine, cast by the vast observation platform overlooking the dock above.

Out of instinct, he looked up and saw the line of crimson armoured warriors bearing down on them with bolter and plasma gun.

Death rained down in a hail of venting promethium and spent electrum. Antiges rolled out of its way into the shadow of the docking clamp. Hargrath was distracted and a fraction slower. He paid for his laxity when a bolt of searing plasma blasted a hole in his torso, cooking the World Eater in his armour. He fell with a resounding clang, the wound cauterised before he hit the ground. Several of his brothers heaved his body towards them, but to act as improvised cover, rather than out of any sense of reverence for their dead comrade.

Antiges replied with barking retorts of his bolt pistol, half-glimpsing the target above between bursts of chipped plascrete and metal as the docking clamp was chewed up around him.

The rest of the World Eaters followed his lead, stowing storm shields and drawing bolt pistols, their weapons adding to the return fire.

Menials, put to flight at the start of the attack, and spilling into the rapidly erupting war zone were ripped apart in the crossfire. The roar of gunfire and the shriek of shrapnel mangled together with their screams.

Antiges pressed up against the closest docking clamp and looked around it, gauging the terrain leading the rest of the way to the *Furious Abyss*. The docks formed a landscape of narrow fire lanes between clamps and fuel tanks. Above was the observation platform, strung on metal struts, and beyond that rings of steel holding fuelling gantries, defence turrets and bouquets of sensor spines.

Antiges slammed himself back against the steel of the docking clamp as bolter fire continued to pin them.

'Captain, we are ambushed!' he yelled into the vox, in an attempt to overcome the din. Despite his volume, the Ultramarine's tone was calm as he cycled through a number of potential battle protocols learned by rote during his training.

There was a moment's pause as the message went through and his captain assessed the options open to him.

'Relief is incoming,' came the clipped reply. 'Be ready.'

AFTER A SECOND bout of return fire, a chain of small explosions erupted across the observation platform, showering frag.

Beyond the destruction and across the dockyard, embarkation ports were opening in the side of the *Furious Abyss*.

Antiges was on his feet and bellowing orders before the resulting smoke had cleared.

'Don't give them time! Hit them! Hit them now!'

The Astartes broke cover and charged, leaving the dead in their wake.

Two hundred robed cohorts in the crimson of the Word Bearers emerged from the *Furious Abyss*, and charged right back.

'Open fire!' shouted Antiges. The Ultramarine felt the immediate pressure wave of discharged bolt pistols behind him as the World Eaters obeyed.

The effect was brutal. Lines of the crudely armoured Word Bearer lackeys fell beneath the onslaught. Bodies pitched into their comrades, jerked and spun as the munitions struck. Blood sprayed in directions too numerous to count and the corpses mounted like a bank of fleshy sandbags, tripping those following. There was only time for a single volley, and the disciplined Astartes holstered pistols before closing with the first of the *Furious's* cannon fodder.

A brutish cohort, scarred and tarnished like an engine ganger, came at Antiges with an axe blade. The Ultramarine met the ganger's roar with the screech of his chainsword, plunging it into the man's chest. The cohort fell, wrenching the weapon from Antiges's hand. The Astartes didn't pause and threw the wretch aside with such force that the corpse spun in the air before crashing into its debased brethren. The Ultramarine drew his short-blade, duelling shield already in hand and cut down a second assailant with a low, arcing sweep.

Rorgath, a World Eater sergeant, came alongside Antiges and forged into the melee with brutal abandon. Limbs fell like rain as he churned through his enemies, his face a grisly mask of wrath without his helmet.

Out of the corner of his eye, Antiges saw another of Rorgath's kin decapitate a cohort officer trying to ram home the charge and extol his warriors to greater fervour. Others disappeared in clouds of red mist and the dreadful din of chainaxes rending bone. Yet, despite the relentless carnage wreaked upon them, the lowly cohorts refused to break, and the killing ground became mired in blood.

'They're fanatics,' grumbled Rorgath, burying his blade in the face on an oncoming cohort.

'Drive them back,' snarled Antiges through gritted teeth, smashing an enemy with the blunt force of his duelling shield. About to redouble his efforts, the Ultramarine fell back, as two or three bodies flew at him. In the madness, he dropped his short-blade, but as he foraged for it in the sea of pressing bodies, he found the hilt of his chainsword. Tearing the weapon loose, Antiges cut a path through bone and flesh to free himself. Hands were grabbing at him to drag the Astartes down, and even as he tried to emerge, bullets rang off his armour. One of the World Eaters yelled in anger and pain. The *Furious Abyss* disappeared from view as more enemy crewmen threw themselves forward.

This was not how men fought. Very few xenos were content to simply die, even when there was something to be gained by it. That was why the Astartes were such lethal warriors; they were the ultimate weapon against any enemy tainted by natural cowardice, since a Space Marine could control and banish his own fear. The Word Bearers had created another kind of enemy, one that even Space Marines could not break.

'Damn you,' hissed Antiges as he threw another man off him, and was sprayed by a shower of blood as Rorgath disembowelled yet another. 'Now we have to kill them all.'

Driving on, pain burst against Antiges's side as a blade or a bullet found its way through his armour. He staggered and it gave the enemy the opening they needed. A sudden flurry of cohorts sprang on the stricken Astartes. Then the weight of the attacks was dragging him down, their death-cries and the smell of their sundered bodies filling his senses.

BRYNNGAR HEFTED HIS last belt of frag grenades at the observation platform. A cluster of explosions rippled over the pitted surface, hewing off chunks of ferrocrete and scorching metal. The assault had achieved its desired effect, forcing the ambushers above Antiges's position back for a few moments, who were unseen from the channel the Space Wolf and his Blood Claws charged down, and switching their attention.

Fire erupted again from the platform before the last of the grenades had even detonated, but this time their focus was upon the Wolf Guard and his squad. Brynngar's highly attuned animal senses picked up on the stink of cordite and blood, and the sporadic clatter of weapon's fire, and he assumed that his brother Ultramarine was otherwise occupied, hence their popularity.

Rujveld slid into cover beside his venerable leader as he appraised the disposition of the ambushers strafing them. Fire streaked down from the observation gallery and prevented them joining the fight beyond.

'They knew we were coming,' Brynngar growled to the stony-faced Blood Claw.

'What are your orders, Wolf Guard?'

Brynngar turned his feral gaze onto his pack brother.

'We bring them down,' he grinned, displaying his fangs. 'Yorl, Borund,' bellowed the Space Wolf captain, and two of his charges abandoned their ready positions to approach their leader.

'Melta bombs,' snarled Brynngar. 'One of those struts.' He pointed to the source of the platform's elevation.

Yorl and Borund nodded as one, priming their melta charges before heading across a gauntlet of open ground that led to the structure. Withering fire struck the first Blood Claw before he ventured more than a few feet, the impacts kicking him off his feet and spinning him around before he fell in a bloody heap.

Borund had greater fortune, a feral war cry on his lips as he reached the base of the platform. Clamping the charge onto one of the struts, he took a hit in the shoulder. Another struck him across the torso as Word Bearers positioned neared the building's base realised what he was doing. Borund pressed the detonator before they could stop him. He roared in savage defiance as the melta bomb exploded, vaporising him in a flare of super-heated chemicals.

The platform held.

Brynngar was about to head into the gauntlet to finish the job when a second explosion erupted after the first. The Space Wolf captain turned away from the sudden blast, an actinic stench prickling his nostrils when he looked back. The sound of wrenching metal followed and the observation platform finally collapsed, kicking up clouds of dust and ferrocrete. The structure was robust and Astartes could withstand worse. There would be survivors.

Unconcerned where the secondary blast had come from, Brynngar got to his feet and howled in triumph. Running across the open to the ruined mass of crumpled metal and broken ferrocrete, he swung his rune axe in preparation for battle, knowing that his Blood Claws were right behind him.

ABOARD THE WRATHFUL, Cestus wore a pained expression as he reviewed the tactical display. Frantic vox chatter was coming in over the ship's array, but it was indistinct and impossible to discern.

The three icons, representing the relative positions of his assault teams had stalled. A silver icon, indicating the Space Wolves and Brynngar's warriors, was moving slowly towards an area obscured by a sudden belt of smoke and bright light, hazing the readout. Judging from the schematic, this was the observation platform.

Cestus assumed that the attack had been successful.

Elsewhere in a flanking channel close by, an azure icon represented Antiges and was shown embroiled in a brutal close-quarters fight against massed enemies. The dark slab of crimson that was the *Furious Abyss* was not far beyond the melee, but it didn't appear as if the

Ultramarine was making progress. All Cestus's subsequent attempts to raise Antiges on the vox had thus far failed. A third icon, depicted in stark white, converged on Antiges's position.

To Cestus's dismay, they were not alone.

TEN

Into the belly of the beast/Sacrifice/My future is written

THE SCREAM OF chainaxes brought Antiges to his senses.
The whine of their spinning teeth turned to a crunching
drone as they bit into flesh and bone.

Antiges saw white armour trimmed with blue, sprayed
liberally with crimson and the Legion markings of a
captain.

Skraal dragged the Ultramarine out of the mess of
bodies. The *Furious*'s crewmen were being bludgeoned
to the ground or thrown through the air, the World
Eaters squad painting every surface with crescents of
gore. Antiges took a moment to set himself, such was
the impact of the second charge from Skraal's World
Eaters.

The captain of the XII Legion was butchering a man
on the floor.

Such reckless murderous enthusiasm was alien to the
Ultramarines and Antiges fought the urge to put a stop
to it. The battlefield was no place for recrimination.

Instead, the Ultramarine looked across the dock, a brief lull in the fighting provided by the sudden appearance of Skraal's forces allowing him to take stock. A clutter of crimson-armoured corpses lay at the end of the central channel, victims of the World Eaters' ferocity. He also saw Brynngar leading his Blood Claws, tangled up in a short-range firestorm with a squad of Word Bearers emerging from the ruin of the collapsed observation platform. The fighting was fierce and it didn't look like the sons of Russ would be able to bolster them.

Skraal heaved a dying man off the floor and cut him in two at the waist with a slash of his chainaxe. It got Antiges's attention.

'Captain,' cried the Ultramarine, seeing a break in the cohort's ranks for the first time, 'drive on to the ship, now!'

Skraal looked back at him. For a split second there was nothing in the World Eater's face but hatred, nothing to suggest that he saw Antiges as anything but another enemy.

The moment passed and the eyes that looked at the Ultramarine belonged to Skraal again. The World Eater picked up his shield from the ground, discarded in his lust for carnage, shook his head to get the worst of the blood out of his eyes, and called to his squad to follow.

'Form up on me, and keep moving!' shouted Antiges, pointing towards the *Furious Abyss* with his chainsword.

A WORD BEARER stumbled out of the wreckage of the platform, strafing wildly with his bolter. Brynngar stepped out of the kill-zone and beheaded the Astartes with a sweep of Felltooth. A second followed and the Space Wolf leapt forward, burying the blade in the Legionary's cranium. A third was dragged from the collapsed building, half-dazed, by Rujveld who executed him with a burst from his bolt pistol.

After the initial slaughter, though, the Word Bearers managed to put up more of a fight. Wreathed in super-heated plasma, Elfyarl fell screaming and Vorik was dismembered by a fusillade of bolter fire.

Brynngar snarled at the losses, whipping another Word Bearer off his feet at the edge of the ruins before lunging down to tear out his throat with his teeth. Howling in fury, the Wolf Guard was about to press on when whickering bolter fire churned up the ferrocrete debris around him. Reeling against the sudden assault, the venerable wolf could only watch as a line of blood stitched up Svornfeld's cuirass. He spun and fell in a lifeless heap.

A second squad of Word Bearers advanced on them, unseen from the original route of attack.

Brynngar unhitched his bolter in the face of this new threat and blew the faceplate off one Word Bearer's helmet and smashed a chunk from the shoulder pad of another as they came on.

'Into them!' he raged, weapon blazing as he charged the enemy.

The howling reply of his remaining Blood Claws was a feral chorus to the brutal bolter din.

ANTIGES THRUST HIS chainsword through the Word Bearer's chest.

As they'd closed on the *Furious Abyss*, the cohorts a bloody mess in their wake, another line of defenders had emerged: fellow Astartes, their erstwhile brothers the Word Bearers. Decked in crimson armour replete with debased scratchings and ragged scrolls of parchment, they were a dark shadow of the proud warriors Antiges remembered.

The Word Bearer jerked as he tried to wrench himself free of the churning blade that impaled him, but then it passed through his spine and all he could do was vomit a plume of blood.

Suddenly, it was real.

These Word Bearers, Astartes and brothers to all Space Marines, were the enemy. Antiges realised in that moment that he hadn't really believed it before. There was no time to consider it further as a second Word Bearer came at him with a power maul. Antiges caught the weapon just before it cleaved through his face, and rammed his knee into the Astartes's stomach, but his enemy stayed locked with him. Behind the lenses of the Word Bearer's helmet the Ultramarine could just see an eye narrowed in anger. There was no brotherhood there.

In a sudden fury of churning steel and wrath, Skraal tore the Word Bearer off Antiges and ripped him apart with his chainaxe. Finishing the grisly work quickly, the World Eater glanced back at his battle-brother.

'Too intense for you, Ultramarine?'

A WORD BEARER's elbow caught Brynngar in the side of the head and the Space Wolf fell back. Rolling out of a second attack, he switched to his bolter and, one-handed, unloaded the magazine into his assailant's stomach. The Word Bearer had life in him yet, though, and Rujveld stalked forward, drawing a knife from a scabbard at his waist. He jammed the point through the gap in the wounded traitor's gorget.

Brynngar grunted thanks to the Blood Claw and moved on into the Word Bearer squad that had set upon them. Combined with the survivors from the platform's destruction, the Space Wolves were hard-pressed. The Wolf Guard was determined to lead by example, however, and scythed through crimson ceramite, the bloody Felltooth clutched in his grasp.

Cutting down an enemy Astartes with a swift diagonal slice across the neck and chest, Brynngar kicked the Word Bearer aside to face a new opponent. Suddenly, the tempo of the battle changed. The fury and ferocity exploding around him dulled and slowed as he stood eye-to-eye with a fellow captain. This was clearly their leader, clearly a veteran if the ruin and subsequent reconstruction of his face was any measure. A two-handed power sword swung freely in his fists, which he wielded like a mace. A trio of Blood Claws lay at the warrior's feet. They had died on that sword, their bodies split in two and spilling organs over the floor of the dock.

'Now face me,' snarled the Wolf Guard and hefted Felltooth in a feral challenge.

The Word Bearer captain drove at the Space Wolf using his body like a battering ram, the blade as its tip. The charge was fast, so fast that Brynngar didn't get out of the way in time and took a glancing blow against his pauldron. White fire surged into his shoulder, but the Wolf Guard mastered the pain quickly and turned with the attack, using its momentum and raking Felltooth down his opponent's back.

The Word Bearer roared and spun on his heel, driving the two-handed blade at him like a spear at first to pitch the Space Wolf off balance and then as a club to bludgeon him to death. A wild swipe slapped the flat edge of the weapon against Brynngar's outstretched arm. His bolter fell from nerveless fingers as the blow struck a muscle cluster, numbed even through his power armour.

Brynngar smashed the brutal sword aside as it came for another slash, and used his forward momentum to get inside his attacker's reach. Pressing a rune on Felltooth's hilt, a long spike slid from the tip of the axe. Brynngar roared in savage exultation as he plunged it deep into one of the Word Bearer's biceps and twisted. The Word Bearer's arm was torn open revealing wet muscle and gore. No pain registered on his face as he leapt towards Brynngar in an attempt to throw him off-balance and bring his sword to bear again.

Using his opponent's momentum, Brynngar lifted the Word Bearer off his feet and smashed him to the ground. He yanked the dazed enemy captain up again, gripping his gorget, and seized his head by the chin. Emitting a terrible roar that flung blood and spittle into his enemy's face, Brynngar rammed the spike of Felltooth through his throat.

The Word Bearer's good eye bulged out as it fought the wracking pain of his imminent death. He coughed up blood, and it sheeted down the front of his armour, covering it with a new wet shade of crimson.

Brynngar spat in his face and let the Word Bearer fall.

Bolter shells blistered the ground around him as yet more Word Bearers converged on them. Brynngar and what was left of his Blood Claws returned fire and sought cover even as they fell back. The attack was short-lived, the Astartes merely dragging away the body of their fallen captain before retreating too.

Indiscriminate and sporadic gunfire kept the Space Wolves at bay as the remaining Word Bearers fell back. Crouching behind the ruin of a disused fuel tanker Brynngar snatched a glance across the battlefield. Skraal and Antiges were advancing towards the *Furious Abyss* with a small combat squad of World Eaters, scattering crewmen from the battleship as they went.

Brynngar envied them. Even before the plasma drives of the Word Bearers' mighty battleship started to power up, he knew that the enemy was leaving. The pinning fire from their retreating assailants was gradually diminishing, and all across the dockyard, enemy Astartes were heading back to embarkation ports in the hull of the vast vessel.

Like the orca, I would've gutted that beast inside out, he thought with dark regret and cried out his lament. Blood flecked from his beard and hair as he threw back his head and the long, hollow note tore from his throat. Taking up the call, his Blood Claws arched their necks back as one and joined the chorus howl.

GUNFIRE SPATTERED DOWN at the Astartes, ricocheting off metal and kicking out sparks.

Together with the Ultramarine, Antiges, and three of his battle-brothers, the World Eater captain had gained the *Furious Abyss*, entering into the belly of the ship through one of the embarkation ports and heading down. Their progress had been arrested inevitably when the onboard patrols had caught up with them at the intersection of a coolant pipe. The fire was coming from one end of the corridor, distant, shadowy figures tramping urgently down the wide, curved diameter of the pipe. Metal instrumentation provided some cover, but the Astartes were as good as dead if they didn't move on quickly.

Skraal took part of the fusillade on his storm shield, casings striking the grating at his feet like brass rain: bolter fire.

Shadows danced against the muzzle flashes. Huge armoured bodies, helmets and shoulder pads: Astartes. Word Bearers.

One of Skraal's warriors, Orlak, cut through a hatch in the ceiling with his chainaxe. The slab of metal clanged down and he hauled himself up swiftly. Rorgath stood point as the Legionaries made their way further inwards. Having lost both his weapons in the brutal melee outside the ship, he slammed the bolter he had scavenged into rapid fire and hosed the conduit, punching ragged holes into the metal. The other World Eaters lent the fire of their bolt pistols, keeping their enemies at bay.

Half the World Eaters were through the hatch before the Word Bearers returned fire. Only Skraal and Antiges remained, the Ultramarine taking over from Rorgath as he unclipped a brace of frag grenades from his belt and rolled them down the conduit. Skraal leapt up the hatch as return bolter fire blazed past him. Antiges followed, the World Eater captain hauling the Ultramarine up as the first of the explosions ripped down the conduit, shredding plating and buying time.

'MOUNTAINS OF MACRAGGE,' breathed Antiges.

The engine room of the *Furious Abyss* was like a cathedral to machinery. It was vast. The criss-crossing ribs of a vaulted ceiling reached through the gloom. The immense hulks of the cylindrical exhaust chambers were decorated with steel ribbing and iron scrollwork, and inscribed with High Gothic text running along their whole length. Multiple levels were delineated by gantries and lattice-like overhead walkways. Word Bearers' banners hung from the web of iron above them, bearing the symbols of the Legion's Chapters: a quill with a drop of blood at its nib, an open hand with an eye in the palm, a burning book, and a sceptre crowned with a skull. The metallic throb of the engines was like the ship's own monstrous heartbeat.

The conduit in the labyrinthine ship had led the Astartes to this place and though the sounds of pursuit were distant and hollow, the enemy would not be far behind.

'Find something to destroy,' said Skraal. 'Get to the reactors if you can.'

Antiges tried to take in the vastness of the engine room. Even with the munitions they had at their disposal and the fact that they were Astartes, they would still have a hard time doing anything that could cripple the *Furious Abyss*.

'No,' said Antiges, 'we drive onwards. Look for ordnance or cogitators. We can't sabotage this vessel attacking blindly.'

Skraal looked back at his squad. The last of them was being dragged up through the hatch. The coolant pipe they had entered through was one of many forming a tangle of pipes and junctions around the exhaust chambers. Between the pipes was darkness and there was no telling how far down it went.

'We might not find our–'

'We're not getting back out,' snapped Antiges.

Skraal nodded. 'Forwards, then.'

Antiges led the Astartes up onto the nearest walkway, above the exhaust chambers. The immense shapes of generatoria loomed towards the ship's stern, connected to the even larger plasma reactors somewhere below. Ahead of them, the walkway wound into a dark steel valley between enormous pounding pistons. Shapes were gathering on a walkway above them, hidden by the solid metal of a control deck. It seemed that the engineering menials had been ordered out of the chamber, which meant that the Word Bearers planned to stop them here.

'Cover!' shouted Skraal, but there was little to be had when the bolter fire from the Word Bearers hammered down at them. Rorgath returned fire with his scavenged bolter, but there was little the others could do with pistols and close combat weapons. One of Skraal's battle-brothers was hit square in the chest and knocked over a guardrail. He fell onto the engine block below and was pounded flat by a piston hammering down on him. Orlak's arm disappeared in a spray of blood and he fell to the walkway. Antiges hoisted him bodily to his feet and dragged him along as more gunfire streaked from above.

'Break for it!' Skraal bellowed, seeing a lull in the fusillade hammering them. Then he was on his feet and running for the cover at the far end of the engine block, where the walkway led up into a great wall of galleries and machinery. Even hurried by Antiges, Orlak lingered behind and was speared through the back by storm bolter rounds. Smoke poured from the backpack of his armour, mixed with a spray of blood.

Orlak: Skraal had led him through a dozen battle-fields. He was a brother, as they all were.

The World Eater captain took that grief and locked it away beneath his consciousness, where it mixed with the pool of rage that he would call on again when the time was right.

Skraal reached cover. The *Furious Abyss* closed around him. He was in an equipment room, the walls covered in racks of hydraulic drills, wrenches and hammers. Human deck-crews fled in wild panic as the World Eaters burst in, followed by Antiges. There were just three left. It was hardly the raiding force they needed to bring the vast ship to heel.

Skraal noticed something inscribed on the ceiling of the chamber.

BUILD THE WORD OF LORGAR FROM THIS STEEL
LIVE AS IT IS WRITTEN

'Move! Move! They're heading down after us!' bellowed Antiges, demanding his attention.

'We need to hold them up. No way we can dodge bolter fire and wreck the ship at the same time,' said Skraal, slamming the portal shut behind them and using a stolen wrench to wedge it.

'Three squads at least,' Antiges replied, his breathing heavy, but measured. 'No way we can beat them.'

'I'll slow them,' said Rorgath, planting his feet and checking the clip in his bolter.

Antiges regarded the World Eater. The white and blue of his armour was already scored by bullet wounds and scorched by plasma burns.

'Your sacrifice will be remembered,' said Antiges, reverently.

No such sentiment was evident from the World Eater's captain, who tossed Rorgath his bolt pistol.

'Give them no quarter,' he snarled, turning abruptly to lead what was left of the raiding party through the tangle of anterooms and corridors. The shouts of pursuers relaying their position followed them like hollow, ghost whispers, and the thud of armoured feet on the floor was dull and resonant in their wake.

Together, Antiges and Skraal moved swiftly across the hinterlands of the engine room and through a doorway in the bulkhead. Not long before they had left the chamber, the fierce bark of bolter fire erupted behind them.

It didn't last long and deathly silence reigned for a moment before their relentless pursuers could be heard once more. Mangled with a cacophony of voices emitted from the ship's vox array, it became obvious that a widespread search had begun. The *Furious*'s warriors were converging on the Astartes. They were getting closer every second.

Passing through an empty storage chamber, Skraal kicked open a door to reveal another corridor. The atmosphere was close and hot, the walls lined with burning torches. The sight was incongruous amongst the decks and trappings of a spaceship, but it also led downwards and prow-wards, in the direction where the Astartes guessed the primary ordnance deck would be.

'What did they build in here?' hissed Antiges, giving voice to his thoughts as they moved down the corridor. The Ultramarine got his answer as he emerged from the far end of the tunnel.

A vast plaza stretched out in front of them. Walls lined with baroque statues of deep red steel rose up into a domed ceiling. The vault at the apex of the massive chamber was hazy with incense and supported by dramatic false columns. Prayers were inscribed on the flagstone floor. An altar and pulpit stood at the far end of a central aisle. There was only one word to describe it: a cathedral. In the supposed age of enlightenment, when all superstition and religion was to be expunged from the galaxy to be replaced by science and understanding, all that the Emperor had decreed was dishonoured by the chamber's very existence.

Antiges found that it left a bitter taste in his mouth and was ready to tear down the effigies and rend this temple of false idolatry to the ground with his bare hands, when a voice echoed out of the surrounding gloom.

'There is no escape.'

The Ultramarine saw Skraal throw himself against a pillar. Antiges swiftly adopted a crouching position, bolt pistol outstretched in a two-handed grip, scanning the darkness. He could just make out the crimson armour at the far end of the cathedral. The speaker, his tone eerily calm and cultured, was sheltering behind the altar. The Word Bearer was not alone.

Booted feet clacking against the stone floor behind the Astartes confirmed the threat. Antiges and the World Eater were covered from both sides of the chamber.

'I am Sergeant-Commander Reskiel of the Word Bearers,' said the speaker, identifying himself. 'Throw down your arms and surrender at once,' he warned, all the culture evaporating.

'After you fired on us and slew our brothers!' Skraal raged.

'This need not end in further bloodshed,' Reskiel added.

Antiges felt the enemy converging on them, heard the faint scrape of ceramite against stone as they closed.

'What is this place, Word Bearer?' asked the Ultramarine, panning his sights first across the pulpit and then further out until he had swept the gloom around them. 'Such religiosity is not condoned by the Emperor. You openly defy his will. Have you reverted to primitive debasement and superstition?' he asked, trying to goad them, trying to find time to devise a plan, expose a weakness. 'Is all Colchis like this now?'

'There is nothing primitive about the vision of our primarch or his home world,' said Reskiel levelly, clearly wise to the Ultramarine's stratagem. Stepping out from behind the altar, the sergeant-commander allowed the diffuse torchlight to bath him in its glow.

He was young, but highly decorated judging by the honour studs and medals on his crimson armour. The trappings of heroism and glory warred with strips of parchment and leaves of tattered vellum scripted in wretched verse.

A squad of Word Bearers emerged into the cathedral behind him, their bolters trained on the shadows where Antiges and Skraal were in cover.

'Show yourselves, and let us speak brother to brother,' said Reskiel, allowing his guardians to move in front of him.

'You are no brother of mine!' shouted Skraal.

'Get ready,' Antiges hissed to his ally as Reskiel raised a hand. The Ultramarine knew, with an ingrained warrior instinct, that he was about to give the order to open fire. He trained his bolt pistol on a cluster of Word Bearers at the front of the advancing guards.

Skraal roared, surging out of cover and throwing his chainaxe. He thumbed the activation stud as it left his hand and the weapon shrieked through the air. With a scream of ceramite on metal, the axe bypassed the guards and sliced clean through Reskiel's wrist, embedding itself in the altar. Shield upraised, a war cry on his lips, the World Eater charged.

Antiges cursed the son of Angron's impetuous battle lust and triggered the bolt pistol, running forward as the muzzle flare gave away his position. Bolt rounds hammered into the approaching Word Bearers and three of the warriors collapsed in a heap against the fury.

Bedlam filled the cathedral. Skraal covered the distance between him and his enemy so fast that none of the opening bolter shots hit him.

Antiges followed, acutely aware that he had foes behind as well as in front. An errant shot clipped his pauldron, another chipped his knee guard and he staggered briefly but kept on into the maelstrom, the name of Guilliman in his furious heart.

'This is sacred ground!' wailed Reskiel, clutching the stump of his arm as blood spurted freely from it. Skraal battered the Word Bearers in his path aside and when he reached the sergeant-commander, backhanded him across the face with his shield by way of a reply, and wrenched his chainaxe from the altar. He spun and slammed the head of the axe into the head of a red-armoured warrior charging behind him. The Word Bearer was thrown off his feet and skidded along the floor on his back, his face a red ruin of bone and shattered ceramite.

The ambushers from behind the two Astartes fell into the fray.

Skraal fought as if possessed by the spirit of Angron, slaying left and right as a terrible bloody rage overtook him. He embraced the cauldron of fury within and used it to kill, to ignore pain. Word Bearers fell horribly before his onslaught, so fierce that those surrounding the assault gave ground and retreated to the cathedral door. The one who called himself Reskiel was dragged out by one of his battle-brothers, the blood clotting on the stump of his wrist as he screamed his choler.

Bolter fire was hammering away towards the rear of the cathedral. Antiges could hear it echoing loudly inside his helmet as Skraal turned from the carnage he was wreaking to look at him.

A line of pain sketched its way down the Ultramarine's back and he realised he'd been hit. This time the shot pierced his armour. Something warm welled in his chest and Antiges looked down to see a wet ragged hole. As his mind suddenly made the connection to what his body already knew, he slumped against a pillar, spitting blood. Lungs heaving, he tried to force his augmented body back into action and cranked another magazine into his bolt

pistol. One hand clamped over the wound, the other triggering the bolter, Antiges resolved to go down fighting. In
the distance, vision fogging, a shadow fell.

White spikes of pain were flashing before his eyes as
he turned to look back at Skraal amidst the bloodbath
at the altar.

'Go,' gasped Antiges.

The World Eater paused for a second, about to run
back in and rescue the Ultramarine. A thrown grenade
exploded near the pillar and Antiges's world ended in a
billow of smoke and shrapnel.

SKRAAL DIDN'T WAIT to see if the Ultramarine had survived. One way or another, Antiges was lost. Instead, he
ran from the cathedral, storm shield warding off the
worst of the bolter fire hammering across the cathedral
towards him.

As he fled into the endless darkness, the shifting of
the vessel's hull echoing as if venting its displeasure, a
thought forced its way into his mind in spite of the
battle rage.

He was alone.

ZADKIEL WATCHED THE battle unfolding through the
docking picters mounted along the hull of the *Furious
Abyss*.

Baelanos had fallen, yet his inert body had been recovered and lay in the laboratorium of Magos Gureod.

He would serve the Word, yet.

Baelanos's dedication to the Word was that of a soldier to his commander, and he had never appreciated
the more intellectual implications of Lorgar's beliefs.
Nevertheless, he was a loyal and useful asset. Zadkiel
would not throw him away cheaply.

Ultis was doubtless buried beneath the rubble of Bakka Triumveron 14. In that, Baelanos had served Zadkiel too. It was another thorn removed from his side, the potential usurper despatched.

Yes, for that deed you will receive eternal service to the Legion.

'We're breached.' Sergeant-Commander Reskiel's voice came through on the vox, down where the engines met the main body of the battleship.

'How many?'

'Only one remains, my lord,' Reskiel replied. 'They made it in through the coolant venting ports, open for the re-supplying.'

'Hunt him down with my blessing, sergeant-commander,' Zadkiel ordered, 'but be aware that you will be making your pursuit under take-off conditions.'

Another thorn, thought Zadkiel.

'Sire, there are still warriors of the Legion fighting on the dock,' countered Reskiel at the news of their imminent departure.

'We cannot tarry. Every moment we stay to fight is another moment for the *Wrathful* to reach strike range or for our stowaway to damage something that cannot be replaced, not to mention the fact that the dockyard's defences might be brought to bear. Sacrifice, Reskiel, is a lesson worth learning. Now, find the interloper and end this annoyance.'

'At your command, admiral. I'm heading into the coolant systems now.'

Zadkiel cut the vox and observed the viewscreens above his command throne. A tactical map showed the *Furious Abyss* and the complex structure of the orbital docks around it. Crimson icons represented the Word Bearer forces still fighting and dying for their cause.

Zadkiel reached back for the vox and gave the order to take off.

ULTIS WATCHED FROM the rubble of the collapsed observation platform as the *Furious Abyss* begin to rise.

The engines of the battleship threw burning winds across the dockyards. Docking clamps and supply hangars melted to slag. Gantries burned and fuel tankers exploded, blossoms of blue-white thrown up amidst the firestorm. Fiery gales whipped around the open metal plaza, cooking cohorts and Astartes alike in the burgeoning conflagration surging across Bakka Triumveron 14. Scalding winds singed his face, even shielded by the wrecked chunks of ferrocrete. He saw the crimson paint on his armour blistering in the backwash of intense heat.

The maelstrom engulfed the bodies fighting outside it and they became as shadows and ash before it, as if frozen in time, eternally at war.

This was not the future he had envisaged for himself as he watched the *Furious Abyss* rise higher from the deck with a blast from its ventral thrusters.

He had been betrayed: not by the Word, but by another on board ship.

A shadow eclipsed the stricken Word Bearer, prone in the rubble.

'Your friends desert you, traitor whelp,' said a voice from above, old and gnarled.

Ultis craned his neck around to see, vision hazing in and out of focus, dimly aware of the blood that he had lost.

A massive Astartes in the armour of Leman Russ's Legion reared over him like a slab of unyielding steel. Bedecked in trophies, pelts and tooth fetishes, he was every inch the savage that Ultis believed the Space Wolves to be.

'I serve the Word,' he said defiantly through blood-caked lips.

The Space Wolf shook the blood out of his straggly hair and grinned to display his fangs.

'The Word be damned,' he snarled.

The Space Wolf's gauntleted fist was the last thing Ultis saw before all sense fled and his world went black.

ELEVEN

Survivors/Aftermath/I will break him

Buoyed upon hot currents of air vented by the *Furious Abyss*, what was left of the assault boats carrying the Astartes strike force made their escape from Bakka Triumveron 14 and back to the *Wrathful* held in orbit around the moon.

Cestus was waiting for the atmospheric craft in the tertiary docking bay when a single vessel touched down. Its outer hull shielding was badly scorched and its engines were all but burned out as it *thunked* to an unwieldy stop on the metal deck.

One assault boat, thought the Ultramarine captain, waiting with Saphrax and Laeradis, the apothecary ready with his narthecium injector. How many casualties did we sustain?

Engineering deck-hands hurried back and forth, hosing down the superheated aspects of the boat with coolant foam, and brandishing tools to affect immediate repairs. One of the officers stood at a distance with a data-slate, already compiling an initial damage report.

Cestus was oblivious to them all, his gaze fixed on the embarkation ramp as it ground open slowly with a hiss of venting pressure. Brynngar and his Blood Claws stepped out of the compartment.

The Ultramarine greeted him cordially enough.

'Well met, son of Russ.'

Brynngar grunted a response, his demeanour still hostile, and turned to one of his charges.

'Rujveld, bring him out.'

One of the Blood Claws, a youth with bright orange hair worked into a mohawk and a short beard festooned with wolf fetishes, nodded and went back into the crew compartment. When he returned, he was not alone. A pale-faced warrior was with him, his hands and forearms encased by restraints linked by an adamantium cord, his face fraught with cuts, and a massive purple-black bruise over one eye the size of Brynngar's fist. Bent-backed and obviously weak, he had a defiant air about him still. He wore the armour of the XV Legion: the armour of the Word Bearers.

'We have ourselves a prisoner,' Brynngar snarled, stalking past the trio of Ultramarines without explanation, his Blood Claws with their prize in tow.

'Find me an isolation cell,' Cestus overheard the Wolf Guard say to one of his battle-brothers. 'I intend to find out what he knows.'

Cestus kept his eyes forward for a moment, striving to master his anger.

'My lord?' ventured Saphrax, the banner bearer clearly noticing his captain's distemper.

'Son of Russ,' Cestus said levelly, knowing he would be heard.

The sound of the departing Space Wolves echoing down the deck was the only reply.

'Son of Russ,' he bellowed this time and turned, his expression set as if in stone.

Brynngar had almost reached the deck portal when he stopped.

'I would have your report, brother,' said Cestus, calmly, 'and I would have it now.'

The Wolf Guard turned slowly, his massive bulk forcing the Blood Claws close by to step aside. Anger and belligerence were etched on his face as plain as the Legion symbols on his armour.

'The assault failed,' he growled. 'The *Furious Abyss* is still intact. There, you have my report.'

Cestus fought to keep his voice steady and devoid of emotion.

'What of Antiges and Skraal?'

Brynngar was breathing hard, his anger boiling, but at the mention of the two captains, particularly Antiges, his expression softened for a moment.

'We were the only survivors,' he replied quietly and continued on through the deck portal to the passageways beyond that would lead eventually to the isolation chambers.

Cestus stood for a moment, allowing it to sink in. Antiges had been his battle-brother for almost twenty years. They had fought together on countless occasions. They had brought the light of the Emperor to countless worlds in the darkest reaches of the known galaxy.

'What are your orders, my captain?' asked Saphrax, ever the pragmatist.

Cestus crushed his grief quickly. It would serve no purpose here.

'Get Admiral Kaminska. Tell her we are to continue pursuit of the *Furious Abyss* at once, with all speed.'

'At your command, my lord.' Saphrax snapped a strong salute and left the dock, heading for the bridge.

Cestus's plan had failed, catastrophically. More than sixty per cent casualties were unacceptable. It left only the Ultramarines honour guard, still stationed aboard ship by way of contingency, and Brynngar's Blood Claws. The Space Wolf's continued defiance was developing into open hostility. Something was building. Even without the animal instincts of the sons of Russ, Cestus could feel it. He wondered how long it would be before the inevitable storm broke.

Here they were, at war with their fellow Legions. Guilliman only knew how deep the treachery went, how many more Legions had turned against the Emperor. If anything, the loyal Legions needed desperately to draw together, not to fight internecine conflicts between themselves in the name of petty disagreements. When the final reckoning came, where would Brynngar and his Legion sit? Guilliman and his Ultramarines were dogmatic in their fealty to the Emperor; could the same be said of Russ?

Cestus left such dark thoughts behind for now, knowing it would not aid him or their mission to dwell on them. Instead, his mind turned briefly to Antiges. In all likelihood, he was dead. His brother, his closest friend slain in what had been a fool's cause. Cestus cursed himself for allowing Antiges to take his place. Saphrax was an able adjutant, his dedication to the teachings of Guilliman was unshakeable, but he was not the confidant that Antiges had been.

Cestus clenched his fist.

This deed will not go unavenged.

'Laeradis, with me,' said the Ultramarine captain, marching off in the direction that Brynngar had taken.

The Apothecary fell into lockstep behind him.

'Where are we going, captain?'

'I want to know what happened on Bakka Triumveron and I want to find out what our Word Bearer knows about his Legion's ship and their mission to Macragge.'

BY THE TIME Cestus and Laeradis reached the isolation cells, Brynngar was already inside, the door sealed with Rujveld standing guard.

The isolation cells were located in the lower decks, where the heat and sweat of the engines could be heard and felt palpably. Toiling ratings below sang gritty naval chants to aid them in their work and the resonant din carried through the metal. It was a muffled chorus down the gloom-drenched passages that Cestus and Laeradis had travelled to reach this point.

'Step aside, Blood Claw,' ordered Cestus without preamble.

At first it looked as if Rujveld would disobey the Ultramarine, but Cestus was a captain, albeit from a different Legion, and that position commanded respect. The Blood Claw lowered his gaze, indicating his obedience, and gave ground.

Cestus thumbed the door release icon as he stood before the cell portal. The bare metal panel slid aside, two thins jets of vapour escaping as it did so.

A darkened chamber beckoned, barely illuminated in the half-light of lume-globes set to low-emit. A bulky shape stood within, with two shrivelled, robed forms to either side. Brynngar had stripped out of his armour, aided by two attendant Legion serfs. The menials kept their heads low and their tongues still. The Wolf Guard was naked from the waist up, wearing only simple grey battle fatigues. His torso was covered in old wounds, scars and faded pinkish welts creating a patchwork history of pain and battle.

Standing without his armour, his immense musculature obvious and intimidating, and with the great mass of his hair hanging down, Brynngar reminded the Ultramarine of a barbarian of ancient Terra, the kind that he had seen rendered in frescos in some of the great antiquitariums.

The Wolf Guard turned at the interruption, the shadow of another figure strapped down in a metal restraint frame partly visible for a moment before the Space Wolf's bulk took up the space again.

'What do you want, Cestus? I'm sure you can see that I'm busy.' Brynngar's knuckles were hard and white as he clenched his fists.

As he had stormed from the tertiary dock after the Space Wolf and his battle-brothers, Cestus had thought to intervene, the idea of torturing a fellow Legion brother abhorrent to him. Now, standing at the threshold of the isolation chamber, he realised just how desperate their plight had become and that victory might call for compromise.

Just how far this compromise would go and where it would eventually lead, Cestus did not care to think. It was what it was. They were on this course now and the Word Bearers were enemies like any other. They had not hesitated when they destroyed the *Waning Moon*, nor had they paused to consider their actions during the slaughter on Bakka Triumveron 14.

'I would speak to you again, Brynngar,' the Ultramarine captain said, 'once this is over. I would know the details of what happened on Bakka.'

'Aye, lad.' The Space Wolf nodded, a glimmer of their old rapport returning briefly to his features.

Cestus glimpsed the prone form of their prisoner as Brynngar turned back to his 'work'.

'Do only what is necessary,' the Ultramarine warned, 'and do it quickly. I am leaving Laeradis here to… assist you if he can.'

The Apothecary shifted uncomfortably beside Cestus, whether at the thought of partaking in torture or the prospect of being left alone with Brynngar, the Ultramarines captain did not know.

Brynngar looked over his shoulder just as Cestus was leaving.

'I will break him,' he said with a predatory gleam in his eye.

'WE HID BEHIND Bakka Triumveron to keep the *Furious Abyss* from sending torpedoes after us. We're heading on course for a warp jump vector as we speak.'

Kaminska was, as ever, on station at her command throne on the bridge. Saphrax was there, also, straight backed and dour as ever. Cestus had headed there alone after leaving Laeradis with Brynngar in the isolation chamber. In the scant reports he'd received from the admiral regarding information gleaned from the assault boat pilot, Cestus had learned a little more of what had happened at Bakka. They'd lost the other two assault boats during the extraction, swallowed up by the fire of the *Furious*'s engines that had turned much of Bakka Triumveron 14 into a smoking wasteland of charred and twisted metal. The tactical readouts aboard ship had disclosed precious little, save that it was chaotic and not to plan. One of Guilliman's edicts of wisdom was that any plan, however meticulously devised, seldom survives contact with the enemy. The primarch spoke, of course, of the need for flexibility and adaptation when at war. Cestus thought he should have heeded those words more closely. It appeared, also, that the Word Bearers had been forewarned of the Astartes' attack, a fact that he resolved to discover the root of. He considered briefly the possibility of a traitor in their ranks aboard the *Wrathful*, but dismissed the thought quickly, partly because to countenance such a thing would breed only suspicion and paranoia, and also because to do so would implicate the Astartes captains or Kaminska.

'What of our prisoner, Captain Cestus?' asked Kaminska, after consulting the battery of viewscreens in front of her, satisfied that all necessary preparations were underway for pursuit.

'He is resting uncomfortably with Brynngar,' the Ultramarine replied, his gaze locked on the prow-facing viewport.

'You believe he knows something about the ship that we can use to our advantage?'

Cestus's response was taciturn as he thought grimly of the road ahead and of their options dwindling like parchment before a flame.

'Let us hope so.'

Kaminska allowed a moment's pause, before she spoke again.

'I am sorry about Antiges. I know he was your friend.'

Cestus turned to face her.

'He was my brother.'

Kaminska's vox-bead chirped, interrupting the sentiment of the moment.

'We have reached the jump point, captain' she said. 'If we hit the warp now, Orcadus has a chance of finding the *Furious Abyss* again.'

'Engage the warp drives,' said Cestus.

Kaminska gave the order and after a few minutes the *Wrathful* shuddered as the integrity fields leapt up around it, ready for its re-entry into the warp.

ZADKIEL PRAYED TO the bodies in front of him.

The Word Bearer was situated in one of the many chapels within the lower decks of the *Furious Abyss*. It was a modest, relatively unadorned chamber with a simple shrine etched with the scriptures of Lorgar and lit by votive candles set in baroque-looking candelabras. The room, besides being the ship's morgue, also offered solace and the opportunity to consider the divinity of the primarch's Word, of his teachings and the power of faith and the warp.

Prayer was a complicated matter. On the crude, fleshly level it was just a stream of words spoken by a man. It was little wonder that Imperial conquerors, without an understanding of what faith truly was, saw the prayers of primitive people and discarded them as dangerous superstition and a barrier to genuine enlightenment. They saw the holy books and sacred places, and ascribed them not to faith or a higher understanding but to stupidity, blindness, and an adherence to divisive, irrelevant traditions. They taught an Imperial Truth in the place of those simple religions and wiped out any evidence that faith had once been a reality to those worlds. Sometimes that erasure was done with flames and bullets. More often it was done with iterators, brilliant diplomats and philosophers, who could re-educate whole populations.

Zadkiel's belief, the root of his vainglorious conviction, was that the Throne of Terra would be toppled, not by the strength of arms wielded by the Warmaster, nor even by the denizens of the warp, but by faith. Simple and indissoluble, the purity of it would burn through the Imperium like a holy spear, setting the non-believers and their effigies of science and empirical delusion alight.

Zadkiel shifted slightly in his kneeling position, abruptly aware that another presence was in the chapel-morgue with him.

'Speak,' he uttered calmly, eyes closed.

'My lord it is I, Reskiel,' the sergeant-commander announced.

Zadkiel could hear the creak of his armour as he bowed, in spite of the fact that he could not see him.

'I would know the fate of Captain Baelanos, sire,' Reskiel continued after a moment's pause. 'Was he recovered?'

Doubtless, the ambitious cur sought to supplant the stricken assault-captain in Zadkiel's command hierarchy, or manoeuvre for greater power and influence in the fleet. This did not trouble the Word Bearer admiral. Reskiel was easy to manipulate. His ambition far outweighed his ability, a fact that was easy to exploit and control. Unlike Ultis, whose youthful idealism and fearlessness threatened him, Zadkiel was sanguine about Reskiel's prospects for advancement.

'Though mortally injured, the good captain was indeed recovered,' Zadkiel told him. 'His body has gone into its fugue state in order to heal.' Zadkiel turned at that remark, looking the sergeant-commander in the eye. 'Baelanos will be incapacitated for some time, captain. This only strengthens your position in my command.'

'My lord, I don't mean to imply–'

'No, of course not Reskiel,' Zadkiel interjected with a mirthless smile, 'but you have suffered for our cause and such sacrifice will not go unrewarded. You will assume Baelanos's duties.'

Reskiel nodded. The World Eater had shattered the bones down one side of his skull and his face had been reinforced with a metal web bolted to his cheek and jaw.

'We have lost many brothers this day,' he said, indicating the Astartes corpses laid out before his lord.

'They are not lost,' said Zadkiel. Each of the slain Word Bearers was set upon a mortuary slab, ready for their armour to be removed and their gene-seed recovered. One of them lay with his eyes staring blankly at the ceiling. Zadkiel closed them reverently. 'Only if the Word had no place for them would they be lost.'

'What of Ultis?'

Zadkiel surveyed the array of the dead. 'He fell at Bakka,' he lied, 'and the Scholar Coven with him.'

Reskiel clenched his teeth in anger. 'Damn them.'

'We will not damn anyone, Reskiel,' said Zadkiel sharply, 'nor even will Lorgar. The Emperor's gun-dogs will damn themselves.'

'We should turn about and blast them out of real space.'

'You, sergeant-commander, are in no place to say what this ship should and should not do. In the presence of these loyal brothers, do not debase yourself by forgetting your purpose.' Zadkiel did not have to raise his voice to convey his displeasure.

'Please forgive me, admiral. I have… I have lost brothers.'

'We have all lost something. It was written that we would lose much before we are victorious. We should not expect anything else. We will not engage the *Wrathful* in a fight because to do so would use up time that we

no longer have to spare, and our mission depends on its
timing. Kor Phaeron will not be late, so neither will we.
Besides, we have other options when dealing with the
Wrathful.'

'You mean Wsoric?'

Zadkiel clenched his fist in a moment of unsup-
pressed emotion. 'It is not appropriate for his name to
be spoken here. Make the cathedral ready to receive
him.'

'Of course,' said Reskiel. 'And the surviving Astartes?'

'Hunt him down and kill him,' said Zadkiel.

Reskiel saluted and walked out of the chapel-
mortuary.

Certain that the sergeant-commander was gone, Zadkiel gestured to the shadows from which a clandestine
guest emerged.

Magos Gureod shuffled into the light of the votive
candles slowly, mechadendrites clicking like insectoid
claws.

'You have received Baelanos?' the admiral asked.

The magos nodded.

'All is prepared, my lord.'

'Then begin his rebirth at once.'

Gureod bowed and left the chamber.

Now truly alone, Zadkiel looked back at the bodies
lying arranged in front of him. In another chamber,
together with the many crew of the *Furious* who had
died, were the enemy Astartes, slain in the engine
room and the cathedral. They would not receive
benediction. They would have refused such an honour even if it could be given, because they did not
understand what prayer and faith meant. They would
never be given their place in the Word. They had forsaken it.

Those Astartes, the declared enemies of Lorgar, were the ones who were truly lost.

AN HOUR AFTER the *Wrathful* had entered the warp, Cestus went to the isolation chambers. Upon his arrival, he found Rujveld still dutifully in his position. This time, though, the Blood Claw stepped aside without being ordered and offered no resistance, it being ostensibly clear that the Ultramarine would brook none.

The gloom of the isolation, cum interrogation, chamber was as Cestus remembered it, although now, the air was redolent of copper and sweat.

'What progress have you made?' the Ultramarine captain asked of Laeradis, who stood at the edge of the room. The apothecary's face was ashen as he faced his brother-captain and saluted.

'None,' he hissed.

'Nothing?' asked Cestus, nonplussed. 'He hasn't yielded any information whatsoever?'

'No, my lord.'

'Brynngar–'

'Your Apothecary has the strength of it,' grumbled the Space Wolf, his back to Cestus, body heaving up and down with the obvious effort of his interrogations. When he turned, Brynngar's face was haggard and his beard and much of his torso were flecked with blood. His meaty fists were angry and raw.

'Is he alive?' Cestus asked, concern creeping into his voice, not at the fate of their prisoner but at the prospect that they might have lost their one and only piece of leverage.

'He lives,' Brynngar answered, 'but, by the oceans of Fenris, he is tight-lipped. He has not even spoken his name.'

Cestus felt his spirit falter for a moment. Time was running out. How many more warp jumps until they reached Macragge? How many more opportunities would they get to stop the Word Bearers? It was irrational to even comprehend that one ship, even one such as the *Furious Abyss*, could possibly threaten Macragge and the Legion. Surely, even the mere presence of the orbital fleet above the Ultramarines' home world would be enough to stop it, let alone Guilliman and the Legion mustering at nearby Calth. Something else was happening, however, events that, as of yet, Cestus had no knowledge of. The *Furious Abyss* was a piece of a larger plan, he could sense it, and one that posed a very real danger. They needed to break this Word Bearer, and quickly, find out what he knew and a way to stop the ship and its inexorable course.

Brynngar was possibly the most physically intimidating Astartes he had ever known, aside from the glory and majesty of the noble primarch. If he, with all his bulk and feral savagery, could not break the traitor then who could?

'There is but one avenue left open to us,' said Cestus, the answer suddenly clear, even though it was an answer muddied with the utmost compromise.

Brynngar held Cestus's gaze, his eyes narrowed as he fought to discern the Ultramarine's meaning.

'Speak then,' he said.

'We release Mhotep,' Cestus answered simply.

Brynngar roared his dissent.

MHOTEP SAT IN quiet contemplation in the quarters made ready for him aboard the *Wrathful*. As ordered, he had not left the relatively spartan chamber since his incarceration after he had vanquished the *Fireblade*. He sat, naked of his armour, in robes afforded to him by attendant Legion serfs, long since departed, in deep meditation. His gaze was fixed upon the reflective surface of the room's single viewport, poring into the unfathomable depths of psychic space and communion.

When the door to his cell slid open, Mhotep was not surprised. He had followed the strands of fate, witnessed and understood the web of possibility that brought him to this point, this meeting.

'Captain Cestus,' muttered the Thousand Son with an air of prescience from beneath a cowl of vermillion.

'Mhotep,' Cestus replied, taken a little aback by the Thousand Son's demeanour. The Ultramarine wasn't alone; he had brought Excelinor, Amryx and Laeradis with him.

'The assault at Bakka Triumveron failed, didn't it?' said the Thousand Son.

'The enemy obviously had prior warning of our intentions. It is part of the reason I came here to meet with you.'

'You believe that I can provide an answer to this conundrum?'

'Yes, I do,' Cestus replied.

'It is simple,' said Mhotep. 'The Word Bearers have made a pact with the denizens of the warp. They forewarned them of your attack.'

'There is sentience in the empyrean?' the Ultramarine asked in disbelief. 'How is it we do not know this? Are the primarchs privy to this? Is the Emperor?'

'That I do not know. All I can tell you is that the warp is beyond the comprehension of you or I, and things exist in its fathomless depths that are older than time as we know it.'

Mhotep paused for a moment as if in sudden contemplation.

'Do you see them, son of Guilliman?' he asked, still locked in his meditative posture. 'Quite beautiful.'

Cestus followed the Thousand Son's gaze to the viewport and saw nothing but the haze of the integrity fields and the bizarre and undulating landscape of the warp.

'Don't make me regret what I am about to do, Mhotep,' he warned, glad of his battle-brothers' presence behind him. The Ultramarine captain had already dismissed the armsmen guarding the door, an order they responded to with no shortage of relief. It was a moot gesture, really; Mhotep could have left at any time, irrespective of their presence. The fact that he had not somewhat mitigated what Cestus was about to say.

That was, before Mhotep pre-empted him.

'I am to be released.' It wasn't a question.

'Yes,' said Cestus, carefully. 'We have a prisoner aboard and precious little time to find out what he knows.'

'I take it conventional methods have already failed?'

'Yes.'

'Small wonder,' said Mhotep. 'Of all the children of the Emperor, the seventeenth Legion are the most fervent and impassioned. Mere torture would not prevail against such ardent fanaticism and zealotry.'

'We require a different tack, one which I do not relish undertaking, but which I am compelled to employ.'

Mhotep stood, setting back his hood and turning to face Cestus.

'Ultramarine, there is no need to convey your reluctance to me. I am sure the account of this day, if such records ever come to pass given our current predicament, will state that you acted under the most profound duress,' he said smoothly, the trace of a smile appearing on his lips before it was lost in the mask of indifference.

'I do not know what powers you possess, brother,' said Cestus. 'I had thought to make you stand trial and answer that question for me. It seems, however, that events have overtaken us.'

'Indeed,' answered Mhotep. 'I am as moved by my duty as you are, Ultramarine. If I am freed then I will fight as hard as any and pledge my strength to the cause.'

Cestus nodded. His stern expression gave away the warring emotions within him, the abhorrence of flouting the Emperor's decree matched against the needs of the situation.

'Gather your armour,' he ordered. 'Brothers Excelinor and Amryx will accompany you to the isolation cell.' Cestus about turned and was walking away with Laeradis when Mhotep spoke again.

'What of the son of Russ? What does he make of my emancipation?'

The bellowing and violent protests of Brynngar were still ringing in the Ultramarine's ears.

'Let me worry about that.'

CESTUS AND LAERADIS were waiting when Mhotep, with Excelinor and Amryx in tow, reached them at the isolation cell. Brynngar and Rujveld had already stormed off in the wake of the Space Wolf captain's explosive discontent.

Cestus nodded to his battle-brothers as they approached. The two Ultramarines reciprocated the gesture and fell in beside their captain.

'The prisoner is within,' the Ultramarine captain told Mhotep, who had reached the door and stood before it calmly. 'Will you require Laeradis's assistance?' he added.

'You can have your chirurgeon go back to his quarters,' replied the Thousand Son, his gaze fixed upon the sealed portal as if he could see through it.

Cestus nodded to his Apothecary, indicating that his duty was done.

If Laeradis thought anything of the slight that Mhotep had delivered, he did not show it. Instead, he snapped a sharp salute to his captain and left for his quarters as directed.

Mhotep thumbed the activation icon and the portal slid open, showing the darkened cell.

'Once it begins,' he said, 'do not enter.' Mhotep turned to face the Ultramarine. 'No matter what you hear or see, do not enter,' he warned, and all trace of superiority vanished from his face.

'We will be outside,' Cestus replied, Excelinor and Amryx grim-faced behind their captain, 'and watching everything you do, Thousand Son.' The Ultramarine captain indicated a viewport that allowed observation into the isolation cell. 'I see anything I don't like and you'll be dead before you can utter another word.'

'Of course,' said Mhotep, unperturbed as he entered the chamber, the door sliding shut in his wake.

MHOTEP STEPPED CAREFULLY into the gloom, surveying his immediate surroundings as he went. Dark splashes littered the floor and walls; even the ceiling was not devoid of the evidence of torture. A suit of armour had been thrown into one corner, together with the body-glove that went beneath it. This was not considered disrobing by a coterie of acolytes. No, this was frenzied: an attempt to get to the soft meat of the flesh and exact pain and profound suffering. Mhotep's expression hardened at such barbarism. Implements, crude and brutish to the Thousand Son's eyes, lay discarded on a silver tray, also speckled in blood. Some of the devices even bore traces of meat, doubtless rent from the unfortunate subject when his tongue failed to loosen under the fists of the Space Wolf. The chirurgeon's methods, then, had been equally ineffective.

'You are quite tenacious,' Mhotep said. There was a trace of menace in his calm inflection as he approached the metal cruciform frame to which the prisoner was affixed. The Thousand Son ignored the rapacious bruising, the cuts, gouges and tears that afflicted the subject's battered body. Instead, he focused on the eyes. They were still defiant, albeit slightly groggy from the beatings the prisoner had been given.

'What compromise you force us to endure,' he whispered to himself, drawing close so that their faces almost touched. 'Tell me, what secrets do you possess?'

The response came stuttering through blood-caked lips.

'I... serve... only... the... Word.'

Mhotep reached for the scarab earring and removed it. He manipulated the small object with his thumb and forefinger, and placed it upon his forehead, where it stayed affixed in the shape of a gold eye, the symbol of Magnus.

'Do not think,' he warned, placing his fingers against the prisoner's skull and pressing hard, 'that you can hide from me.'

When Mhotep's fingers penetrated the flesh, the screaming began.

TWELVE

Sirens/Screams and silence/Here be monsters

CESTUS'S TEETH CLENCHED at the horrific noises emanating from within the isolation chamber. Excelinor and Amryx followed their captain's example, stoically bearing the sounds of psychic torture, secretly glad that they were not the subject of Mhotep's attentions.

Through the viewport, the isolation cell was shrouded in shadow. Cestus could see Mhotep from the back only. The Thousand Son moved almost imperceptibly as he stood before the prisoner who, by contrast, spasmed intermittently as his mind was ransacked.

On several occasions, when the screaming was at its height, Cestus had wanted to go in and end it, abhorred at the mental damage being inflicted on what was once a brother Astartes, but he had stopped himself every time, even warning off Excelinor and Amryx from taking action. Instead, the two battle-brothers had turned away from the viewport, leaving

Cestus alone to observe the imagined horrors of the Word Bearer's torture.

Twice already, he had angrily ordered worried arms-men away, after they had come to investigate the sound, fearing another warp attack as they patrolled the decks.

As the shipboard vox crackled, issuing a warning, obliquely, they were right.

'Captain Cestus, come to the bridge at once. We are under attack!'

LOATHE AS HE was to leave Mhotep, albeit with Excelinor and Amryx, Cestus had little choice but to do as bidden. He reached the bridge quickly and Saphrax quickly apprised him of the situation.

The alert had come when several unknown projectiles had been expelled from the vicinity of the *Furious Abyss*, and were snaking across the warp towards the *Wrathful*. At first it was believed that the missiles were in fact tor-pedoes launched in a punitive attempt to dissuade pursuit. That assumption was crushed in the moment when Admiral Kaminska's helmsmistress, Venkmyer, had identified their erratic trajectory and the truth had been revealed.

'Sirens,' Kaminska breathed, looking up at the tactical display before her that showed the inexorable advance of the creatures. A dark atmosphere seemed to pervade the bridge, and the admiral looked uncomfortable because of it. Her uniform was in slight disarray – she had clearly been roused from quarters when the alert had come in – and only added to her apparent sense of unease. 'I had thought such things were void-born myths.'

'They are the denizens of the empyrean,' Cestus told her, the disquieting mood affecting him less acutely.

Something was awry. The Ultramarine captain put it down to the sudden appearance of the warp beasts. 'Can we avoid them, admiral?'

Kaminska's face was grave as she considered the path of the warp creatures on the tactical display in front of her command throne.

'Admiral,' Cestus said sternly, snapping Kaminska free of the dark mood that had suddenly ensnared her.

'Yes, captain?' she gasped, face pale and unsteady in her command throne.

'Can Orcadus find a way around these creatures?'

Kaminska shook her head. 'We are on a collision course.'

Cestus turned to Saphrax.

'Ready the honour guard and have them gather on the assembly deck at once; Amryx and Excelinor, too.' He didn't want to leave Mhotep alone, but the warp creatures threatened the safety of the ship and he would need all of his battle-brothers to defend it. On balance, it was a risk worth taking.

'Captain,' said Kaminska as the Ultramarine was leaving.

Cestus turned and looked at her, noticing that Helmsmistress Venkmyer had moved to her aid. Kaminska warned off her second-in-command with a glance.

'What is it, admiral?' Cestus asked.

'If these creatures are indeed native to the warp, how are we to stop them?'

'I don't know,' answered the Astartes and then left the bridge.

QUITE WHAT THE warp looked like was a question that could never be answered. The human mind was not designed to comprehend it, which was why only specialised mutants like Orcadus could look upon it, and even then with a third eye that did not truly perceive it, merely filtering out the parts that would otherwise drive him mad.

Certainly, there was something ophidian or shark-like about the creatures that closed in on the *Wrathful*. In truth, they neither intercepted nor followed it, but stalked it from all directions at once, creeping up from the past and gliding in from the future to converge on the point of fragile space-time that held the *Wrathful* in its bubble.

They had eyes, lots of eyes. Their bodies were writhing strings of non-matter, which could take on any shape, because they had no true form to begin with, but there were always eyes. They had wings, too, which were also claws and fangs, and masses of pendulous blubber to keep them warm against the nuclear cold of the warp's storms. They burned and shimmered with acid, and shed daggers of ice from their scales. They had been born in the abyss, and had never been forced by the tyranny of reality into one form. To stay the same from one moment to the next would have been as alien to them as the warp was to a human mind.

Lamprey mouths opened up. The predators made themselves coterminous with the *Wrathful*, forcing themselves into unfamiliar frames of logic to avoid annihilation by the protective energy fields that surrounded the ship.

The minds inside were brimming with the potential for madness, delicious insanity to be suckled upon. The predators fed normally on scraps: moments of emotion or agony, powerful enough to bloom in the warp and be consumed. Here there were lifetimes worth of sensation to be drained, enough for any one of the wraiths to become bloated and terrible, a whale drifting through the abyss big enough to feed upon its own kind.

Thousands of bright lights flickered in the ship, each one both a potential feast, and a gateway for the non-physical predators.

One of them found an unprotected mind and, easing itself painfully into the rules of reality, forced its way in.

THE SCREAMS WERE the first signs that anything was wrong on the lance deck.

The lances, immense laser cannon hooked up to the plasma reactors in the ship's stern, had been silent since the duel with the *Furious Abyss* outside the Solar System. The gun gangs still tended to them, because lasers were temperamental, especially when they had to funnel the titanic levels of power that could surge through a laser lance, and the gun gangs were constantly busy hammering out imperfections in focusing lenses and cleaning the laser conduits, which could misfire if any blemish refracted too much power in the wrong direction.

One ganger fell from his perch high up on the inner hull, where he had been aligning one of the huge mirrors. He hit the ground with a wet crump that told the gang chief that he was most certainly dead. It was a sound he had heard many times before.

The gang chief was in no hurry to see what had become of the fallen ganger. Deaths meant hassle. The gang would be one short, so someone would have to be drafted from somewhere else on the ship and the *Wrathful* had lost plenty of men already, and they were in the abyss.

For a man to die in the abyss was bad luck. Some said if you died in the warp you never got out, and even with the suppression of religions in the fleet you couldn't stop a void-born superstition like that.

The dead man, however, was not dead. When the gang chief reached the body he saw it mewling like a drowning animal, writhing around on its back with its wrists and ankles shaking as if it was trying to right itself.

The gang chief expressed displeasure that the man was still alive, since he would undoubtedly die soon and carting him off to the sick bay was another inconvenience the gun crews didn't need.

The dying man's body distended with the cracking of ribs. One side of his body split off from the other, organs separating as his pelvis split. His sternum snapped free and false ribs pinged against the laser housing beside him. His body rippled up from the floor into a writhing, pulsing arch of flesh and bone, drizzling blood onto the gunmetal deck. The crewman's head lolled to one side, its jaw wrenched at an angle, its eyes still open.

The space within the arch twisted and went dark. The predator forced its way through, spilling out onto the floor like the contents of a split belly, feeling blindly, eyes blinking as they evolved to absorb light.

Then the screaming started.

IT WAS CARNAGE in the lance decks, absolute carnage.

The warning icons had blazed through the ship, coupled with frantic vox chatter about monsters and the dead coming back to life, before it cut off ominously. Reconnoitring with his battle-brothers on the assembly deck, Cestus had led the honour guard, fully armed, to the lance decks and there they stood to bear witness to the horror.

The Ultramarine captain wondered, for a moment, whether he had been wrong all along, whether the Imperial Truth itself was wrong, and that the hells of those primitive faiths really did exist to be given form in the lance decks. He dismissed his doubts as heretical, crushing them beneath his iron-hard resolve and his loyalty to Roboute Guilliman. Even still, what he saw warred with what he desperately tried to believe. Bodies were painted across the walls in ragged smears of skin and muscle. The faces of the gang ratings were ripped open in expressions of horror, and stared out from heaps of torn limbs. Flesh and viscera were draped across high girders ahead, or over the massive workings of the lances themselves. The focusing mirrors and lenses were sprayed with blood. The living writhed in a single mass, smearing themselves with gore and sinking their teeth into one another.

Spectral threads of glowing black wrapped around the spines of the bleeding revellers. The threads led up to the ceiling of the lance deck where a titanic mass of darkness squatted, a seething thing of eyes and mouths gibbering and chuckling as it manipulated the lance deck's crew into further depths of suffering.

Cestus was an Astartes. He had seen extraordinary, horrible things: amorphous aliens that consumed their own to be ready for battle; insect-things that broke up into swarms of seething, biting horrors; whole worlds infected or dying, whole stars boiling away in the death throes of a species, but he had never seen anything like this.

'Weapons free,' he raged.

A brutal chorus of bolter fire rang out to his order, puncturing the mass of flesh and exploding it from within. Thestor swung his heavy bolter around and added his own punishing shots to the salvo.

Terrible screeching filled the tight space and resonated in his battle helm, auditory-limiters struggling
to modulate the horrible keening of the damned ratings.

The dangling threads held by the warp creature began
to sever one by one as the munitions of the Astartes
struck and detonated with fury. It snarled its displeasure, revealing row upon row of fine needle-like fangs
and a slathering spectral tongue that appeared to taste
their essence. Like a lightning strike, the tongue lashed
out and speared Thestor through his cuirass. He bellowed in pain, heavy bolter fire flaring as he triggered
the weapon in his death throes. The honour guard scattered as the errant shells strafed the deck, and Thestor
shook and went into spasm as he was lifted into the air,
impaled on the warp spawn's tongue.

'Burn it!' cried Cestus in desperation. 'Burn it all!'

Morar stepped forward with his flamer and doused
the tunnel in roaring, white-hot promethium. Thestor
and the creature's transfixing tongue were immolated in
cleansing fire. The warp spawn reeled, shrieking in
anger as it recoiled from the attack. Morar swept the
cone of intense heat downward, cooking the conjoined
mass of the dead ratings.

As the warp spawn gave ground, Cestus noticed
patches of ichorous fluid spattering the deck in its wake.

If it can bleed, he thought, we can kill it.

'Advance on me,' cried the Ultramarine captain.
'Courage and honour!'

'Courage and honour!' his battle-brothers bellowed
in reply.

BROODING IN THE temporary barrack room afforded to
the Space Wolves onboard the *Wrathful*, Brynngar had

heard the alert screaming through the ship and had mustered his warriors.

Tracking the commotion to the lower lance decks, he and his Blood Claws were unprepared for the sight that greeted them as they descended into the gloom. It was a charnel house. Flayed flesh lined the walls and blood slicked the floor. Bones, still red with gore, lay discarded in mangled piles. Screams were etched upon the visages of skulls, locked in their last moments of agony.

The bloody massacre was not, however, what gave the Space Wolf captain pause. It was the nightmare creature, tearing at chunks of flesh with its teeth. At their approach, the beast, a luminous, shark-like horror, turned, its lipless maw smeared with blood, its swollen belly engorged.

'Here be monsters,' Brynngar breathed and felt a quail of something unfamiliar, an alien emotion, trickle down his spine.

He found his courage quickly, baring his fangs as he howled.

The Space Wolves launched at the creature, blades drawn.

MHOTEP STAGGERED FROM the isolation chamber, not surprised to see that he was alone. He had broken the traitor, though it had not been easy. He felt the sweat of his exertions beneath his helmet and was breathing heavily as he stepped into the adjoining corridor. Of the subject known as Ultis, for he had given his name before the end, there was precious little left. A drooling cage of flesh and bone were all that remained. His conditioned defences, ingrained by years of fanatical indoctrination, had been tough to break, but as a result, when they had fallen, they had fallen hard. Only a shell remained, a gibbering wreck incapable of further defiance, incapable of anything.

Exhausted as he was, Mhotep groaned when he detected the rogue presence onboard the ship. Mustering what reserves of strength he had left, he made for the lance decks.

MORAR WAS DEAD. His bifurcated body lay in two halves across the deck. Amyrx was badly wounded, but alive. He slumped against an upright, beneath a metal arch, a chunk of flesh ripped from his torso.

A dark mass was boiling down the corridor behind Cestus, even as the honour guard faced off against the first warp predator, torrents of semi-liquid flesh bursting through doorways in a flood. Eyes formed in the mass, focusing on the Astartes.

The Ultramarine swivelled his body around, barking a warning before his bolter blazed, the muzzle flare lighting up the dark around him. A long tongue of dark muscle thrashed blindly past him from the creature's gaping mouth, and Cestus threw himself out of its path. Laeradis, desperately ministering to the wounded Amyrx, was not so lucky. The membrane lashed around him, sending spines of pain throughout his body. The Apothecary screamed as the flesh suddenly dried and split open, fist-sized seeds spilling from the fibrous interior.

The seeds burst into life, tiny buzzing wings shearing through the shells and long sharp mandibles splintering out. Laeradis was eviscerated in the storm in a bloody haze of bone, flesh and armour.

Cestus cried out and swung his bolt pistol back around. He picked off the insectoid creatures with precise shots as they buzzed towards him, letting out his breath to steady his aim. He caught the last with his free hand. Cestus mashed it into the wall before it could chew through the ceramite of his gauntlet.

With the two warp creatures on either side, the Ultramarines were being crushed into a tight circle.

Even as he continued to pummel the second warp fiend with bolt pistol fire, he heard Saphrax bellow the name of Roboute Guilliman, punctuated by the retort of his weapon. The burning flare of expelled plasma lit the side of his face, and the Ultramarine captain knew that their other special weapon bearer, Pytaron, was still with them. Muzzle flashes blazing, Lexinal and Excelinor continued to fire their bolters, war cries on their lips.

The chorus of battle raged as the warp predators closed, weaving and twisting impossibly from the worst of the Ultramarines' fusillade, shrieking and screeching whenever they were struck and forced back.

Cestus checked the ammo-reader on his bolt pistol. His remaining rounds wouldn't last long. Divided as they were, he and his battle-brothers would be unable to destroy either creature like this. With little recourse left, he made his decision.

'All guns with me!' he cried. 'In the name of Guilliman, concentrate fire.'

With no hesitation, the Ultramarines turned their combined fire onto one of the warp creatures. Not expecting the sudden storm, the beast was caught unawares. Desperately trying to weave and jink out of harm's way, it was struck by a barrage of bolter rounds. Super-heated plasma scorched its flank and a precise salvo from Cestus struck it in the eye. A keening wail emanated from the dread creature as it shuddered out of existence, expelled from the bubble of real space within the *Wrathful*. However, the victory proved costly, as the second creature surged, unhindered, to the Ultramarines' position, suddenly buoyed by the presence of three more of its kin.

Cestus and his battle-brothers turned as one, defiant war cries on their lips as they prepared to sell their lives dearly.

The rending of flesh as their bodies were torn asunder, the stench of blood and the sound of shredding bone failed to materialise.

Poised with jaws outstretched, ready to devour the Astartes, the warp creatures were assailed by a blazing crimson light that bathed the corridor in an incandescent lustre. The beasts recoiled and shrank before him, snapping ineffectually at the air as the building aura seared them.

'Warp spawned filth!' spat a voice behind Cestus, echoing with power. 'Flee back into the abyss and leave this plane of existence.'

Shielding his eyes against the brilliance of the light, Cestus saw Mhotep striding towards them, a cerulean nimbus of psychic energy coursing over his armoured body. He held a golden spear in his outstretched hand.

'Down, now!' he cried and the Ultramarines hit the floor with a crash of ceramite.

The spear arced over their heads like a divine bolt of lightning and pierced the first warp beast, tearing through its slithering flank and slathering the deck with dark grey, spilling gore.

Its death cry reverberated in the confines of the vaulted tunnel, the metal uprights screaming before it. Then it was gone, leaving an actinic stench in its wake.

The kindred beasts came at him, enduring the furious energy that the Thousand Son had unleashed, but were driven back as Cestus and his honour guard crouched on their knees and delivered a punishing salvo.

'Blind them,' Mhotep cried, plucking his spear from the air as it returned to him as if magnetised to his gauntlet.

The Ultramarines obeyed, aiming for the hideous black orbs that served the shark-like predators as eyes. More screeching filled the corridor as the shots found their marks, rupturing the glassy orbs. Mhotep cast his spear again and another of the creatures was thrust back into the immaterium.

The last predator turned in on itself and re-formed. It grew fresh eyes, dripping with glowing ichor. It extruded a frill of tendrils from what Cestus assumed was its head end, and they became tough jointed limbs tipped with claws. Snakelike tongues whipped from its mouth.

A hail of fire struck it and it was blasted into a gory mess upon the deck.

Curious, ringing silence filled the void where the eruption of bolters and the bark of shouting had been. Red-tinged gloom from the emergency lights drifted back into focus after the monochromatic battle flare of muzzle flashes and psychic conflagration.

Cestus surveyed his battle-brothers. Amyrx lay still against the upright, injured but alive. The service of Laeradis and Morar, though, had ended, their final moments awash with blood and pain. The rest had survived. A weary nod from Saphrax confirmed it.

Breathing hard, a strange, subdued exultance at their victory sweeping over him, Cestus looked back around at Mhotep.

The Thousand Son staggered, the crimson light extinguished.

'They are gone,' he breathed and fell hard onto the deck.

THIRTEEN

Legacy of Lorgar/Proposition/Honour duel

As Skraal delved deeper into the *Furious Abyss*, the world around him got stranger. The ship was the size of a city, and just like a city it had its hidden corners and curiosities, its beautiful clean-cut vistas and its dismal bordellos of decay.

Though supposedly newly fashioned, the vessel felt very old. Its concomitant parts had spent so many decades being built and rendered in the forges of Mars that they had acquired a history of their own before the battleship was ever finished, let alone launched. It had a presence, too, a kind of impalpable sentience that exuded from its steel walls and clung to its corridors and conduits like gossamer threads of being.

Skraal passed under a support beam, his chainaxe held out warily in front of him, and saw the signature of a Mechanicum shipwright inscribed in binary. The passageway of steel looked like an avenue in a wealthy spire-top, the low ceiling supported by caryatids and columns; a nest of shanties, perhaps the lodgings of the menials, who had once laboured to build the ship, their ramshackle homes abandoned between two generatorium housings: the vessel was intricate and immense. The World Eater saw chambers he could only assume were for worship, with altars and rows of prayer books etched in the Word of Lorgar. A temple, half wrought in stone and symbiotically merged with deep red steel, was housed in a massive false amphitheatre, its columned front and carved pediment providing a medieval milieu. The wide threshold was lit by braziers of violet fire. Skraal thought he had seen something moving inside and took care to avoid it.

The World Eater had no time for distractions. The denizens of the *Furious Abyss* hunted him, and even in a ship as vast as it, the chase would not last indefinitely. Melta bombs and belts of krak grenades clanked against his armour as he moved, reminding him of their presence and the urgency with which he needed to put them to some use.

In a fleeting moment, when Skraal had paused to try and get some kind of bearing, he thought of Antiges.

The Ultramarines believed themselves to be philosophers, or kings, or members of the galaxy's rightful ruling class. They did not appreciate the purity of purpose that could only be found in the crucible of war as did Skraal's Legion. They were most concerned with forging their own empire around Macragge. Antiges had demonstrated his warrior spirit, though, fighting and dying in the cauldron of war, driven by simple duty.

Skraal mourned his passing with a moment of silence, honouring his valourous deeds, and, in that moment, he made a promise of revenge.

A great set of double doors carved from lacquered black wood blocked the World Eater's path. Skraal could not turn back from the barrier, incongruous like so much of what he had witnessed on the *Furious Abyss*. Instead, he pushed the door open. There was light inside, but still the silence persisted, so, he entered into what was a long, low chamber. Beyond it was a gallery full of artefacts. Tapestries lined the walls, displaying the victories and history of the Word Bearers. He saw a comet crashing down to their native earth of Colchis and a golden child emerging from the conflagration left from its impact. He saw temples, their spires lost in a swathe of red cloud, and lines of pilgrims trailing off into infinity. It was a world stained with tragedy, the gilded palaces and cathedrals tarnished, and every statue of past religious dynasts missing an arm or an eye. In the middle of this fallen world, like a single point of hope, was the smouldering crater of their saviour's arrival.

The ceiling was a single endless fresco depicting Lorgar's conquest of Colchis. Here it was a corrupt place cleansed by the primarch, whose image shone with the light of reason and command as robed prophets and priests prostrated themselves before him. Armies laid down their arms and crowds cheered in adulation. At the far end of the museum the story ended with Colchis restored and Lorgar a scholar-hero writing down his history and philosophy. This epilogue ended with a truth that Skraal knew, the Emperor coming to the world to find Lorgar, just as he had come to the World Eaters' forgotten home world to install Angron as the Legion's primarch.

The paintings, frescoes and tapestries gave way to trophies displayed on plinths and suspended from the vaulted ceiling. Skraal ignored them and pressed on.

'You look upon the soul of our Legion, brother,' boomed a voice suddenly through the vox-casters in the gallery.

Skraal backed up against the wall, which was painted with an image of Lorgar debating with a host of wizened old men in a Colchian amphitheatre.

'I am Admiral Zadkiel of the Word Bearers,' said the voice, when the World Eater answered with silence. 'You are aboard my ship.'

'Traitor whoreson, does your entire Legion cower behind words?' Skraal snapped, unable to contain his anger.

'Such a curious term, World Eater,' the voice of Zadkiel replied, ignoring the slight. 'You dub us traitors, and yet we have never been anything but loyal to our primarch.'

'Then your lord is also a traitor,' Skraal growled in return, hunting the shadows for any sign of movement, any hint that he was being stalked.

'Your own lord, Angron, calls him brother. How then can Lorgar be regarded as a traitor?'

Skraal cast his gaze around, trying to locate the picter observing him or the vox-caster broadcasting Zadkiel's voice. 'Then he has betrayed my primarch and in turn his Legion.'

'Angron was a slave,' said Zadkiel. 'The very fact shames him. He despises what he was, and what other men made of him. It is from this that his anger, that the anger of all the World Eaters stems.'

Certain that there was no one else in there with him, Skraal started moving cautiously through the gallery, looking for some way out other than the double doors at either end. He would not be swayed by Zadkiel's words, and focused instead on the hot line of rage building inside him, using it to galvanise himself.

'I saw the echo of that anger at Bakka Triumveron,' said Zadkiel. 'It was enacted against the menials that drowned in their own blood at the hands of you and your brothers.'

Skraal paused. He had thought no one knew of the slaughter he had perpetrated at the dock.

'Angron sought to bring his brothers closer to him in that aspect, did he not?' Zadkiel was relentless, his words like silken blades penetrating the World Eater's defences. 'It was the Emperor's censure that forbade it, the very being that holds you and your slave primarch in his thrall. For what is Angron if not a slave? What accolades has he won that the Angel or Guilliman have not? What reward has Angron been given that can equal the empire of Ultramar or the stewardship of the Imperial Palace granted to Dorn? Nothing. He fights for nothing save by the command of another. What can such a man claim to be, other than a slave?'

'We are not slaves! We will never be slaves!' Skraal cried in anger and carved his chainaxe through one of the museum's stone pillars.

'It is the truth,' Zadkiel persisted, 'but you are not alone, brother; yours is not the only Legion to have been thus forsaken,' he continued. 'We Word Bearers worshipped him, worshipped the Emperor as... a... god! But he mocked our divinity with reproach and reprimand, just as he mocks you.'

Skraal ignored him. His faith in his Legion and his primarch would not easily be undone. This Word Bearer's rhetoric meant nothing. Duty and rage: these were the things he focused on as he sought to escape from the chamber.

'Look before you, World Eater,' Zadkiel began again. 'There you will find what you seek.'

Despite himself, Skraal looked.

There, within an ornate glass cabinet, forged of obsidian and brass and once wielded by Angron's hand, was a chainaxe. Decked with teeth of glinting black stone, its haft wrapped in the skin of some monstrous lizard, he knew it instinctively to be Brazentooth, the former blade of his primarch.

The weapon, magnificent in its simple brutality, had taken the head of the queen of the Scandrane xenos, and cleaved through a horde of greenskins following the Arch-Vandal of Pasiphae. A feral world teeming with tribal psychopaths had rebelled against the Imperial Truth, and at the mere sight of Brazentooth in Angron's hand they had given up their revolt and kneeled to the World Eaters. Until the forging of Gorefather and Gorechild, the twin axes Angron now wielded, Brazentooth had been as much a symbol of Angron's relentlessness and independence as it was a mere weapon.

'Gifted unto Lorgar, it symbolises our alliance,' Zadkiel told him. 'Angron pledged himself to our cause, and with him all the World Eaters.'

Skraal regarded the chainaxe. Thick veins stuck out on his forehead, beneath his skull-helmet, exacerbated by the heat of his impotent wrath.

'It is written, World Eater, that you and all your brothers will join with us when the fate of the galaxy is decided. The Emperor is lost. He is ignorant of the *true* power of the universe. We will embrace it.'

'Word Bearer,' Skraal said, his lip curled derisively, 'you talk too much.'

The World Eater shattered the cabinet with a blow from his fist and seized Brazentooth. Without pause, he squeezed the tongue of brass in the chainaxe's haft, and the teeth whirred hungrily. The weapon was far too heavy and unbalanced for Skraal to wield; it would have taken Angron's own magnificent strength to use it. It was all he could do to keep the bucking chainblade level as he put his body weight behind it and hurled it into the nearest wall.

Brazentooth ripped into a fresco depicting Lorgar as an educator of the benighted, thousands of ignorant souls bathing in the halo of enlightenment that surrounded him. The image was shredded and the weapon, free of Skraal's hands, bored its way through, casting sparks as it chewed up the metal beneath.

'You're doomed, Zadkiel!' bellowed Skraal over the screech of the chainblade. 'The Emperor will learn of your treachery! He'll send your brothers to bring you back in chains! He'll send the Warmaster!'

The World Eater hurled himself through the ragged tear in the museum wall and fell through into a tangled dark mess of cabling and metal beyond.

Zadkiel's laughter tumbled after him from the vox-caster.

ZADKIEL SWITCHED OFF the pict screens adorning the small security console at the rear of the temple. 'Tell me, chaplain, is everything prepared?'

Ikthalon, decked in his full regalia including vestments of deep crimson, nodded and gestured towards a circle, drawn from a paste mixed from Colchian soil and the blood that had been drained from the body of the Ultramarine, Antiges.

The Astartes inert body lay at its nexus, his cuirass removed and his chest levered open to reveal the congealed vermillion mass of his organs. Symbols had been scratched on the floor around him, using his blood. His helmet had been removed, too, and his head lolled back, glassy-eyed, its mouth open as if in awe of the ritual he would facilitate in death.

'It is ready, as you ordered,' uttered Ikthalon, the chaplain's tone approaching relish.

Zadkiel smiled thinly and then looked up at the sound of shuffling feet. An old, bent figure ascended the steps at the temple entrance and the candles on the floor flickered against its cowl and robe as it entered between the pillars.

'Astropath Kyrszan,' said Zadkiel.

The astropath pulled back his hood, revealing hollow sockets in place of his eyes as inflicted by the soul-binding.

'I am at your service,' he hissed through cracked lips.

'You know your role in this?'

'I have studied it well, my lord,' Kyrszan replied, leaning heavily on a gnarled cane of dark wood as he shuffled towards Antiges's corpse.

Kyrszan knelt down and held his hands over the body. The astropath smirked as he felt the last wreaths of heat bleeding from it. 'An Astartes,' he muttered.

'Indeed,' added Ikthalon. 'You'll find his scalp has been removed.'

'Then we can begin.'

'I will require what is left after this is done,' added Ikthalon.

'Don't worry, chaplain,' said Zadkiel. 'You'll have his body for your surgery. 'Kyrszan,' he added, switching his gaze to the astropath, 'you may proceed.'

Zadkiel threw a book in front of him. Kyrszan felt its edges, ran his fingers over its binding, the ancient vellum of its pages and breathed deep of its musk, redolent with power. His spidery digits, so sensitive from a lifetime of blindness, scurried across the ink and read with ease. The script was distinctive and known to him.

'What… what secrets,' he whispered in awe. 'This is written by your hand, admiral. What was it that dictated this to you?'

'His name,' said Zadkiel, 'is Wsoric and we are about to honour the pact he has made with us.'

IN THE HOURS that followed, the warp was angry. It was wounded. It bled half-formed emotions, like something undigested: hatred that was too unfocused to be pure, love without an object, obsession over nothing and gouts of oblivion without form.

It quaked. It thrashed as if being forced into something unwilling, or trying to hold on to something dear to it. The *Wrathful* was thrown around on the towering waves that billowed up through the layers of reality and threatened to snap the spindly anchor-line of reason that kept the ship intact.

The quake subsided. The predators that had homed in on the disturbance scented the corpses of their fellow warp-sharks in the *Wrathful*, and hastily slunk back into the abyss. The *Wrathful* continued on its way, following eddies left by the wake of the *Furious Abyss*.

'HAS THERE BEEN any change?' asked Cestus as he approached Saphrax.

The banner bearer stood outside the medical bay, looking in at the prone form of Mhotep, laid as if slumbering, on a slab of metal.

'None, sire. He has not stirred since he fell after the battle.'

The Ultramarine captain had recently been tended to by the *Wrathful*'s medical staff, an injury sustained to his arm that he had not realised he had suffered making its presence felt as he'd gone to Mhotep's aid. In the absence of the dead Laeradis, the treatment was rudimentary but satisfactory. The bodies, what was left of them, of the Astartes, two of the Blood Claws included, had been taken to the ship's morgue.

Cestus's mind still reeled at what he'd witnessed on the lance decks and the powers that the Thousand Son had unleashed. Truly, there was no doubt as to his practising psychics. That in itself left an altogether different and yet more pressing question: Brynngar.

The Wolf Guard had also been down in the lance decks, though Cestus was not aware of it until the battle was over, and had banished three of the warp spawn with his Blood Claws. The artifice of the Fenrisian rune priests, in their fashioning of Felltooth, was to thank for it. For once, reunited at the centre of the deck, Brynngar had curtly disclosed how the creatures parted easily before the blade and fled from the Space Wolves' fury. The Ultramarine believed that some of the account was embellished, so that it might become worthy of a saga, but he did not doubt the veracity at the heart of Brynngar's words.

It mattered not. Whatever the Wolf Guard intended to do about Mhotep and, indeed, Cestus, he would do regardless. Right now, the Ultramarine captain had greater concerns, namely, that the traitor had been broken, for Saphrax had discovered his shattered body in the isolation chamber, but that whatever secrets he had divulged were denied to them while Mhotep was incapacitated. It felt like a cruel irony.

'Do you know what we do with witches on Fenris, Ultramarine?'

Cestus turned at the voice and saw Brynngar standing behind him, glowering through the glass at Mhotep.

'We cut the tendons in their arms and legs. Then we throw them in the sea to the mercy of Mother Fenris.'

Cestus moved into the Space Wolf's path.

'This is not Fenris, brother.'

Brynngar smiled, mirthlessly, as if at some faded remembrance.

'No, it is not,' he said, locking his gaze with Cestus. 'You give your sanction to this warp-dabbler, and in so doing have twice besmirched my honour. I will not let his presence stand on this ship, nor will I let these deeds go unreckoned.'

The Space Wolf tore a charm hanging from his cuirass and tossed it at the Ultramarine's feet.

Cestus looked up and matched the Wolf Guard's gaze.

'Challenge accepted,' he said.

BRYNNGAR WAITED IN the duelling pit in the lower decks of the *Wrathful*. The old wolf was stripped down to the waist, wearing grey training breeches and charcoal-coloured boots, and flexed his muscles and rotated his shoulders as he prepared for his opponent.

Arrayed around the training arena, commonly used for the armsmen to practise unarmed combat routines, were what was left of the Astartes: the Ultramarine honour guard, barring Amryx, who was still recovering from his injuries, and a handful of Blood Claws. Admiral Kaminska, as the captain of the ship, was the only non-Astartes allowed to attend. She had forbidden any other of the crew from watching the duel. The realisation that the Astartes in the fleet were turning on one another was a sign of the worst kind, and she had no desire to discover its effects upon morale if witnessed by them first hand.

She watched as Cestus stepped into the arena, descending a set of metal steps that retracted into the wall once he was within the duelling pit. The Ultramarine was similarly attired to Brynngar, though his training breeches were blue to match the colour of his Legion.

At the appearance of his opponent, Brynngar swung the chainsword in his grasp eagerly.

The assembled Astartes were eerily silent; even the normally pugnacious Blood Claws held their tongues and merely watched.

'This is madness,' Kaminska hissed, biting back her anger.

'No, admiral,' said Saphrax, who towered alongside her, 'it is resolution.'

The Ultramarine banner bearer stepped forward. As the next highest ranking Astartes, it was his duty to announce the duel and state the rules.

'This honour-duel is between Lysimachus Cestus of the Ultramarines Legion and Brynngar Sturmdreng of the Space Wolves Legion,' Saphrax bellowed clearly like a clarion call. 'The weapon is chainswords and the duel is to blood from the torso or incapacitation. Limb or eye loss counts as thus, as does a cut to the front of the throat. No armour; no fire arms.'

Saphrax took a brief hiatus to ensure that both Astartes were ready. He saw his brother-captain testing the weight of his chainsword and adjusting his grip. Brynngar made no further preparation and was straining at the leash.

'The stakes are the fate of Captain Mhotep of the Thousand Sons Legion. To arms!'

The Astartes saluted each other and levelled their chainswords in their respective fighting stances:

Brynngar two-handed and slightly off-centre, Cestus low and pointed towards the ground.

'Begin!'

BRYNNGAR LAUNCHED HIMSELF at Cestus with a roar, channelling his anger into a shoulder barge. Cestus twisted on his heel to avoid the charge, but was still a little sluggish from the earlier battle and caught the blow down his side. A mass of pain numbed his body, resonating through his bones and skull, but the Ultramarine kept his feet.

Blows fell like hammers against Cestus's defensive stance, his chainblade screeching as it bit against Brynngar's weapon. Teeth were stripped away and sparks flew violently from the impact. Two-handed, the Ultramarine held him, but was forced down to one knee as the Space Wolf used his superior bulk against him.

'We are not in the muster hall, now,' he snarled. 'I shall give no quarter.'

'I will ask for none,' Cestus bit back and twisted out of the blade lock, using Brynngar's momentum to overbalance the Space Wolf.

The Ultramarine moved in quickly to exploit the advantage with a low thrust, intending to graze Brynngar's torso, draw blood and end the duel. The old wolf was canny, though, and parried the blow with a flick of his sword, before leaning in with another shoulder charge. It lacked the sudden impetuous and fury of the first, but jolted Cestus's body all the same. The Ultramarine staggered and Brynngar swept his weapon downward in a brutal arc that would have removed Cestus's head from his shoulders. Instead he rolled and the blade teeth carved into the metal floor of the duelling pit, disturbing the streaks of old blood left by the World Eater's earlier contest.

Cestus came out of the roll and was on his feet. There was a little distance between the two Astartes gladiators, and they circled each other warily, assessing strength and searching for an opening.

Brynngar didn't wait long and, howling, hurled his body at the Ultramarine, chainsword swinging.

Cestus met it with his blade and the two weapons came apart with the force of the blow, chain teeth spitting from their respective housings.

Brynngar cast the ruined chainsword haft aside and powered a savage uppercut into Cestus's chin that nearly shattered the Ultramarine's jaw. A second punch fell like a piston and smashed into his ear. A third lifted him off his feet, hammering into the Ultramarine's gut. The sound of Brynngar's grunting aggression became dull and distant as if Cestus was submerged below water, as he fought to get his bearings.

He was dimly aware of falling and had the vague sense of grasping something in his hand as he hit the hard metal floor of the duelling pit.

Abruptly, Cestus found it hard to breath and realised suddenly that Brynngar was choking him. Strangely, the Ultramarine thought he heard weeping. With a blink, he snapped back into lucidity and smashed his fists down hard against Brynngar's forearms, whilst landing a kick into his sternum. It was enough for the Space Wolf to loosen his grip. Cestus head-butted him in the nose and a stream of blood and mucus flowed freely after the impact.

Feeling the ground beneath him again, Cestus ducked a wild swing and lashed out beneath Brynngar's reach. The Ultramarine wasn't quick enough to avoid a backhand swipe and took it in the side of the face. He was reeling again, dark spots forming before his eyes, hinting that he was about to black out.

'Yield,' he breathed, sinking to his knees, his voice groggy as he pointed to the Space Wolf's torso with the chainsword tooth clutched in his outstretched hand.

Brynngar paused, fists clenched, his breathing ragged and looked down to where Cestus was pointing.

A line of crimson was drawn across the Space Wolf's stomach from the tiny diagonal blade in his opponent's grip.

'Blood from the torso,' Saphrax announced with thinly veiled relief. 'Cestus wins.'

FOURTEEN

Hunted/A single blow/We are all alone

TIME HAS LITTLE meaning in the warp. Weeks become days, days become hours and hours become minutes. Time is fluid. It can expand and contract, invert and even cease in those fathomless depths of infinite nothing; endless everything.

Leaving the gallery and Zadkiel's echoing laughter behind him, Skraal had fled into the pitch dark.

Crouching in the blackness with naught but the groans of the *Furious Abyss* for company it felt like the passage of years, and yet it could have been no more than weeks or as little as an hour. Heaving, shifting, baying, venting, the vessel was like some primordial beast as it ploughed the empyrean tides. Sentience exuded from every surface: the moisture of the metal, the blood, oil and soot in the air. Heat from generatoria became breath, fire from blast furnaces anger and hate, the creak of the hull, dull moans of pleasure and annoyance. Perhaps this awareness had always existed and lacked only form to give it tangibility. Perhaps the skeleton the adepts of Mars had forged provided merely a shell for an already sentient host.

The World Eater decided that his thoughts heralded the onset of madness at being hunted for so long, the thin talons of paranoia pricking his skull and infecting his mind with visions.

After his discovery in the gallery, he had gone to ground, questing downwards through the inner circuitry and workings of the *Furious Abyss* in some kind of attempt at preservation. It was not cowardice that drove him, such a thing was anathema to the Astartes: a World Eater was incapable of the emotion. Fear simply did not have meaning for them. No, it was out of a desire to regroup, to plan, to achieve some petty measure of destruction that might not at least escape notice, that meant something. Into the heat and fire he'd passed arches of steel, vast throbbing engines and forests of cables so thick that he'd needed to cut them down with his chainaxe. It was in this manufactured hell that he'd found refuge.

Bones lay on the lower decks, pounded to dust by pistons, though some were intact. They were the forgotten dead of the *Furious*'s birth, sucked into machinery or simply lost and left to starve or die of thirst in the ship's labyrinthine depths.

During his flight into this cauldron, Skraal had seen things. The dark had played with him, the heat, too, and the endless industrial din. Glowing eyes would watch the World Eater, only to then melt away into the walls. A landscape had opened up before him, its edges picked out in darkness: a vast land of bloody ribs and palaces of bone, with mountains of gristle and labyrinths carved down into plains of rippling muscle. Humanoid shapes danced in rivers of blood as the whole world swelled and fell with an ancient breath.

Then it was gone, replaced by the darkness, and so he had driven on.

Here in the searing depths, he'd found some respite.

It could have been days that he'd lingered in meditative solitude, listening to the pitch and pull of the vessel, marshalling his thoughts and his resolve so as not to give in to insanity. Way down in the stygian gloom, Skraal couldn't hear the vox traffic, didn't sense the patrols at his heels and so didn't know if he was still hunted.

Sheltering in a crawl space large enough to accommodate his power-armoured frame, within a cluster of pipes and cables, the World Eater snapped abruptly to his senses. Disengaging the cataleptic node that allowed him to maintain a form of active sleep, Skraal became aware of a shadow looming in the conduit ahead. He was not alone.

The passing of menials was not uncommon, but infrequent. Skraal had listened to their pathetic mewlings as they serviced and maintained the ship, with disgust. Such wretches! It had taken all of his resolve not to spring out of his hiding place and butcher them all like the cattle they were, but then the alarm would have been raised and the hunt begun anew. He needed to think, to devise his next move. Not gifted with the tactical acumen of the sons of Guilliman or Dorn, Skraal was a pure instrument of war, brutal and effective. Yet now he needed a stratagem and for that he required time. Survival first, then sabotage; it was his mantra.

That doctrine dissolved into the ether with the shadow. No menial this, it did not mewl or bay or weep,

it was silent. It was something else, massive footfalls resonating against metal with every step, and it was
seeking him. Skraal extracted himself from the crawl
space and bled away into the darkness, eyes on the
growing gloom he left behind him, and went onwards
into the *Furious Abyss*.

'THEY TAIL US ever doggedly, my lord,' uttered Reskiel as
he considered the reports of Navigator Esthemya
clutched in his gauntlet.

Zadkiel appeared sanguine to the fact that the *Wrathful* continued to follow them into the warp as he
regarded the scrawlings on the cell wall of one of the
ship's astropathic choir.

It was a spartan chamber with little to distinguish it.
A narrow cot served as a bed, a simple lectern as a place
to scribe. Function was paramount here.

'Wsoric is with us,' he said, emboldened enough in
the surety that they had sealed their pact with the
ancient creature to speak his name, 'and once he reveals
his presence, the pawns of the False Emperor will learn
the folly of their pursuit. The horrors endured thus far
will be as nothing compared to the torture he will visit
upon them.'

'Yes, my lord,' Reskiel said humbly.

'We are destined to achieve our mission, Reskiel,' Zadkiel went on, 'just as this one was destined to die for it.'
The admiral turned the corpse of a dead astropath over.
It was lying in the middle of the cell in a pool of its own
blood. The face was female, but twisted into a rictus of
fear and pain so pronounced that it was hard to tell.
Black, empty orbs stared out from crater-like sockets.

Communications were difficult even for those who
claimed the warp as an ally, and the messages of the

Furious's astropathic choir were proving ever more unreliable and difficult to discern. Zadkiel had some skill at divination, however, and carefully deconstructed nuances of meaning, subtle vagaries of sense and context in the symbolic renderings of the dead astropath.

'Anything?' asked Reskiel.

'Perhaps,' said Zadkiel, sensing the desperate cadence in the sergeant-commander's voice. 'Once we reach the Macragge system we will have no further need of them,' he added. 'You need not fear us floundering blind in the immaterium, Reskiel.'

'I fear nothing, lord,' Reskiel affirmed, standing straight, his expression stern.

'Of course not,' Zadkiel replied smoothly, 'except, perhaps, our intruder. Do the sons of Angron hold an inner dread for you sergeant-commander? Do you recall all too readily the sting of our erstwhile brother's wrath?'

Reskiel raised his gauntlet to the crude repairs of his face and cheekbone almost subconsciously, but then retracted it as if suddenly scalded.

'Is that the reason that our interloper still roams free aboard this ship?' Zadkiel pressed.

'He is contained,' Reskiel snarled. 'Should he surface then I will know, and mount his head upon a spike myself!'

Zadkiel traced a shape out of the dense scribblings on the wall, deliberately ignoring the sergeant-commander's impassioned outburst.

'Here,' he hissed, finding the meaning he sought at last.

The astropath had written the message in her vital fluids, the parchment pages of her symbol log overloaded with further crimson data and strewn about the cell floor like bloodied leaves.

'The crown is Colchis,' said Zadkiel, indicating a smeared icon. 'These ancillary marks indicate that this dictate comes from a lord of the Legion,' he added, a sweep of his gauntleted hand encompassing a range of symbols that Reskiel could not fathom.

Astropaths rarely had the luxury of communicating by words or phrases. Instead, they had an extensive catalogue of symbols, which were a lot easier to transmit psychically. Each symbol had a meaning, which became increasingly complex the more symbols were added. The Word Bearers fleet had their own code, in which the crown was modelled after the Crown of Colchis and represented both the Legion's home world and the leadership of the Legion.

'Two eyes, one blinded,' continued Zadkiel. 'That is Kor Phaeron's Chapter.'

'He asks something of us?' asked Reskiel.

Zadkiel picked out another symbol from the miasma, most of which was eidetic doggerel coming out in a rush of mindless images and non-sequitous ravings, a coiled snake: the abstract geometrical code for the Calth system.

'His scouts have confirmed that the Ultramarines are mustering at Calth,' Zadkiel answered, 'all of them. There are but a few token honour guards not present.'

'Then we will strike them out with a single blow,' stated the sergeant-commander confidently.

'As it is written, my brother,' Zadkiel replied, looking up from the scrawlings and offering a mirthless smile. He finished examining the astropath's message and brushed the flakes of dried blood from his gauntlets.

'All is in readiness,' he said to himself, imaging the glory of their triumph and the plaudits he, Zadkiel, would garner. 'Thy Word be done.'

* * *

CESTUS FILLED HIS time with training regimens and meditation, in part to occupy his mind whilst the *Wrathful* traversed the warp, but also to recondition his body after the brutal duel with Brynngar.

Something had possessed the Space Wolf during the fight, Cestus had felt it in every blow and heard it in the Wolf Guard's battle cries. It was not a change in the sense that the warp predators took on the form of the *Fireblade*'s crew. No, it was something less ephemeral and more intrinsic than that, as if a part of the gene-code that made up the zygotic structure of Leman Russ's Legion had been exposed somehow and allowed free rein.

Base savagery, that was how Cestus thought of it, an animalistic predilection let slip only in the face of the Space Wolves' foes. Was the warp the cause of this loosening of resolve? Cestus felt its presence constantly. It was clear that the crew did also, though they appeared to be more acutely afflicted. Armsmen patrols had doubled over the passing weeks. Rotations of those patrols had also increased and prolonged exposure to the warp even whilst in the protective bubble of the *Wrathful*'s integrity fields took its toll.

There had been seventeen warp-related deaths after the attack on the lance decks, the entirety of which had been fusion-sealed in the wake of the horrors perpetrated there. Damage sustained whilst in battle against the Word Bearers' ship had rendered the weapon systems inoperable in any case, and no one on the *Wrathful* had any desire to tread those bloody halls again. Suicides and apparent accidents were common, one rating was even murdered, the perpetrator still at large, as the products of warp-induced psychosis made their presence felt.

Of the *Furious Abyss*, there had been little sign. It continued to plough through the empyrean, content to let the *Wrathful* follow. Cestus didn't like the calm; trouble invariably followed it.

A stinging blow caught the Ultramarine captain on the side of the temple and he grimaced in pain.

'You seem preoccupied, my lord,' said Saphrax, standing opposite him in a fighting posture. He twirled the duelling staff in his hands with expert precision as he circled his captain.

The two Astartes faced each other in one of the vessel's gymnasia, wearing breeches and loose-fitting vests as they conducted the daily ritual of their training katas. Routine dictated the duelling staff as the weapon of choice for this session.

Cestus's body was already bruised and numb from a dozen or more precise blows landed by his banner bearer. Saphrax was right; his mind was elsewhere, still in the duelling pit facing off against Brynngar.

'Perhaps, we should switch to the rudius?' Saphrax offered, indicating a pair of short wooden swords clutched by a weapons servitor, two amongst many training weapons held by the creature's rack-like frontal carapace.

Cestus shook his head, giving the battle-sign that he had had enough.

'That will suffice for today,' he said, lowering the staff and reaching for a towel offered by a Legion serf to wipe down his naked arms and neck.

'I don't like this, Saphrax,' he confessed, handing the duelling weapon back to the servitor as it approached.

'The training schema was not satisfactory?' the banner bearer asked, unlike Antiges, unable to penetrate the deeper meaning of his captain's words.

'No, my brother. It is this quietude that vexes me. We have seen little in the way of deterrent from the *Furious Abyss* for almost two weeks, or at least as close to two weeks as I can fathom in this wretched empyrean.'

'Is that not a boon rather than a cause of vexation?' Saphrax asked, commencing a series of stretching exercises to loosen his muscles after the bout.

'No, I do not think so. Macragge draws ever closer and yet we seem ever further from finding a way to stop the Word Bearers. We do not even know of their plan, damn Mhotep in his coma state.' Cestus stopped what he was doing and looked Saphrax in the eye. 'I am losing hope, brother. Part of me believes the reason they have ceased in their attempts to destroy us is because they do not need to, that we no longer pose a significant threat to their mission, if we ever did.'

'Put your belief in the strength of the Emperor, captain. Trust in that and we shall prevail,' said the banner bearer vehemently.

Cestus sighed deeply, feeling a great weight upon his shoulders.

'You are right,' said the Ultramarine captain. Saphrax might not possess the instinct and empathy of Antiges, but his dour pragmatism was an unshakeable rock in a sea of doubt. 'Thank you, Saphrax,' he added, clapping his hand on the banner bearer's shoulder while nodded in response.

Cestus wrenched off the vest, sodden with his sweat, and donned a set of robes as he padded across the gymnasium to the antechamber, where Legion serf armourers awaited him.

'If you do not need me further, captain, I shall continue my daily regimen in your absence,' said the banner bearer.

'Very well, Saphrax,' Cestus replied, his thoughts still clouded. 'There is someone else I need to see,' he added in a murmur to himself.

BRYNNGAR SLUMPED FORLORNLY onto his rump in the quarters set aside for him by Admiral Kaminska. He was alone, surrounded by a host of empty ale barrels, his Blood Claws isolated to the barracks, and belched raucously. He had come here after losing the honour duel, speaking to no one and entertaining no remarks, however placatory, from his fellow Space Wolves. The old wolf's demeanour made it clear that he wished to be alone. Not everyone got the message.

Brynngar looked up from his dour brooding when he saw Cestus enter the gloomy chamber.

'Wulfsmeade is all gone,' he slurred, impossibly drunk despite the co-action of the Space Wolf's preomnor and oolitic kidney. The beverage, native to Fenris, was brewed with the very purpose of granting intoxication that overrode even the processes of the Astartes' gene-enhanced physiognomy, albeit temporarily.

'You keep it, my friend,' Cestus replied with mock geniality, despite his apprehension.

Brynngar grunted, kicking over his empty tankard as he got up. The old wolf was stripped out of his armour and wore an amalgam of furs and coarse, grey robes. Charms and runic talismans clattered over his hirsute chest, the nick from the chain tooth still visible, though all but healed.

'You seem well recovered, Ultramarine,' grumbled the Wolf Guard, irascibly. Brynngar's belligerence had not dimmed with the passage of hours in the warp.

In truth, Cestus still felt the ache in his jaw and stomach in spite of the larraman cells in his body speeding up the healing process exponentially. The Ultramarine merely nodded, unwilling to disclose his discomfort.

'Now it is done,' he said. 'You are an honourable warrior, Brynngar. What's more, you are my friend. I know you will abide by the outcome of the duel.'

The Space Wolf fixed his good eye on him, pausing as he hunted around for more ale to quaff. He snarled, and for a moment Cestus thought he might instigate another fight, but then relaxed and let out a rasping sigh.

'Aye, I'll abide by it, but I warn you, Lysimachus Cestus, I will hold no truck with warp-dabblers. Keep him away from me or I will visit my blade upon his sorcerer's tongue,' he promised, drawing closer, the rustle of his beard hair the only clue that the Space Wolf's lips were actually moving. 'If you stand in my way again, it will be no honour duel that decides his fate.'

Cestus paused for a moment, matching Brynngar's intensity with a stern expression.

'Very well,' the Ultramarine replied, and then added, 'I need you in this fight, Brynngar. I need the strength of your arm and the steel of your courage.'

The old wolf sniffed in mild contempt.

'But not my counsel, eh?'

Cestus was about to counter when Brynngar continued.

'You'll have my arm, and my courage, right enough,' he said, waving Cestus away with his clawed hand. 'Leave me, now. I'm sure there's more to drink in here somewhere.'

Cestus breathed in hard and turned away. Yes, Brynngar remained in the fight, the Ultramarine had gained that much, but he had lost something much more potent: a friend.

* * *

CESTUS DID NOT have much time to lament the ending of Brynngar's friendship as he made for the bridge. Down one of the *Wrathful's* access corridors, he received a vox transmission that crackled in the receiver node on his gorget.

'Captain Cestus,' said Admiral Kaminska's voice.

'Speak admiral, this is Cestus.'

'You are required at the isolation chambers at once,' she said.

'For what reason, admiral?' Cestus replied, betraying his annoyance at the admiral's brevity.

'Lord Mhotep is awake.'

ONCE CESTUS HAD left, Brynngar found a last barrel of Wulfsmeade and guzzled it down, foam and liquid lapping at his beard. He cared little for the revival of the Thousand Son and slumped back into melancholy, their passage through the warp affecting him more than he would admit.

A haze overtook his vision and he could smell the scent of the cold and hear the lap of Fenrisian oceans.

Brynngar wiped his eyes with the back of his hand and remembered standing atop a jagged glacier with nought but a flint knife and a loincloth to cover his dignity.

This was not a punishment, he recalled, recognising the place from his past, it was a reward. Only the toughest Fenrisian youths were considered for the test. It was called the Blooding, but so rarely did a Space Wolf speak of it that it barely needed a name at all.

Faced with the bleak white nightmare of the Fenrisian winter, Brynngar had found the bone of a long-dead ice predator and had fixed his knife to it to make a spear.

He had stalked patiently, following the short-lived tracks of the prey-beast across the ice and tundra.

When he had killed it, it had put up a mighty fight, because even the most docile of Fenrisian creatures were angry monsters. After consuming its flesh, he had skinned it, and worn the skin as a cloak as if part of the beast's essence lived on within him. Without its fur and flesh, he would have died during the first night. He had then sharpened its bones into more blades, in case he lost his knife. He wove a line from its tendons and made a hook from a tiny bone in its inner ear, using it to pull fish from the sea. He split its jawbone in two and carried it as a club.

Brynngar trekked his way back towards the Fang, using faint glimpses of the winter sun to show him the way as he descended the glacier. Upon a rugged place of razor shards, the ice collapsed to pitch him into a sickle-tooth den. He fought his way free of the scaly predators with his jawbone club. Onwards he pressed, and a frost lynx ambushed him, but he wrestled the writhing feline to the ground and bit out its throat, saturating himself in gore. The journey was long. He had killed a skyblade hawk with a thrown bone knife. He had scaled mountains.

When, finally, he saw the gates of the Fang ahead, Brynngar understood the lesson that the Blooding was supposed to teach him. It was not about survival, or fighting, or even the determination required of an Astartes. Any prospective Space Wolf who made it to the Blooding had already shown that he had those skills and qualities. The Blooding's message was far harder to learn.

'We are all alone,' Brynngar muttered, having drained the last of the Wulfsmeade.

Briefly, his mind wandered back to the Blooding. He remembered that an enormous, shaggy, black wolf had appeared on a crag overlooking the path he was to take. It had watched him for a long time, and he had known that it was a wulfen: the half-mythical predators said to be born from the earth of Fenris to winnow out the weak. The wulfen had not approached him, but Brynngar had felt its eyes watching him for days on end. He wondered if the creature's gaze had ever left him.

The same wulfen was now sitting before him, regarding Brynngar with its black eyes. The Wolf Guard returned its gaze and saw his face mirrored in the beast's pupils.

'You're alone,' he said. 'We're pack animals all of us, but that's just... that's just on the surface. We cling to the pack because if we did not there would be no Legion. We are alone, all of us. There might as well be no one else on this bloody ship.'

The Wulfen did not reply.

'Just you and me,' said Brynngar, huskily.

The Wulfen shook itself, like a dog drying its fur. It growled powerfully and stood up on all fours. It was the size of a horse, its head level with the Space Wolf's.

The Wulfen bowed down and picked something up off the floor with its jaws. With a flick of its head he threw it at Brynngar's feet.

It was a bolt pistol. The grip was plated with shards of the bone knife that Brynngar had been carrying when he arrived at the Fang after his Blooding. His fishhook hung from the butt of the gun on a thong made from animal tendon. Skyblade talons and frost lynx teeth decorated the body of the weapon in an intricate mosaic depicting a black wolf against the whiteness of a Fenrisian winter.

'Ah,' said the Wolf Guard, picking the weapon up, 'that's where it got to.'

FATE WAS A lattice of interconnecting strands of potential realities and possible futures. Eventualities flowed in bifurcating lines and paradoxes. Destiny was unfixed, existing purely as a series of outcomes, and even the most infinitesimal action had consequence and resonance.

Mhotep regarded the myriad strands of fate in his mind. Focusing on the silence and solace of the isolation chamber, visions sprang unbidden to his mind. Glorious mountains of power rose up before him. Galaxies boiled away in the distance, points of burning light on an endless silver sky. Infinite layers of reality fell, each one teeming with life. Mhotep's concepts of history and humanity saw endless cities springing up like grass and withering away again to be replaced by spires greater than those on Prospero. Mhotep's memories flared up against the sky and became whole worlds.

Subsumed completely within the meditative trance state, he saw the magnificence of the Emperor's Palace, its golden walls resplendent against the Terran sun. He saw the finery and gilded glory torn down, artistry and mosaic replaced by gunmetal steel. The palace became a fortress, cannons like black fingers pointing towards an enemy burning from the sky above. Driven earth and waves of blood tarnished its glory. Brother fought brother in their Legions and changeling beasts loped out of the dark at the behest of fell masters.

War machines soared, their titanic presence blotting out the smoke-scarred sun. Thunder boomed and lightning split the blood-drenched sky as their weapons spoke. Laughter peeled across the heavens and the

Emperor of Mankind looked skyward where shadows blackened the crimson horizon. Light, so bright that it burned Mhotep's irises, flared like the luminance of an exploding star. When he looked back, the battlefield was gone, the Emperor was gone. There was only the isolation chamber and the escaping resonance of purpose drifting out of Mhotep's consciousness.

'Greetings Cestus,' he said, noting the Ultramarine's presence in the room as he shrouded the disorientation and discomfort he felt after leaving the fate-trance.

'It is good to have you back with us, brother,' said Cestus, who had lingered at the threshold, but now stepped fully into the chamber to stand in front of his fellow Astartes.

Mhotep turned to face the Ultramarine and gave a shallow bow.

'I see you still do not see fit to offer better accommodations.'

Prior to the Thousand Son's revival, Cestus had ordered that as soon as he awoke and his vital signs were confirmed, Mhotep should be taken at once to the isolation chamber. There existed no doubt of his abilities. It meant that he had defied the edicts of Nikea, and it meant that he had a connection to the warp. Whether it was one he could exploit or would need to sever, Cestus did not yet know.

'You come to learn of what I gleaned from Brother Ultis,' Mhotep stated, content to guide the conversation.

The Ultramarine found his prescience unnerving.

'Don't worry, Cestus, I am not probing your mind,' added the Thousand Son, sensing his fellow Astartes' unease. 'What other possible reason could there be for you to have been summoned to my presence so urgently?'

'Ultis: that is his name?'

'Indeed,' Mhotep answered, parting the robes he wore to sit upon the bunk in the chamber. The Astartes armour had been removed during his time in the medibay. There it lay still, with the rest of the Thousand Son's accoutrements. Cestus noted, however, that Mhotep still wore the scarab earring, glinting in the depths of his cowl from the ambient light in the room, and remained hooded throughout the exchange.

'What else did you learn? What do the Word Bearers plan to do?'

'Formaska is where it begins,' Mhotep answered simply.

Cestus made an incredulous face.

'The second moon of Macragge. It's a barren rock. There is nothing there.'

'On the contrary, Ultramarine,' countered Mhotep, lowering his head. 'Everything is on Formaska.'

'I don't understand,' said Cestus.

Mhotep lifted his head. His eyes were alight with crimson flame. 'Then let me show you,' he said as Cestus recoiled, lunging forward to thrust his open palm against the Ultramarine's head.

FIFTEEN

Desecration/Communion/Visions of death

SKRAAL SURGED THROUGH the dark and the heat, rising now, exploiting conduits and pipes and using any means he could to secrete his ascent up the decks of the *Furious Abyss*. Finally he arrived, incredulously, at the place where weeks before he had fled, leaving Antiges to his death. He had returned to the temple.

Skraal found that Antiges remained, too.

Dismembered in his armour, the dark blue of the ceramite almost hidden by the red sheen of blood, the World Eater could only tell it was Antiges by his Chapter symbols. Little more than a collection of body parts existed now. What lay before him on a pall, attended by silent acolytes could barely be considered a corpse. Antiges's head was missing.

Skraal had heard of the inhabitants of feral worlds who dismembered their foes or sacrificed humans to their heathen gods. The World Eaters had their own warrior traditions, most of them bloody, but nothing to compare to the religious mutilation he had seen among the savages. To see Astartes, especially the self-righteously sophisticated Word Bearers, doing thus, shocked Skraal as much as the moment that the *Furious Abyss* had turned on the Imperial fleet.

The galaxy was changing very quickly. The words of Zadkiel, spoken so many days ago in the gallery, echoed back at him.

The World Eater shrank deeper into the shadows as he saw Astartes entering the chamber. One, the warrior he had fought earlier in the temple during his escape, he recognised. It was not with a little satisfaction that he saw the metal artifice attached to the Word Bearer's face where Skraal had broken his jaw and shattered his cheekbone.

A darkly-armoured chaplain accompanied the warrior, Reskiel. One of the demagogues of the Legion, the chaplain wore a skull-faced battle helm with conjoined rebreather apparatus worked into the gorget and carried a crozius, the icon of his office.

Silently, Reskiel gave the acolytes orders. As if understanding on some instinctive level, they bowed curtly and proceeded to lift what was left of Antiges on a steel pall. Together, they raised him up onto their shoulders and, led by the chaplain, left the room.

Reskiel lingered in their wake, probing the shadows and, for a brief moment, Skraal thought he was discovered, but the Word Bearer turned eventually and followed the macabre procession.

Loosening the grip on his chainaxe, the World Eater went after them.

Tailing the enemy at a discrete distance, Skraal was led down a pathway lined with statues that flowed towards what he assumed was the prow of the ship. He had previously steered clear of the vessel's forward sections, preferring to hide himself in the industrial tangle of the stern-ward engine decks, but a greater understanding of his enemy was worth the risk. Continuing his pursuit, the World Eater found himself in darkness, lit only by candles mounted in alcoves.

Watching intently, Skraal witnessed the pallbearers saying a prayer at a set of blast doors – the exact words were indiscernible, but their reverence was obvious – before continuing into a dim chamber beyond.

Using the shadows like a concealing cloak, Skraal moved into the room. As he got further inside, he realised that it was an anatomy theatre. A surgeon's slab dominated the centre of the room, surrounded by circular tiers of seating, though they were not occupied. Whatever ritual or experiment was to be performed here was a clandestine one.

The chaplain, the vestments he wore across his armour fringed with black trim, beckoned the acolytes forward.

The debased creatures, hunch-backed and robed, slunk to the table as one. Sibilant emanations pierced the silence softly as they took the disparate sections of Antiges's corpse and laid them out on the slab. Obscene and profane, the gorge in Skraal's throat rose and his anger swelled at the sight of the act. Taken apart like that: it was as if Antiges was no more than a machine to be stripped down or meat cleaved at the butcher's block.

Coldness smothered the anger and bile within Skraal, as if his blood had been drained away and replaced with ice. It was as if a film of dirt overlaid him, and choked him all at once.

Skraal had done terrible things. At the Sack of Scholamgrad and the burning of the Ethellion Fleet,

innocents had died. Even at Bakka Triumveron, he
had killed in cold blood for the sake of slaking his
thirst for carnage, but this was different. It was calcu-
lated and precise, the systematic and ritual
dismemberment of another Astartes so invasive, so
fundamentally destructive that his essence was forever
lost. There would be no honours for him, no clean
death on the field of battle as it should be for all warriors; there was dignity in that. No, this was an
aberration, soulless and terrible. To think of a fellow
Astartes being so shamed and by one of his battle-
brothers... it took all of Skraal's resolve not to wade in
and kill them all for such defilement.

Stepping forward, the chaplain approached the table,
the acolytes retreating obsequiously as he picked up
one of Antiges's arms to inspect it.

'There is no head?' he asked, setting the limb back
down as he turned to his fellow Word Bearer.

'Wsoric required it,' replied Reskiel.

'I see, and now our omniscient lord would have us
yoke this body for further favours of the warp.' There
was an almost contemptuous tone to the chaplain's
words.

'You speak out of turn, Ikthalon,' Reskiel snapped.
'You would do well to remember who is master aboard
this ship.'

'Be still, sycophant.' The chaplain, Ikthalon, fashioned his retort into a snarl. 'Your allegiance is well
known to all, as is your ambition.'

Reskiel moved to respond, but was cut off.

'Hold your tongue! Think on the fate of those left at
Bakka Triumveron. Think of Ultis before you speak of
whom is master. In this place,' he said, spreading his
arms to encompass the macabre surgery, 'you supplicate

yourself to me. Zadkiel's wizened astropath has had his
turn and sealed the pact with Wsoric, now I will divine
what I can from what remains. Speak no further. I have
need to concentrate, and you try my patience, Reskiel.'

The other Word Bearer, cowed by the tirade, retreated
back into the shadows to let the chaplain work.

Skraal kept watching with abhorred satisfaction, but
was intrigued by the obvious dissension within the
Word Bearers' ranks.

'Warrior's hands,' said Ikthalon, gauntleted fingers
tracing Antiges's palm as he resumed his morbid exam-
ination, 'strong and instinctive, but I will need more.'
The chaplain gestured at the former Ultramarine's torso.
'Open it.'

One of the acolytes took a las-cutter from beneath the
slab and sheared through the front of Antiges's breastplate. The gilded decoration split off from the ceramite
and clattered to the floor. The Word Bearers ignored it.
Once the acolyte with the cutter retreated, Ikthalon
inserted his fingers into the cut. With a grunt of effort,
he forced the Ultramarine's chest open.

The complex mass of an Astartes's organs was
exposed. Skraal could make out the two hearts and
third lung, together with the reverse of the bony breastplate that fused from every Astartes's ribs.

The chaplain dug a hand into the gory dark and
extracted an organ. It looked like the oolitic kidney, or
perhaps the omophagaea. Ikthalon regarded it coolly,
putting the organ down and yanking out a handful of
entrails. He cast them across the slab, and stood for a
long time peering into the loops of tissue and sprays of
blood.

'Macragge suspects nothing,' he hissed, discerning
meaning from the act. Running a finger through the

bloody miasma, he added. 'Here, that's our route. It lies open to us.'

'What of Calth?' Reskiel asked from the darkness.

'That is unclear,' Ikthalon replied. 'Kor Phaeron has no obstacles, save any he makes for himself.' The chaplain peered into Antiges's open chest again. 'There is veining on the third lung. Guilliman is represented there as just a man. Not a primarch, just a man ignorant of his fate.' Ikthalon's voice dripped with malice.

The chaplain looked further, his gaze lingering for a moment on one of Antiges's hearts before his head snapped up quickly.

'We are not alone,' he snarled.

Reskiel's bolter swung up in readiness and he barked into the transponder in his gorget.

'In the anatomy theatre, now!'

A troop of four Word Bearers barged into the room, weapons drawn.

'Spread out,' Reskiel bellowed. 'Find him!'

Skraal backed out of the chamber. He forged back the way he had come and split off from the candlelit path, kicking open a maintenance hatch and dropping into a tangle of wiring and circuitry. He stormed ahead, relying on the ship to hide him for a little longer. He wanted to feel rage, and be comforted by it, but he couldn't reach it. He felt numb.

VISIONS RACED INTO Cestus's mind as he felt all of tangible reality fall away around him. At once, he was suspended in the depths of real space. Formaska rolled beneath, its laborious orbit somehow visible. Silvered torpedoes struck suddenly against its surface at strategic points across the moon. Miniature detonations were discernible as a slow shockwave resonated over it in ripples of destructive force. Cestus saw tiny fractures in the outer crust, magnifying with each passing second into massive fissures that yawned like jagged mouths. Formaska glowed and pulsed as if it were a throbbing heart giving out its last, inexorable beat. The moon exploded.

Debris cascaded outwards in shuddering waves, miniscule asteroids burning up in the atmosphere of nearby Macragge. A fleet suspended in the planet's upper atmosphere was destroyed. Impossibly, Cestus heard the screams of his home world's inhabitants below as the detritus of Formaska's death rained upon them in super-heated waves of rock.

Something moved in the debris field, shielded from the thundering defence lasers of Macragge's surface. Getting ever closer, the dark shape breached the planet's atmosphere. The vision shifted to the industrial hive of the cities. A cloud of gas boiled along the streets, engulfing the screaming populous.

The image changed again, depicting other ships, great vessels of the Crusade, held in orbit at Calth hit by an errant meteor storm. Cestus watched in horror as they broke up against the onslaught, the stylised 'U' of his Legion immolated in flame. The meteor shower struck Calth, forcing its way through the planet's atmosphere to where his battle-brothers mustered below. Cestus roared in anguish, furious at his impotence, screaming a desperate warning that his brothers and his primarch would never hear.

The scene changed once more as the void of real space became metal. As if propelled at subsonic speed, Cestus flew through the tunnels and chambers of a ship. Through conducts, across heaving generators, beyond the fire of immense plasma-driven engines, he came at last to an ordnance deck. There, sitting innocuously amongst the other munitions, was a lethal payload. Though he could not explain how, he knew it at once to be a viral torpedo and the effective death warrant of Macragge.

World killer.

The words resolved themselves in the Ultramarine's mind, taunting him, goading him.

Cestus railed against the sense of doom, the fathomless despair they evoked. He bellowed loud and hard, the only name he could think of to repel it.

'Guilliman!'

Cestus was back in the isolation chamber. He saw Mhotep sitting across from him. The Thousand Son's face was haggard and covered in a sheen of sweat.

Cestus staggered backwards as recall returned, wrenching his bolt pistol from its holster with difficultly and pointing it waveringly at Mhotep.

'What did you do to me,' he hissed, shaking his head in an effort to banish the lingering images and sensations.

'I showed you the truth,' Mhotep gasped, breathing raggedly as he propped himself up against the wall of the cell, 'by sharing my memories, the memories of Ultis, with you. It is no different to the omophagea, though the absorption of memory is conducted psychically and not biologically,' he pleaded.

Cestus kept his aim on the Thousand Son.

'Was it real?' he asked. 'What I witnessed, was it real?' he demanded, stowing the bolt pistol in favour of grabbing Mhotep by the throat.

'Yes,' the Thousand Son spat through choking breaths.

Cestus held him there for a moment longer, thinking that he might crush the life out of the fellow Astartes.

Exhaling deeply, Cestus let Mhotep go. The Thousand Son doubled over coughing as he gasped for breath and rubbed his throat.

'They do not plan to attack Calth, or destroy Macragge. They want to conquer them both and bring the Legion to heel or vanquish it if it does not yield,' said Cestus, his thoughts and fears coming out in a flood.

Mhotep looked up at the frantic Ultramarine, and nodded.

'And the destruction of Formaska is where it will begin.'

'The ship,' Cestus ventured, beginning to calm down. 'That was the *Furious Abyss*, wasn't it? And the viral payload is the method of extermination for the people of Macragge.'

'You have seen what I saw, and what Ultis knew,' Mhotep confirmed, regaining his composure and sitting up.

Cestus's gaze was distant as he struggled to process everything he'd learned, together with resisting the urge to vomit against the invasive psychic experience. He looked back at Mhotep, a suspicious cast to his eyes and face.

'Why are you here, Mhotep? I mean, why are you really here?'

The Thousand Son gazed back for a moment and then withdrew his hood and sighed deeply.

'I have seen the lines of fate, Ultramarine. I knew long before we made contact with the *Furious Abyss*, back when we were on Vangelis, that my destiny lay with this ship, that this mission, *your* mission, was important.

'My Legion is cursed with psychic mutation, but my lord Magnus taught us to harness it, to commune with

the warp and fashion that communion into true power.'
Mhotep ignored the growing revulsion in Cestus's face
as he spoke of the empyrean, and went on. 'Nikea was
no council, Ultramarine. It was a trial, not only of my
lord Magnus but of the entire Thousand Sons Legion.
The Emperor's edict wounded him, like a father's disap-
proval and chastisement would wound any child.

'What I told you at Vangelis, that I sought to improve
the reputation of my Legion, in the eyes of the sons of
Guilliman if no other, was in part true. I desire only to
open your eyes to the potential of the psychic and how
it is a boon, a ready weapon to use against our enemies.'

Cestus's expression was stern in the face of Mhotep's
impassioned arguments.

'You saved us all in the lance deck,' said the Ultramarine. 'You probably did the same when we fought what
became of the *Fireblade*. But, your ambition overreaches
you, Mhotep. I have stayed Brynngar's hand, but from
this point on you will remain here in isolation. If we are
successful and can reach Macragge or some other Imperial stronghold, you will face trial and there, your fate
will be decided.'

Cestus got to his feet and turned. As he was about to
leave the room, he paused.

'If you ever invade my mind like that again, I will execute you myself,' he added and left, the cell door sliding
shut behind him.

'How narrow your mind is,' Mhotep hissed, focusing
at once on the reflective sheen of the cell wall. 'How
ignorant you are of what is to come.'

SIXTEEN

Fleet/Kor Phaeron/A storm breaks

'That,' said Orcadus, 'is Macragge.'

The Navigator had received instructions from his admiral that whilst they were still in the warp he should make regular reports of their progress. The appearance of the Ultramarines' home world, albeit through the misted lens of the empyrean, was worthy of note and so he had summoned her.

The observation blister was a chamber on the same deck of the *Wrathful* as the bridge and within walking distance. The room was usually reserved for formal gatherings, when officers came together to formalise some business within the Saturnine Fleet. Its grand transparent dome afforded a view of space that lent gravitas to the matters at hand. In the warp, of course, it was strictly off-limits and its eye was kept permanently closed.

The eye was open, but the dome was masked with heavy filters that kept all but the most mundane wavelengths of light out of the blister.

Admiral Kaminska faced away from the Navigator and actually followed Orcadus's gaze through a mirror screen that offered a hazy representation of what he was seeing. To look at the warp, even filtered as it was, would be incredibly dangerous for her.

'If you could see it as I can,' Orcadus hissed, allowing a reverent tone to colour his voice. 'What wonders there are out in the void. There is beauty in the galaxy, for those who can but see it.'

'I'm happy staying blind,' said Kaminska. The view through the filters and reflected by the mirror screen was heavily distorted, but she could make out a crescent-shaped mass of light hanging over the ship. Though she had no frame of reference, she had an impression of enormous distance.

'Macragge,' muttered Orcadus. 'See how it glows, the brightest constellation in this depth of the abyss? All those hard-working souls toiling at its surface; their combined life-spark is refulgent to my eyes. Ultramar is the most heavily populated system in the whole segmentum and the minds of its citizens are bright and full of hope. That is what I mean by beauty. It is a beacon, one that shines amidst the malice and bleakness of the empyrean tide.'

Kaminska continued to regard the dim mirror image of the warp through the minute aperture offered by the filters. Old space-farers' tales were full of the effects the naked warp could have on a human mind. Madness was the most merciful fate, they said: mutation, excruciating spontaneous cancers and even possession by some malfeasant presence all featured prominently. Kaminska felt a flicker of vulnerability, and was glad that only the Navigator was there with her.

'Is this why you summoned me?' she asked, having little time or inclination for a philosophical debate concerning the immaterium. Her mind was on other matters, namely the sudden revival of Mhotep and Cestus's meeting with the Thousand Son. She hoped it would yield some good news.

'No,' Orcadus answered simply, puncturing the admiral's introspection, and pointing to a different region of the warp. It was a dim mass of glowing bluffs, like the top of endless cliffs reaching down into blackness. Above the cliffs was a streak of red.

'I am not well-versed in reading the empyrean tides, Navigator,' she snapped, weary of Orcadus's eccentricities, which were ubiquitous amongst all the great Navigator houses. 'What am I looking at?'

'Formations like these cliffs are common enough in the abyss,' he explained, oblivious to Kaminska's impatience. 'I am steering us well clear of them, and I am certain that our quarry has taken the same route. The formation above them, however, is rather more troubling.'

'Another world, perhaps?' ventured Kaminska. 'There's plenty of new settlement out here near the fringe.'

'I suspected that, but it is not a planet. I believe it is another ship.'

'A second vessel?'

'No. I think it is a fleet.'

'Are they following us?' asked Kaminska, a knot of dread building in her stomach.

'I cannot tell. Distance is relative down here,' the Navigator admitted.

'Could it be the Ultramarines? Their Legion was heading for Calth.'

'It is possible. Calth could be its destination, I suppose.'

'If not, then what is the alternative, Navigator?' Kaminska didn't like where this was going as the knot in her stomach became a fist.

'It could be another Legion fleet,' said Orcadus, leaving the implication hanging.

'You mean more Word Bearers.'

'Yes,' the Navigator confirmed after a moment's pause.

LORD KOR PHAERON of the Word Bearers scowled. 'He's behind schedule,' he said. Aboard the *Infidus Imperator* he and his warriors made their inexorable course towards Ultramar, the great flagship leading the dread fleet of battleships, cruisers, escorts and frigates towards their destiny.

The arch commander of the Legion, favoured of Lorgar, was immense in his panoply of war. Seated upon a throne of black iron, he towered like an all-powerful tyrant, the surveyor of all his deadly works. Votive chains, festooned with tiny silver skulls, and icons of dedication, arched from his shoulder pads to his cuirass. A spiked halo of iron arced across his mighty shoulders, fixed to his armoured backpack. The stout metal gorget fixed around his neck was forged into a high and imperious collar that bore the symbol of the Legion. The tenets of it were etched ostensibly across every surface of Kor Phaeron's armour in the epistles of Lorgar. Parchments unfurled like ragged, script-ridden pennants from studded pauldrons; seals and scraps of vellum covered his leg greaves like patchwork.

In the eyes of the arch-commander there burned a relentless fervour that flowed outwards and ignited the room. It was almost as if any who fell beneath his glowering gaze would be immolated in righteous fire should they be found wanting. His voice was dominance and zeal, his Word the dictate of the primarch. This would be his finest hour, as it was written.

Six Chapter Masters of the Word Bearers stood behind Kor Phaeron, each resplendent in their respective panoplies. They still managed to fill the immense council chamber of the *Infidus Imperator* with their presence. Above them curved a great domed roof hung with smoking censers. The floor was a giant viewscreen, showing a stellar map of the space surrounding Ultramar.

'Our most recent reports indicate that Zadkiel was being followed,' said Faerskarel, Master of the Chapter of the Opening Eye. 'It is possible that he is just showing caution.'

'He has the *Furious Abyss*!' roared Kor Phaeron. 'He should have been able to see off anything that stood in his way. Zadkiel had better know the consequences for us all if we fail.'

Deinos, Master of the Burning Hand Chapter, stepped forwards. 'Lorgar shows Admiral Zadkiel all honour,' he said. In keeping with the name of his Chapter, Deinos's gauntlets were permanently wreathed in flames from gas jets built into his vambraces. 'It was written that we will succeed.'

'Not,' said Kor Phaeron, measuredly, 'that we will do so without great loss. Calth will fall and the Ultramarines with it, that is already decided, but there is plenty of scope for our Legion to lose a great many brothers, and we certainly shall if Zadkiel cannot fulfil his mission.'

'My lord, surely Zadkiel makes his own fate? We should be minded only with the progress of our own fleet.' It was Rukis, the Master of the Crimson Mask Chapter, who spoke. The faceplate of his helmet was wrought to resemble a fearsome red-skinned snarling creature.

'I will not allow our brother to fail us,' hissed Kor Phaeron, intent on the stellar map and the alleged progress of the *Furious Abyss*. 'I had not wanted to use my hand in this matter, but it seems that circumstances allow no other recourse. Much is written of Zadkiel's success and its bearing upon our own. To prosecute the war on Calth, we must risk nothing. Is that understood?'

The Chapter Masters' silence constituted their agreement. Skolinthos, Master of the Ebony Serpent Chapter, broke the quietude once his assent and that of his brothers was clear. Skolinthos's oesophagus had been crushed in the early years of the Great Crusade when it was the Emperor whom the Word Bearers vaunted above all others. His voice crackled sibilantly through a vocal synthesiser on his chest, the honorific of his Chapter somehow perversely apt given his affliction. 'Then how might we assist the admiral?'

'There are still words newly written,' said Kor Phaeron, 'that you do not know of. They concern the warp through which we travel. We can reach Zadkiel even though the *Furious Abyss* lies many days ahead of us. Master Tenaebron?'

Chapter Master Tenaebron bowed in supplication behind his lord. The Chapter of the Void was probably the least respected among the Word Bearers Legion for it was by far the smallest, with less than seven hundred Astartes. There was little glory in its history, used moreover as a reserve force that enacted its missions behind the front line. This grim,

dishonourable purpose fell to the Void and
Tenaebron, their master, did not complain, for he
knew that his Chapter's true role was to create and test
new weapons and tactics for the rest of the Legion. It
had not gone unnoticed that Lorgar's most recent
orders to Tenaebron had concerned the exploitation
of the Word Bearers' psychic resources.

'I trust you will require the use of the supplicants?'
said Tenaebron.

'How many remain?' asked Kor Phaeron, votive
chains jangling as he shifted in his throne.

'One hundred and thirty, my lord,' Tenaebron replied.
'Seventy here on the *Infidus*, thirty on the *Carnomancer*
and the remainder are spread throughout the fleet. I
have ensured they are kept in a state of readiness; they
can be awakened within the hour.'

'Get them ready,' Kor Phaeron ordered. 'How many
can we afford to lose?'

'More than half would compromise the masking of
the Calth assault,' Tenaebron answered humbly.

'Then be prepared to lose them.'

'Understood, my lord. What will you have them do?'

Kor Phaeron cracked his knuckles in annoyance.
There could be no doubt that he had hoped everything
would go more smoothly than this. Zadkiel's mission
was supposedly easy. The assault on Calth would be far
more complex, with much more to go wrong. If Zadkiel
could not fulfil his written role, then the problems at
Calth would be magnified greatly.

'Give me a storm,' said the arch-commander, darkly.

TENAEBRON LED KOR Phaeron down into the supplicant
chambers of the *Infidis Imperator*. The arch-commander
had since dismissed the other masters to their respective

duties, ignoring their obvious surprise at his bold stratagem. The *Infidis Imperator* was a great and mighty flagship that almost rivalled the immensity of the *Furious Abyss*. It took some time to traverse the proving grounds and ritual chambers, the ranks of Word Bearers honing their battle-skills with bolter and blade in the arenas. Down here, upon every surface, the Word was ubiquitous. Sentences inscribed on bulkheads and support ribs, tomes penned by Lorgar on pulpits overlooking halls and seminary chapels, libraries of lore, the vessel was drenched in the primarch's wisdom and zealotry.

The ship had once been known as the *Raptorous Rex*, a vessel devoted to the Emperor, who had plucked Lorgar from Colchis and placed the Word Bearers at his command. It was a temple to another, more willing and appreciative idol now, the False Emperor of Mankind having been stricken from its corridors.

Tenaebron reached the narrow, high chamber, like a steel canyon, where the supplicants resided. Held in glass blisters on the walls, each served by a bulky life support system feeding oxygen and nutrients, the supplicants slumbered. Curled up and naked, twitching with the force of the power held in their swollen, lacerated craniums it looked like they were dreaming. Their eyes and mouths had grown shut. Some had no facial features at all, their bodies abandoning the need to breathe, eat or experience externally.

A trio of Word Bearers Librarians saluted their Chapter Master as Tenaebron examined the vital-signs on a pict screen, slaved to the individual life supports, in the centre of the room. The Librarians bowed deeply as Kor Phaeron walked in, and genuflected silently before him.

'Rise,' he intoned, and the Librarians obeyed. 'Is everything in preparation?' he asked, directing the question at the Chapter Master.

Tenaebron consulted the data on the pict screen, turned to his lord and nodded. 'Marshal the storm,' he growled. 'Let them be broken by its wrath.'

The Chapter Master nodded again, and proceeded to order his Librarians to activate the cogitators hooked up to the supplicants' blisters. Kor Phaeron left Tenaebron to his duties without further word.

Up on the walls the supplicants stirred, as if the dream had become a nightmare.

ZADKIEL ARRIVED ON the bridge as the storm broke.

The vista below him was bathed in strobing hazard lights as if lashed by lightning. Complicated symbolic maps of the warp shone on the three main viewscreens and indicated that it was in violent flux. Bridge crew, Helmsmaster Sarkorov barking orders at them, bent over their picters, faces picked out in the green glow of reams of scrolling data.

'The warp rebels!' hissed Zadkiel.

'Perhaps not,' muttered Ikthalon. The chaplain, having left Reskiel to his pursuit of their stowaway, had been summoned to the bridge and stood alongside the command throne. 'The supplicants were recently animated. It was probably a foreshadowing of the empyrean's current state of turmoil. I believe that a higher purpose is at work. Confidence, it seems, in our ability to prosecute this mission, is waning.' Ikthalon was careful to keep the barb well-hidden, but the implication at Zadkiel's ineptitude was still there.

The admiral ignored it. The warp storm, and its origin, was of greater concern to him at that moment

'Kor Phaeron?' he wondered.

'I can think of no other, save our arch lord, who would intercede on our behalf.'

Zadkiel sneered as another thought occurred to him.

'It is Tenaebron, no doubt, trying to claim for the Chapter of the Void that which belongs to the Quill.'

'He is ever ambitious,' Ikthalon agreed, keeping his voice level.

Zadkiel assumed his position on the command throne.

'It would be rude,' Zadkiel sneered, 'to deny Tenaebron his sliver of victory. It will be eclipsed utterly by our own. Helmsmaster Sarkorov,' he snapped, 'press on for Macragge. Let the warp take the *Wrathful*.'

Cestus was thrown against the wall as the *Wrathful* shuddered violently. He was heading back to the bridge in order to convene with Kaminska and the remaining Astartes when the storm wave hit. Debris was flung throughout the corridors, medi-bays were in disarray as desperate orderlies fought to hang on to the wounded, armsmen were smashed against bulkheads and ratings fell to their deaths as the *Wrathful* pitched and yawed. A terrible metallic moaning came from the engine sections as the ship fought to right itself. Cestus could feel the structure flexing and straining through the floor, as if the vessel was on the verge of snapping in two under the strain.

The Ultramarine made his way through the mayhem until he reached the bridge, blast doors opening to allow him access. The crew clung to their posts, Helmsmistress Venkmyer issuing frantic orders set against the unearthly calm of servitors running through their emergency protocols. Drenched in crimson gloom from vermillion alert status, the bridge looked bloody in the half-light.

'Navigator Orcadus, report!' snapped Kaminska, gripping the sides of her command position as the shaking *Wrathful* threatened to dethrone her.

'A storm,' Orcadus's voice said over the bridge voxcaster, the Navigator sounding strained, 'came out of nowhere.'

'Evade it,' ordered Kaminska.

'Admiral, we are already in it!' replied the Navigator.

'Damage control to your posts!' bellowed Kaminska. 'Close off the reactor sections and clear the gun decks.'

Cestus reached the admiral. 'This is the Word Bearers' doing,' he shouted against the din of warning sirens and frantic reports from the crew. Another wave slammed into the *Wrathful*. Bursting pipes vented vapour and gas. Crewmen were thrown off their feet. A viewscreen was sheared off its moorings and fell in a shower of sparks and shattered glass, landing in the middle of the bridge.

'Orcadus, can we ride it out?' asked Kaminska, her eyes on the Ultramarine.

'I see no end to it, admiral.'

'Captain Cestus?' she asked of the Astartes.

'If we drift here and ride it out, the *Furious Abyss* escapes,' Cestus confirmed. 'There is no choice left to us but to drive through it.'

Kaminska nodded grimly. If they failed it would mean the destruction of the ship and the deaths of over ten thousand crew. Her order would condemn them all to their fates.

'Engage the engines to full power!' she ordered. 'Let's break this storm's back!' she snarled with fire in her eyes. 'We'll teach the warp to fear us!'

* * *

FROM WITHIN THE confines of the isolation cell, Mhotep could hear the anarchy outside. He ignored it, poring over the reflective sheen of the polished gunmetal walls instead. A window of fate opened up to him as he channelled his powers. Panic reigned on the *Wrathful*. He saw fire, men and women burning, thousands sacrificed upon the altar of hopeful victory. They became ghosts in his mind's eye, their penitent souls devoured hungrily by the warp and scattered into atoms until only residue remained.

Death awaited on this ship: his death. The certainty of that fact instilled calm in him rather than fear. His place amongst the myriad strands of fate was fixed.

The vista changed and Mhotep's mind ranged beyond the *Wrathful* and into the churning abyss. The *Furious Abyss* loomed through the haze of resolution as a new scene presented itself. The vessel was immense, like a city laid on its side and falling towards the *Wrathful*. Thousands of gun ports opened up like mouths, the primed, glowing barrels of magna-lasers and cannon like tongues ready to roar. The *Furious Abyss* was utterly hideous, a monstrosity of dark crimson steel, and yet the beauty of its majesty overcame any aesthetic offence.

Mhotep drifted further across the gulf, through ersatz reality. As his mind expanded, he could taste the warp, the endless flavours, sounds and sensations of the abyss, calling to him. Probing tendrils pricked at his sanity and the Thousand Son attempted to disengage. He couldn't, and panic rushed into him like a flood. Mhotep mastered it quickly, recognising at once that he was in peril. The warp had seen him and it sought to drive his mind asunder.

It showed him visions of destruction, the spires of Prospero aflame and his Legion cast into the warp. In another vista, he knelt before a throne of black iron in supplication before the icon of the Word Bearers. Screams filled his ears, together with the howling of wolves.

Mhotep clawed back some semblance of control. He fashioned the image of a cyclopean eye in his mind. It glowed with scarlet radiance, and, as if following a beacon to safe harbour, Mhotep used it to guide himself away from the clutches of the empyrean. He emerged at last, drained of all will, of all strength and collapsed to the floor of the cell. The metal was cool against his cheek. Though hard and unyielding, it was the most invigorating salve he had ever felt. He had resisted, though the lines of fate had been laid open to him. Mhotep knew, as he slipped into unconsciousness, what the visions had been about. It was not a lure into madness; it was something far more sinister and invasive. It was temptation.

'THEY ARE LOST,' said Zadkiel, smiling with malice. He looked up at the centre viewscreen, showing little emotion as alarming numbers scrolled past the symbol representing the *Wrathful*. He looked more thoughtful than triumphant. 'Do we have any readings from their engines? Are they still void-worthy?'

'No readings,' Sarkorov replied. 'The storm is too strong.'

'I have seen enough,' Zadkiel said, his response was curt. 'Continue at all speed.'

'You won't wait until we are certain of the *Wrathful*'s destruction?' counselled Ikthalon, a sliver of doubt evident in his voice at Zadkiel's order.

'No, I will not,' answered the admiral. 'Our mission is to reach Macragge in time for Kor Phaeron's assault. I cannot tarry here in order to make certain of what is inevitable. We need to be out of this region and back on our way. Return to your chambers, chaplain. Have the supplicants watch for the *Wrathful*'s death throes. Even in a warp storm such as this, that many deaths should make some ripple.'

'As you wish, my lord.' Ikthalon bowed and left the bridge.

The *Furious Abyss* resumed its former heading in short order. Kor Phaeron's plan had worked in so far as they were undamaged by the storm. Whether it had also put paid to the *Wrathful* did not concern the admiral.

A petty creature might have been angry at his lord's meddling, but Zadkiel was sanguine. Let lesser minds worry on such things. The Word would play out as written. Nothing else mattered.

SEVENTEEN

Strategy/Out of the warp/Formaska in sight

CESTUS TURNED HIS head away as the warp glared against the *Wrathful*'s port side.

The force of it shone through the metal of the ship's hull, as if the *Wrathful* was made of paper, transparent against the light of the abyss. Cestus heard screams and laughter as men's minds were stripped away by it. He threw himself against the housing of a torpedo tube entrance, willing himself not to look. Saphrax and Brother Excelinor were beside him and they too averted their gaze.

Cestus had left the bridge almost as soon as he'd arrived. He'd gathered his fellow Ultramarines to patrol the corridors, knowing full well what awaited them and the crew of the *Wrathful*. Two teams of what was left of the honour guard and Brynngar's wolves moved through the decks and corridors in an effort to steel resolve, and snuff out manifesting psychosis wherever they found it.

Cestus hoped the presence of the Astartes would be enough. The need for them to be the Angels of the Emperor was greater than any other.

'It is as if the warp is at their very beck and call,' bellowed Excelinor, his voice tinny through his Corvus-pattern nose cone.

Cestus did not reply, for he knew of the terrible truth of his battle-brother's words. Moving defiantly down the corridor, the infernal light of the empyrean was scarlet through his eyelids. Silhouettes of bodies fell in the blazing vista; men and women fell to their knees, weeping and screaming; a gunshot rang out as an officer turned his sidearm on himself. The sound of a female voice was contiguous with it, reciting paragraphs from the Saturnine Fleet's rules and regulations in an effort to stave off the madness.

Visions forced their way into the Ultramarine's mind: the beneficent Emperor, mighty upon his golden throne and the majesty of the Imperial Palace, and Terra, the beacon of enlightenment in a galaxy surrounded by darkness. Then he saw it burning, continents peeling off and red gouts of magma boiling away into space.

He was an Astartes. He was stronger than this.

'Do not give in to madness,' he cried aloud to all who could still listen. 'Hold on and heed the Imperial Truth.'

For a brief moment, it looked like that the warp would engulf them, but then the visions melted away and the screaming ebbed and died. The ship was still again. The *Wrathful* had emerged on the other side.

Cestus breathed hard as the blazing light diminished, leaving a painful afterglow. He adjusted quickly and opened his eyes to see that his brothers were still with him. The shadows came back, too, swallowing the dead. The Ultramarine nodded slowly to Saphrax and

Excelinor and opened up communications through his gorget as he surveyed the carnage around him.

'Admiral, are you still with us?'

There was a pause before the vox-link crackled and Kaminska's voice replied.

'We are through the storm,' she said, similarly breathless. 'Your plan was successful.'

'Medical teams are required at my location as well as fleet morticians,' Cestus informed her.

'Very well.'

'Admiral,' Cestus added, 'as soon as recovery is underway, I request your presence in the conference chamber.'

'Of course, my lord. I shall be there momentarily. Kaminska out.'

HALF AN HOUR later, when the crews began to organise themselves into shifts to recover the bodies and the wounded, Kaminska had Helmsmistress Venkmyer tour the worst-hit sections of the ship and make a report of their losses.

In normal circumstances, Kaminska would have done this herself, demonstrating to the crew that their leader cared about the deaths and the terrible tragedy that had befallen them. More urgent matters pressed for her attention, however, and she was not about to ignore the request of an Astartes.

So, she had made her way to the conference chamber as bidden. Within, the remaining Astartes force awaited her.

'Welcome, admiral,' said Cestus, standing at the edge of the oval table with Saphrax to his right and his other battle-brothers arrayed around him. The Space Wolf, Brynngar, sat opposite with his warriors, but did not acknowledge the admiral's arrival.

'Please sit,' the Ultramarine captain said sternly, despite trying to soften his mood with a small smile.

Now the council was assembled, Cestus surveyed the room, looking into the eyes of each person present.

'It is beyond all doubt,' he began, 'that the Word Bearers are in league with the warp. They are utterly lost.'

Hardened faces returned his gaze as the Ultramarine articulated what they already knew in their hearts.

'With such dark allies at their disposal, together with the *Furious Abyss*, they are a formidable opponent,' Cestus continued, 'but we have a slim hope. I have discovered the nature of the Word Bearers' plan and how it is to be employed.'

Brynngar twitched at the remark. The Space Wolf clearly knew of the methods that the Ultramarine had used to discover the information they needed. He also knew of Mhotep's subsequent revival. The absence of the Thousand Son from the conference spoke volumes as to his demeanour on that matter.

'Make no mistake,' Cestus began, 'what the Word Bearers are planning is audacious in the extreme. In assaulting Macragge, there are several factors that any enemy must consider before committing his forces,' he explained. 'Firstly, the planetary fleet held in high orbit consists of a flotilla of several cruisers and escorts. It would not be easy for any foe, however determined or well-armed, to break through without significant losses. Should he be successful, though, the enemy must then face the static orbital deterrents on the surface: Macragge's battery of defence lasers.'

'And the *Furious Abyss* is supposed to achieve this feat?' scoffed Brynngar. 'Impossible.'

Cestus nodded in agreement.

'Had you asked me the same an hour ago I would have concurred,' the Ultramarine admitted. 'The Word Bearers strategy has two key elements. It all begins at Formaska, which the Word Bearers plan to hit with cyclonic torpedoes to destroy it.'

'I know little of Ultramar,' growled the Wolf Guard, 'but Formaska is a dead moon. Why not use their cyclonics against Macragge directly?'

'A direct assault against Macragge would be suicide. Its defence lasers would cripple their fleet before they made landfall and render any attempt to subdue Guilliman untenable,' he explained. 'The debris from Formaska's destruction will achieve their ends indirectly. The Legion will divert forces to the aid of Macragge caught in the asteroid storm of the moon's demise and the Word Bearers will strike as they are divided and take them utterly by surprise.'

'I've seen it,' said Brynngar, 'on Proxus XII. An asteroid passed too close and came apart. It was a feral planet. Those people thought the world was ending. Fire was falling from the sky. Every impact was like an atomic hit. It won't destroy Macragge, but it'll kill millions.'

'That is not all,' Cestus continued. 'The *Furious Abyss* will then use the debris like a shield, allowing them to get past the warning stations and satellites around Macragge and draw close enough for a viral payload to be effective. Only that ship is powerful enough to weather the inevitable storm of fire from the defence lasers. The death toll from the viral strike will be near-total. Guilliman and the Legion will be divided, some of our forces probably destroyed on Macragge, when the remainder of the Word Bearers' fleet will strike. I do not know whether we could recover from such a blow, should it succeed.'

'What then, is to be done?' the Wolf Guard asked gruffly.

'We are nearing Macragge and soon will be out of the warp,' said the Ultramarine, a nod from Kaminska confirming his words. 'So too are our enemies. It will require discipline, guile and timing.' Cestus paused, and looked around the room again, his gaze ended on Kaminska. 'Most of all it will require sacrifice.'

Space ruptured and spat out the *Furious Abyss*, edged hard in the diamond light of Macragge's sun.

Shoals of predators shimmered out alongside it, like sea creatures leaping around the bow of a ship. Caught in the anathema of reality, they coiled in on themselves and seethed out of existence, their psychic essence dissipating without the warp to sustain them.

The *Furious Abyss* looked little worse than it had when it had left Thule. The attack of the escort squadron had destroyed some of the gun batteries on its dorsal and ventral surfaces, and there were countless tiny pockmarks on its hull from the impacts of doomed fighter craft that had crashed into it after their crews had lost their minds. Those scars did nothing to diminish the majesty of the vast scarlet ship, however. It took a full minute to emerge from the warp rift torn before it, and in those moments the warp was full of nothing but slabs of hull plating and engine cowlings all streaming into real space.

Every warning station around Macragge instantly recognised the scale of the ship and demanded its identity. No reply was forthcoming.

The image of Macragge filled the central viewport on the bridge of the *Furious Abyss*. Flanking it were tactical readouts of the system, which were full of early warning stations and military satellites.

'There it is,' said Zadkiel. 'Hateful is it not? Like a boulder squatting in the path of the future.'

Magos Gureod stood beside Zadkiel, mechadendrites clicking like insectoid limbs, withered arms folded across his chest.

'It evokes no emotion,' the magos replied neutrally.

Zadkiel sniffed his mild contempt at the passionless Mechanicum drone.

'As a symbol, it has no equal,' he said. 'The majesty of a stagnant universe. The ignorance of the powerful. The Ultramarines could have done anything with the worlds under their dominion, and they chose to forge this tired echo of a past that never was.'

Gureod remained unmoved. He had come to bear witness to the launching of the torpedoes that would end a world, the unbridled destructive forces yielded by the mech-science of Mars's devotion to the Omnissiah. The magos was standing in the position once occupied by Baelanos, who had fallen at Bakka.

'I take it your presence means that my former assault-captain has been recovered?' Zadkiel snapped, annoyed at Gureod's unwillingness to bask in his self-perceived reflected glory.

'He dreams fitfully, my lord. When the sus-an membrane failed and he roused, somewhat unexpectedly, I was forced to take more drastic methods to secure him,' said the magos.

'See that he does not waken again until the transition is complete. Once Formaska is destroyed, we shall be joining Kor Phaeron's forces on the ground. Baelanos is to be part of that invasion force.'

'Yes, my lord.' Gureod said, showing no fear.

Zadkiel turned his attention back to the viewport.

All was in place now. He would lead the assault that would be remembered forever in history.

A few moments passed. Then the bridge vox-units crackled.

'Awaiting your mark, admiral,' said Kor Phaeron's voice, transmitted across the system from Calth. Even at these relatively short distances, only the most advanced system could allow communication between the two ships without the need for an astropath.

'It shall be forthcoming,' said Zadkiel, turning his attention to another viewscreen. 'Master Malforian,' he intoned, awaiting the grizzled countenance of his weapon master.

The nightmarish visage of the badly injured Word Bearer was forthcoming.

'At your command, my lord,' Malforian responded.

'Open the frontal torpedo apertures and load the first wave of cyclonics,' Zadkiel commanded with relish. 'It begins at Formaska. Let us unleash devastation and bring about a new era of man.'

Sarkorov snapped orders at the bridge crew, and despatched runners as the *Furious Abyss* prepared for battle stations. The navigation crew began orienting the ship towards Formaska, its prow arc aimed like a sniper's sight on his kill.

The moon was on the screen. Deep lava-filled gulleys wormed their way across its continents, broken by boiling seas.

'The primitives of ancient Macragge thought Formaska was the eye of a god, and that it was bloodshot with anger,' Zadkiel said, to himself more than the unappreciative Magos. 'Sometimes, when the lava fields grew, they thought the eye had opened and looked down on them as prey. They prophesied the day when the god would finally decide to reach down and consume them all. That day has arrived,' he concluded.

'Admiral,' the sibilant voice of Chaplain Ikthalon came through on the bridge vox.

'What is it, chaplain?' Zadkiel snapped.

'The supplicants are stirring,' Ikthalon told him. 'There is movement in the warp. It seems that our pursuers have yet to give up the fight.'

'See that they do not interfere,' snarled Kor Phaeron from the long wave vox, before Zadkiel could reply. 'I'm bringing the fleet into an assault pattern. Guilliman knows we are here by now. Fulfil your mission, Zadkiel.'

'So it is written,' replied Zadkiel, 'so it shall be.' He returned to Malforian. 'Your status, weapon master?'

'A few more minutes, my liege,' Malforian replied. 'We are encountering some problems with the torpedo apertures.'

'Inform me as soon as we're ready to fire the cyclonics,' ordered Zadkiel, his tone betraying his impatience at the unforeseen delay.

'My lord,' Helmsmaster Sarkorov interrupted, 'the *Wrathful* is coming abeam. They are priming weapons.'

Zadkiel exhaled his annoyance. He should have excised this thorn from his side long ago.

'Malforian,' he barked into the vox, 'send all targeting solutions to the bridge once the Imperial lap dogs are in our sights. The *Wrathful* does not deserve the honour of dying as a part of this history, but we shall grant them that honour nonetheless.'

The *Wrathful* appeared on the left viewscreen. She had lost half her guns down one side and was followed by a tail of wreckage tumbling out of her ravaged engine and cargo areas. Her hull was weathered and pitted by the lashes of the warp, covered in the tooth marks of empyrean predators.

Zadkiel smiled maliciously when he saw the wrecked ship. He would derive great pleasure from this.

'Let us finish her.'

THE WRATHFUL LIMPED from the warp and went immediately to battle stations. Aft thrusters burning as hot as they were able, the once formidable Imperial vessel drove head on towards the waiting form of the *Furious Abyss*. Diverting power to its port side, the great ship turned grindingly slowly on its aft axis until its still-functioning broadsides were presented to the foe.

Beams of azure light lit up all the way down the *Wrathful's* flank, and in seconds the blazing fury of her lances was unleashed. Explosions rippled down the armoured hull of the *Furious Abyss*, together with the immense blast flares of shield impacts. These wounds were a mere sting to a beast such as this and the Word Bearer vessel responded with a devastating salvo.

As the crimson light rays of the *Furious's* broadside cannons spat out, the *Wrathful* was already moving, trying to bring the enemy vessel's prow abeam of their lances. The shields of the Imperial ship disintegrated against the assault and the aft decks were raked by deadly fire, explosive impacts sending out chunks of debris and spilling swathes of crew. Still, the *Wrathful* endured, its last ditch manoeuvre bringing it away from the deadly barrage. Torpedoes soared from the vessel's prow, followed by a second volley from the lances. Again, the *Furious* was stung and dorsal cannons swung in their mounts to bring their munitions to bear. Incendiaries crumpled against the *Wrathful's* swerving prow, fully extended broadsides punching ragged holes through its hull armour.

Annoyed at the tenacity of this little wasp, the mighty *Furious Abyss* turned to present its full armament against their aggressor. The damage sustained by the *Wrathful* had slowed it, but even still it could have fled if it had wanted to. Instead, the Imperial vessel stood its ground, making a defiant last stand. Lances flashing, the *Wrathful* poured everything it had left at the Word Bearers. It wasn't enough. The *Furious Abyss* had turned, and, now, it unleashed devastation.

ZADKIEL OBSERVED THE short-lived battle from the bridge. The *Wrathful* was in their sights. The might of his ship was at his disposal.

'Crush them,' he snarled.

Malforian replied his affirmation. Light and fire filled the viewscreen a moment later as the *Furious*'s guns wrecked the Imperial vessel. Its engines died, and great fissures were rent in its hull as it slowly drifted, pulled by the gravity well of Formaska. As the *Wrathful* fell away, sparks flashed sporadically, rendering it in a grim cast, as vented coolant pipes billowed in hazy plumes.

'I had expected more from a son of Guilliman,' Zadkiel admitted. 'How could such a desperate plan ever succeed? The Ultramarines are deserving of their death warrant.'

'Lord Zadkiel.' It was Sarkorov again.

Zadkiel turned to face him.

'What is it, helmsmaster?' he snapped.

'Shuttles, my liege,' he explained, 'heading for the port side.'

Zadkiel was nonplussed.

'How many?'

'Fifteen, my lord,' Sarkorov replied. 'Too close for lances.'

Zadkiel paused for a moment, still confused as to this latest Imperial gambit. The answer came swiftly.

'They seek to gain entry through the torpedo apertures,' he said.

'Should I give the order to close them, Lord Zadkiel?'

'Do it,' Zadkiel snapped, 'and engage dorsal cannons. Bring them down!'

EIGHTEEN

Gauntlet/Infiltration/Dark dreams

BRYNNGAR SMILED AS the shuttle shuddered, spirals of flak and countermeasures hammering against its hull.

Rujveld and the Blood Claws sat in the tight crew compartment with him. They were strapped down in their shuttle couches, braced across the shoulders, chest and waist. The engines were screaming, and intermittent flashes from the explosions outside threw sharp light into the compartment. The small vessel was armoured, but it wasn't designed to take this punishment. Every bolt and stanchion was straining with the speed.

'Do you hear it, lads?' he roared above the din, utterly at ease.

His Blood Claws, even Rujveld, looked back perplexed.

'It is the call to combat,' he told them proudly. 'Those are the arms of Mother Fenris! That's the embrace of war!'

The Wolf Guard howled and the Blood Claws howled with him.

Beyond the vision slits, it and several other shuttles soared through the void towards the *Furious Abyss*. Deployed before the suicide attack, the *Wrathful*'s feint had given them the time they needed to close the gap. It had provided a chance to reach the gaping apertures of the vessel's torpedo tubes before being scattered into debris by its guns.

DORSAL GUNS PULSED and rocked in their turrets as the *Furious Abyss* sought to obliterate the attacker's force. In the third shuttle, Cestus saw three of his sister vessels explode under a hail of flak. They broke and split apart, their desperate speed abruptly arrested as if they were a sail boat breaking up on the rocks of some ragged cliff line. The bodies of naval armsmen spilled from the crew compartments, frozen in spasms of pain as they were exposed to the void.

Three of his battle-brothers were alongside the Ultramarine captain: Lexinal, Pytaron and Excelinor helping to fill up the compartment with their armoured bulk. They stared impassively into space as the flash of explosions was thrown through the viewports, and the armoured hull shook. Their lips moved as they swore silent Oaths of Moment.

Cestus did the same, watching three more shuttles shredded apart by heavy turret fire.

'Come on,' he urged through gritted teeth, the gaping maw of the torpedo aperture getting ever closer. 'Come on.'

'IMPACT IN ONE minute!' said the vox from the shuttle's pilot.

'One minute from mother's love!' shouted Brynngar, taking a firm grip on Felltooth. Embarkation would need to be swift; there could be enemy forces already in position to repel any boarders. For a moment, he wondered whether or not Cestus had made it through the fusillade. Putting the thought out of his mind, he took up the battle cry once more. They were almost in.

'She's waiting for us there! Mother Fenris, mother of war!'

'Mother of war!' yelled the Blood Claws. 'Mother of war! Mother of hate!'

A few feet from the aperture, a stray round struck the left aerofoil of the shuttle and it spiralled wildly out of control. Exploding shrapnel shattered the front viewing arc; the sound of breaking armourglas could even be heard in the troop compartment. The pilot died with a shard of hot metal in his neck, before the icy cool of space froze him and his desperate co-pilot to their flight couches. Brynngar's shuttle dipped sharply away from the aperture and downward into another void entirely.

A SHUTTLE EXPLODED, its nose sheared off by a shell casing thrown out of the *Furious Abyss*'s gun decks. The remaining craft looped up beneath the battleship's ventral surface, the valleys and peaks of the city-sized ship streaking past.

Cestus saw another vessel explode, the bursting shrapnel shredding much of its frontal arc. It dipped, engines blazing ineffectually, and fell downward until it was lost from view behind a slab of crimson hull.

Ahead, the torpedo apertures were closing.

'More speed!' Cestus roared into his helmet vox.

The blazing shuttle engines screeched even louder.

A snatched glimpse through the viewport showed a third shuttle, banking sharply in an attempt to avoid the flak fire and arrow back towards the battleship. Its retro engines flared as it braked. It didn't slow fast enough and slammed into the hull beside the torpedo aperture. The fat metal body crumpled under the impact and split. Broken bodies were cast into the void. They were wearing the blue armour of the Ultramarines.

Saphrax and Amryx are dead, thought Cestus bitterly.

Twisting sharply, the shuttle found a way through the rapidly diminishing aperture. As the *Furious Abyss* swallowed them, Cestus thought he heard the explosions of the shuttles following them as they crashed against the sealed hull.

'Brace!' yelled the pilot.

Tortured metal boomed. Cestus was thrown against the restraints of his grav-couch and felt them stretch and pull against his cuirass.

A terrible twisting, howling sound, like a metal earthquake, filled the Ultramarine's ears.

'Umbilicals away!' said the pilot's voice.

The hatch in the roof of the passenger compartment slid open. White vapour filled the shuttle. 'Pressurising!' shouted the pilot.

Cestus knew what was next and hammered the icon on his chest that would disengage the harness. It came apart quickly and he was on his feet, his battle-brothers beside him. Excelinor, Pytaron and Lexinal, two with bolters low slung and another carrying a plasma gun: they would have to be enough. Cestus checked the load in his bolt pistol and unsheathed his sword, thumbing the activation stud that sent frantic lines of power coursing through the blade.

'Courage and honour!' he yelled, and his battle-brothers returned the battle cry.

Explosive bolts detonated like gunshots. The second hatch was flung open, and the long dark throat of the torpedo tube opened up above them.

Cestus stormed through the short umbilicus, through the hatch and into the tube. It sloped upwards and was wide enough for an Astartes to walk with his head bowed. Its ribbed metal interior was caked in ice. The shuttle had pumped air into it, and the vapour in that air had frozen instantly.

'Move!' ordered the Ultramarine captain, and headed upwards.

As Cestus led the way up the torpedo tube, the sounds of thundering guns and shell impacts echoed dimly through the structure of the *Furious Abyss*, a terrible chorus welcoming them onto the ship.

Cestus saw light ahead: the fires of a forge. He had his bolt pistol up in front of him, ready to fire. The light was coming through a thick armourglas window in a heavy hatch, sealing the far end of the tube.

'Charges!' he ordered.

Excelinor and Pytaron reacted quickly, planting a cluster of krak grenades around the weak points of the hatch. Charges primed, the Astartes retreated as one. A few feet from the entrance, Cestus bellowed, 'Now!'

A muffled explosion radiated through the tube, echoing off the concave interior, and the hatch fell away in a shower of sparks and fire.

Combat protocols and stratagems learned when he was a neophyte and honed in countless conflicts throughout the Great Crusade cycled through Cestus's battle-attuned mind. Bursting onto the ship, the Ultramarines found themselves amidst the massive workings of an ordnance deck: torpedo cranes, ammunition and fuel hoppers; cavernous spaces criss-crossed with gantries and crowded with gangs of sweating menials were all in abundance.

With tactical precision, the Astartes fanned out. Cestus drove forward with Lexinal, the punch of his battle-brother's plasma gun backing up the ferocity of the Ultramarine captain at close quarters.

A group of deck hands came at them with a clutch of heavy tools. Cestus swept low through their clumsy attacks and rose quickly, cutting through two with a savage criss-cross strike and killing a third with a head-butt. Barking fire from his bolt pistol put paid to two more. An actinic flash sent the temperature warnings in his battle-helm spiking as a beam of plasma ignited a fuel hopper. Fire blossomed in plumes of orange and white, twinned with billowing smoke. A squad of rushing armsmen were incinerated in the blaze and the heavy stubber mount, hastily erected above, was thrown to oblivion.

Left and right, Excelinor and Pytaron let rip with their bolters, creating a deadly crossfire that shredded anything that dared to advance through it. They surged steadily into the deck, despatching targets with brutal efficiency, but these were only ratings and armsmen. Cestus knew that the Astartes of the Word Bearers would be coming. They had to act quickly and disable the cyclonics before the real threat arrived. Without the destruction of Formaska, the Word Bearers could not fulfil their plan and get close enough to Macragge to unleash the viral strain.

His super-advanced mind skipping ahead to the tactical tasking to come, Cestus almost missed the scarred-faced officer flying at him with a power mace.

This one was Astartes, although he wore a half-armour variant of full battle-plate. Most of the bottom half of his face was destroyed and had been replaced with a metal grille. Deep pink scar lines ran like fat veins up his jaw and across his cheek bones.

'Quail before the might of the Word,' he bellowed, voice metallic and resonant through the augmetics.

Cestus parried a deft swing of the mace with his power sword. Arcs of miniature lightning danced across the two weapons as they were locked in a brief, pyrotechnic struggle. The Ultramarine broke away and brought up his bolt pistol, only for the grille-faced Word Bearer to smash it out of his grasp. Pain lanced through Cestus's fingers, even though his armour bore the brunt of the blow, numbing his shoulder.

'Lorgar will guide us to victory,' snarled the Word Bearer, allowing his fervour to fuel his swings, though they dulled his accuracy.

Cestus wove out of the death arc from an overhand smash designed to finish him and brought his blazing blade onto the Word Bearer's bare head. Slicing through flesh, bone and, eventually, armour, he sheared the warrior in two, the corpse flopping on either side of the blow.

'Know that Guilliman is righteous,' Cestus snarled, gritting back the pain to reclaim his fallen pistol. Re-armed, he drove on into the building firestorm, focused on the killing.

'WHERE ARE THEY?' demanded Zadkiel.

'All over the gun decks,' came the reply from one of Malforian's subordinates. In the weapon master's absence, Zadkiel assumed that he was dead or otherwise incapacitated. 'Reports say they're Astartes.'

'They'll be going for the torpedo payload,' said Zadkiel, mainly to himself.

The admiral turned his attentions to his helmsmaster. 'Sarkorov, are we in position to launch?'

'Yes, my lord, but we cannot deploy the torpedoes while the deck is contested.'

Zadkiel swore beneath his breath.

'Reskiel,' he snarled into the throne vox with growing annoyance.

The sergeant-commander responded after a moment's pause.

'I'm calling off the hunt for our interloper. Gather your brethren and head for the ordnance decks at once. Destroy any Astartes you find on that deck. Do you understand?'

Reskiel replied in the affirmative and the vox link died.

'If the attack is to be delayed, I will return to my sanctum,' said Magos Gureod, already blending away into the darkness.

'Do as you must,' Zadkiel muttered, his agitation obvious, the veneer of calm ever slipping. 'Ikthalon,' he snarled into the vox, a plan forming in his mind.

'My lord,' the sibilant voice of the chaplain replied.

'Wake the supplicants.'

THERE WAS NO need to spare the supplicants. The *Furious Abyss* had reached its destination. The mission was over. Their role had been to help with the manipulation of the warp and fend off attacks against the ship. Zadkiel's order meant using them to destruction.

The streams of nutrients were replaced with psychoactive drugs. Restraints snapped apart and cortical stimulators crackled, waking the supplicants from their comatose state to halfway between sleep and waking, where sensations and nightmares alike were real. Some of the supplicants, the ones whose mouths and throats still worked, moaned and mewled as they slithered out of their restraints onto the floor. Some convulsed as unfamiliar impulses flooded their muscles. One or two died, their hearts finally giving out.

As part of his chaplain's attire, Ikthalon drew a heavy scarlet cowl over his battle-helm to prevent excess psychic energy from staining his mind, and moved carefully among the waking supplicants, inspecting readouts and checking for swallowed tongues. One by one, he switched off the inhibitor circuits, the loops of psychoactive material that kept the supplicants' minds from feeding back into the *Furious Abyss*. The cogitators hooked in to the debased creatures' consciousness fed them the image of the ship's prow, the engineering works behind the plasma lance and the ordnance decks below.

Finally, the supply of stupefying narcotics and soothing brain-wave instigators was cut off and the supplicants were given their last silent orders.

CESTUS SPRAYED A gantry with bolter fire. Bodies plummeted and crumpled against his fury. The Ultramarines had gained a foothold on the primary ordnance deck, but Cestus could still see no sign of the Space Wolves. He hoped that they had not shared the same fate as Saphrax. The schematic as witnessed in the vision bestowed upon him by Mhotep filled his eidetic memory. The cluster of cyclonics destined for Formaska was at the end of the deck, doubtless in mid-transit to the torpedo apertures. The viral payload was secured in a drop chamber in the hull. There was no way to get to it.

They would have to hobble the Word Bearers' plan at its first juncture.

Barking fire from a pair of pintle-mounted cannons set up on a loading platform above had the Ultramarines pinned for a moment. Cestus's battle-brothers regrouped behind a pair of empty fuel bowsers and the housing of a torpedo crane.

Lexinal, plasma gun cradled in his gauntlets, slid in beside Cestus.

'What now, captain?' he asked as the barrage above them intensified.

Cestus memorised an open stretch of deck and then the huge metal cliff face of the *Furious Abyss*'s prow, broken by the loading mechanisms and the torpedo tubes. He visualised an industrial tangle on the other side, including giant hoppers stacked with further munitions and the rearing masses of arming chambers where yet more ordnance was stored.

'We have to clear the deck and then get to the munitions store and deploy our melta bombs,' he replied.

'What about Brynngar?' Lexinal asked, using a break in the fusillade to fire off a snap shot that bathed the loading platform in super-heated plasma. The screams died in the raging battle din.

'Once we take out the cyclonics, we link up with whoever is left and do what damage we can,' said Cestus, once Lexinal had resumed cover.

The Ultramarine nodded his understanding.

Cestus relayed the same order through his helmet vox on a discrete frequency in Ultramar battle-cant to Pytaron and Excelinor. The two battle-brothers flanked the captain's position, heavy-duty munitions crates in front of them being chipped apart by persistent fire.

Cestus glanced between the two bowsers. The *Furious*'s crewmen, in dark scarlet overalls and fatigues, had been hit hard by the shock of the assault. Dozens of them lay dead around the torpedo hatches or shot down from the gantries and cranes. The Astartes has exacted a heavy toll, but the enemy were regrouping and reinforcements covered their losses in short order.

There was no time to delay.

'On me,' Cestus cried, 'battle formation theta-epsilon, Macragge in ascendance!'

He vaulted the bowser, bolt pistol flaring and lasgun impacts spattered his cuirass. Cestus held his sword in salute stance, in front of his face and the upright blade deflected energy blasts from his battle-helm. Twin bolters blazed, cross-shaped muzzle flashes glaring, as Excelinor and Pytaron moved in staggered battle formation to Cestus's left. Lexinal took the right flank, firing his plasma gun in controlled bursts to prevent the deadly weapon from overheating.

Towards the last third of the deck, they broke up, each taking a channel into the industrial tangle of machinery. Troops of armsmen had mobilised and came at Cestus with shock mauls and lengths of spiked chain. The Ultramarine captain cut them down, Guilliman's name a mantra on his lips. Amidst the killing, he noticed an access portal to the ordnance deck and wondered why the Word Bearers' Astartes had not yet shown themselves.

'Link up and force through to the cyclonics,' Cestus ordered through his helmet vox as he moved into a labyrinth of munitions.

His battle-brothers obeyed and together they converged on a pair of cyclonics, still harnessed in their mobile racking.

Shots spattered from gantries above, most of the las-bolts and hard rounds smacking into cranes and clusters of machinery. Cestus saw a lucky shot ricochet from Lexinal's breastplate and he staggered. A second burst from a heavy cannon somewhere above them raked his leg greave and he was down. Out of the corner of his eye, Cestus saw a group of armsmen converging on the prone Ultramarine. A las-bolt clipping his pauldron, Cestus twisted as he ran, slamming a fresh magazine in his bolt pistol and discharging a furious burst into the armsmen. Two disappeared in a red haze, another crumpled to the ground nursing the wet crater in his stomach. Cestus didn't see the rest. Lexinal was getting to his feet when a round struck an active fuel bowser. The resulting explosion engulfed the Astartes in coruscating flame, the blast wave throwing him half way across the deck.

The Ultramarine captain averted his gaze, muttering a battle-oath, and refocused ahead.

'Deploy incendiaries,' Cestus ordered when they finally reached the first batch of cyclonics. Pytaron unclipped a melta bomb from his armour, disengaging the magna-clamp that kept it in place. Excelinor provided covering fire with his bolter.

'Brynngar!' Cestus shouted into his helmet vox, crouching beside Excelinor as he desperately tried to make contact. 'Brynngar respond.'

Dead air came back at him. Either the wolf had been killed or he was in another part of the ship where they couldn't reach him.

'Charges deployed,' reported Pytaron. As he turned to his captain, a heavy round struck him in the neck, piercing his gorget. He clutched the wound with one hand, the melta bomb detonator in the other, and fell to one knee as blood streamed down his breastplate.

Larraman cells within Pytaron's body worked hard to slow the bleeding and speed up clotting, but the wound was serious. Even an Astartes enhanced physiology would be unable to save the battle-brother.

'Take it,' Pytaron said, gurgling his words through blood.

Cestus took the detonator, his hands around Pytaron's.

'You will be honoured…' Cestus's voice trailed away as the air around him suddenly turned cold, receptors built into his battle-plate registering a severe drop in temperature. For an awful second, he thought that the deck had de-pressurised and the void would claim them all.

With the cold came screaming: a thousand voices, echoing out from the inside of Cestus's head.

It was not the void, reaching into the ship to freeze them solid. It was something far worse. Prickling talons probing his mental defences like ice blades reminded Cestus of his earlier encounter with Mhotep aboard the *Wrathful*.

'Psyker!' he hissed with sudden realisation. 'Psyker!' he shouted this time to get Excelinor's attention. 'We are under attack.'

One of the *Furious Abyss*'s crewmen stumbled out into the open. He clutched an autogun loosely in one hand, his arm hanging down by his side. With his other hand, he appeared to be trying to tear out his own tongue.

Cestus shot the man in the chest. He bucked violently and fell still against the deck. He then turned and saw Excelinor slowly raise his boltgun to his head.

'No,' Cestus cried, yanking his fellow battle-brother to his senses.

'Voices in my head… I can't stop them,' whispered Excelinor through his vox, still struggling with his bolter.

'Fight it!' Cestus snarled at him, feeling the shreds of his own sanity slowly being devoured by the unseen force of the warp. They had to get out, right now. The Ultramarine captain seized Excelinor's arm, the world starting to blur around him, and hauled him towards the access portal.

'Come on,' Cestus breathed as the floor shifted beneath him and the walls began to melt.

Try as he might, Cestus could not keep himself from falling into madness. The last thing he remembered was his fist closing on the detonator and the rush of fire.

'THEY THINK IT's alive,' breathed Zadkiel, standing before his command throne, 'This ship has been a part of them for so long that the supplicants regard it as an extension of their own bodies. No. It is a host, in which they are parasites. There won't be a mind left intact among them. The enemy will be driven mad long before we kill them.'

'Your orders, admiral?' The voice of Sergeant-Commander Reskiel through the throne vox interrupted Zadkiel's monologue.

'You have gained the area outside of the ordnance deck?' he asked, imagining the warriors of Reskiel looming in the corridor intersections.

'Yes, my lord,' Reskiel answered. Just prior to entering the ordnance deck, the sergeant-commander and his warriors had been ordered to secure the exits, Zadkiel having no desire for his forces to be caught up in the psychic attack.

'Although, a massive detonation destroyed much of the tertiary access points, as yet, we have been unable to break through,' Reskiel added.

'Is it possible that the Astartes escaped the deck?' the irritation in Zadkiel's voice obvious, even through the vox link.

There was a short pause as Reskiel considered his response.

'It is possible, yes.'

'Find them, Reskiel. Do it or do not return to my bridge.' Zadkiel cut the vox link abruptly.

The admiral turned to a secondary force of Word Bearers, who had assembled behind him.

'Secure the ordnance deck, port and starboard access portals. Get in there and recover what is left of our cyclonic payload.'

'Yes, my lord,' said a chorus of voices from the assembled Word Bearers.

'Do so, now!' Zadkiel raged and the clattering sound of booted feet erupted behind him as the Word Bearers deployed.

The infiltrators had to be stopped. Despite the psychic assault, Zadkiel needed to be sure that any further loose ends had been tied up. Nothing must prevent the bombardment against Formaska. Without it, the rest of the plan could not proceed. He would not allow his soul to be forfeit from Kor Phaeron's rage at his failure. Success was inevitable. It had to be. It was written.

MACRAGGE'S NATIVES, THE people who had been there before the Emperor's Great Crusade had rediscovered them, had believed in a hell that was very specific in its

cruelties. Its circles each held a certain breed of sinner,
all suffering punishments appropriate to their mis-
deeds. The further in a dead man went, the more
horrible and varied his punishments became, until the
very worse of the worst – traitors to Macragge's Battle
Kings, and those who had betrayed their own families –
were held in the very centre in a series of torments that
a living mind could not comprehend and upon which
the legends refused to speculate.

Those beliefs had survived alongside the Imperial
Truth, as folk tales and allegories. Macragge's circles of
hell were the subject of epic verse, cautionary tales and
colourful curses.

Cestus was, at that moment, in the circle of hell
reserved for cowards.

'Run!' shouted the taskmaster. 'You ran from everything! You sacrificed everything to run! Run, now, as
you did in life! Never stop!'

Cestus was blinded by tears. His hands and feet
screamed at him, cut to tatters. Behind him, a miniature
sun rolled towards him, blistering the skin on the back
of his torso and legs. It was relentless, never slowing, as
it ground its way along the vast circular track, bounded
by walls of granite, its light flickering against the stalac-
tites hanging from the cave ceiling overhead.

The floor was covered in blades, swords dropped by
failed soldiers as they fled the battlefield. As the ball of
fire approached, the sinners fled, tearing themselves on
the blades to escape the fire. Their punishment was to
flee forever.

Cestus remembered being told of this hell by drill
sergeants on Macragge, in the half-remembered time
before Guilliman's Legion had taken him from among
hundreds of supplicants to be turned into an Ultramarine.

This hell was halfway through the levels of hell, for while cowards were despised on Macragge theirs was a pathetic sin, a sin of failure, and not comparable to the treachery of murder punished closer to hell's heart. It compounded the punishment, not only to suffer, not only to know the weight of failure, but to be reminded that even in sin a coward was lacking.

Cestus stumbled and fell. Steel bit into his hands, his knees and his chest. A blade slid through the softer skin of his lips and he tasted blood. He coughed, desperate for it to end. It felt like he had been there for years, the relentless sun driving him on.

The taskmaster was a drill sergeant of Macragge, the same kind of man who had ordered him to march and fight and strive as a child. Cestus remembered the fear of failure, of letting his betters down. He got to his feet and somehow the flesh was still screaming.

'I am not a coward,' he gasped. 'Please... I am not a coward.'

The taskmaster's whip lashed down. It was a tongue of flame from the sun, scoring a red-black line of agony against Cestus's back. 'You all but murdered your battle-brother because you feared to take his place!' the taskmaster shouted. 'You doomed your fellow warriors because you feared failure! And now you beg for your just punishment to end! What are these but the actions of a coward? And you wore the colours of Guilliman! What shame you have brought to your Legion!'

'I have never run!' yelled Cestus. 'Not once! I never backed down! I never turned from the enemy! Fear never made my choice!'

'Do you deny?' shouted the taskmaster.

'I deny! I deny you! The Imperial Truth has no room for hells! The only hells are those we make for ourselves!'

'Another lifetime, Lysimachus Cestus, and you will break!'

The sun roared closer. It swelled up, angry and orange. Dark spots flared on its surface. Flaming tongues licked out at Cestus, searing the soles of his feet, the backs of his legs. One wrapped around his face and he moaned as it burned through his skin, his cheek and nose, his ear. Cestus fought to escape, but the blades snagged him. One leg was trapped by hooks between the bones and he felt steel scraping along his shin, flaying skin and muscle away. One hand was stuck, too, pierced through by the barbed head of a spear.

'I am not a coward!' yelled Cestus. He tore himself free of the bladed ground. Muscle and blood sloughed away. 'I know no fear!' He turned around and walked on what remained of his feet, into the heart of the sun.

ADMIRAL KAMINSKA SAT in her command throne in front of the blast doors leading to the bridge of the *Wrathful*. The doors were closed, the bridge sealed off against the secondary explosions wracking the ship. Another huge explosion thundered up from the generatoria deep in the stern. The *Wrathful* was breaking up. Formaska's weak gravity well was slowly dragging it into a death spiral. There, upon the barren rock, they would be broken. That was, if a catastrophic reactor collapse didn't destroy the ship completely first.

Kaminska felt curiously calm as they drifted through the void, completely at the whim of gravity. There was still a trace of underlying disquiet at the edge of her senses, however, as if the feeling she had experienced before had remained, but she'd become inured to it.

She had known when Cestus proposed his plan and spoke of sacrifice that this would be her last mission. She wore her full admiral's regalia and had instructed all of her bridge staff to do the same. There would be honour in this final act. They had fought a giant in the form of the *Furious Abyss*, and they had lost, but like the fly irritates the bison, perhaps it would be enough to distract their enemy long enough for the Angels of the Emperor to do what they must.

'Helmsmistress,' said Kaminska, her eyes on the forward viewscreen and space as scattered debris from her ship spiralled slowly past, 'dismiss the bridge crew, yourself included. You are to evacuate the *Wrathful* at once and take the saviour pods. May fortune favour you in the void.'

'I'm sorry, admiral. I cannot speak for the rest of the crew, but I will not obey that order,' answered Venkmyer.

Kaminska whirled in her command throne and fixed her helmsmistress with an icy glare.

'I am your captain, and you will do as I bid,' she said.

'I request to remain onboard the *Wrathful* and go down with the ship,' Venkmyer responded.

For a moment, Kaminska looked as if she were about to erupt into a fit of apoplexy at such insubordination, but the determined expression on her helmsmistress's face made the ice soften and melt.

Kaminska saluted Venkmyer and her bridge crew.

'You do me great honour.' Kaminska was about to smile proudly when the feeling of unease intensified and she realised it was emanating from her helmsmistress.

'No, admiral,' Venkmyer replied, and from the obvious demeanour of the crew around her, they were all in agreement. 'We are honoured.'

Venkmyer raised her hand to return the naval salute when she suddenly clutched her stomach. She grimaced in pain and fell to the deck, convulsing violently.

Helms-mate Kant, standing close by, went immediately to her aid.

'Officer Venkmyer,' shouted Kaminska getting off her throne to go to her helmsmistress's aid. She stopped short when she saw her breath misting in front of her. A profound chill filled the bridge as if it were suddenly converted into a meat locker.

Eyes wide as Venkmyer bucked and thrashed, she drew her naval sidearm.

Armed or not, it wouldn't matter. It was already too late for them all.

MHOTEP WAS MEDITATING in the isolation chamber, his gaze fixed on the reflective surface of the speculum in his wand. Abruptly, his glazed expression bled away and he was at full awareness again.

It was time.

The Thousand Son got to his feet. His gaolers had allowed him to wear his battle-plate and the heavily armoured boots resonated against the metal floor. He approached the locked cell door and raised his hand. Chanting eldritch words in a sibilant tongue, the door dissolved before Mhotep's open palm, disintegrating back into atoms. The Astartes stepped through and was struck immediately by a profound sense of emptiness. The corridors were utterly bereft of life. He knew the *Wrathful* had only a skeleton crew, but this was something else: an absence of existence that smacked of the otherworldly. Mhotep drew the psychic hood over his head, securing it firmly to the scarab-shaped clasps on his gorget. He drew the wand out before him and

activated it. The small stave extended into the spear
again and a small crackle of energy played down its
length as if reacting to the air around it. This ghost ship
in which he walked had a phantom. Mhotep knew it for
certain.

Calmly, the Thousand Son walked down the narrow
passageways that would lead him to the bridge, where
he knew his destiny awaited. The lines of fate had been
very specific. This was the path he had chosen, despite
the efforts of the *other* to try and change his mind, to
will him into divine madness.

Mhotep reached the bridge without encountering a
single soul. It was as if the crew had been devoured
utterly. He moved his hand in a swift chopping motion
and the sealed blast doors opened, venting a small
cloud of pressure.

Carnage greeted him as the Thousand Son stepped
into the chamber. It was as if the bleeding heart of the
Wrathful had been laid open upon the surgeon's slab.

The heart of the ship, of course, was its crew. Their
blood and viscera painted the walls, an incarnadine
portrait rendered by an obscene and demented artist.
Skin was flayed from bone, organs eviscerated.

A bizarre skeleton ribbed the walls and ceiling, the
concomitant elements harvested from the slain crew
members, changing the bridge into a macabre
ossuary.

Mhotep ignored the abattoir stink assailing his nostrils, even through his battle-helm, the wet redness of
the chamber cast starkly in the intermittent flare of
warning lamps. He saw Admiral Kaminska, slumped
against the floor, a pistol in her hand.

'Get out of her,' she breathed, blood flecking her lips
as she spoke.

Standing before them both, an insane grin etched upon her face, was Helmsmistress Venkmyer. She was bloody and her toes, pointing downward in her boots, just scraped the floor as if she were a marionette held limply by its strings.

'Get out!' Kaminska urged again, struggling to stand as she fired her pistol on empty at the abomination that used to be her second-in-command.

The Venkmyer-puppet lashed out, her arm extending as if it were made of clay, and sheared off Kaminska's head with its talon-like fingers. The admiral dead, the creature's arm shrank back into position, glistening with blood.

'You dwell within,' said Mhotep calmly, taking a step forward as he mustered his psychic resolve. 'Come forth.'

The Venkmyer-puppet grinned back at him.

'I am a servant of the crimson eye. I am a vassal of Magnus the all-knowing,' said Mhotep, taking another step as he reaffirmed the grip on his spear. 'Come forth.'

Eerie quiet had descended like a veil and the temperature readings in the Thousand Son's helmet were registering sub-zero. He saw miniature icicles of hoarfrost building on his gauntlets. A faint white patina was emerging slowly on his cuirass as he advanced.

Still, the Venkmyer-puppet did not answer.

'I know you are here!' cried Mhotep, his voice resonating around the bridge. 'You have been here all along! You cannot hide from me. I have the eye of Magnus!' Mhotep levelled his spear at Venkmyer as if she was a wild beast poised to attack.

'Come forth,' he hissed, and the briefest flash of recognition appeared on Venkmyer's face, but was swallowed by agony.

The thing that used to be the helmsmistress opened its mouth and the jaw distended to reveal a hollow maw of deep red. A gush of blood spewed outwards, coating Mhotep in its sickly gore. The Thousand Son did not falter against the crimson tide and held his ground.

The sound of cracking bone filled the air as Venkmyer's spine was ripped out of her back and arced up and over her head like a scorpion's sting. Her neck snapped, and her jaw distended further, tendons severing. Beneath her tarnished uniform, her ribs writhed as a shape fought to free itself from the flesh and bone sack of her body. Convulsions wracked her and the head came apart in a shower of gore and matter.

A shape of raw muscle emerged, unfolding and opening like a bloody flower. Venkmyer's hands became claws and enhanced musculature spread across her ravaged body in a riot. Wet and pink, the muscle swelled until a hard, black carapace formed over it. What had once been Venkmyer, little more than a conduit for something to wrench itself into existence, grew exponentially until it had to crouch to fit into the chamber. The nubs of horns sprouted from a bulbous head from which eyes like pits of tar blinked maliciously. A slit ran across the near-featureless head like the cut from a surgeon's scalpel and a wide mouth opened from it, revealing rows of razor teeth. Talons like scythe blades scraped along the floor from distended, simian-like arms. A long, sinewy tail spilled from its back made of tough muscle-bound vines and twisted spine.

'There you are…' said Mhotep, looking up at the towering abomination, '…Wsoric.'

It was a thing of the warp, a daemon made flesh, and it stared at the Thousand Son, allowing its malign presence to wash over him.

'I am gorged,' the thing gurgled, drooling blood as its mouth deformed to make the words, 'but there is always room for more.'

Mhotep knew then that the beast had been aboard the ship for weeks, devouring souls to gather its strength. It had been the temptation in his head that had almost made him slip into madness. It had fanned the flames of the Space Wolf's enmity against him. It had fostered the madness that had claimed the lives of so many of the crew.

Mhotep brandished his spear and a corona of crackling energy arced over it.

'Feeding time is over,' he promised.

The seventh circle of hell, two steps closer to the heart of damnation, was for rebels: those who had cast off the natural order, who had defied their betters or refused to accept their place in the world. In ages past, those who had taken up arms against Macragge's Battle Kings had found themselves here, alongside children who had turned against their parents, and deviants and agitators of every kind.

It was a machine – a vast, complex, endless construction of cogs and steel that churned through the seventh circle. Rebels had failed to realise that they were required to be a part of a larger machine, and so the seventh hell was to educate them in their place. Sinners became a part of that machine, bent and stretched into component parts. The machine never let them alone, always twisting them or thrusting a piston through them, until they gave up their individuality in the hope of ending the pain. The seventh hell was not just a punishment, it was a lesson, and it would break the pupil's spirit in the telling.

Cestus's spine was bent backwards. Spurs of metal were slid in at his wrists, down through the muscle of his arms and into his chest. Metal merged with the back of his skull and snapped it back every few seconds as the teeth of a cog hammered by behind him.

This circle of hell was dark and dripping with blood. Other sinners were everywhere, their bodies so deformed by the machine that they were little more than cogs or cams of gristle and bone, facial features barely discernible. A few others were new and their bodies were still resisting. They screamed, bones poking through their skin and muscles ripping.

'Cestus!' cried someone above him. Cestus tried to look back, grimacing as metal pushed through the skin of his scalp.

It was Antiges. The Ultramarine had been stripped of his armour and was bolted spread-eagled to a cog. His limbs were being forced around to follow the circle of the cog. His shins and forearms were being bent into curves and they looked like they would shatter at any moment. Another, smaller cog inside the larger was fixed to his back, slowly twisting his spine. Already, his torso looked lopsided and his head had been forced down onto one shoulder.

'Antiges!' gasped Cestus. 'I had thought you were lost.'

'I am,' said Antiges, a brief lull in his suffering before the agony returned. 'So are you. Fathers of Macragge, this pain... I cannot suffer it much longer. If only there were some... some new death, some oblivion.'

'This is the hell for rebels,' said Cestus. He felt a note of panic in his mind as the spurs in his forearms and chest began to force apart, drawing his arms behind him. 'We are not rebels. We were always loyal sons of

Macragge! We served the Imperial Truth until the end! Nothing was worth more to us than our duty.'

'Your duties were on Terra,' said Antiges. 'You took a ship and left your post. You took us all on your mission to Macragge, and damned the rest! There was no duty that told you to gather your fleet and abandon Terra. That was your personal crusade, Cestus. That was your rebellion.'

'I had a duty to Macragge and to my battle-brothers. Everything I did, I did because it was demanded of my by my Legion! Loyalty drove me on!'

'Loyalty, Cestus, to yourself.' Antiges threw his head back and screamed. One leg shattered, snapping at the shin. The other one was wrenched apart at the knee. A shoulder followed, the bone torn out of the socket. Skin split and Antiges's arm was held on only by a few tendons. His eyes rolled back and his breathing turned ragged. An Astartes could take pain that would kill a normal man, but even Antiges had his limits.

'Brother!' shouted Cestus. 'Hold on! Do not leave me! Fight!'

Cestus's part of the machine hummed with power diverted to the engines chugging away beneath him. He felt his arms forced back further and a sharp pressure in his back. His head was forced back, too, snapping back and forth as it was ratcheted tight into the top of his spine.

The pressure in his chest was tremendous. An Astartes's ribs were fused into a breastplate of bone, and Cestus could feel them grinding as it made ready to split down the middle. The pain grew and the Ultramarine could feel nothing else, only the awful inevitability of his breaking.

'I am no rebel!' shouted Cestus, drawing resolve from a pit of strength he didn't know he had. 'I only serve! My Legion is my life! I do not belong in this hell of Macragge, and so this hell is not real! I am no rebel! I defy you all!'

Somewhere, a taskmaster turned a rusting wheel and the machine shuddered with power.

Cestus's chest split open. He screamed. Hot air shrieked through his organs. His legs kicked frantically and both his arms snapped. His neck broke, but the pain did not die, and his body was forced to accept the form of the machine.

'I defy you,' gasped Cestus with his last breath.

NINETEEN

Pack mentality/Wsoric/Reunion

BRYNNGAR STALKED ON all fours amongst the steaming carcasses of the pack. He had rent them apart with tooth and claw, his furred muzzle stained with their blood. They had challenged him and he had proved he was dominant. Upon the snowy, Fenrisian plain, his feral eyes cast across a silver ocean so still that it was like glass. He sniffed the air, the scent of something drifting towards him on the cold breeze. Long wolf ears pricking at the faintest sound of disturbed tundra, he saw a shape above him, moving stealthily up a craggy peak under a shawl of snow.

Another wolf still lived and was stalking him.

Brynngar emitted a baleful howl that echoed across the soaring mountains. Its challenge was met by another.

The hackles rose on Brynngar's back as the other wolf loped into view. He was smaller, but lean and well-muscled. Reddish, brown fur covered his lupine body and he pawed at the ground with blood-red claws.

Brynngar growled at the red wolf's approach, a deep and ululating sound that resonated through his body. The challenger stepped down onto the plain and they began circling each other, the old and venerable grey versus the youthful red. Death was the only outcome. The only thing that was uncertain was whether the duel would claim them both.

Ribbons of wolf flesh still clung to Brynngar's fangs. The blood taste was intoxicating, and the scent set his feral senses aflame. With a roar, he dived at the other wolf, biting and clawing with savage abandon. So furious was the attack that the red wolf was bowled briefly off balance. He twisted in Brynngar's jaws, scraping wildly with his claws and biting down against the grey's back. The wolves broke apart, both bloodied and full of fury. This time the red wolf attacked, launching a swift assault that saw him rake his claws down Brynngar's flank. The old, grey wolf yelped in pain and skidded away across the ice plain on all fours, before regrouping to charge again.

The red wolf slashed a claw across Brynngar's muzzle as he came at him, but the old grey was not to be deterred. Ignoring the pain, Brynngar locked his jaw around the red wolf's neck and bit down. Claws raked his flank as the red wolf's back legs kicked out in desperation. Brynngar could hear his opponent's frantic breathing, and feel the hotness against his fur, the vapour cooling in the cold. With a grunt of effort, he snapped the red wolf's neck. It yelped just before it died, and fell limp in Brynngar's jaw. The old wolf shook the corpse loose and howled in triumph, blood drizzling from his maw as he brandished gory fangs.

The silver ocean was before him once more and Brynngar felt it call to him. Snow spilled across its mirror sheen in fat, white drifts. It fell upon the ground where Brynngar stood, covering up the spilled blood of the slain wolves. The old grey was about to lope off when a shadow fell across the ice plain. He looked up and for a moment could see nothing through the heavy snowfall. Then, slowly, a figure resolved itself. It was a black wolf, easily twice his size, sitting on its haunches watching him calmly. There was no challenge in its posture; Brynngar detected no threat in either its tone or manner. It merely watched. The grey wolf had seen this black furred beast before. He approached it slowly, warily and stopped as the black wolf got up. Its eyes bored into him and it opened its mouth as if to howl.

'Look around you,' said the black wolf, and though it spoke the words of man, Brynngar the grey wolf understood.

'Look around you, Brynngar,' said the giant black wolf again. 'This is not Fenris.'

BRYNNGAR WOKE FROM a dream straight into a nightmare. Rujveld lay dead at his feet. The Blood Claw's throat had been ripped out and vital fluids pooled around his corpse. Brynngar tasted copper in his mouth and knew at once that he had killed him. Out of the corner of his eye, the Wolf Guard saw other grey-armoured forms and realised that he had slain all of his kinsmen. He shut his eyes against the horror, willing it to be his fevered imagination, but when Brynngar opened them again he knew it was not.

The Wolf Guard got unsteadily to his feet. The last thing he remembered was approaching the *Furious Abyss*. Their shuttle had been hit and they'd crashed in a place of darkness. The rest was lost. He had emerged onto what he thought was Fenris. He knew that this was some form of psychic lie. He clenched his fists at the thought of being manipulated by witchcraft. It had cost the lives of his battle-brothers. He had been damned by it.

Senses returning, Brynngar looked around. The chamber was gloomy in the extreme, but felt large and tall. It was some kind of armoury. He stood face-to-face with a suit of dreadnought armour. Startled at first, the Wolf Guard took an instinctive step back and reached for Felltooth. When he realised that the sarcophagus of the mighty war machine was empty and dormant, he relaxed. There was another dreadnought next to it, similarly harnessed, made ready for the warrior who would become entombed within it for all time or until they fell in service to the Legion.

The armoury was vast and well-stocked. There were crates of munitions, stacked in rows. They joined ranks of bolter clips, fuel cells and harnessed grenades. It was the hulking presence of the dreadnoughts, however, that caught the Space Wolf's attention. Next to the second war machine, there was another and another, and another. Brynngar gazed up and across the chamber, his enhanced eyesight adjusting to the darkness. At least a hundred dreadnoughts filled the massive armoury hall, their somnambulant forms held fast in racks and rows. Weapon systems, great piston hammers, power flails, autocannons, heavy bolters, twin-linked flamers and missile pods, were arrayed next to them, waiting to be attached to the dreadnought body. Brynngar balked at the firepower on display and the thought of thousands of these armoured leviathans going to war in Lorgar's name.

Brynngar's ears pricked up; he'd lost his battle-helm at some point he could not recall. A slab of metal slid away from a bare wall in the armoury hall and a shaft of wan red light issued through the gap. A tall, thin shadow was waiting outside and, with the way open, it moved into the room. It was clad in black robes and Brynngar detected the glint of a metal artifice at its back: Mechanicum.

The magos turned when it noticed the Astartes in the armoury. Without preamble, it came at the Space Wolf, a mechadendrite drill emerging from the folds of its robes. Brynngar slashed the mechanical arm of the weapon, oil spilling from the severed metal limb like blood, and brought Felltooth down onto the hapless magos with a roar. The creature gurgled as it died, in what might have been an expression of pain or regret. It twitched for a moment as if its mechanical body was taking time to realise that it was already dead, before at last it lay still.

The red light continued to issue from the portal opened by the magos.

Brynngar had no idea where it led, but perhaps he could find some vulnerable location on the ship and do some damage, making the sacrifice of his Blood Claws and his own terrible act worth something. Maybe even the Ultramarine was still alive and he could find him. These thoughts running through his mind, the Wolf Guard took a step towards the portal, but stopped when he heard the shift of metal in the chamber, followed by the pressure-hiss of a disengaging harness.

Brynngar turned towards the sound, his accentuated hearing pinpointing its location exactly, and paused. He did not have to wait long for the source of the disturbance to reveal itself.

'I serve the Legion eternally,' a scratchy voice, said, emitted from a vox-caster out of the darkness. Heavy metal footfalls like the *thunk* of giant hammers hitting metal, echoed in the armoury as a massive dreadnought emerged from the shadows.

The thing was an abomination, only part-way through the procedure of interment. The armoured sarcophagus hung open revealing a translucent blister pod in which a naked form was surrounded in amniotic fluid. The viscous material clung to the body, casting the enhanced musculature of the entombed Astartes in a dull sheen through the blister.

It walked unsteadily and one of its arms was missing, disconnected cabling flapping like cut veins, doubtless still awaiting the weapons of destruction through which it would express the art of war. The other arm, though, was more than ready, a massive, spiked hammer swinging from it. A faint energy crackle played along its surface, casting stark flashes onto the dreadnought as it primed the deadly weapon subconsciously. A sense of palpable menace came from the metal monster that towered over Brynngar. The old wolf took a step back, swinging Felltooth in readiness. The armour of his opponent looked thick and he hoped that the rune axe could pierce it.

'My enemy,' droned the dreadnought lumbering forward to close off the exit to the armoury as a flare of recognition coloured its tone and demeanour. 'Ultis must die,' it added, pausing for a moment as if suddenly confused, before it refocused on the Space Wolf and continued, 'You will not gain the ship.'

Brynngar knew this warrior. He had killed him once already, at Bakka Triumveron.

'Baelanos...' it said with machine coldness.

The assault-captain.

'Didn't I kill you once, already,' growled the Wolf Guard.

'...Destroy you,' the dreadnought replied, the sarcophagus closing up over the blister.

'Round two,' Brynngar whispered as Baelanos the dreadnought charged.

MHOTEP CRASHED THROUGH the blast doors of the bridge, and skidded across the floor of an adjoining corridor. Fire wreathed his armour and scorch marks tarnished it from where the daemon had burned him with its breath. The force of the blow was such that Mhotep tried to claw at the corridor walls to slow his passage, but the wood veneer and metal tore away in his grasp, revealing bare wiring and fat cables that spat sparks and flame. The Thousand Son struck a bulkhead at the corridor's intersection and crumpled to a halt, pain lancing his back and shoulder.

Heat coiled from the edges of Mhotep's armour. The faceplate of his helmet had taken the worst of the impact and he ripped it away, half-melted, leaving the rest of the headgear intact, together with the psychic hood. Discarding the battle-helm face plate, Mhotep got to his feet. Three claw marks were cut so deep into his cuirass that they bled. The Astartes staggered at first, but drew on his psychic reserves to steel himself. Forcing one foot in front of the other, banishing the pain, he made his way back to the bridge.

Wsoric stepped from the shattered blast doors, metal squealing as the daemon pushed its immense bulk through the ragged hole left by Mhotep. The beast would meet him halfway.

As it got closer, Mhotep saw that the black armour carapace was cracked in places and faintly glowing ichor seeped from minor cuts on its body.

It could be hurt, at least. Mhotep clung to that small sliver of hope as he readied his spear. With a muttered incantation, he sent an arc of crimson lightning towards the daemon. The creature shied away at first, using its muscular forearm to fend off the psychic assault, but the cerulean energy quickly died and Wsoric emerged unscathed.

'Like an insect,' said the daemon, its voice accompanied by the slither of muscle and the cracking of bone, 'you are harder to kill than your feeble frame suggests.'

'I am Astartes. I am an avenging angel of the Emperor of Mankind,' Mhotep challenged, using the brief respite to marshal his strength. Though he was weak and in pain, the Thousand Son was careful not to show weakness, not even to contemplate defeat. For if he did, the daemon would seize upon it and all would be lost.

'I am your doom,' Wsoric promised and came forward with preternatural speed.

'As I am yours,' Mhotep hissed.

Talons like blades scythed the air and Mhotep's spear spat golden sparks as he used it to parry the blow. He was staggered by the force of it and took an involuntary step back, boots grinding metal. He lunged with his spear, igniting the tip in an aura of crimson fire, and pierced Wsoric's side. The daemon's skin felt like iron, and the resonance of the blow rippled down Mhotep's forearm and into his shoulder. The effect was numbing and he nearly dropped the weapon. Wsoric's pain bellow was immense, and the Thousand Son winced against its intensity before withdrawing.

With the servos in his armour assisting his muscles, Mhotep leapt backwards, the tattered robes of his armour flapping like a cloak, and landed, spear in hand, before the daemon could retaliate.

'You have failed here, spirit,' he said, filling his voice with absolute certainty. 'Wraith of times past, I name thee. Native thing of the warp, I shall send you back there. However much you hunger, you are known to me and you will not prevail. You will be banished by the light of the Emperor.'

'You know nothing,' Wsoric sneered, 'of what we are.' The terrible wound in its side was already healing. 'You are misled and you know not of your fate.'

An image flashed briefly in Mhotep's mind, of the spires of Prospero burning and the howling of wolves. It was the same vision he'd seen when Wsoric had first tried to subvert him and it came back like a recurring nightmare to haunt him.

Mhotep focused, determined not to give in, and slowly the image faded away like smoke.

'I am Mhotep, Thousand Son of Magnus the Red. The wisdom of Ahriman flows within me.' The affirmation steeled him and power coursed through his body. Wsoric's body, all muscle and blemished skin like the hide of a diseased corpse, shuddered with what the Thousand Son could only think was laughter. The daemon's bloody lips peeled back from its dog-like skull and its pure black eyes shimmered wetly in sunken sockets of gore. One of Wsoric's hands turned in on itself with a foul sucking sound, forming a wide orifice, which the monster aimed like a gun. The daemon roared with effort and a bolt of purple fire spat from its hand. Mhotep couldn't get out of the way quickly enough and the blast caught his pauldron, hitting him hard enough to throw him, spinning, down the corridor. The Thousand Son was on his feet as soon as he landed, feeling the armour down one side char with the heat and the exposed skin of his face blistering.

Wsoric fired again, a heavy chain of caged fire spitting from his hand. The monster was laughing loudly, a horrendous gurgling sound that sprayed blood from its throat. Mhotep rolled around the intersection, tumbling into another corridor as lances of fire tore through the bulkhead.

The stink of burning metal filled his nostrils and wretched heat plagued his skin, but Mhotep was not about to give up. Once the conflagration had died down, he swung back around the intersection. From his outstretched palm, he sent a boiling mass of crimson fire against the daemon, which coursed over its weapon-arm, searing it shut.

'The Word Bearers will not succeed,' he said, rushing forward with his spear. The Emperor knows he is betrayed! Lorgar will not escape his justice!'

'I care nothing for Lorgar's dogs,' roared Wsoric. 'They are beholden to the will of the warp, the ancient ones that dwell in the empyrean. The slave Lorgar is merely a tool in the fashioning of our grand design. Mankind will fall as Old Night returns to the galaxy, shrouding it in a second darkness. You will all be slaves!'

Astartes and daemon clashed. Mhotep ran his spear through Wsoric's side while the daemon swatted him against the corridor wall with a sweep of its gargantuan claws. Before the Thousand Son could recover, it seized upon his skull and started to squeeze. Mhotep could hear the bone cracking inside his head as dark spots flecked his failing vision.

'Your Emperor can plot and cower all he likes,' said Wsoric. 'What has the warp to fear from him?' he taunted, exerting more pressure.

'Knowledge…' hissed Mhotep through clenched teeth, '…is power.' Twin beams of light seared from his eyes, burning Wsoric's face and torso. The daemon recoiled, loosing its grip and Mhotep rammed his spear into its neck. Shrieking in pain, Wsoric let him down and the Thousand Son clattered to the floor, the spear still embedded in the daemon's neck.

With a massive effort, Mhotep got up and threw the daemon off, a mental shield forming in his mind and crystallising in the air before him. Wsoric was angry, its red raw flesh charred and bleeding ichor. The fresh spear wound had not closed.

Wsoric came at the Thousand Son again, tearing through the psychic shield as if it was parchment.

CESTUS FELL FLAT on his face, dry heaving. He couldn't tell which way was up. He was cold, appallingly cold, as if he was wrapped in ice or exposed to the naked void.

The feeling of his body coming apart was an agonising echo in every bone and tendon. To turn like that from a living, breathing man to a piece of mangled meat, to be trapped in that transition, feeling his spine cracking and his chest splitting, had been as obscene as it was tortuous. He felt violated, as if his flesh didn't belong to him any more.

Cestus opened his eyes.

He was in the last circle of hell. It was an endless shaft of blackness, reaching up and down for infinity. Hundreds of long, thin blades penetrated the darkened void, hanging down from above and spearing down forever. On these blades were impaled traitors to Macragge. They slid, centimetre by centimetre, down into the black.

Cestus stood on a thin spur of rock reaching from the wall of this circle of hell. He saw the faces of the condemned, locked in eternal screams as the blades bit slowly through them.

'You have as many circles of sin as hell itself,' said the taskmaster, standing behind Cestus. The Ultramarine

got a good look at him for the first time, as burly as an
Astartes, dressed in tarnished steel armour such as that
worn by Macragge's ancient Battle Kings. He wore a
leather apron stained with blood and sweat. His face
was like a solid slab, features worn down by an eternity
serving in hell. The whip in his hand was as cruel and
ugly a weapon as Cestus had ever seen.

'I'm not a traitor,' said Cestus.

'Neither are these,' said the taskmaster, pointing with
his whip towards the damned souls sliding their way
into eternity. 'They think they are. Theirs is a sin more
of arrogance than treachery. They thought they really
had the capacity to betray their fellow man, but in truth
they are just petty thieves and killers: unremarkable. To
be a true betrayer, you need power to turn against your
brother. Very few ever possess it. That the virtue in
acquiring that very power should be so tainted by the
act of betrayal, that is the truth of the sin. That is what
makes it fouler still than anything else.'

Cestus looked down at his body. His armour was
gone and he wore the deep blue padded armour of an
aspirant of Macragge, with the crest of the Battle Kings
on his chest. It was what he had worn when he had first
stepped up to the Ultramarines' chaplain and declared
that he believed he was ready to join the sons of Guilliman. It was tattered and torn, stained with the blood of
a thousand battles. 'I am no traitor, imagined or otherwise. I have never turned on my brothers.'

'As for you, Lysimachus, where do you really belong?
You are an Astartes, with all the power and brutality that
brings. You're a murderer, too, given all the people and
xenos you have killed, do you truly believe that not one
of them could have been undeserving of their fate?
Think of all those sins, and that is without the mission

you died fighting. You led a whole fleet to its destruction. You allowed your battle-brothers to die in vain. You protected a psyker, knowing full well that he was in breach of the Council of Nikea: all of this to fight your fellow Astartes. Where, captain, do we start with you?'

Cestus looked down over the edge of the precipice. The true heart of hell was there. Something enormous roiled down, barely visible against the darkness. A vast maw ground traitors between its teeth. Thousands of eyes accused them with every flash of pain.

'None of this is real,' said Cestus.

The Ultramarine smiled despite his surroundings as the clarity of understanding washed away all doubt like blue water.

'I am not dead and this is not hell,' he affirmed.

'How can you be sure?' asked the taskmaster.

'Because I may be guilty of everything you have said. I have led men to their deaths, and killed and maimed, and turned on fellow Astartes, but I am no traitor.'

Cestus stepped off the ledge, and fell into the last hell.

PAIN, REAL TANGIBLE pain, slammed into Cestus as he hit the ground. He had escaped. Somehow, through resolve and belief in himself, he had shrugged off the psychic glamour, the cage of his own mind, and emerged intact.

The booming of the big guns hammered at him through the floor and recollection returned.

He was on the *Furious Abyss*. Cynically, he wondered if it might have been more prudent to stay in hell.

Cestus's body ached and he tested himself for injuries. He was bruised and rattled, but otherwise fine and he still had his armour. Getting to his feet, he saw Excelinor beside him. In his fever dream, he must have dragged his battle-brother along with him, although, the Ultramarine captain had no idea where he actually was.

Cestus felt a pang of grief in his heart. Excelinor was dead. It was possible that under the psychic assault the Astartes's sus-an membrane had shut his body down into stasis. It hardly mattered; there would be no waking him.

Cestus crouched over his fallen battle-brother and rested his arms across his chest, placing the short-blade in his grasp in a death salute. The Ultramarine captain could do little more. He stood up again and backed up against a wall, ignoring the throbbing in his head. He felt his armour dispensing painkillers into his system and detected his altered physiognomy at work, enabling him to move and fight.

Scanning his surroundings, Cestus gathered that he was no longer outside the ordnance decks. He had no idea how he had got to this place and assumed that he had staggered through the tunnels of the *Furious Abyss* in a psychic-induced delirium, some innate survival instinct carrying him from immediate danger. It looked like a barracks. He dredged flashes of schematic implanted in his mind by Mhotep. Several dormitories made up the deck and there was temple at the far end. It was the only exit.

Treading cautiously, assuming that the deck must be largely unoccupied or he would've been discovered already, Cestus made for the temple.

The chamber was anathema to everything the Emperor had taught them to believe. It opposed the era of enlightenment that the Great Crusade was meant to usher in for mankind, the banishment of barbarian customs and the value of the empirical over the superstitious. The temple flouted everything the Astartes stood for.

It was a place of worship, but of what craven deities Cestus did not know. An altar sat against one wall and there were pews arranged for prayer. The chamber was dressed with deep scarlet banners with crimson embroidery. The Ultramarine tried to focus on the designs, but found he couldn't as they appeared to squirm and congeal before his eyes.

Several small bloodstained objects stood on the altar. Cestus realised that they were severed fingers, hundreds of them. An image of the *Furious*'s crewmen lining up to mutilate themselves in the name of Lorgar filled his mind. Cestus shook it away and forced himself to focus. His mind was still reeling. He had been to hell. The aftertaste of it was in his mouth and his body remembered the feeling of being wrenched apart.

The sound of footsteps snapped his attention to the present. They were approaching fast: voices barked orders and armoured bodies clattered through a doorway nearby.

Though it rankled to hide, Cestus moved swiftly to the far end of the room where he could disappear into a shadowy alcove. It stank of old blood and decaying flesh. For the span of the *Furious*'s short life, the crew had used it constantly for their devotions. Books were piled up behind the altar nearby, each one with the rune of an eight-pointed star on the cover. Cestus averted his gaze, unwilling to learn of the myriad forms of damnation that awaited him within those pages.

'There! The blood trail's in here. Guns up and execute!' It came from inside the room.

Cestus slid his bolt pistol from his holster and risked a glance around the altar. A squad of five Word Bearers had entered the room and were sweeping every corner with bolters. One wore an open book worked into the breastplate of his armour, words upon it inscribed in gold intaglio. Cestus assumed that he was a Legion veteran given command of the squad.

'Check the barrack rooms,' growled the veteran, with a voice like churning gravel. The Word Bearer cradled a low-slung melta-gun, a short-range weapon that burned through armour and flesh like parchment. It was an Astartes killer, the perfect hunting weapon.

The veteran and two others were left in the temple. The squad fanned out at a silent battle-sign from their leader and were working their way through the pews.

Cestus needed to act, while he still maintained the element of surprise. Unclipping a pair of frag grenades from his belt, he thumbed the activation icon on each and rolled them slowly across the ground.

One of the Word Bearers reacted to the sound and swung his bolter around to fire. Frag exploded in his face before he could pull the trigger, ripping off part of his helmet. A secondary detonation erupted beneath the other Astartes, the impact accentuated in the close confines, and took off his leg at the armour joint.

Spits of flame and a storm of splinters still clouding the air, Cestus was up and drilled a shot through the first Word Bearer, exploiting the fact that his head armour was compromised. A puff of red mist came from the back of the Word Bearer's head before he died.

The Ultramarine heard the telltale whine of the melta-gun powering up and threw himself aside as the Word Bearer veteran discharged the deadly weapon. His sight line was cluttered with debris and the shot burned through the still falling, one-legged Word Bearer, who slumped to the ground with a smoking crater through his torso.

Cestus was up in moments, leaping over the pews and pumping rounds from his bolt pistol. The veteran, the last Word Bearer standing in the temple, saw the Ultramarine, but reacted too slowly. Before he could swing his melta-gun around for a second shot, bolt-rounds punched him in the arm and torso. The veteran spun and bucked with the impacts. As Cestus reached him, he had already drawn his power sword and lopped off the falling veteran's head with a grunt of effort. Ignoring the sanguine gore pouring from the veteran's neck, Cestus pushed on and regained the corridor outside the temple that led to the barrack rooms. A surprised Word Bearer, alerted by the gunfire, emerged from one of the chambers. Cestus shot him through the lens in his battle-helm and the enemy Astartes crumpled with a muffled cry.

A second Word Bearer sensibly employed more caution, using the extended grip of his bolter so that he could reach around the doorway and blindly strafe the corridor. Cestus hugged the wall as the shots streamed past, muzzle flash blazing. An errant bolt-round struck his pauldron armour, sending a chip spinning into Cestus's face. He was without his battle-helm and fought the urge to cry out when the shard cut into his flesh and embedded there. Instead, he rolled his body over the wall, descending into a crouching stance and squeezed his bolt pistol trigger in an attempt to force his aggressor back into the chamber.

The weapon clicked in his grasp. It seemed so loud and final, despite the roar of battle filling Cestus's ears.

The Ultramarine's mouth formed an oath as the Word Bearer, who must have heard the dry shot, came out from his hiding place, laughing.

Instinctively, Cestus hurled his power sword. The blade spun end over end and *thunked* hard through the shocked Word Bearer's gorget, impaling him through the neck. The Astartes staggered, arms splayed at first as he struggled to comprehend what had just happened to him, dark fluid leaking down his breastplate like a flood. Cestus followed the sword's path at a run, smacking the boltgun out of the stricken traitor's hand and wrenching the power sword free, taking the Word Bearer's head with it.

'My brother, my enemy,' Cestus breathed after he took a moment to take stock, regarding the carnage of the dead Word Bearers around him.

Five Astartes slain, albeit traitors, by his hand; a temple devoted to heathen gods; enlightenment and the pragmatism of science and reason abandoned for superstition. Cestus felt the galaxy darkening even as he sheathed his power sword and discarded the Word Bearer's unusable bolter clips. Grimacing, he tugged the ceramite chip from his face and then he pushed on. Somewhere ahead, he knew, was an armoury.

BRYNNGAR LEAPT ASIDE as the power hammer crashed down onto the deck. Rolling to his feet, the Space Wolf could only watch as Baelanos, awesome in his dreadnought armour, wrenched the weapon free from a crater filled with sparking wires and torn metal. Cables ripped out with the hammer head were snarled around the weapon's spikes like intestines.

Baelanos grunted as he righted himself, confusion still warring within him, and charged again.

Brynngar ducked beneath the wild sweep of the hammer this time, the solid metal face whistling past his head like a death knell. The Space Wolf moved in with Felltooth and landed a fearsome blow to Baelanos's armoured flank. The rune axe *spanged* against the reinforced ceramite frame and bit deep, but the Word Bearer dreadnought didn't slow. Baelanos's momentum carried him thundering into the Space Wolf, his machine bulk like a battering ram. Brynngar was smashed aside and lost his grip on Felltooth. He skidded on his front across the deck, friction sparks kicked up from his armour spitting in the Space Wolf's face. Brynngar grimaced and got up, drawing a knife from his belt. The monomolecular blade was honed to beyond razor sharpness and could scythe open power armour with the proper amount of pressure. The only downside was its appalling reach, and Brynngar doubted whether a thrown blade would even irritate his goliath enemy.

Roaring a battle-cry, the old wolf launched himself at Baelanos, who was still turning, flashing in and out of lucidity. With every attack from the Space Wolf, though, the dreadnought's memory was renewed.

Clinging to the Word Bearer machine's weapon arm, Brynngar rammed his knife blade into the armour joint that sealed the sarcophagus in an attempt to prize it open. Baelanos spun hard, armoured feet stomping up and down, and his torso twisting as he sought to dislodge his opponent. Brynngar dug in, wrapping his legs around the dreadnought's shoulder as he pushed the blade two-handed until it reached the hilt.

Baelanos, realising that he couldn't shake the Space Wolf loose, decided to ram the Astartes into the armoury wall and charged headlong into it. Brynngar saw the empty dreadnought suits coming towards him at speed and realised that he was about to be crushed. He swung aside at the last moment, violently thrown clear as Baelanos careered into the dormant armour with a deafening *clang*. Dislodging himself quickly, the

Word Bearer turned and stomped towards the prone Space Wolf, still dazed from his hurried dismount, intending to crush him beneath his feet.

With a groan of pain, Brynngar rolled aside, but Baelanos was getting quicker and caught him a glancing blow with the power hammer as the Space Wolf struggled to rise. White fury filled Brynngar's body and for a moment he was back at Fenris, though now a man, standing upon the shores of the silver-grey ocean. Brynngar ducked a second swipe of the giant hammer that would have shattered his skull and ended the duel then and there. He saw Felltooth in flashes, but couldn't reach the weapon's haft to wrench it free. Brynngar also saw that the sarcophagus had sprung open, the collision forcing it loose with the Space Wolf's knife lodged in the joint. The amniotic blister lay unprotected. Brynngar went for his bolt pistol, but found it wasn't there. He cursed loudly. He must have lost it during the crash or at some point in the psychic fever dream.

Blood drooled from the Space Wolf's mouth and nose, matting in the hair of his beard. His leg felt leaden and unresponsive. His body ached as if stuck with red-hot pins. This was the end. Unarmed and injured, even a warrior of Brynngar's prowess could not hope to hold out against a dreadnought. Baelanos seemed to sense that inevitability and moved in slowly, as if savouring the kill.

The Space Wolf realised that he was laughing. The action of it hurt his chest. The shadow of the dreadnought eclipsed him completely and Brynngar closed his eyes, imaging the ocean.

'Fenris,' he whispered.

A bolter shot, stark and hollow, resounded in the armoury. Brynngar's eyes snapped open to see a smoking hole in the blister, fracture lines emanating outwards from the puncture crater. Baelanos was rocked backwards, a gurgling sound emanating from his vox-emitter. Viscous, amniotic fluid spilled out from the crack like brine.

The Space Wolf ran forward, despite a new pain flaring in his leg, and ripped Felltooth free from the dreadnought's bulk. He carved a line down the blister as Baelanos flailed in desperation and it cracked apart. The fluid gushed out, taking the incumbent Astartes inside with it. Baelanos flopped out of the shattered blister, half suspended by the circuitry and cables linking him to the dreadnought armour. A second shot from the still unseen bolt pistol struck him in the chest and thick blood oozed from the wound. The dreadnought fell backwards, hitting the armoury floor with a resounding clang, and was still. Brynngar crawled on top of it, straddling the machine, and tore into the wasted body of Baelanos with his rune axe until there was nothing left.

'Try coming back from that,' he breathed savagely.

Resonating footsteps made the Space Wolf turn around to regard his saviour. Skraal emerged from the gloom, bolt pistol still smoking in his outstretched fist.

'Thought you were dead,' grunted the old wolf and promptly collapsed.

MHOTEP FORCED THE end of his arm back into his shoulder joint. The pain didn't mean anything. The grimace on his face was from frustration that the arm, and with it his spear, would be weakened. He heaved down a couple of deep breaths and backed up against a bulkhead.

The battle against Wsoric had passed beyond the corridor outside the bridge and had progressed to the senior crew quarters, chambers allocated to him before he'd been confined to isolation. They were relatively close to the bridge, should an emergency necessitate the presence of any senior crew. That fact meant little, in the face of certain death, save that the trail of destruction left by their battle was short-lived.

As he regarded the collapsed ceiling, the wreckage of two decks punctuated by a few intact support stanchions and columns still smouldering, Mhotep came to realise that he was the last living being on the command deck. The Thousand Son had lost sight of the daemon when he'd been smashed through the deck and landed in the chamber below. Wsoric could be anywhere. He tasted blood in his mouth and knew the fused carapace of his ribs was broken. His breathing was ragged, which indicated a punctured lung and his shoulder burned.

In truth, the fight was not going as he'd hoped.

'You resisted,' said the daemon. 'I turned your brothers against you, showed you the path and you refused it. That was folly.'

Mhotep tried to follow the sound of Wsoric's voice, but it came from all around him.

'Do you realise how fragile the Emperor's house is? How easily his sons will war with one another? It took nothing to make the wolf turn on you and little more for the puritan captain to abandon your defence.'

Mhotep ignored the goading, and tried to focus. It was dark in the crew quarters, all power having died on the *Wrathful* and he closed his eyes, relying instead on his psy-sight to guide him. Life support was dead too and the air was growing stagnant without it. Mhotep kept his breathing steady, so as not to use up too much oxygen.

'The Imperium will fall,' Wsoric promised, 'and the galaxy will bathe in blood and fire. Humanity's dominance is at an end.'

Mhotep cast about the chamber. His psy-sight showed him a grey, shadow world that was indistinct and grainy. Corpses of the slain officers who had died in their quarters flickered briefly like dimming candles. A voracious life spark, red and angry, got Mhotep's attention. He saw the daemon form. Its skin was like incandescent fire, constantly burning, and ribbed horns curled from its snarling head. A hide of thick, black hair covered its back from where immense, tattered wings extended, and its clawed feet raked the floor.

'I see you,' he whispered and threw his spear.

The daemon roared in agony as the golden spear impaled its neck. Mhotep's eyes snapped open and Wsoric became the fleshy abomination once more, transfixed by his weapon. He ran headlong at the creature, trying to make the most of the small advantage he had gained.

The daemon twisted, enduring the pain it brought as the spear tip tore at its ephemeral flesh. Its gaping maw split open all the way down through its torso and, just as Mhotep reached it, the daemon vomited a hail of burning bone shards. The Thousand Son took a shard in his leg that pierced his battle-plate with ease. Limping backwards, he ripped the spear out of Wsoric's neck, ichor spewing in its wake and thrust again, shredding through the muscle of the daemon's shoulder.

With a lurch of straining steel, the deck collapsed, Astartes and daemon plunging into a dark void below. They landed in a dead space in the hull, separating the crew quarters from the lower industrial decks. A freezing gloom persisted there, criss-crossed with support beams. Mhotep rolled off the creature, which had taken the brunt of the fall, and staggered backwards.

Wsoric rose with the screech of sundered metal. The struts around it were already damaged. The ship was breaking apart. The daemon roared its anger, preparing to vent its wrath when the supports gave way. Together, they tumbled down into the cold blackness.

THE SOUND OF the ocean receded as Brynngar came around. The scarred visage of the World Eater in his battle-helm looked down on him.

'You're a sore sight for my eyes,' grumbled the old wolf and got to his feet. Brynngar's body felt bruised with the effort, and the pain down one leg made him stagger at first before he righted himself. Blood flecked his beard and armour.

'How long was I out?' he asked, aware that they were still in the armoury hall.

'Just a few minutes,' Skraal replied, 'but we've no time to rest. Word Bearers are patrolling the ship looking for us.'

'Been hunting you for a while, eh?' guessed the Space Wolf, taking in the rents and burns on Skraal's armour. He could almost imagine the fevered look in his eyes, the kind of nervous expression that any man on the run might adopt after being chased for long enough. The World Eater was already volatile. Shaken up as he was, he might crack at any moment.

'Several weeks… I think.' The son of Angron came across a little dazed as his time aboard the ship had dulled his sense of what was real and what were merely phantoms of the mind.

'Did anyone else get aboard?' Brynngar asked, swinging Felltooth to better remember the strength of his arm. The old wolf noticed that the red-limned portal was still open.

'I am the only survivor,' Skraal responded curtly and headed for the light.

'You know where that leads?' asked the Wolf Guard, noting the nonchalant way the World Eater approached the doorway.

'The corridor beyond will get us to the engine deck.'

'We need to reach ordnance and destroy the cyclonic payload,' said Brynngar, 'and how do you know that we can reach the engines from there?'

'He knows because I told him,' said a familiar voice from the gloom that sent the hackles on the back of Brynngar's neck rising.

'Destroying the cyclonics is no longer viable,' he added, emerging out of the penumbra.

'Cestus.' Brynngar growled when he said it.

The Ultramarine slammed a fresh clip from the armoury's stores into his bolt pistol and nodded to the Space Wolf.

'There is but one opportunity left to us,' Cestus said. 'The easier course is no longer possible. We must walk the harder road. It is the only one open to us.'

Brynngar's silence held the question.

'We must destroy the ship,' said Cestus.

TWENTY

Contention/Avenge me/Immolation

'DESTROY THE SHIP?' Brynngar laughed as he limped after his battle-brothers. When Cestus went to aid him, he snarled, 'I'm fine,' before continuing.

'This is the single largest and most powerful vessel I have ever seen. A few incendiaries,' the Space Wolf indicated the grenade harness he still carried 'will not see to its ruin.'

'Have you lost your mind as well as your honour, son of Guilliman?'

'Neither,' Cestus replied. 'The *Furious Abyss* can be destroyed. In order to do it, we must reach the engines and the plasma reactor that fuels them. If we can overload them with an incendiary payload of our own the resulting explosion will commence a chain reaction that cannot be averted by the ship's fail safes and redundant systems.'

Brynngar seized Cestus by the shoulder. The Space Wolf's eyes were full of anger.

'You knew this and yet said nothing?'

'It was irrelevant before,' Cestus returned, shaking free of the Wolf Guard's grip. 'Our only way in was through the torpedo tubes, which made the cyclonics our obvious and most immediate target. There was no way of knowing we could've made it this far into the ship for an assault on the main reactor to be even possible.'

'Leaving aside the matter of how you even know this,' snarled the Wolf Guard, 'how do you plan on getting close enough to destroy it? Have you seen the size of this vessel; it will be like a labyrinth in the engineering decks. We might never find it.'

'I can guide us. It will take minutes,' Cestus replied curtly. He was about to head off when Brynngar grabbed his arm again.

'I don't know what pact you have made with the witch that cowers aboard the *Wrathful* and what secrets you may be privy to,' growled the Space Wolf dangerously, 'but know this: I will not abide sorcery in any form. Once we gain the reactor and set this ship burning, our alliance is at an end, Ultramarine.' Brynngar let Cestus go, and stalked away, taking a bolt pistol from the armoury and making ready at the open portal.

'So be it,' said Cestus grimly to himself and went to join his battle-brothers.

THE FURIOUS ABYSS had been forced out of position during the battle with the *Wrathful*. Formaska glowered well to its starboard side, Macragge scarcely less ominous well below it. The planet's local defence fleet was also in sight, lingering above Macragge's upper-atmosphere. With the supplicants dead, the *Furious*'s surveyor-dampening systems, which had allowed it to ambush the *Fist of Macragge* were no longer effective.

Slowly, the vessels were moving into defensive positions. Without knowledge of the Word Bearers' intentions or their defection from the Imperium, though, the Macragge fleet was cautious and had yet to engage. They would try to hail them first. It was all the time that the *Furious Abyss* would need to realign, destroy Formaska and thus cripple the fleet in one stroke. The *Wrathful* was gone from the massive ship's viewscreens, now little more than a chilling tomb of dead lights and lost souls, as it floundered in the void without power. Gravity would claim it.

Orders were relayed down to the *Furious Abyss*'s engine rooms to engage the directional thrusters and orient the ship back towards Formaska. The ordnance decks had been retaken, although the damage done by the enemy' assault was extensive in some areas. The explosive discharge from a rapidly detonated melta bomb cluster had been ill-targeted, but destructive. The repair crews were hard at work clearing debris and expelling corpses into the void, but reaching operational status again would take time. It meant, although the cyclonic payload was intact, the launch would be delayed further.

Zadkiel felt his glory slipping through his grasp even as he listened to the toiling of the ratings on the ordnance deck. He shut down the vox link and closed his eyes, trying to master his anger.

Opening them again, Zadkiel looked at the positional display on one of his command throne's viewscreens. The *Furious* had yet to change its heading and reset the launch vectors for the torpedoes.

'Gureod,' he barked into the vox array.

Silence answered.

'Damn it, magos, why are the engines not engaged?'

Nothing again. Now the magos was just mocking him.

'Reskiel,' snarled Zadkiel, his tone impatient.

'My lord,' said the voice of the sergeant-commander, the thudding retort of gunfire audible in the background.

'Get to engineering and find out why the ship has stalled.'

'My lord,' said Reskiel again, 'we are at engineering. The enemy are here. They move through the ship as if they know every tunnel and access conduit. My squad is moving in to eliminate–'

The sound of a thunderous explosion broke the vox link for a moment. Crackling static reigned for a few seconds before Reskiel returned. 'We have made contact. They are at the edge of the main reactor approach...'

Frantic cries and the screams of Word Bearers punctuated the chorus of bolter fire before the vox link went dead.

Zadkiel clenched his fist, and bit out his next words.

'Ikthalon, lead three squads down to engineering. Seek those curs out and destroy them!' Zadkiel's veneer of calm cracked and fell away completely. He was shaking with apoplectic rage.

Ikthalon had returned to the bridge following the death of the supplicants and had, until now, observed proceedings with silent deference.

'No, my lord,' he responded in his usual sibilant cadence, adding, 'I have endured your ineptitude for long enough. It threatens the glory of Kor Phaeron and our Lord Lorgar.' Zadkiel heard the chaplain draw his bolt pistol from its holster.

'I had thought you impudent, Ikthalon,' said the admiral calmly, his composure returning as he turned to the chaplain. Zadkiel saw that he did indeed have his pistol trained upon him.

'I did not believe you to be stupid.'

The chaplain's posture was neutral and unassuming.

'Stand down,' he said simply, lifting the pistol a fraction to emphasis his point.

Zadkiel bowed his head. In the corner of his eye, he saw Ikthalon start to lower his weapon. It would be the chaplain's last mistake.

Zadkiel moved swiftly to the side, his rapier-like power sword drawn fluidly. The bucking report of the bolt pistol sounded on the bridge, but Ikthalon's shot, confounded by the admiral's sudden movement, missed.

Zadkiel slid the blade through the chaplain's gorget, smacking the bolt pistol from his grasp at the same time.

'Did you think I would leave this bridge, my bridge, to a snake like you?'

Ikthalon could only gurgle in reply.

Zadkiel ripped away the chaplain's battle-helm. Underneath it, Ikthalon was scarred, his face a mass of burn tissue, his ravaged throat a wreck of scabrous flesh. He stared into the chaplain's pink-tinged eyes with intense hate.

'You thought wrong,' he hissed, and pushed Ikthalon off the blade to land with a clang of ceramite on the deck. The chaplain floundered at first, trying to speak, clutching ineffectually at his throat, but was then still, the blood pooling slowly beneath him.

Zadkiel turned to Sarkorov.

'Clean that up and monitor all stations. You have the bridge. As soon as we are in a state of readiness again, inform me at once,' ordered Zadkiel.

Pale-faced at the chaplain's sudden death, the helms-master snapped a ragged salute and gestured to a group of Legion serfs to act as a clean-up crew.

Zadkiel stalked away, wiping the blood off his blade. He would deal with the infiltrators and be damned to ignominy if he was going to let them interfere any further with his plans. Besides, it would not look favourable in the eyes of the arch-commander if he needed his lackeys to deal with their enemies. No, the only way to be sure was to kill them all himself.

RESKIEL WAS PLEASED. Though he had lost several of his squad fighting the loyalists, he had them boxed in, having forced them into a tunnel that he knew was a dead end. The sound of gunfire had abated, but the roar of the primary reactor and all the workings of the ship were still incredibly loud inside his battle-helm.

Using Astartes battle-sign, he signalled for the three warriors with him to descend from the upper stacks where they'd spread out and exploited their vantage point to coral the loyalists into a death trap. For a moment, Reskiel lost sight of two of his warriors as they moved into position.

Reaching the ground floor of the engineering deck, they converged on the tunnel. That was when Reskiel first realised that something was wrong. One of his warriors was missing.

'Where is Vorkan?' he hissed through the helmet vox.

'I lost sight of him as he changed position, sergeant,' one of the others, Karhadax, replied.

Reskiel turned to the second Word Bearer, Eradan.

'I was watching the Space Wolf and the Ultramarine,' he said by way of explanation.

A cold chill ran down Reskiel's spine despite the heat of exertion and the warmth of the engineering deck.

'What of the third? What of the World Eater?'

The hunters had suddenly become the prey.

Eradan's neck and chest exploded outwards in a rain of blood and flesh, the whirring of chain teeth visible through all the gore.

'I'm right here,' said Skraal, his voice dead of all emotion, as the Word Bearer he had slain fell face forward onto the deck. He killed Karhadax next, cutting off his head as he charged. Whatever oath or battle cry the Word Bearer was about to shout died on his lips as his decapitated head hit the ground. Skraal kicked the still-flailing body out of his path and came at Reskiel.

To the sergeant-commander's credit, he did not flinch in the face of the killing machine before him, and even managed to put a bolt round through Skraal's thigh before the World Eater buried his chainaxe into him.

Skraal tore his bloodied weapon out of the still quivering body as Cestus and Brynngar emerged from the tunnel. It was with some degree of satisfaction that the World Eater had killed Reskiel. He had slain Antiges and chased him like a dog through the bowels of the ship. Four other Word Bearers lay within the tunnel nearby, variously punctured with bolter wounds and cleaved by blades. They were the other remnants of Reskiel's hunter squad, despatched by the Astartes.

'Next time, you're the bait,' Brynngar growled at Skraal, who smacked his chainaxe against the deck to dislodge some of the flesh snarled up in its blades.

'There will be more,' said Cestus, ramming a fresh clip that he'd taken from the armoury hall into his bolt pistol.

'There's always more,' growled Brynngar, eager not to linger. 'Lead on.'

Warning klaxons were sounding everywhere as the search for the Astartes saboteurs intensified and found its focus. Red hazard lights flashed with insistent inter-mittence and the shouts of the distant hunters echoed through the metal labyrinth of piping conduits and machinery. Gantries overhead provided only a curtailed view of the maze below, but Cestus instructed them to seek what cover they could whilst moving swiftly.

Determined to inflict as much damage as possible en route to the main reactor, the three Astartes had moved through the secondary reactors, systematically wrecking them as they went. Already reactor three had shut down, several coolant pipes torn free of its side and its crews scythed down with bolter fire at their dead man's handles. Escaped coolant poured down from it in a scalding thunderhead of steam.

Cestus despatched a reactor crewman emerging from a control room with a snap shot from his bolt pistol. Another came from the opposite aisle of conduits. The Ultramarine killed him too.

The death dealing was indiscriminate. Fighting in and amongst the close confines of the pipe-works was like guerrilla warfare. Despite the overwhelming forces arrayed against them, the loyalist Astartes had a chance in this arena. Numerous improvised booby traps, sim-ple frag grenade and tripwire arrangements, had been left in their wake, and the occasional explosion behind them meant that Cestus knew when their enemies were closing. Only the frag and krak grenades were used for traps. They would need the melta bombs for the main reactor. Once they reached it, they would need to infil-trate the protective shielding and plant the explosives into the reactor swell. That was, assuming the reactor's immense radiation didn't kill them first. It was a journey that Cestus planned on making alone and not one he was expecting to come back from.

A fusillade of bolter fire from a gantry above them got the Ultramarine's attention, tearing up sections of piping.

The Word Bearers had found them.

ZADKIEL WATCHED THE Astartes scurry into cover as his squads opened fire from the main access gantry. From his vantage point, he could see the whole reactor section, like an ocean of darkness with the reactors, immense steel islands, connected by a flimsy spider's web of catwalks, coolant pipes and maintenance ladders. He recognised the armour of three Legions amongst the saboteurs, and knew that this was the last of them: the last desperate attempt to try and make a difference.

'It will do you no good,' Zadkiel whispered to himself and turned to his sergeants. 'Grazious, hound them from up here. The rest of us will press on to the main reactor and intercept them.'

The sergeant saluted, snapping an affirmative response as Zadkiel departed.

'Such impudence,' Zadkiel muttered as he headed towards the main reactor.

It would end, here and now, with the death of the Ultramarines.

MHOTEP DRAGGED HIMSELF along the floor of the ordnance deck.

The air was still thick with the stench of death. Dried blood caked the walls and the bulkheads on either side were sealed with super-hot torches.

The Thousand Son rolled onto his back with effort and peered up at the rent in the ceiling far above, through which he'd plummeted. Wsoric had fallen with him. Craning his neck to look down the charnel house gangway, Mhotep saw rotting corpses on either side, prickling with frost as the void penetrated the *Wrathful*'s hull. Breathing was difficult, the air was thinning, and with the life support inoperative it would not replenish itself. Pain kept the Astartes moving. The red hot needles in his body let him know he was alive and still fighting.

He was dying. Mhotep knew this, but death held no fear for him. It was fate, his fate, and he embraced it. Struggling to his feet, the hellish agony intensified, and for a moment, Mhotep thought he might pass out.

Wsoric was a short distance away, squatting over a heap of corpses. They were the remains of the ratings and gang masters that had been sealed in when the deck was quarantined. Already lost to madness, Mhotep could only imagine what they had thought, half frozen from the cold of space, when the daemon approached them. Perhaps they had welcomed it. Perhaps they had forfeited their souls.

Wsoric stood and arched its neck. Distended flesh bulged and writhed as it consumed the last of the survivors in body and in doing so claimed their souls.

The daemon turned, an apparition in the blackness of the abattoir its kind had created, smiling at the Thousand Son's pitiful attempt to escape it.

'I ever hunger, Astartes,' it told him. 'The thirst for souls is never slaked. It is like an eternal keening in my skull upon this plane. You will quiet it for a time,' it promised, heading for Mhotep.

The Thousand Son fell as he went to flee the daemon. Blood was seeping from his cuirass where Wsoric had raked him with its claws. Bloody and battered, the Astartes had been granted a short reprieve when the creature detected the mewling terror from within the deck. It had found the ratings easily, drawn by the scent of their fear. Mhotep had been made to watch as the daemon butchered them.

'I will drink of your hope and bravery until you are hollow,' promised Wsoric.

Mhotep dragged himself up, using his spear as a crutch. He would meet his destruction face-to-face and on his feet. Outstretching his palm, a nimbus of scarlet light played about his finger tips.

Wsoric was almost upon him, and reached out, crushing the Thousand Son's hand in his taloned fist.

Mhotep screamed in agony as his bones were splintered even within his gauntlet. He dropped the spear and sagged, only held up by the strength of the daemon.

'Still you fight, insignificant speck,' it said, mouth forming into a feral sneer. 'To think that one such as you could kill one such as I.'

The daemon's booming laughter flecked caustic spittle and dead blood into Mhotep's face.

'I wasn't trying to kill you,' muttered the Thousand Son, looking up at the beast as he unclipped something from his belt. It was an incendiary grenade.

'What do you intend to do with that, little man?' asked Wsoric with an obscene smile.

'You have tarried here too long,' said Mhotep. 'At any moment you could have swum across the empyrean to the *Furious Abyss*, or back into the immaterium, but your gluttony for reaping souls has undone you warp beast. Look!'

Wsoric's flesh was leaking ichorous fluid as the psychic energy required to keep it in the material universe broke down. Its form was becoming gelatinous and ephemeral. Mhotep had detected the creature weakening all the time he fought it. Every psychic exertion had taken its toll, sloughing away some of the matter that kept it stable and in existence.

'I wasn't trying to kill you,' said Mhotep with his failing breath, 'just to keep you here for long enough.' He thrust his free hand forward, punching through Wsoric's melting skin and releasing the grenade's detonator.

The daemon snarled in rage and sudden fear.

'Puny human, I will feast upon your…'

Mhotep was thrown back by the blast as Wsoric exploded from the inside, destroyed by the dissolution of its corporeal body.

Lying in an expanding pool of his own blood, Mhotep could see through one of the aiming ports in the ordnance deck's starboard wall. Roaring fire burned at the edges of the *Wrathful*'s armoured hull as the ship, caught in the moon's gravity well, hurtled towards Formaska. He imagined the rivers of lava on its barren surface, the crags and mountainous expanses, and smiled, accepting his doom.

THE NOISE OF THE main reactor, even closed off within its housing, was immense. Beyond, Cestus knew there was an approach corridor, designed to enable close maintenance of the reactor when not in use. Beyond that was the incandescent core of energy. To step into it meant certain death. It was a sacrifice he was willing to make.

Using Astartes battle-sign, the Ultramarine indicated for Brynngar to take up position on the opposite side of the armoured hatch that led into the approach corridor. The Space Wolf obeyed swiftly and was about to cleave

into the first layer of shielding when a hail of bolter fire
rebounded off the metal, forcing him into cover. Cestus
followed, Skraal next to him. The Astartes saw a squad
of Word Bearers in firing drill formation on a lofted
gantry, led by a commander in gilded, crimson armour.
So resplendent and arrogant did he look, that Cestus
assumed at once that he was the captain of the ship.

'We are honoured,' he said sarcastically, shouting at
Skraal to be heard.

The World Eater nodded. He had recognised the
captain too, the one he knew to be called Zadkiel: the
taunting orator who had tried to twist his loyalty and
prey upon his inner weakness. Skraal despised that.
Crouching as he ran, he left cover and disappeared for a
moment behind a riot of piping. He emerged, bolt
pistol blazing. One of the Word Bearers pinning them
was pitched off the gantry, clutching his neck. The
gilded captain stood his ground at first, but took a step
back when a second Word Bearer was spun off his feet,
a smoking hole in his chest-plate.

'Skraal, no, it's suicide!' Cestus cried as he watched
the World Eater gain the stairway and head straight at
the Word Bearers. There was no way he would make it
before they perforated him with bolter shells.

'Come on,' Brynngar bellowed, hacking into the
armoured hatch with the sudden respite. 'Make his sacrifice worthwhile.'

With the Word Bearers occupied, Skraal had given his
comrades the time they needed to cut their way into the
reactor and finally end the *Furious Abyss*.

Cestus was on his feet and cleaved into the hatch with
his power sword. The metal fell away with a resounding
clang as it struck the deck. A backwash of heat flowed
from the approach corridor sending the radiation

warnings flickering on the Ultramarine's·helmet display to critical.

'Bandoleers,' Cestus cried, holding out his hand for the belt of melta bombs that Brynngar carried.

'It's a one way trip,' said the old wolf.

Cestus stared at Brynngar, nonplussed.

'Yes, now hand them over.'

'Not for you,' said the Wolf Guard and punched the Ultramarine hard in the battle-helm.

Cestus fell, half-stunned by the sudden attack, and through his blurring vision he saw Brynngar enter the approach corridor.

'Both of us need not die here. Avenge me,' he heard the Space Wolf say, 'and your Legion.'

SKRAAL TOOK THE gantry steps three at a time. About halfway up his bolt pistol ran dry and he tossed it, focusing instead on his chainaxe. As he emerged into view, the Word Bearers fired. One round tore through his pauldron, another stuck his thigh, a third hit his chest and he staggered, but the fury was upon him and nothing would prevent him from spilling the blood of the enemy. All those weeks fleeing like an animal, caged in the depths of the ship like a… like a slave. That would not be his fate.

Two more shots to the chest and Skraal struck his foes. A Word Bearer came at him with a chainsword. The World Eater swatted the blow aside and carved his enemy in two across the torso. A second went down clutching the ruin of his face where Skraal had caved it in. Another lost an arm and screamed as the World Eater booted him off the gantry to his death below.

Then Skraal faced the gilded captain, standing stock still before him as if at total ease. Bellowing Angron's name, Skraal launched himself at Zadkiel, preparing to dismember him with his chainaxe.

The Word Bearer captain calmly raised his bolt pistol and shot Skraal through the neck. With a last effort, the World Eater lashed out.

Zadkiel screamed in pain as his bolt pistol was cut in two, three of his fingers sheared off with it through the gauntlet.

Smiling beneath his battle-helm, the World Eater felt his leg collapse beneath him. The spinal cord was abruptly severed and a terrible, sudden cold engulfed him, as if he had been plunged into ice.

Vision fogging, he saw Zadkiel standing above, blood dripping from his severed fingers as he drew a long, thin sword.

'I am no slave,' Skraal hissed as the last of his vital fluid pumped out of him freely.

'You have never been anything else,' said Zadkiel savagely, and thrust the blade precisely through Skraal's helmet lens and into the World Eater's eye.

The dead Astartes shuddered for a moment, transfixed on the Word Bearer's sword, before Zadkiel withdrew it with a flourish and Skraal crumpled to the deck. Wiping his blade on the corpse, and with a brief glance at his ruined hand, he turned to his sergeants.

'Now kill the other two.'

CESTUS SHRUGGED OFF his disorientation and went for the hatch, but the barrage of fire resumed, cutting him off from the wolf.

'Damn you, Brynngar,' he bellowed, knowing that it was useless.

Soon the engineering deck would be immolated by fire. The chain reaction that followed after the main reactor's destruction would be cataclysmic. Cestus didn't want to be there when that happened. Anger burned within him at the death of his battle-brothers, the base treachery of the Word Bearers. He wanted Zadkiel, and although there was little chance of reaching him on the engineering deck, the Ultramarine knew where he would find him.

Cestus made his way to the shuttle bay.

BRYNNGAR POWERED THROUGH the access corridor, waves of radiation washing over him, and tore apart the first line of shielding that led further into the reactor core chamber. He pummelled a second bulkhead with his fists. The sense of descent into the beating heart of the ship enveloped Brynngar as he crawled on his hands and knees through the final access conduit.

Ripping away the last barrier of shielding, now several metres below the surface of the engineering deck, he passed the threshold of the reactor core's inner chamber. A blast of intense heat struck him at once, his armour blistering before its fury, and for a moment the wolf recoiled. A deep cone fell away from a narrow platform over which the Space Wolf was perched. Hot wind, boiled up by the lake of liquid fire churning at the nadir of the cone, whipped his hair. Brynngar felt it burning, his skin too, as the intense radiation ravaged his flesh.

Beautiful, he thought as he regarded the glowing reactor mass below: raw, incandescent energy that boiled and thrashed like a captured thunderhead.

Priming the melta bombs around his waist, the Space Wolf closed his eyes. It was a hundred-metre drop down into the reactor core. Its smooth, angled walls were bathed in light.

Brynngar stepped off the narrow platform and fell. The first explosion was like a thunderclap.

Storms ravaged the platinum sky as Brynngar stood upon the edge of the silver Fenrisian ocean. The tide was high and the waves crashed against the icebergs, shattering the ice-flows with pounding surf. He was dressed in only a loincloth, with his knife tucked into a leather belt and his baleen spear thrust into the hard-packed snow. Out beyond the glowing horizon, there was a keening echo. The great orca was calling to him.

Brynngar took his spear and dived into the ice-cold waters. Light was rising on the horizon, the storm receding. As he swam, he felt a strange sensation. It felt as if he was going home.

THE SUDDEN RELEASE of explosive power rippled through the main reactor. The conical structure ruptured and the plasma roared out. It fell in a massive fountain of fire, drenching the whole reactor section in a monstrous burning rain. Bolts of it punched through machinery and walkways, and through the bodies of Zadkiel's warriors. Secondary explosions tore up from the minor reactors as a terrible chain reaction took hold. There was a deep and sonorous *crump* of force as one of the engines shattered apart with the backwash of energy.

A chunk of reactor housing shot like a missile right through the main chamber of reactor seven, which echoed the explosion with a huge expanding flood of ignited plasma. Emergency systems slammed into place, but there was no way to seal the breach when plasma was free and expanding within the hull.

Reactors two and eight were breached, emptying their plasma into the reactor section's depths. The hapless menials still at work in the labyrinth were devoured in the sudden flood. The level of plasma reached the base of reactor seven, which blew its top, throwing a second burst into the air like a vast azure fountain.

Heat-expanded air ripped bulkheads open. The hull gave way, the inner skins breaching and filling with plasma before the outer hull was finally torn open and a black-red ribbon of vacuum-frozen fuel bubbled out of the *Furious Abyss*'s wounded flank.

Zadkiel crawled away from the destruction as his ship began to destroy itself from within. He reached the portal, sealing it shut before the few survivors of his squad could get through. He watched, curious and detached, as a bolt of plasma fell like a comet and ripped the gantry apart on which they stood. Survival instincts got Zadkiel to his feet. Reaching the vox, he ordered the abandon ship and proceeded to head for the shuttle bays before it was too late.

TWENTY-ONE

Eve of battle/Face-to-face/Still we'll fight

THE BANNERS OF the Word Bearers, deep crimson with the emblems of the Legion's Chapters, barely stirred in the artificial air of the Cloister of Contrition. Kor Phaeron knelt alone in front of the altar, which was crowned with the image of Lorgar, the Prophet of Colchis. The primarch's image, carved from porphyry and marble, was brandishing the book in which he had first written the Word.

The arch-commander was praying. It was this faith that set the Word Bearers apart. They understood its power. Lorgar had been an exemplar of what a man could achieve when he realised his full potential. Indeed, Lorgar had become much more even than that. Each Word Bearer prayed to commune with himself, with the forces of the universe, to discover the means to unlock their latent strength so that they might use it to do the work of Lorgar. On the eve of battle, it was prayer that made the Word Bearers ready.

Footsteps echoed through the cloisters. It was a place of worship large enough to house three Chapters of battle-brothers, or all of the *Infidus Imperator*'s crew, and the echoes lasted for several seconds.

'I am at prayer,' Kor Phaeron told the intruder, the powerful cadence of his deep voice exacerbated by the acoustics of the temple.

'My lord, we have received no signal,' came the disembodied reply.

It was Tenaebron, Chapter Master of the Void.

'Nothing?' asked Kor Phaeron, incredulity masking his anger as he turned to look upon his subordinate.

'The supplicants on the *Furious Abyss* were activated,' replied Tenaebron, 'and some time after, a psychic flare was detected: very powerful.'

'Formaska?'

'Assuredly not, Lord Kor Phaeron.'

The arch-commander stood up. Bareheaded, he was resplendent in his prayer vestments and towered over the Chapter Master. 'You must be certain of this, Tenaebron,' he said, a warning implicit in his tone.

'Formaska still exists,' the Chapter Master replied. Compared to most Astartes he looked old and weak, and some who did not know the Legion's ways might have thought he was a veteran, half-crippled in body, whose role was to advise and lead from afar. In truth, his small wet eyes and sagging, mournful face concealed a warrior's soul, which he could back up with the force staff scabbarded on his back and the inferno pistol at his side. Even that was of little significance compared to the horrible injuries that Tenaebron could inflict on an enemy's mind.

'Zadkiel has failed,' he added unnecessarily.

Kor Phaeron thought for a moment, turning back to the altar as if the statue of Lorgar could advise him.

'Follow,' he said at length, and marched towards the great doors at the far end of the cloister. Kor Phaeron threw them open.

Hundreds of Word Bearers knelt in prayer, by the light of a thousand braziers, filling the cathedral to which the Cloisters of Contrition adjoined. Each one was deep in his prayers, seeking some greater self within him that could win this fight in the name of Lorgar and seal the truth of the Word. Almost the entire muster of the Chapter of the Opening Eye, that which was being transported by the *Infidus Imperator*, was assembled, with Chapter Master Faerskarel in the front row.

Faerskarel stood up and saluted at the arch commander's approach. 'Lord Kor Phaeron,' he said, 'is it time?'

'Zadkiel has failed,' said Kor Phaeron. 'Soon the fleet's presence will be revealed and Calth will be waiting for us. It is time. This will not be the massacre of which we have spoken. This will be a fight to the end, and Calth will not give up its victory easily. We must wrest it from the enemy as we have always done.'

Faerskarel said nothing, but turned to his Word Bearers, who stood to attention as one.

'Word Bearers!' shouted Kor Phaeron. 'To your drop pods and gunships! Now is the time for war, for victory and death! Arm and say your final prayers, for the Ultramarines are waiting!'

CESTUS REACHED THE shuttle bay quickly. In the ensuing panic once the abandon ship had been declared, few enemies opposed him. Those that did were mainly zealous ratings or blood-hungry menials and he despatched them with bolt and blade.

The deck beneath the Ultramarine shuddered and lurched to the side and, for a moment, Cestus struggled to keep his feet. He heard the first of the explosions from the main reactor as they'd ravaged the ship. Now, further internal detonations were erupting across all decks as the chain reaction set in place by Brynngar's sacrifice tore the *Furious Abyss* apart.

The rest of the crew, the cohorts of Word Bearers and the officers of the bridge, had yet to reach the bay. As plumes of fire spat up from the bowels of the ship like white-orange jets through the deck, and the infrastructure of the shuttle bay disintegrated around him, Cestus doubted that they ever would.

Crossing the metal plaza of the bay was like running a gauntlet, as vessels exploded in storms of shrapnel and debris fell like rain. Cestus saw a rating crushed beneath a hunk of fallen arch, the corpse's hand still twitching in its death throes.

Hundreds of small antechambers bled off from the main bay, each housing a quartet of shuttles, racked in a two by two arrangement. Cestus stepped into the first antechamber he could find that wasn't wreathed in fire or sealed shut by wreckage.

Stepping over the threshold, he saw a solitary figure lit up by the warning strobes set into the shuttle runways. It was gloomy in the chamber, but Cestus recognised the livery of the armour before him.

'Word Bearer,' he called out.

The figure turned, about to step into the first shuttle, and regarded the Ultramarine coldly.

'So you are the one who I am to thank for this,' he said calmly, looking around the room as he opened his arms.

Cestus returned the Word Bearer's contempt and drew his power sword. The arcing lightning coursing down the blade lit the Ultramarine in a grim cast.

'You are Zadkiel,' Cestus said as if it were an accusation. 'I thought the captain was meant to go down with his ship.'

'That will not be my destiny,' Zadkiel replied drawing his sword. Energy crackled down its blade too. It was longer and slightly thinner than the Ultramarine's weapon, master crafted by some Martian artificer no doubt, the aesthetic flourishes added by a Legion artisan.

'I have your destiny right here,' Cestus promised him, and thought of Antiges slain in battle, his battle-brothers killed by the warp predators aboard the *Wrathful*; of Saphrax and his warriors smashed against the hull, their honour denied them; of Skraal and Brynngar sacrificed upon the altar of victory and hope. 'This is where your words end.'

'You are a fool, Ultramarine,' snarled Zadkiel, 'ignorant of the power of the galaxy. Gods walk among us, Astartes. Real gods! Not ghosts or ciphers or interloper aliens, but beings of true power, beings who pray back!' Zadkiel's eyes blazed suddenly with fervour.

Cestus knew this was the religiosity for which the Emperor had once scolded Lorgar's Legion. Zadkiel was a fanatic, all the Word Bearers were. It was all they had ever been. How could their duplicity and deception have gone unnoticed for so long?

'We have spoken with them. They hear us!' continued Zadkiel. 'They see the future as we do. The warp is not just a sea for ignorant space-farers to drown in. It is another dimension far more wondrous than real space. Our reality is the shadow of the warp, not the other way around. Lorgar and the intelligences of the warp have the same vision. For the warp and our reality to become one, where the human mind has no limits! True enlightenment, Ultramarine! Can you imagine it?'

'I can,' Cestus said simply. There was pity in his eyes. 'It is a nightmare and one doomed to fail.'

Zadkiel sniffed his contempt.

'You underestimate the power of the Word,' he scoffed.

'Talk is cheap, fanatic,' Cestus snarled, casting aside his helmet so that his enemy could see the face of his slayer, and launched himself at the Word Bearer.

A massive energy flare lit the room in actinic radiation as the two power swords clashed: Cestus's broad-bladed spartha versus Zadkiel's rapier-like weapon.

Sparks cascaded as the two Astartes raked down each other's blades before withdrawing quickly. Cestus let anger fuel his blows and crafted an overhead cut that would cleave into the Word Bearer's shoulder. Zadkiel foresaw the attack, though, and rolled aside, thrusting the tip of his blade into the Ultramarine's thigh. Cestus grimaced as the tip went in and recoiled, swiping downward to force Zadkiel back.

'I am an expert swordsman, Ultramarine,' Zadkiel told him, goading his opponent carefully, 'as martially skilled as any of the sons of Guilliman. You will not best me.'

'Enough words,' Cestus roared. 'Act!' He smashed his blade, two-handed, against Zadkiel's defence. The Word Bearer wove away from the blow, using the Ultramarine's momentum to overbalance him, forging his parry into a riposte that pierced Cestus's shoulder beneath the pauldron. A second stinging blow cut a gash across the Ultramarine's chest and he staggered back.

Breathing hard, using the precious seconds his retreat had given him, Cestus sank into a low fighting posture and went to drive in beneath Zadkiel's guard. The Word

Bearer turned, casually avoiding the Ultramarine's lunge and placing a fierce kick in his guts.

Doubling over, Cestus felt a sharp pain in his side. There was a flash of blazing light, and he felt heat on his exposed skin as Zadkiel's power sword came close. Searing agony filled his world utterly as the Word Bearer plunged the blade deep into the Ultramarine's leg. Cestus fell to one knee, dizzy with pain. Another blow struck him in the chin. It felt like a punch, and he fell over onto his back.

Cestus brought his blade up just in time as Zadkiel launched himself at him, lashing his rapier down against the Ultramarine's improvised guard. It hovered near to Cestus's face, his power sword the only thing preventing it from cutting his head clean off. All the while, the shuttle bay and the *Furious Abyss* disintegrated around them.

'Give it up,' hissed Zadkiel, pressing the blade ever closer to Cestus's throat.

'Never,' the Ultramarine snarled back.

'Calth is dead, Ultramarine!' shouted Zadkiel. 'Your Legion is doomed! Guilliman's head will be mounted on the Crown of Colchis and paraded all the way to Terra! Nowhere is it written that one such as you can change the Word!'

Once, when Cestus was a mere aspirant, one of hundreds drawn from the valleys of Macragge to be judged before the sons of Guilliman, he had scrambled up the steps of the Temple of Hera. He'd defied the whips of the previous year's failed aspirants, who lashed at the youths as they tried to be the first to reach the top. He had hunted through the forests of the Valley of Laponis. He had learned there, not just that the weak gave up and the strong persevered; he had learned that at a far earlier age, or he would never have been considered an aspirant at all. He had learned that perseverance did not just make the difference between success and failure. It could change the test, and create victory where none had been possible. Will alone could change the universe. That was what made a mere man into an Ultramarine.

It was will alone that allowed Cestus to throw off his attacker in the shuttle bay antechamber, crushing the ruin of Zadkiel's severed fingers in his fist to loosen the Word Bearer's hold. It was will alone that brought him to his feet, and will alone that made him cut Zadkiel's sword, hand and all, from his wrist as he hefted it.

Clutching the stump of his arm where Cestus had cleaved it, the Word Bearer got to his knees and bowed his head.

'It means nothing, Ultramarine,' he said with finality. 'It is the beginning of the end for your kind.'

'Yet, still we'll fight,' he said, and with a grunt Cestus cut off Zadkiel's head.

The Word Bearer's lifeless body slid to the ground, as the rest of him rolled across the deck. Cestus sank to one knee beside him and found that he could no longer carry his sword. It clattered to the floor and the Ultramarine pressed his hand against his side. There was blood on his gauntlet. Zadkiel had struck him a mortal blow after all.

Cestus laughed at the ludicrousness of it. It had felt like nothing more than a sting of metal, so innocuous, yet so deadly.

The world was turning to fire around Cestus as he fell bodily beside Zadkiel. The sound of rending metal told him that the integrity of the shuttle antechamber would not hold for much longer.

The *Furious Abyss* was all but destroyed, the plan for it to cripple the Legion in tatters. The thought gave Cestus some solace in the moments before he died. As his cooling blood pooled around him, he thought of Macragge and of glory, and was finally at peace, his duty ended at last in death.

'This conclusion to the Word is no conclusion at all, for it shall go on. The future as it is written is but the merest fraction of the wonders that will be unveiled by my vision. When mankind and the warp are one, when our souls are joined in an endless psychic sea, then the truth of reality will be open to all and we shall enter an aeon where even the most enlightened of us shall be revealed to have been groping in the darkness for some truth to sustain us.

Yes, the wonders I seek are but the beginning, and for our enemies, those who would defy the future and attempt to crush the hopes of our species, the pain is only just beginning, too. Our enemies will fight, and they will lose, and destruction will be visited upon them, for it is written. Even beyond those first battles there is a purgatory of the soul that the most tormented of our foes cannot imagine. Yes, for those who will deny their place in the Word, these hateful birth pangs of the future will be but a splinter of their suffering.'

– The Word of Lorgar